QUEEN OF CROWS

Queen of Crows

A NOVEL

S.L. WILTON

atmosphere press

TABLE OF CONTENTS

CHAPTER ONE 3

CHAPTER TWO 13

CHAPTER THREE 27

CHAPTER FOUR 34

CHAPTER FIVE 47

CHAPTER SEVEN 66

CHAPTER EIGHT 80

CHAPTER NINE 90

CHAPTER TEN 100

CHAPTER ELEVEN 114

CHAPTER TWELVE 127

CHAPTER THIRTEEN 134

CHAPTER FOURTEEN 145

CHAPTER FIFTEEN 156

CHAPTER SIXTEEN 165

CHAPTER SEVENTEEN 176

CHAPTER EIGHTEEN 189

CHAPTER NINETEEN 199

CHAPTER TWENTY 207

CHAPTER TWENTY-ONE 216

CHAPTER TWENTY-TWO 223

CHAPTER TWENTY-THREE 230

CHAPTER TWENTY-FOUR 239

CHAPTER TWENTY-FIVE 247

CHAPTER TWENTY-SIX 255

CHAPTER TWENTY-SEVEN 262

CHAPTER TWENTY-EIGHT 272

CHAPTER TWENTY-NINE 279

CHAPTER THIRTY 289

CHAPTER THIRTY-ONE 299

CHAPTER THIRTY-TWO 308

CHAPTER THIRTY-THREE 318

CHAPTER THIRTY-FOUR 327

CHAPTER THIRTY-FIVE 334

CHAPTER THIRTY-SIX 343

GLOSSARY 353

"When wyverns suggest one change their ways, one should listen."

Serek-jen, Scourge of the East

CHAPTER ONE

Castle Kersey stood on a high mound in the center of the Timber River across from the city of Kersey. The fast-flowing water protected the gray stone fortress on all sides. A plethora of dark-blue and white banners decorated the mighty keep.

Half a millennium old, the castle had survived many a wyvern's aerial attack, spanning the reigns of untold Warrior Kings and Queens of the Sword. However, no woman had ruled in Kersey in more than five generations.

Inside the keep, Sophia Pendergast sat with her back to her cluttered vanity. She giggled as Celeste, her handmaiden, read aloud from a frowned-upon collection of ribald poetry. Heat grew on the rims of Sophia's ears before migrating to her cheeks. She clamped a hand over her mouth but laughed heartily as Celeste provided some vigorous hip gyrations to accompany the rhyme.

Horns blared from the gatehouse roof. Horses' hoofbeats echoed from the bailey stones below. Celeste snapped the volume closed, hid it among the folds of her gown, and swept an auburn lock behind an ear.

Sophia jumped, then dashed to the balcony rail. In the bailey armed men rushed to dismount. Some ran up the stairs leading to the battlements, scattering a raucous flock of chickens. The ancient hawsers groaned as the oxen bawled while powering the giant windless. The iron bridge telescoped into itself as it withdrew across its cinnamon-colored pilings.

The men wore Kersey's colors but carried no banners and no infantry accompanied them. Sophia turned to Celeste. "Knights, a lot of them, but I don't see my father."

Celeste joined her on the balcony. They watched as grooms struggled to remove the sweating horses from the bailey. Sophia could glean no more details from her vantage point. "I'm going down there," she said, turning away from the rail.

"You can't. The scandal of it. The princess can't be seen mingling with knights without proper escort. Not to mention, you're wearing an indoor gown and your hair isn't done."

Sophia fingered the thin, almost sheer lace covering her décolletage. She shook her head. "Hog's tail! Father mingles with knights all the time." She tossed her thick braid behind a shoulder.

"Mind your tongue, my Princess. Your father is a Warrior King. And a man. Achaea's divine word allows men to do as they please."

"Hog's tail twice! Cassandra's divine wiles influence Achaea's decisions. Besides, most of those knights have helped train me. They're almost brothers. You may stay here if you like."

Sophia strode to the iron-bound door. Her silk slippers hissed on the tile floor. Her fingers touched the ornate brass handle as the thumping of someone running in boots pounded up the outer staircase. Sophia withdrew and took a halting step back behind a brocade decorated chair. Celeste stood near the well-oiled weapons resting in their storage rack next to the stand supporting Sophia's helmet, hauberk, and shield.

Three loud bangs rattled the door. It burst open and slammed on its hinges. Josiah Tarkenton filled the doorway. Reddish-brown spots soiled the white lion embroidered on his surcoat's front. His black eyebrows seemed knitted together, the long vertical scar on his face pulled at the corner of his frown.

He dropped to a knee and lowered his eyes. "Two hundred pardons, my Princess. I wouldn't dare intrude on your apartment, but these are dark times and decorum must be set aside."

"You may rise, Sir Josiah. What has brought you here so poorly announced? And where is my father? You *are* his right hand." Sweat, blood, and oil odors wafted from his person. She wrinkled her nose. She would ask Father to require his men to bathe before calling on her.

Josiah rose and stepped into the room. He gestured at Celeste. "Come, girl. Take your Princess's hand."

Celeste stepped close and placed a calloused palm on Sophia's sleeve. Sophia leaned into Celeste's body heat, her mind racing. A tremor rushed through her insides.

"Now you frighten me, Sir Josiah. What's happened? Where's Father?" Sophia stared into his brown eyes. Sweat beaded in the graying stubble on his jaw. Through the dirt and soot on his face, the ancient scar glowed with an inner heat, as if the wound were fresh.

"In your eighteen years I've never had to deliver such news as this." He shifted his eyes to the floor, drew a deep breath, then looked at her again. "We've been betrayed, my Princess. Last night we camped opposite Fraysse's army. Cavale and your father argued over tactical concerns. Today that bastard went over to King De Leon at the critical moment. And that pig's ass Pendergast and his company arrived after the rout began. Too late to be of any help. Your father has fallen. He is among the slain. The battle is lost, but not the war. Not yet."

Sophia's knees trembled, then buckled. Celeste and Josiah grabbed her arms, holding her upright.

Father had never lost a contest in the lists. Sophia gathered her wits. Josiah was known for his pranks. She steadied her stance and glared at him. "Truly? You think this is a jest? We are not amused. Perhaps you should confine your foolishness to the unseemly and silly. This tale rings poorly here. I'll beg Father to punish you for this tasteless trick."

Josiah's frown grew deeper. "I do not jest, my Princess. Your father has been struck down. De Leon made a pact with mountain ogres. Six of them were committed to the fight at the worst time for us. Your father cleaved two and his wizard conjured a sheet of flame incinerating another. The wizard was too slow casting a shield spell for your father. Damn wizards. Your father fell."

"Not true. It can't be true..." Sophia turned from Josiah to Celeste, as if not looking at him would expose the lie. "Where is his body?" She looked over her shoulder. "Show me your proof."

He stared at the floor. "We couldn't retrieve his body. We were overwhelmed before a litter could be brought. Your father's corpse became a prize on the field, changing hands several times. Many good men were killed or maimed trying to retrieve him, including his wizard. Your uncle, King Bruce De Leon, has your father's body. He'll likely send it to Fraysse to be displayed as a trophy in his castle's bailey."

"You tell tales, Sir Josiah." Sophia pulled away from them and tugged at her braid as a hollowness crept through her body. She held her chin aloft but steadied herself with a hand on her sword's pommel. The sword, light, sharp, and balanced, a gift from father three years past. Her first real weapon. Its grip granted her comfort, normalcy, and control.

"I do not lie, Princess. I don't make jests. Not today. We have no time to mourn. Come, we must take you to the Lord Bishop. You must accept the throne within the hour. The army's morale falters. In spite of your father's courage and the slaying of the remaining ogres, they believe we are leaderless. It's time for you to break from Cassandra, take up the sword and embrace Achaea, setting prophecy on its path."

"Prophecy?"

"The men must see your ensign. They must know you will lead. You will fight. That pig's ass Pendergast will likely see your father's death as an opportunity to seize the throne for himself. We must act quickly. I have Odette preventing anyone from approaching the Lord Bishop until you arrive at the sanctuary." Josiah pushed a cold object into Sophia's hand. Her father's signet ring. The blue stone tinted with flakes of dry blood. "Even after the coronation, your reign will be vulnerable until the Solstice."

Sophia looked from the ring to Josiah. She found no words. Emptiness crept through her, an insidious serpent, clinging to her heart, constricting her lungs and stifling her mind's grasp.

"Two hundred pardons, my Princess, this and his sword are all we have of him." Josiah stared at the floor.

It must be true. Sophia choked down nausea as she clenched the ring in her fist. She stared at her father's favorite general, adviser, and friend. The man Father trusted above all others. His intense eyes met hers and softened for a moment. The look replaced immediately with hard determination. Her mind clawed at his words, but understanding wouldn't come.

Josiah jerked his head at Celeste, then toward the open door. "Bring her, girl. Bring her to the sanctuary. We have no time for reflection."

Celeste stepped toward Sophia. "The princess isn't dressed to be seen outdoors, Sir Knight. It will take at least an hour to dress her properly."

Josiah turned at the doorway. "I said we have no time. Bring her!" Then he was gone.

Sophia allowed Celeste to hold one hand and throw an arm around her waist. She let herself be guided down the stairs. They left the massive keep, navigated around a large puddle, and across the bailey to the sanctuary.

A few men-at-arms inclined their heads in acknowledgment but whispered among themselves at her passing. She should have been embarrassed dressed as she was, but no shame or words came. Her mind remained numb. Father joined Mother in Hecuba's tower. She was beginning a new life as an orphan. She was about to be their queen.

Sophia balked at the sanctuary's steps. A pair of white ducks with their downy offspring trailing behind, muttered as they waddled past the young women. Sophia glanced at the afternoon sky. Black smoke rolled from the sanctuary's chimney. The king was dead. She turned to Celeste. Her confidant's brilliant green eyes, the eyes Sophia always wished were hers, were clouded with grief. Celeste's full lips pressed into a tight line, nearly disappearing among the strawberry freckles on her cheeks.

"Is this truly happening?"

Celeste squeezed Sophia's hand and spoke in a soothing tone, "You knew this day would come."

Sophia's insides churned. "But Father was to pass the throne to me at the Solstice and remain as my advisor. I'm not ready for this."

Celeste flashed a wry grin. "I've heard no honest person ever is."

"A woman hasn't ruled Kersey in more than a century."

"It's prophecy. When women, one a child, rule two of the three enlightened kingdoms, the wyverns will rejoin the alliance. Peace will come to all three." Celeste tugged on Sophia's arm.

"That's not prophecy, it's a fairy tale. Regardless, I'll be ruling one kingdom and I'm not a child."

"A flood starts with a single drop of rain. Come, my Princess, this is your coronation."

They entered the sanctuary, a small imitation of the great temple at Oxted. Kersey's colored banners hung on the walls. Between them, shining brass and silver adornments depicted Achaea going about his great deeds, creating their world from within the forming fire. Slaying the first wyverns with nothing more than a glare. Claiming his mate, the god of mothers and mother to them all, Cassandra. Others showed Hecuba judging the dead in her tower.

The commoners loved shiny things. The gods provided them for the people here in this house. The three-foot-tall brass rendering of the gods stood upon the altar. A heavily muscled Achaea, Cassandra with her comically enormous breasts, and Hecuba, always watching and frowning. They held hands round the forming fire. Below a haze of spicy incense smoke, the statuary glittered like a faraway beacon.

Sophia blinked twice. She would have to embrace Achaea as a warrior. Accept her calling as a Queen of the Sword and put Cassandra's care for hearth and home out of her mind for the time being.

The bishop stood with an acolyte near the altar. Sweat glistened on his face and darkened the armpits of his white vestments. Sophia couldn't remember seeing him so flustered. More than a dozen knights stood in an arrow-straight row to one side of the aisle. Fresh from the battlefield. The iron stench of blood mixed with sweat and soil radiated from their unclean boots. Josiah hovered near the bishop. The Black Wyvern, her father's sword, held loose before him, its point resting on the floor.

Her father's ministers and advisers, with their ladies, stood on the other side of the aisle. Sophia sucked in a deep breath and forced herself to make eye contact with them. They smelled of rose water and perfumes. Combined with the odor from the other side it created a strangely garden-like aroma. Sophia returned her attention to the knights.

Her father's cousin and vocal opponent, Mallet Pendergast, stared at Sophia as Celeste ushered her past him. His insolent smirk never faded. Josiah said he'd arrived late to the battle. Yet he was here and Father was not. Sophia raised her chin and forced a smile anyway. The arrogant ass. He'd always felt himself better suited for the throne than Father.

Stewart Odette, her father's youngest knight, stood near the front with head bowed. A blood-soaked rag covered his left hand. His sweat-dampened black ringlets hung nearly obscuring his smooth face, and his broad shoulders slumped. Sophia's mind cried out for him to gaze upon her with his marvelous blue eyes and commanded he tell her it hadn't happened. If he truly sought her love, he'd expose the experience as a horrible dream.

Stewart glanced at her with a pain-filled expression. His eyes softened, meeting hers for a moment. He blinked before returning his gaze to the floor. Sophia and Celeste walked past him.

The bishop guided Sophia into an adorned, backless chair near the altar. Without polite manners he nudged Celeste aside. The bishop glanced at Josiah, then licked his lips.

"We're pressed for time, Lord Bishop. Proceed with the short version of the ceremony," Josiah said.

"Very well." He turned to the acolyte. Accepting ceremonial items, he set them in Sophia's hands. A gold scepter in her right and a brass bejeweled egg in the other. He placed her father's silver coronet on her head. It was too large and slipped, covering her eyes.

The bishop pushed the coronet up with a finger and smiled at her. "We'll have it fixed when time permits," he whispered. "Certainly, before the Solstice."

"Get on with it, Lord Bishop, the enemy may be approaching," Josiah snapped.

"Yes, yes. I understand, Sir Knight. The vagaries of war are not lost on me, but the princess is not properly prepared. She's not wearing the cloak. The coronet doesn't fit. She hasn't walked and prayed the pillars. This is all quite irregular."

A murmur, instigated by Pendergast, rumbled through the gathered knights and ministers.

"For want of a fat pig's ass," Josiah said over his shoulder. He thrust the sword into Stewart's hands, then ripped a banner from the wall and approached Sophia.

"By your leave?" Josiah bowed at her side.

Sophia held the coronet in place with a finger, juggling the egg at the same time. She nodded. Josiah draped the banner over her shoulders. He turned to the bishop. "You cling too closely to Achaea's teachings. We all have for far too long. Perhaps if we'd heeded Cassandra, this war with Fraysse could've been avoided. Regardless, the Princess wears a cloak. You may proceed."

Sophia allowed her mind to wander, ignoring all the bishop said. She held the egg in a precarious two-fingered grip while she rubbed the ring stuck loosely on her thumb. Father was never without it. It was the real sign of his power and authority. This was no prank. Father was dead. She was to be their leader. Was she ready for this? There was the war to tend to and a myriad of other duties. Could the ring grant her some insight? Did it have a magic that would guide her?

The audience chorused, "Allegiance to the queen."

Sophia flinched. She blinked as she glanced at Celeste. What came next? Where in the ceremony were they? Celeste rolled her eyes in rebuke, then jerked her chin toward the bishop.

The bishop took the scepter and egg from her, then handed her the sword Father had held so many times. It was heavier than hers but well-balanced and manageable. Sophia stood, then raised its black blade. The knights sounded their approval, thumping their chests with their fists.

"You are now Queen of Kersey." The bishop gestured at the statue of the nude figures on the altar. "May you, with the gods' help, reign long and wisely. May you not draw that weapon without reason; may you not sheath it without honor."

Sophia held the sword aloft with one hand. The yellow stones representing eyes on the wyvern's-head pommel glared at her. The Black Wyvern was Father's recognition of Mother's house. Now the weapon and the realm were hers. The wyvern's unblinking eyes challenged her. Did she have what it would take to rule Kersey?

Josiah knelt before her. "My Queen, the enemy is sure to approach. May I have your leave?"

Sophia lowered the sword, resting its point on the floor. "Wait." She examined the faces of those gathered. Most seemed hopeful; a few, including Pendergast, stared at her through narrow lids. Sophia gathered her thoughts for a moment. "I did not wake today expecting this responsibility. I know little of diplomacy and less of war. Know this though, my father's fight is mine. I appoint Sir Josiah Tarkenton as my general and my chief advisor. Tell the people his words are mine."

"I am humbled by my Queen's confidence. I have taken the liberty to order the unfurling of the ensign bearing the Eastern Lion; it's now your flag. May we raise it to inspire the men?"

"Certainly, Sir Josiah." The coronet slipped, covering Sophia's eyes again.

CHAPTER TWO

Bruce De Leon didn't follow up his victory at Persimmon Field with a direct assault or siege at Castle Kersey as expected. Rather, he sent Fraysse's army onto the plain west of Kersey, where it laid waste to the farms and small villages. Daily, new columns of black smoke rose against the summer sky, scarring the brilliant blue as if a wyvern clawed it.

From her apartment, Sophia imagined vultures feasting on the corpses of her father's people. She swallowed hard. Her people. Refugees flocked to the castle, setting up tents and shacks on the outskirts of the city. A smelly, noisy shanty town.

Father hadn't provided any insight about such an extreme event. What could she do? The people needed to return to their farms. She'd called a formal meeting of her generals. She must have what was left of her army do something to remedy the situation. The crier, limping across the bailey, announced the top of the hour. Sophia turned away from her balcony and went straight to her council room.

"I want Fraysse's army driven from our lands," Sophia said, opening the meeting. She looked around the large table. The men looked so different without their hauberks and weapons. Even though she'd seen many of these men in social settings, the coarse fabrics and somber colors they wore made them look smaller and older than she remembered.

"My Queen, your throne is precarious. We must solidify your hold and claim. There are those in your court, some sitting here now, who would see you deposed. You must know well, there are many who don't believe in a woman's right to rule," Josiah said. His unblinking gaze caused two ministers to look away. Pendergast's nostrils flared at Josiah's stare.

"The people are being attacked. They cry out for their queen to protect them," Sophia said.

"And you will, but you must let our agents secure your hold on power. The search for a new wizard is ongoing. It is still four months until the Solstice when Achaea and the people will hear you affirm your right to reign. By then I'll have gathered an army large enough to confront Bruce De Leon. Achaea knows, we lost far too many men at Persimmon."

"How many exactly?"

Josiah shrugged. "We don't have exact numbers. Few knights were lost. Among the commoners, perhaps one in ten was slain, another three or four wounded or captured. The rest scattered, deserting, most likely returning to their homes."

"Perhaps every nobleman with a horse shouldn't have abandoned them," Sophia said. Josiah's face morphed from serious concern to smoldering anger. She bit her lip.

Pendergast slapped the tabletop and burst into laughter. "Every man with a horse..."

Josiah's lips disappeared in a tight thin line. His left eye ticked above the hideous scar. "If my Queen were a man, I'd demand satisfaction for such an insult. Perhaps Mallet Pendergast, sorely missed at Persimmon, will stand now as your champion."

Sophia regarded her general as Pendergast slowly rose, closing his fist on his dagger.

"I don't need the queen's request to stand against you, Tarkenton," Pendergast said.

Sophia motioned for him to sit back down. She'd made a mistake, insinuating cowardice among her knights. She needed those men, she had to save face while still offering an apology. "That was poorly spoken on my part, Sir Knight." She inclined her head at Josiah. "My inexperience is sometimes unrestrained. We have greater concerns than fighting among ourselves."

Josiah held his chin high, but his lips remained tight as he cast a poisonous glare at Pendergast. Pendergast returned the venom.

"Regardless, we must solidify your hold on power or all else will count for naught." Josiah didn't remove his eyes from Pendergast.

"I am your queen. I want something done about Fraysse's predations. Do not forget, my father as well as most of you here, trained me in both martial skills and tactical concepts. I do understand what I'm speaking about."

Josiah's grimace deepened. "We know your skills well. However, I'm speaking of political matters, not tactical concerns. We need a stable throne before winter brings a wyvern."

Sophia glanced at each member of her council. Their faces hard and unreadable. "Regardless, I want something done about Fraysse's army."

"Waiting until your army is reformed will serve the greater good, my Queen. In the meantime I've ordered fast-moving mounted companies to conduct raids and probes to harass De Leon's troops."

Sophia pursed her lips. Patience had never come to her easily.

***

During five days of polite arguing, Sophia was surprised Pendergast approved of her plan and supported her position while Josiah remained opposed. At last, she overruled Josiah's objections. She ordered him, with most of her knights, onto the plain to stop the slaughter. On the fourth day of Josiah's foray against the enemy, Sophia stood on the royal balcony staring at the setting sun.

Celeste hovered behind her, inside the apartment proper. "You must eat something. The gods know you can't rule without keeping your strength."

Sophia ignored the stern tone. Celeste expected to nanny Sophia's future children as her mother had been Sophia's nanny. "How many do you think have been slain today?"

"I don't know and neither do you. Maybe it's been a good day and Achaea has allowed your knights to meet the enemy. Maybe only men from Fraysse have been butchered today."

Butchered. There was no word more appropriate. Four years past, Father summoned her to a battlefield in the aftermath of the beer rebellion. He called it a victory. The dismembered and gutted corpses she'd seen there still gave her pause. The cries and groans of the maimed were more appalling. Josiah criticized Father for bringing her there. Father's response, "She needed to see it at least once."

Sophia shuddered. "There has been no message. Surely if there'd been a victory Sir Josiah would've sent word. I fear all may be lost. I fear I'll own the shortest reign in Kersey's history. A poor commentary on a Queen of the Sword and my house." Sophia turned to face Celeste.

"It will certainly be the most frugal. Come, eat your supper." Celeste indicated the white linen-covered dining table, set with silver cutlery and blue candles. A tray with her meal, a portion of roast pork, whipped potatoes, and spring beans, rested before her seat.

"Share it with our soldiers. I have no appetite."

Celeste pursed her lips. "You're spoiling them. Those on

the walls grow fat, while your gowns drape from your shoulders like they were tossed on some peddler's hanger. Not to mention, during this morning's sword practice you grew light-headed. You're not eating enough."

Sophia folded her arms on her chest, then gestured at the door with her chin. "You're becoming too comfortable expressing your opinions. After all, I am your queen."

Celeste bowed and picked up the tray. She backed to the door. "By your leave, my Queen. But know this, in the lower half they say Sir Stewart Odette favors a woman with a bit of meat on her bones."

Sophia stifled a laugh, then threw a scarf at Celeste. "Go, evil woman. You know nothing of Sir Stewart's preferences or the sweet words he has shared with our wiry self."

Celeste laughed as she opened the door. "You've told me all about those sweet words. You need to fatten up a little." She escaped through the doorway.

Sophia turned to the balcony. The thought of Stewart's playful eyes and square chin brought warmth to her heart. The soft youthful whiskers framing his lips garnered a tremor in her fingers. Had she, a plain-looking woman, won his heart or was it her station he flattered? Beautiful Celeste harbored no such worries. Most men fawned over her.

How would Celeste know what sort of woman he liked? Common women were always available for noblemen to entertain themselves. No one really expected commoners to keep their purity. Had Stewart lain with Celeste? Sophia shook her head. If he had, Celeste would've told her about it.

Even so, she'd prayed Cassandra would sway Father to choose him for her. Stewart was out there with Josiah. She'd ordered him into danger. He had no wife. Now the choice fell to her. She could pick him, but did his heart belong to her? Even being the queen, she couldn't force him to love her. The war was more important. She would wait for Stewart to take the first step.

Riders appeared on the west road. The fading light glittered from their spear points. Sophia's heart leapt to her throat, but her hope to see Stewart dashed when they drew nearer the castle. The black stag's head on a pale blue ensign announced they were Pendergast's men. Stewart had said more than once he wouldn't be found a corpse among them. Still, perhaps they brought news of a victory.

The captain of the guard shouted a challenge to the soldiers when they halted near the river. Sophia couldn't hear their response. Pendergast's party was large, easily numbering a score. More than needed to deliver a message. Perhaps it was indeed good news. She turned from the balcony and went to the door. Her two personal guards, good men too old for campaigning, snapped to rigid attention.

"I'll be going to the audience hall. You may lead on," Sophia announced in the hall outside her apartment.

Both men stepped toward the stairs and responded in unison, "As you wish, your Grace."

Celeste met them at the foot of the staircase. She grabbed Sophia's elbow, stopping her, then whispered in her ear.

"Take care, my Queen. A rumor races through the lower half. Sir Pendergast may be here for less than honorable reasons. You must choose your guards with caution."

Sophia stared into Celeste's wide eyes. "Truly? Where did you hear this?"

"It's going around. Coin has changed hands. You may be in danger."

Sophia glanced at her guards. Josiah had picked them himself. They stood a few feet ahead. Both met her gaze with nothing more nefarious on their faces than curiosity at the delay.

Pendergast may have designs on the throne, but he'd stood as her champion when she'd insulted Josiah. And he'd supported her desire to send troops to meet Fraysse's army. Achaea's teachings had inspired Pendergast to keep his place.

Still, with Josiah in the field and a small garrison guarding the castle...Sophia looked back at Celeste. "Come with me. You'll be another witness, just in case." She motioned for her guards to move on.

The receiving hall always felt stuffy and formal. Especially when eight ministers, their wives, and secretaries were in attendance. It was no different now, and dark. More light needed to be let in. Should the room be made more welcoming?

Sophia fluffed out her skirt before sitting on the plain, uncomfortable chair someone had the audacity to call a throne. Father often told her the chair was uncomfortable to remind the one sitting on it of their responsibility. She resolved to spend as little time sitting on it as tradition and decorum would allow.

She perused the portraits of her ancestors. Stoic, handsome men with confident eyes stared back at her. A Queen of the Sword, a grandmother six or seven generations removed, glared as well. Her eyes cold and amber. Could Sophia hope to measure up to those who'd ruled before? She needed to commission a portrait of Father. After all, he belonged among them. After the war, of course. All the nicer things waited on the war's end.

Several of Sophia's ministers approached her. Celeste stood near the wall, out of the way, but in Sophia's peripheral vision. One of the ministers exchanged some minor details of logistics with Sophia. She listened until Pendergast was announced. She waved the minister to silence when half a dozen soldiers, wearing gambesons in her colors, came in and took their position along the wall under the portraits. Their spear butts resting on the floor, their arms relaxed. She looked down the line; not one of them met her gaze.

Sophia bit the inside of her lip, then gestured for the doors to be opened.

Pendergast paused at the threshold. He lifted his camail

and unfastened the chin strap, then removed his helmet. He handed it to his squire, a pimple-faced boy several years younger than Sophia. Pendergast's hauberk sparkled in the lamp light as he approached Sophia. Her stomach quaked. His sauntering carriage and bold stare spoke volumes about his disregard for her authority.

Father would have him executed for walking into that hall with such a disrespectful attitude openly displayed. Sophia glared. If she ordered his execution in these trying times, could Kersey afford to lose a knight as skilled as Pendergast?

He stopped, appropriately, at three arm's lengths from her. His dark eyes glittered. Wisps of gray on the point of his chin granted him a falsely distinguished look. Father had mentioned Pendergast as a potential husband. While he was handsome and brave enough, Sophia shuddered. Thankfully Father had acquiesced to her refusal to even consider such an arrangement.

"Queen Sophia, greetings. I bring a peace proposal and a most generous gift from your uncle, Bruce De Leon, King of Fraysse." Pendergast's deep voice boomed in the small hall.

The arrogance, putting on theater for his own amusement. "Sir Mallet, Cousin, I am unsettled one of my most trusted knights should be in converse with the enemy, lacking my behest. And armed men accompany you to my hall." Sophia gestured at the half-score men behind him.

Pendergast smirked. He turned to one of his men and accepted a wooden box, grasping its rope handles. He placed the box on the edge of the dais before Sophia's feet.

"All will be clear when you have accepted this gift." Pendergast resumed the respectful distance if not the proper bearing.

Sophia swallowed hard. The box was too small to contain coins of any significant value but too large for transporting gemstones. Incense or rare spices perhaps? Without removing her eyes from Pendergast's she gestured for a minister to open the box.

A caustic odor rolled from within. The minister looked, then dropped the lid. "By the gods. Your father's head, your Grace." His face twisted, he recoiled.

Sophia's soldiers standing along the walls snapped their spears against their shoulders. Pendergast's men grasped their sword hilts and stood ready. Pendergast held out his hands, palms toward the walls.

"Wait. There's no need for violence. I've brought a peace proposal and you haven't yet heard it," Pendergast said.

Sophia stared at the box. A crackling came to her mind's ear. The same one she'd heard as a child when she'd been angry. Crackling like the kindling of a fire. She wanted to approach the box, to expose the lie, but the crackling told her it wasn't a lie. Her guts crawled, then clenched. She dragged her eyes from the box and snarled at Pendergast.

"How dare you come to my hall in this manner with this." She pointed at the box. "High treason in the presence of witnesses. I can have you executed where you stand."

"Executed? Who will carry out such an order?" Pendergast exaggerated looking all around.

Sophia perused the hall. "Give me your sword and I'll tend to it myself."

Pendergast laughed. "I have no doubt. However, as I see things, I'm giving the orders here. This hall is mine. It was always meant to be mine. Our common grandfather never should have chosen your grandfather as his heir." Pendergast jabbed a finger in her direction.

Sophia crossed her arms on her chest. The nerve of that pig's ass, pointing at her as if she were a misbehaving child. Besides, she wasn't even born when her great-grandfather chose his heir. Did she have enough men to overpower Pendergast's party?

"My father was the elder brother and should have taken the throne. Instead, he languished in your grandfather's shadow. I in turn have been forced to stand in your father's. I will not stand in any woman's shadow, least of all yours, Cousin." Pendergast took a step closer.

"Treason!" the bishop shouted. "Our queen has been properly chosen and installed. You have no standing, Sir Knight."

"Silence, Priest." Pendergast jabbed the irreverent finger at the bishop. "You'll speak when I tell you to. Achaea will affirm my standing at the Solstice."

Pendergast returned his attention to Sophia. "Your father, with his lenient attitude toward the Crows and disregard for Achaea's teachings, didn't belong on that seat. And now, Achaea's students know we can't have a woman trying to bring prophecy to fruition. Achaea forbids it. Men rule in the enlightened kingdoms just as Achaea rules the afterlife. Only men can deal with wyverns and other men. Had you been born male I'd kill you out of hand, but as a woman you have another value."

Sophia's bodyguards positioned themselves between her and Pendergast, drawing their swords. Their blades chimed as they cleared their scabbards. The air grew in weight, pressing on Sophia's chest. She moved her hands to her thighs, steadying a growing trembling. Men and women along the walls held their breath.

Pendergast raised his hands before him. The bronze stag's head decorating his baldric flashed as his arms moved. "Everyone remain calm. There's no need for bloodshed."

"You'll not harm our queen," one of the bodyguards said. "You've already committed high treason. If you flee now, you may make it to Fraysse before you're captured and summarily executed."

Pendergast chuckled, more a growl, and took another step toward the throne. Sophia's protectors assumed an on-guard stance, blades vertical and legs spread.

Sophia stood and raised her chin. If the scum meant to slay

her, she'd face him eye to eye. Her knees shook and the room seemed extraordinarily hot. She forced down nausea.

"Bruce De Leon has agreed to end the war if certain conditions are met," Pendergast said.

"Treason," a minister muttered.

Sophia sniffed and held a hand up to the minister. Mist welled in her eyes; she fought it off. What would Josiah have her do? She had to buy time to think. "What is this proposal?"

"He demands the ten sections currently in contention be ceded to his realm. An annual tribute of four hundred weights be delivered to him before the blooming of the trilliums on Ballast Hill, each of the next ten years. And to ensure compliance, and guarantee peace along the new border, I replace you on the throne."

Pendergast stood defiant as though Sophia had no choice. Would her men fight for her? Did she have any men? Perhaps Pendergast mustered the coin to buy them all. Where were Josiah and Stewart? The crackling echoed in her mind's ear. Mother always told her it was her bad side and she should ignore it. Sophia shoved it aside now.

She returned her gaze to Pendergast's smug face. "Your crown will matter not. You'll be Fraysse's puppet and the people will be destitute. Those ten sections are the most fertile lands in the kingdom."

Pendergast jerked his head at the soldiers along the wall. "Don't count on these men, they're with me.

"Those are the terms. If you accept, I'll hold you here in Castle Kersey as a hostage. You can continue to enjoy your life of privilege. If you decline, you and all those in court refusing to swear loyalty to me will be executed. Their families as well. Choose."

Sophia turned her back to Pendergast. Let him strike now, the traitor. Refusal sprang to her tongue. She bit it and wrung her hands. It wasn't the time to be impulsive. Pendergast certainly had the nerve to kill her and her ministers, but was he truly willing? How many would face the executioner with her? If she sacrificed herself the resulting chaos might allow her loyal men's families time to escape. She might be able to purchase them that time.

Celeste bit down on her lip, discreetly crossed her fingers, and raised an eyebrow. She was advising Sophia to accept. A quick survey of her ministers' faces showed every emotion, from fear to gloating. Clearly her soldiers had betrayed her and sending Josiah away from the castle had been a huge mistake.

"Traitor!"

Sophia turned as one of her bodyguards lunged at Pendergast, sword forefront.

Pendergast's squire sprang into the bodyguard's path and was run through. The boy grabbed the blade and cried out for his mother; then, with a gasp, slid from the keen shaft and collapsed. His severed finger twitched on the floor.

Those in the room stared at the fallen boy in silence for a blink, then Pendergast grabbed for his sword and jumped back. Several of Pendergast's men leapt forward, attacking Sophia's bodyguard. The other bodyguard joined the fray. Steel rang, sparks flew, men grunted and cursed with their efforts.

Another of Pendergast's men was stabbed through the gut. Pendergast's men forced her bodyguards back toward her. She jumped aside, knocking over the throne.

Her reign rested on the sword arms of those two loyal, old men. And she didn't even recall their names. Her soldiers stood along the wall but made no move to intervene. If she survived this ordeal and her throne could be righted, she'd never again hold court while unarmed.

The fighting upset the box. Her father's head, coated in tar, rolled free, then stuck to the carpet. The sightless black eyes shone, seeming to stare at Sophia. An anguished cry escaped her lips, sounding far away to her ears.

One of her guards' blood splattered across her shoes and her gown's hem, soaking the carpet near her father's head. A moment later the other bodyguard fell.

"Stop!" Sophia shouted. "No more." She looked each soldier in the eye, every man lowered his. Traitors. Her guards' swords lay out of reach. She glanced at the portraits of her forefathers. The shortest reign in Kersey's history.

Sophia knelt at her bodyguard's side and brushed the hair from his face.

"Two hundred pardons, your Grace. I've failed you." The guard coughed. Bright red, foaming blood appeared on his lips.

"You have served me well. You carry your honor and my gratitude to Hecuba's tower. She will reward you."

Pendergast's men hovered near her, but hesitated, looking over their shoulders at their lord. Sophia stood when her guard passed. She faced Pendergast's men and their gleaming blades. Let them strike now if they possessed the nerve to murder a queen.

Pendergast sheathed his sword and scowled at Sophia.

More than her life hung on her decision. Several ministers', their families', and of course, Celeste's. She rose to her full height and lifted her eyes to the portraits of her ancestors. "I accept the terms."

Pendergast ordered his men to stand aside. He stepped up to Sophia with a mirthless grin. She frowned. How could that disgusting traitor share her blood?

He held out his hand. "The signet ring."

Sophia moved her foot away from the pool of blood creeping across the carpet. She yanked the ring from her neck, breaking the fine chain which held it. She slapped the ring into Pendergast's palm.

"The honest, brave blood spilled in this room will haunt your reign, Cousin." Sophia drew her shoulders back and stood waiting for his response.

The ass turned his back to her. She was the queen, anointed by the gods. If she'd concealed a dagger on her person, she would've plunged it into the base of his neck, piercing his black heart.

"Take her and her Crow to her apartment. A guard outside at all hours," Pendergast said. "Make no mistakes, assume nothing. The Lady Pendergast is highly skilled with blade and staff. I assisted in her training myself."

Four men with the stag's head on their surcoats stepped forward and motioned for Sophia to precede them.

Sophia shook Celeste's hand from her arm and raised her chin. "Achaea will not allow this treachery to go unpunished. Heed my words, all of you." She stared down her traitorous soldiers and ministers. "Sir Mallet's fate is set and you will all share in it."

Pendergast glanced over his shoulder and whispered. "You know full well the gods only exist for the Crows." He looked to his men. "Take her away."

CHAPTER THREE

In less than a quarter-hour, Pendergast's men tore down her ensign and replaced it with his stag's head. Then the refugees from the destroyed villages were cast out into the city and their meager shelters burned, creating an eerie glow over the muddy streets.

The next morning Sophia watched from her balcony as men from Fraysse came and went in the bailey below. Their ghastly crimson flags and plumes were a blight on her castle and realm. She wished a wyvern would come raze the castle, but a wyvern usually came in winter. So it had been the last four years.

Sophia turned to her loom. She would forsake the lion symbol and replace it with the heraldry of Mother's house, a wyvern. If the wyverns wouldn't raze the castle, then she'd become the wyvern. The Kersen Wyvern, a beast of yore. Under her new banner she'd raze the fortress herself, in a manner of speaking.

The rumor that Mother's great-grandmother had been part wyvern always brought a smile to her. It was whispered that Hecuba allowed her descendent, when faced with death, to become a wyvern rather than succumb to human frailty.

The women in her Mother's family attributed many strange happenings to their ancestor. It was said that she could see the future and cast powerful magic against her enemies. It was all utter nonsense, stories to entertain children.

Three days passed as slowly as a ponderous glacier might recede. Sophia remained locked in her suite. Celeste tended to Sophia's wants, but only Celeste was allowed to leave the apartment and then only when she'd been given specific errands to run.

In the early evening of her third day as a prisoner, gentle knocking sounded at her door. Sophia looked up from her loom. A nod sent Celeste to answer it. Pendergast leaned against the jamb. He flashed a toothy smile and presented a green bottle with an etched unicorn on the neck. A bottle from Burkett's vineyards. No telling how long it had been in Father's cellar.

"Good evening, Cousin. May I come in and share this fine vintage with you?" Pendergast slurred.

Sophia covered her parted lips with her fingers. Pendergast presented a fashionable, handsome figure in his wool vest and white, bell-sleeved shirt. What did he want? "You currently rule this castle, Cousin. You may go where you wish."

Pendergast took a shaky step, then paused, rocking, his balance unsteady. He looked around, then turned to Celeste and thrust the bottle at her. "Pour for us, Crow."

Celeste accepted the bottle, allowed a shallow curtsy, then turned away. Sophia draped a scarf over her work and stood, offering Pendergast a seat at her tea table.

He plopped his large frame on the dainty chair and laughed when it creaked. "You need some real furniture, Cousin."

"I rarely entertain guests as robust as you." Sophia arranged her gown's skirt and sat across from him.

Pendergast laughed, a pleasant, disarming sound.

Celeste placed wide-bodied, long-stemmed crystal glasses for them. She held out the bottle and a corkscrew. "If you'd be so kind, my Lord."

Pendergast pulled the cork and handed the items back. "Pour, then leave us. Go get some exercise. Work up the muscle to open a wine bottle."

He chuckled to himself and leered at Celeste's behind as she left before turning his eyes to Sophia. With a carnal grin he raised his glass to his lips.

Sophia sniffed her glass's contents, mellow, fruity, typical of Burkett's vineyards. She hesitated, eying Pendergast over the rim.

He gulped half his portion. "Poison? If I wanted you dead your head would be on a spike, next to your father's, just the other side of the bridge. To this point, your being alive serves me better. Drink, Cousin."

Sophia took a sip. The wine's taste matched its aroma, a hint of acidity making it interesting. Even though she enjoyed the taste, she forced a blank look onto her face and set the glass aside. "Very nice, thank you. To what do I owe this visit?"

"You know it's nothing personal, my rising to the throne?"

Of course, it was personal. Nothing could be more personal. She was a woman and he was a man. He thought himself more qualified, more entitled. And he'd usurped the throne, not risen to it.

"If prophecy was to come to pass and the wyverns of old accepted peace, what would a nobleman do to achieve fame, fortune, and glory? No, peace may be something women and children wish for, but men must have the challenge of a worthy foe," he said.

"Can a man not find fame and glory in raising his people to prosperity? In making peace with the wyverns?"

"Bah! That sort of glory is for women and politicians." He gestured with his glass, slopping a bit over the rim. "For men who falsely believe dying in their beds at an old age is somehow noble. The sort of man who never tastes life, because he hasn't faced Hecuba's tower and won."

Sophia laced her fingers in her lap. "You speak glibly of death, Cousin, and yet you leave me alive."

"As I said, your life has another, more valuable purpose. I've come to offer you an opportunity to return to a more normal routine." Pendergast refilled his glass and splashed a bit in hers. "Yes, perhaps I will allow you to roam the halls, use the library, perhaps even attend your martial exercises when the weather permits."

"And what exactly will I have to do in exchange for this kindness?"

He smiled. "Accept me as your King and be friendly."

"Friendly?"

"Yes. Lady Sophia, you're an attractive woman. That pleases me." Pendergast's brown eyes glittered in the lamp light as they paused at her breasts, then slowly returned to her face. He placed a calloused hand on hers. "If you would become my willing consort, it would make my claim all the more legitimate. If you gave me a son, it would quell the misgivings among many of those with more traditional beliefs."

Sweat dampened Sophia's armpits. She tugged on her braid. Pendergast was clearly drunk, but had his mind left him? She moved her mouth, but couldn't utter a sound. Did tradition oppose his reign? Would those traditionalists support her over Pendergast? She glanced at the blanched knuckles on her fingers, wrapped around the chair's arm.

"Would living as my wife be so horrible?" He asked.

Sophia sought a neutral answer but found none. How could she escape this fate? Surely Cassandra hadn't set this course for her. Her disgust and revulsion must have shown on her face.

Pendergast's eyes narrowed, his color rose. He dropped his glass and leapt to his feet. The shattered crystal crunched beneath his boot. His powerful hands pinned her wrists to the chair's arms. He squeezed, hard. Sophia clamped her tongue with her teeth, preventing a squeal of pain. His face lingered near hers. His breath sour, like cheap, poorly fashioned homemade spirits.

Sophia turned her face away.

Drunk, but not incapacitated. Pendergast rubbed his prickly chin whiskers against her cheek. He whispered in her ear. His breath hot. "I'll take what I please as well as go where I please."

Pain wracked Sophia's forearms. She gritted her teeth. "Rape will certainly bring honor and prestige to your reign, Cousin."

Pendergast pushed her chair back on its rear legs, Sophia's feet dangled. She jerked forward, closer to Pendergast, keeping an awkward balance.

"You need to work on your restraint, Lady Sophia. It may soon cost you your head."

Frantic pounding on the door interrupted.

Pendergast blew a blast of acrid breath in her face then rose, releasing his grip. The chair slammed back on all fours.

"What is it?" He bellowed.

The door opened. A young page stood in the doorway. "My Lord, an envoy from Lord Bruce De Leon has arrived and requests an immediate audience."

Pendergast cast a glare at Sophia.

Go to your master's call, Cousin. Sophia bit her lip, preventing herself from saying it out loud.

Pendergast turned on his heel and strode from the room.

Once Pendergast left, Celeste returned and listened to Sophia's recounting of the meeting.

Celeste's eyes grew wider with each revelation. "You aren't hurt, are you?"

"No. Frightened for sure, but I'm not injured."

"Well, I don't have any good news for you. In the lower half, they say most of your knights paid homage to Lord

Pendergast and now serve him. Sir Josiah remains loyal, but he and those few with him have been declared outlaw. Anyone who assists them in any way will suffer the gallows. The lower half is whispering Lord Pendergast has murdered many of your former ministers. Their wives and children too. Slaughtered them in the dark without trial or mercy. And he's seized their property."

Sophia groaned. She'd hoped to spare her loyal ministers by acquiescing to Pendergast's demands. "It would seem Sir Mallet is tightening his grip on the throne while enriching himself."

"He's also repealed your father's reforms. Under penalty of the lash, the common folk can no longer speak to nobles unless addressed. The grievance courts have been disbanded. The commoners no longer have a voice. It's Lord Pendergast's opinion the Crows are of no value. He's raised the taxes on them as well. Cassandra knows the poorest will struggle to survive on what he's left them."

Sophia gathered her knitting and moved to the window chair. Father never approved of the slur. She seldom used "Crows" and thought to ban its use in her presence. "Father always said higher taxes on the poor only reduced the realm's coffers. Sir Mallet may have to learn that the hard way. Hopefully the people can outlast him."

"Hope isn't a plan."

"Truly spoken." Sophia gazed out the window. A bat darted back and forth in the light before disappearing into the darkness. "I don't see any way to remove my cousin without help. Outside help. Are there any rumors of unrest among the men-at-arms or Sir Mallet's guards?"

Celeste closed the window before facing Sophia. "Not that I've heard. Not yet anyway."

"Could you get a dagger from the armory or a stout knife from the kitchen?" Sophia returned her gaze to Celeste.

The redhead grimaced. "I'm not allowed in the kitchen. I

may be able to flirt my way into the armory. I've done something like that before."

No doubt flirting had gotten Celeste many baubles and favors from men. Sophia frowned. "On second thought, that may be too much of a risk. Any man you toyed with would remember you." She had to think of a different tactic. "Are there not poisons in the market? Poisons that work quickly with a single dose?"

"Of course, if one knows where to ask. What are you thinking?"

"You are allowed to go to the market without escort, yes?"

"I am, but the guards search me and my parcels when I return. Looking for letters and signs from the resistance they say. Mostly the animals use the policy as an excuse to grope me."

"For now, groping can't be helped. Tomorrow you will tell Sir Mallet I've suddenly taken ill and you must go to the apothecary and secure medicine. Although I doubt he will, if he suggests a healer, tell him it's a childhood ailment and you know what is needed. Purchase some of this poison and disguise its packaging. Then we will wait and stay vigilant. My cousin will make a mistake and we will take advantage."

"Are you sure of this course? A lot can go wrong."

Sophia rubbed her eyes. "I see no useful alternative. Are you with me? Can you get the poison?"

"I'll see to it first thing in the morning, my Queen."

CHAPTER FOUR

The next afternoon Sophia finished her luncheon of potato soup. Pounding shook her door. It swung open before Celeste reached it. Pendergast strode in, displaying no ill effects from his previous night's drinking. He glanced around the room, then turned to Celeste. "Leave us. Go find something useful to do. Don't linger about in the hall eavesdropping."

Celeste curtsied and made wide eyes at Sophia from behind his back on her way out. She pulled the door closed.

Pendergast stood between Sophia and the cutlery. She looked for a weapon. Her soup spoon wouldn't do at all. She stepped to her knitting basket. The spindly wooden needles sprouted from a skein. A sad choice, but better than nothing. She let her hand linger near the basket.

Pendergast seemed to ignore her as he meandered about her suite, humming an old tune. He picked up a porcelain figurine depicting a wyvern. He examined it, then put it back before looking at one of a war-dog. Sophia thought to object. They were her things, passed down from Mother's family. He had no right, but she held her tongue, waiting.

"I see you've recovered from your ailment, Cousin. That pleases me." His gaze settled on her.

"Thank you, I'm feeling much better." Sophia held her lips tight. Although she was naturally pale, he clearly didn't think she looked sick. She shouldn't have had Celeste brush and braid her hair that morning.

"I have news for you. News for us both actually." Pendergast stepped closer to her.

"What news, Cousin?" Her breath caught in her throat. Had he killed Josiah or the others; what of Stewart? Sophia clutched the neck of her gown, hoping to appear frail.

"Bruce De Leon is coming to Castle Kersey. He has decided to amend the peace agreement."

A patter of relief tripped through her core. At least this wasn't about Josiah or Stewart. "How so?"

"As you have spurned my generous offer, he wishes to claim you as a war prize."

Sophia gasped. Even as Lord De Leon's niece she'd be less than his mistress, a plaything. Entertainment for his boring evenings. Little more than a common whore in his castle. Why would Achaea ask her to suffer such an insult? Why would Cassandra allow it? "You would permit him to claim me?"

"I have little choice. You've rejected me, making the matter trivial. Of course, if you were to change your feelings for me…"

Trivial to him. Sophia couldn't think of it as such. Take him as a husband or become a whore in her uncle's fortress. Cassandra should intervene, soften Achaea's heart, urge him to show the men they were wrong. "I cannot accept your offer, as I do not love you. And I will not go with him."

Pendergast smiled a mirthless grin that did not include his eyes. "Love has little to do with such affairs." He slid a small, sheathed dagger from his belt. Sophia sucked in a sharp breath and grasped one of her knitting needles.

Pendergast scoffed, his face growing dark. He laid the dagger on her table. "You always were one to improvise when disarmed, weren't you? If you're going to try to kill a man with that," he gestured at her knitting basket. "Strike suddenly. Aim for the throat. You may hit something vital."

Sophia let go of the needle and clasped her hands before her waist. Why was he here? To torment her? To show her he was in command of the situation?

Pendergast patted the weapon where it lay. "No, Cousin. I'd have you use this dagger. It's much more effective."

"What would you have me do with it? Kill myself?" Sophia swallowed a catch in her throat. Surely, he didn't want her to try to attack him.

"Not hardly, but that's your decision alone." The smirk returned. "No, I'd suggest you conceal it on your person. That Crow of yours is always skulking about the castle. Have her help you hide it."

"And?" Sophia wrinkled her brow.

"And when the time is right, rid us both of Bruce De Leon." Pendergast stared at her, his face set, hard, and cold.

Sophia blocked a laugh before it was fully formed. "You think he will receive me without bodyguards at his side?"

"Of course not. However, Cassandra knows a man will rarely enjoy a woman's charms before an audience. De Leon's guards will be close by, but if you strike true, as you've been taught, he'll be in Hecuba's tower before they can react."

"Even so, it's probable they'll kill me. You'd be rid of two problems at once. What do I get in return for this...sacrifice?"

Pendergast growled. "I'll care for your Crow. See to it she's comfortable into her old age. And you'll have avenged your father's death. Revenge carries its own satisfaction."

Sophia stared back at Pendergast. He was lying. He didn't even know Celeste's name. Celeste would suffer a horrible fate once she was gone. Could she turn this around? Perhaps she could convince Bruce De Leon to kill Pendergast. She could willingly offer herself to him in exchange. Did she have the charms to sway him so? Could something so banal compel him to do it? Even though he was Mother's brother Sophia had met her uncle only once and didn't know him well enough to judge.

Pendergast interrupted her thoughts. "I'll leave this weapon. You decide your fate, but remember this, nothing goes on in this castle that I'm not made aware of." He turned and left, banging the door on its hinges, leaving it open.

Sophia picked up the dagger. Small, its blade only six inches long. Long enough in any event. It was an expensive weapon, with a tight, stacked-leather handle. She checked its sharpness with her thumb, then returned it to its sheath. She carried it to her chair where she sat looking out at the gray, featureless sky. It would rain later, probably in the evening. Did her allies have a place to keep dry?

A flock of starlings flashed past the window. The castle's flags stretched, snapping in the wind, bending their staffs. A storm was coming. Sophia tightened her jaw, yes there was indeed a storm coming. She would be that storm.

Celeste returned and Sophia told her of Pendergast's suggestion.

"It seems he has eyes on Fraysse's throne as well," Celeste said after the telling.

Sophia stared at the bleak sky. Could she murder her uncle, Father's rival? Should she? After the assassination, should she survive, she'd forever have to be wary. There was no good solution. Every path led to Hecuba's tower. She allowed a long mournful sigh.

"We have several days before any action needs to be taken. We'll wait for a sign or an opportunity." Sophia forced a half-hearted smile.

***

Days crawled past. Sophia and Celeste settled into a routine. Sophia alternated working on her ensign and embroidering a smaller version. Celeste used her spare time and seamstress skills to alter one of Sophia's more fashionable gowns to conceal the dagger in the bodice.

Pendergast made no other visits and while Celeste was out running errands Sophia was left alone inside the prison of her mind.

The gibbet stood near the city center, in view of her balcony. A young man's body hung there for two days. Had he helped those supporting her? Perhaps he was nothing but a common thief. Why did Pendergast think it a good thing to keep him dangling there, displayed like an obscene trophy?

Father executed criminals too. It was sometimes necessary, but he never kept their bodies from their families, nor left them on display. Pendergast was using terror as a means of controlling the commoners. Perhaps it was a sign of weakness. How could she turn that against him?

Father. Father would never have ended up in this predicament. Sophia missed his advice. She looked up at the balcony outside the apartment her parents had shared. Now Mallet slept there. Father's warm laughter and Mother's twittering echoed faintly in her memory. She could barely remember the sound of Mother's voice. How long before she lost Father's as well? Sophia set her face in a scowl. They weren't there to guide her. She must find her own way.

Celeste swept into the apartment, carrying a bundle containing sundry items, a bottle of wine and a bag of hard candy. "Your moods have been far too dark lately. Candy is just the remedy."

Sophia smiled. "It doesn't go well with what we need to discuss."

"Candy goes with anything," Celeste said.

"Not plotting murder."

Celeste paused unpacking and looked at Sophia with her nose wrinkled. "Who are we murdering today?"

"Sir Mallet must be killed. Soon. Can we use the poison?" Sophia asked, stepping close to Celeste and lowering her voice.

"If we're caught, we'll both join that poor boy on the gallows."

"If we do nothing, we'll both be sent to Fraysse. Who's to say what will become of us there. Even if we escape without killing Sir Mallet, where would we go?"

Celeste looked up at the ceiling for a moment. "The poison will be hard to use. He has three tasters and I'm not allowed in the kitchen. You'd think he doesn't trust me."

"If I invite him here for wine or something, could we do it then?"

Celeste shrugged. "He'd almost certainly suspect."

"True, but he's a man. If I offer him, well, you know..." Sophia splayed her fingers wide, palms up. "He may not be so cautious."

Celeste frowned. "That's a dangerous plan. I can't name all the things that could go wrong. Not to mention, it's well known in the lower half how rough Lord Pendergast is in the bedroom. And how are you going to explain your sudden change of mind about laying with him?"

Sophia glanced at Cassandra's portrait. "I'll lie. I'll tell him I don't want a man from Fraysse to be my first. I'm Kersen after all."

"That lie is a dry goat. He'll never fall for it."

"He has to fall for it. You'll have to convince him. We'll use the poison, but I'll wear the gown with the dagger just in case."

Celeste shook her head. "He's a monster and you'd be alone with him. You'll be taking a huge risk. He may not suspect poison, but he'll demand you return the dagger as soon as he steps through the door."

"If Bruce De Leon arrives and Sir Mallet is still alive, we'll both be handed over to my uncle. Our chance will be gone completely."

"I don't like it. There has to be another way." Celeste placed both palms on the table and stared into the distance.

"There isn't. As soon as Sir Mallet is dead, I'll send word for Sir Josiah and the others to return in haste. We'll be ready to deal with my uncle when he arrives."

"Who will carry that word?"

Sophia stared at her feet. Who indeed? "We'll have to tell at least one of the knights. One who was reluctant to join Sir Mallet."

Celeste nodded. "I know the one, but you've got to know there'll be trouble with those loyal to Lord Pendergast."

"We'll keep his body hidden here. A secret. We won't tell anyone until we know Sir Josiah has been told of Sir Mallet's death."

Celeste's frown mimicked an artisan's sad mask.

"Are you with me?"

"Of course, but I don't like this plan. Too much is left to chance."

"Do you have another plan?"

Celeste's frown deepened, but she shook her head.

"Fine. Tomorrow afternoon you will deliver the invitation to Sir Mallet, for the following day. Tell whatever story you must, but convince him to come, alone. Then speak to the knight, but don't tell him too much. Only hint about something happening."

Celeste sighed, shook her head, and tossed a piece of candy into her mouth. "As you wish, my Queen."

***

In the wee hours, next morning, tapping on Sophia's door roused her from sleep. Celeste sprang from her pallet. Her auburn hair poking from her cap, a comical mess. She grabbed a bread knife from the table.

Sophia rose and turned up the lamp before calling, "What is it?"

A muffled voice whispered a reply, but Sophia made no sense of it. She set aside her quilt, then flung a cape across her shoulders and gathered it at her throat before curling her fingers around the hilt of her dagger. She poked her chin at the door. Celeste held her knife at her side and opened the door.

Stewart swept in and dropped to a knee at Sophia's feet. His face thin and drawn. A fox the hounds had long pursued. He smelled unwashed, his surcoat torn and soiled. Even so, Sophia's heart leapt and she threw her arms around his neck, crushing his face to her breast.

Stewart pushed gently away and rose. His cheeks aglow in the lamp light. "My Queen, Sir Josiah has sent me to fetch you to him. We must flee. Our presence may be detected at any moment. Quickly, gather what you need for travel in the wild and follow me."

"How did you get in here and what of the guards?" Sophia said.

"We can talk when you're safe." Stewart turned to Celeste. "Gather clothing for travel in the wild. Be quick about it, girl. We must leave at once."

"Leave? Where are we going?" Sophia asked.

Celeste shook off her sleeping cap, ripped open a wardrobe, and grabbed a few items, throwing them on Sophia's bed. She gathered other items from the vanity and added Sophia's hunting boots to the pile.

"We've assembled enough loyal men to make an escape. Sir Josiah will explain his plan when we're away. I can say, he intends to go to Tegine for help. Come, my Queen, there's little time."

"Celeste and I have formed a plan to kill Sir Mallet. That plan will return me to the throne tomorrow. Running away seems at odds with that. Now that you're here we can attack him directly."

Stewart frowned. "We have a plan as well, but it doesn't include getting us all killed trying to murder Pendergast. He is too well-guarded and our force is too small. Come with us. There is a less direct, but effective route back to your throne. However, I can't say I approve of the plan in its entirety.

Regardless, we are pressed for time. You must see the change in circumstance and act accordingly. It's not the time to be stubborn, my Queen."

Sophia stared at Stewart. "I don't have the patience for one of Sir Josiah's convoluted games of court intrigue." She raised the dagger. "When this will provide an immediate result."

Stewart gently held her wrist and gestured at the dagger with his chin. "That may not yield the result you wish. Particularly if it gets us all killed. We don't have the men for an assault on Pendergast's person. That would be a foolish act when another, safer route stands open."

Sophia pulled her wrist away and dropped her hand to her side. "How long will this plan take?"

Sophia followed Stewart's eyes as he glanced at Celeste. She fashioned Sofia's quilt into a carrying bag of sorts. He returned his gaze to Sophia. "Several weeks, my Queen. Longer than you'd like, but it offers a sure result."

Josiah's loyalty to Father never faltered. She should trust him and his judgment now. And escaping into the wild with Stewart had an appeal all its own. "I don't like it, but very well. I place my reign in your hands."

Before Celeste hefted the quilt, Sophia added her wyvern embroidery. Stewart took Sophia's hand and led her out the door. She struggled to subdue the heat rushing about her core at the touch of his hand.

The hall was dimly lit and the staircase nearly dark. Her prison guard lay on the floor, a black puddle spread from his neck. Sophia sucked in half a breath and looked away as she passed.

Sophia stiffened at the head of the stairs. Shadowy figures lingered halfway down. Stewart tugged her hand. "Loyal men. Men that will see you back on the throne."

He led the group to the main floor, then into what Sophia thought was a storage room. They stood in the dark. The presence of nearby people crushed against Sophia's mind even though no one touched her. A candle flickered to life as two men wrestled a stove aside revealing a narrow door. Stewart led Sophia, Celeste, and a half dozen common soldiers into the passage. It was a brief commute through a stone corridor to the castle's outer wall.

They turned to the left and, after a short walk inside the perimeter, passed through another disguised door into a sloping passageway. The earthen walls smelled damp. A torch sputtered to life fouling the atmosphere and stinging Sophia's eyes. It took ten minutes to return to the fresh morning air.

Sophia gazed around in the growing dawn's half-light. She stood under a lean-to a quarter-mile from the castle's walls. Newly fashioned barrels surrounded her. The fresh-cut, raw wood gave off a pine odor. The cooper's workshop stood across a muddy path from a wainwright. This was a side of Kersey too poor for Sophia to have ever visited. Even Celeste may not have ventured to this side of the city.

The castle, the only home she'd ever known, loomed in the growing light. Even knowing the finery of her apartment, from here the building appeared a cold-gray fortress. Its crenellated walls menacing like a great beast's teeth. The four cupolas, while occupied by guards, were dark. The many banners and flags hung limp in the quiet air. Did her people see it that way too? A symbol of power they couldn't possess?

Josiah came from inside and approached her. "I'm pleased to find you well, my Queen. I'll take you to a safe house. You can change into traveling clothes while I make our last-minute preparations."

Stewart stood to Josiah's side. Sophia wrinkled her lips. "Where are we going?"

Josiah gestured at the building. "We'll discuss it when we're away from any walls that may be listening."

He took her to a small dwelling. Like most homes in Kersey, it was a grassy mound covering a wooden frame. The only protection from wyverns the poor could muster. Josiah bid her go inside while he and several men made ready to move on.

Sophia ducked her head stepping down through the doorway and wrinkled her nose at the interior of the house. Its dirt floor provided an earthy smell while the human occupants provided another, less pleasant aroma. Her privy had more space than this whole house and smelled better.

There was a rough-hewn table worn smooth from use and two stools in the single room. A weak flame in a pit provided the only light. The smoke curled in a lazy spiral and exited a hole in the plain wood ceiling. A sleeping place stood to one edge of the round room and everything shared the same color, brown. Sophia sat on a stool after wiping ineffectually at its seat.

A woman, with pure white hair drawn into a severe bun, wearing a threadbare, wool habit, looked up from the fire pit and approached Celeste. The old woman's face carried the plague's pockmarks. A lucky survivor.

"May I offer you some tea this morning, your Grace?" The woman asked.

"Certainly. That's most gracious of you," Celeste said. She dropped her bundle on the floor.

The old woman presented Celeste with a glazed, terracotta cup. Celeste handed it to Sophia.

Sophia sipped the beverage, then winced. "This tea is quite weak. Little more than warm water."

"Two hundred pardons, your Grace. I'll put on a new pot." The woman avoided looking directly at Sophia.

Celeste patted the woman's arm. "You'll do nothing of the kind. The tea is fine."

Sophia stared wide-eyed at Celeste. The tea wasn't fine, it was awful. A new pot was a splendid idea.

Celeste set her nanny face, then bit the inside of her cheek. "Rationing, my Queen. For the war effort, as well as the new taxes. You remember?"

Sophia wrinkled her brow. She'd heard nothing of rationing. Why hadn't Father told her? And why did this woman fail to address her directly? Pendergast's stupid rules. She forced a fake smile. "Oh yes, of course. I'd forgotten. The tea is satisfactory, quite delicious, and refreshing. Thank you." She grimaced, then sipped again.

Another woman, clutching a small, dirty-faced, straw-haired girl, squatted near the sleeping pallet, watching from the deeper shadow. When Sophia looked at them the woman lowered her eyes and turned the girl's face away with a finger.

"Where is your man?" Sophia said.

The old woman addressed Celeste. "My oldest son was lost to a wyvern two years past. My husband was taken by the plague the wyvern left behind. My youngest son, lost in the war. My sister and I live here with my niece, your Grace."

Everyone knew wyverns didn't cause plague. Exposure, starvation, and over-crowding brought the plague. Sophia's mind raced for a consolatory response but found none. She'd lost her mother to the plague and her father to the war. What could she say?

Celeste raised both eyebrows at her.

"I'm sorry to hear that," Sophia said at last.

Josiah ducked through the doorway. Two knights followed him. One, Stewart; the other Sophia recognized, but didn't recall his name. She cursed herself. These knights were risking their lives and the lives of their families for her crown, the least she could do was remember their names. And her bodyguards had already given their lives. Rationing? Names? She was a terrible queen.

"My Queen, we're ready to leave. I'd assumed you'd be dressed for the trip. We'll wait outside for you, but be quick. Pendergast must have discovered your escape by now."

Sophia allowed a smile as she gazed at Stewart. Even unwashed he presented a dashing sight. He flashed a warm grin and a wink in return. Her belly fluttered, but she returned her attention to Josiah. "Sir Josiah, how did you know of those secret passages? And why wasn't I told of them?"

Josiah jerked his head at the knights, they left the house. He turned back to Sophia. "Your father kept them a secret. Until now you had no reason to know about them. Change your clothes. We must leave."

Josiah was testing her patience. "Where are we going?"

Celeste pulled a sturdy canvas, olive-green hunting suit from her bundle and held it out to Sophia.

"It's safer for these women and the other commoners if we discuss all of this later. Get changed, my Queen. We're running out of time." Josiah turned and left the home.

CHAPTER FIVE

Sophia's entourage of six knights, slightly more than a score of common soldiers, Celeste, and one mule, slipped out of Kersey on foot, ahead of the dawn. They wove among the numerous mound homes, passing some early risers who stared wide-eyed at the procession.

Josiah led north on the road. They crossed Fish Hook Ridge then went only another mile before he announced they would forsake the road to avoid being seen and slow the pursuit. They plunged into the forest west of the road.

Going was difficult. Small trees and saplings, struggling for their share of sunlight, impeded the company's progress. The slow-growing oaks competed with the rapid proliferation of maples, birches, and elms, all pushing through the litter earlier logging left behind.

Sophia followed directly behind Josiah. The rest of her company strung out behind in single file. She swatted at swarms of small, darting insects. They could only be seen from the corner of the eye. Waving at their erratic flight paths only seemed to embolden them as they zeroed in on her nose.

An hour before noon Josiah called for a halt in a small glen shielded behind towering pines. Sophia plopped down on a fallen log and kicked off her boots. She rubbed her feet. The damp, earthy aroma combined with the near silence of the place left her chilled. She shuddered. The thick, green boughs surrounding them cast foreboding shadows. Even the men seemed reluctant to make a noise.

"Sir Josiah, why are we walking? This trip would go much faster and be more comfortable if we rode. Or even better, employed a carriage. And where are we going?"

Josiah glanced from the gathered knights. "Horses are expensive, my Queen. They're also noisy and easy to track in the wild. Besides, more than half our commoners have never ridden. We'll be better served walking, at first anyway. We'll go to Tegine and ask Lord Henry De Roederio for help and protection. He was always on good terms with your father and has no love for De Leon or Pendergast."

"I defer to your judgment. How far away is this castle at Tegine?"

Josiah cast a wide-eyed stare at Sophia. "Hecuba's privy, did you not spend any time studying the maps and documents your father provided?"

Sophia shrugged. "They were boring. I found more interesting pursuits. You know as well as I, Father planned to abdicate and place me on the throne at the Solstice. He would then become my closest advisor. I thought I'd have time for maps, tariffs, and decrees later."

Josiah shook his head and pointed. "The city, Tegine, lies one-hundred-forty miles to the north. Castle Roederio stands less than a mile north of the river. Under normal circumstances it would take six to eight days to walk there. At this pace twelve, maybe fourteen days."

"One-hundred-forty miles? I can't walk that far. Not through this forest. On a road perhaps, but this ground is rough and it's easy to trip and fall. And what can be done about these insects? They annoy our person."

Josiah swatted away a bee. "My Queen, you must carry on.

If you go back, Pendergast will turn you and your girl over to your uncle. De Leon would only keep you as his plaything until he lost interest. Whether he laid with you once or a hundred times, the novelty would eventually wear off.

"Then you would be seen as a burden, perhaps even a scandal. So, you'd be sent on some frivolous errand in the bowels of his castle where you'd be strangled in a dark alcove and your body thrown in the river. You must walk to Tegine if you think to have any chance of regaining your throne."

Sophia's guts churned. Would her uncle truly have her strangled? She glanced around. Several of the men sat nearby, silent, watching. Their faces showed the same concern she'd seen outside the sanctuary three weeks earlier. What would Father say to them?

Josiah gestured at Celeste. "And your girl? She's a Crow. Although precious to you, she has no other station. Bruce De Leon would allow her to be passed around among his barons until one of them, in a moment of drunken brilliance, decided a game afternoon's sporting event would involve turning her loose in the forest so boar-hounds could chase her down and tear her apart."

Sophia's churning guts turned to rising bile. She allowed her eyes to grow wide. "Sir Josiah, are there no honorable men in Fraysse?"

"Yes. However, when it comes to women, honor can have some shifting guidelines. During war rapine is commonplace. Women often become nothing more than prizes. Not all of Achaea's canons are pleasant conversation around hearth and table."

"Father would never have allowed such a thing. Bruce De Leon must be a beast."

"You have some less than honorable men in your court. Pendergast and Cavale as examples. Both are strong voices for Achaea and his ways. Never forget, war is expensive, in both blood and treasure. An army is not cheap. It must be fed, equipped, and paid. Often the men take their payment where they find it.

"Don't fool yourself. Although your father loved your mother more than a man could, he was a man. When plague took your mother, he didn't forego the charms and company of women. After a proper period of mourning of course. That said, he's gone. We must deal with those still here."

Sophia cast her eyes at the ground and scratched the sole of her foot on an exposed tree root. Surely Father never forced himself on any woman, nor stood aside and allowed it to happen. It was too ridiculous to contemplate. Although, he was a man, and men needed that sort of attention. No, the notion was outrageous. She would pray for Cassandra to soften the hearts of the men she came in contact with.

Celeste patted Sophia's shoulder. "You're stronger than you think. Besides, neither of us are whores and I certainly can't outrun dogs."

Stewart ran his hands over his dark-curly mane, approached and sat next to her. He gathered some rocks and pinecones. He placed them one at a time on the ground in front of her, naming each a different city or castle. In a few moments he created a passable representation of their world.

Josiah rubbed the back of his neck. "Take ten minutes to learn the lay of the land. Then we must move on." He turned away and spoke with another of the knights in low tones.

Stewart drew on the ground with a stick. "Just a reminder, my Queen, this line, the Great River, is our border on the west with Fraysse. This one, Rolling River, is our border on the north and northeast with Tegine."

When Stewart looked at her, she smiled. A shy grin with a touch of pink rose on his cheeks. The churning in her belly smoothed to warmth and giddy excitement. He looked back at his map, drawing another line.

Sophia leaned closer placing a hand on his mail-covered shoulder. "And beyond the steppe, the escarpment, and through the pass lies Oxted?"

Celeste snorted and looked away.

Sophia ignored Celeste's protest of her questioning the obvious.

"That's correct. I understand you've been to the great temple," Stewart said.

"Yes, last year. Father felt it important I be properly impressed with the gods. Their statues are much larger than those in our sanctuary. Of course, my transport and company were grander then."

Stewart chuckled. Sophia's chest warmed. The crinkle at the corner of his eye when he laughed always pleased her. Her heart settled the matter. She would pick him for her consort as soon as she was back on her throne. War or not.

"So, you've become a student of the gods and their teachings?" Stewart grinned.

Sophia shook her head. "Only so much as needed to understand and influence the common folk and keep the wyverns at bay."

They looked as a panting archer rushed to Josiah's side. "We've intercepted Pendergast's hounds. We think we killed them all, but it's hard to say. Their handlers are dead for certain."

"Casualties?" Josiah asked.

"We lost a lot of arrows in the forest, but no men."

"Spears are available. Take food and drink for your men." Josiah turned to Sophia. His scarred face carved in stone, a pitiless knight. He rubbed out the map with his foot. "All right. We have a long trek ahead of us. We'll not get to Tegine cowering in the forest. If you're ready to move on, my Queen."

"Very well." Sophia pulled on her boots and rose. She gave Stewart another glance. Yes, when she was back on her throne, she'd have him. She'd have him all to herself.

***

They walked for two days, arriving at the pond where Josiah planned to replenish their water skins. The pond was covered with a thick green slime, reeking of something rotten. The tiny insects returned and bedeviled them at every breath. The mule pushed the slime aside with her nose and drank her fill, but the men conversed about the merits of the water and the risks of a fire, finally deciding to move on to a creek a few days ahead.

The next day, Josiah came to Sophia with a limp water skin. He held it out to her. Sophia licked her dry lips, glanced at a few men resting on the forest floor, then shook her head.

"Let the men drink it, Sir Josiah."

Josiah frowned. "The men are fine. Drink."

"They run ahead and on our flanks. I'm sure their need is greater."

"You're the queen, it's not necessary for you to go without. The men are fine." Josiah offered the skin again.

Sophia straightened to her full height, squaring her shoulders. Even so, she looked up to meet Josiah's grim face. It wasn't him testing her, but Achaea and Cassandra themselves. If she were to be queen, thirsty as she was, she had to refuse.

"The men labor and risk their lives for my crown. Let them have what I can give. I'll drink when we get to the creek."

Josiah allowed a grin and a wink, then slapped the skin's stopper home. He inclined his head a bit. "So be it." He turned to the gathered soldiers. "All right, loiter-sacks, gawking at her Grace won't get us to Tegine. Get off your asses and get moving."

The men drained the last water skin with the next morning's meal. Sophia struggled, choking down her tiny ration of hardtack and jerky. She turned to Celeste and grinned. "I do believe the vines at Burkett couldn't produce a wine of fine enough quality to improve this fare."

Celeste laughed. "At this point even a sip of water would be lovely."

"And a bath. We both smell awful. Like a hound's pen, I believe the saying goes."

Celeste laughed. "About now I could drink an entire tub."

Stewart brushed an errant ringlet from his cheek. "We'll reach the creek at midmorning tomorrow, ladies. All will be well then." He shared a warm smile with Sophia. She batted her eyes, then looked away. She must avoid showing favoritism for the time being. She needed to disguise her attraction and intention.

Richard De Margot, another of her knights, said, "In the morning we'll gather dew from the leaves. Pitiful as the amount may be, it will fortify us enough to make it to the creek."

Sophia returned a practiced, receiving-line smile. "I'm sure it will suffice, Sir Richard."

Before the sun rose, in the quiet hours of the next day, Sophia nudged Celeste awake and they searched for broad leaf trees among the pines. The queen reduced to licking dew from leaves. She never would've thought it could happen. And yet, squatting behind a tree trunk to answer nature's call, while men surrounded her, was getting to be commonplace. Sophia went from branch to branch trying to relieve her parched demand. Long before she slaked her thirst Josiah called for them to move on.

As predicted, they arrived at the creek midmorning, but it was a dry, rocky scar cutting east and west through the heavy forest. Many of the younger men dropped to the ground and looked about in despair.

"Cassandra's tits." Josiah summoned the knights to him. They argued in low tones.

Sophia touched her dry lips with an equally dry tongue. Celeste plopped on a rock and blew at a stray strand of hair. She'd surely have something clever to say if she wasn't so thirsty. The dry creek sapped Sophia's strength reserves. She wanted to drop to her knees and bawl. She couldn't. Not there, in front of the men.

Sometimes desperation demanded one muster up a possessed determination, Sophia did so. No one could die of thirst in her realm. The gods knew she didn't rule over the Anakat Desert.

She stepped up on a log and looked in both directions down the creek bed. Behind her the knights continued to argue. She pointed at two soldiers standing nearby. "You two men, go east for a mile. Look for a pool with water in it. If you find one, return here with all speed. If you don't find anything, come back and we'll take assessment." She pointed at another two men. "You two, do the same going west."

The men hesitated, looking to the group of knights. Josiah was the de facto leader of their company. Sophia was about to issue her demand again when Josiah growled, "You heard her Grace. Who are you to refuse? Get moving. Look for water and report back."

Half an hour later the eastern scouts returned, they'd found nothing. A few minutes later, the western pair came back.

"What did you find?" Sophia asked.

"Your Grace, there's no water in the creek bed as far as we went, but there's a cottage with full rain barrels just over a mile away," the older man said. "There didn't seem to be anyone about."

"Cottage? Who lives in the middle of the forest so far from others?" Sophia said.

Josiah shrugged and grinned. "Someone who will share their water, or else. Come, let's go meet this hermit."

Before they came in sight of the cottage, their mule pulled at the lead rope, snorted, stomped, and brayed.

"She can smell the water," Stewart said. "It's a good sign, but with all the racket our approach won't go unnoticed."

Josiah called for a halt. The men spread out in a thin line on either side of him. Sophia went to his side. The cottage sat precisely in the center of a round clearing several yards north of the creek bed. Massive pines stood like a fence on the perimeter. The cottage door was closed. It wore dirty white shutters flanking glass windows. Faded red walls supported a thick thatched roof.

"Wood cutter maybe. Most likely a crazed recluse," Josiah whispered.

The company waited in spite of their mule's insistence. At last Josiah took a few steps into the clearing. A cackling laugh bounced among the trees.

CHAPTER SIX

A high-pitched male voice echoed about the clearing surrounding the cottage, leaving doubt as to the owner's location. "Visitors! Armed men wandering the forest. Outlaws and harlots no doubt. You'll find nothing for you here."

Sophia turned in a full circle as she stepped into the clearing. The speaker remained hidden.

Josiah crossed his arms, then grunted. "Outlaws? A fat pig's ass. We are in the company of Her Majesty, Queen Sophia Pendergast of Kersey. If you're a loyal subject we'll be asking your help. If not, we'll deal with you appropriately."

A shimmer not unlike heat rising from a bonfire hid the woodpile for a moment, then a man appeared, seated on the woodpile with a foot on the splitting stump. He wore deer hide with the hair still on. His hat's ear flaps stuck straight out from his head like a gull's wings. He was old, but not ancient.

Sophia exchanged wide eyes with Josiah and Stewart. Celeste raised an eyebrow and pursed her lips. The mule reared, bawled and tried to flee. Two men regained control of the animal a few yards out of the clearing. Sophia looked back at the old man.

He pointed a polished quarterstaff at Josiah. "I don't

answer to any sovereign. Queen, is it? Strange. Will the prophecy be fulfilled?" The man hopped up quicker than Sophia would've thought possible. He took a few steps toward them without lowering his staff.

"This is delicious! Come closer. Let my old eyes have a look at you. I've never been introduced to a queen, or a king for that matter. I did have an unfortunate meeting with a prince once, but that's a story I'd rather not share. Let's have a look at this delicious queen."

Sophia took a step. Josiah blocked her path with his massive arm. He closed a fist on his sword's hilt.

"We've told you who we are. What is your name, old man?" Josiah said.

The man stopped a couple yards from them and leaned on his staff. "You've told me the queen's name, not yours."

Celeste swept around Sophia and Josiah's arm, then stepped up to the old man. She held out her hand. "My party is loyal to me. That should be sufficient identification. Your cottage is within the borders of my realm. It's only polite you tell me your name, good sir," she said.

The man eyed Celeste, then placed his staff on his shoulder and bowed at the waist. "Thomas Dearing, at your service."

Rather than kissing it, he grasped Celeste's wrist and turned her palm up to him. He let the staff rest on the ground and dug in a pocket. He sprinkled what appeared to be lint over her fingers, then traced a dirty nail across her palm.

Josiah drew his sword, taking a half step forward. Sophia clamped a hand on his arm. A blue jay squawked, seeming to mock the mule's snorting and stomping.

"Ah. I see it all now," Thomas said with a conspiratorial grin. "Queen of Kersey, deposed by a usurper. Fleeing through the forest to Tegine. Expecting help from the aristocrats there."

Sophia wrinkled her brow. Was this man a seer? A wizard? Surely, he possessed some arcane power. Was he dangerous?

"Take caution there, Delicious. Tegine has an unstable throne. You may be better served going to the temple at Oxted. Seek help from Achaea's Paladin," Thomas said.

Josiah held his sword in a casual grip. "We need—"

"Water. I know." Thomas released Celeste's wrist. "However, this young woman isn't your queen. Bold enough to be. But a Crow, more likely the queen's handmaiden." He jabbed his scraggly whiskers at Sophia. "That one is the queen, if indeed you speak the truth. It's impolite to try to deceive your host."

"Truly spoken, Wizard. If an apology is needed, consider it given. We are sorely in need of water," Sophia said.

Thomas stared at the sky. His face twisted in silent concentration. He returned his eyes to Sophia and smiled. "Apology accepted."

"In the presence of the queen you'll address her properly or suffer the consequence," Josiah said.

"Of course. Two hundred pardons, your Grace."

Sophia inclined her chin and flashed her practiced smile.

Thomas beamed then gestured at his brimming barrels. "It hasn't rained in ten days, but I can allow you to drink your fill. If properly compensated."

"We have no treasure. You'd be so vile as to sell water?" Sophia said.

"One man's silver is another man's water. However, I will trade water for something of value. What does your Grace have to trade? Some jam perhaps?"

Josiah grunted. "I'll grant you twenty inches of steel if you don't give us water."

"Spoken like a knight, but I negotiate with the queen." Thomas's smile never wavered.

Sophia stepped up to Thomas as Celeste retreated. He stood only an inch taller than her. She cast her most demure smile at his dark eyes, then grabbed his ear flaps and jerked him to his knees. "I am the queen and the queen is through negotiating. Share your water, Wizard."

"If you plan to rule through violence and intimidation perhaps your being sacked is best for the people," Thomas said.

"Treason!" Stewart shouted taking a step toward Thomas while drawing his sword. Josiah held out his other arm, blocking Stewart's path.

"I treat people the way they treat me." Sophia released her grip on Thomas's hat, smoothed his coat, then grabbed his beard and twisted. Thomas yelped.

"Water is free in my realm, but I see you'd extort the needy. Perhaps I should leave this matter to my knights. I'm certain their judgment will be fair, swift, and final."

"More threats? I see diplomacy isn't in your nature." Thomas groaned.

The wizard knew her lack of compromising skills. She had to pass this test and get water for the men. Sophia glanced at Josiah and grinned. She returned a hard look to Thomas. "These are dark times and decorum must be set aside."

"You'd risk me putting a spell on you?" Thomas asked.

Threaten her? She could respond in kind. Sophia drew her dagger. "Can you conjure faster than I can strike?"

Thomas groaned again, then held his hands open to her. "All right, all right, your Grace. There's no need for this to get any uglier. You found my cottage, that's a sign of a sort. Help yourselves to the water. I have plenty to spare."

Josiah sheathed his sword as the men and mule rushed toward the rain barrels. "A wise choice, Dearing. I haven't killed a traitor in almost ten days."

Thomas flashed a smile. "Let's make it eleven, shall we?"

Josiah cast a frown at the man.

"What of the creek? Why is it dry?" Sophia asked, sheathing her dagger.

Thomas clambered to his feet and straightened his ear flaps, then dusted off his knees. "A wyvern in the east dams it up if there's a war. To flood the land near it or deny water to those far away." He scratched his nose. "I assume there's been another war?"

***

Sophia and Josiah walked a few yards into the forest and spoke in low tones. "Do you think there's any merit in Thomas's suggestion we go to Oxted?" Sophia asked.

Josiah ran a hand over his salt and pepper hair. "Maybe, but the temple is greedier than a miller's son. I considered it, but I think we'll have better luck proceeding to Tegine."

Sophia gazed at a blue jay, its colors those of Kersey. It sat on a limb near them and appeared to be listening. She returned her attention to Josiah. "True enough. The temple always wants offerings before doing anything."

"Indeed, and we have little to offer. It's settled then?" Josiah leaned, stretching his back.

"Yes. We go to Tegine."

***

Shortly after leaving Dearing's cottage, the forest became even older, more wild and remote. The trees grew tall with massive trunks a man couldn't wrap his arms around. Moss, like unruly beards, clung to the bark. The air was damp. Rotting vegetation permeated the air, creating a closed, dreary atmosphere.

Sophia watched for the rumored red wolves. Giant predators, waiting for a chance to fall upon the unsuspecting. Webs or other unseen obstacles brushed her cheek on every other step. The humidity rose and sweat streamed down her temples and seeped into her private parts. Celeste tried to wipe Sophia's brow from time to time. The soldiers trod on, but rarely got more than an arm's length from each other.

Their normal banter replaced with apprehensive silence.

When they stopped for the night, the company gathered close. Josiah ordered a small fire for the first time since they'd entered the forest. Sophia ate her ration and enjoyed a long draught from a water skin.

"What arcane power do you think that fellow, Thomas, possessed? And why didn't he use it against us?" Sophia asked her gathered knights.

Josiah scoffed. "Magic rarely stands up to a good blade well employed."

Stewart and Richard voiced their agreement. Another grunted his disdain for magic and its practitioners.

Celeste poked a stick in the flames. "He's a carnival huckster, nothing more. A clever fellow who used parlor tricks to convince some baron to fund his little house, while he performs lip service in exchange."

Sophia looked at her friend. "You think it so? How did he know all those details about us?"

Celeste leaned her head to one side before tossing her stick into the fire. "He's smart and observant. He didn't read anything on my palm, he noticed my hands weren't as soft as a noblewoman's would be. He guessed at the rest."

Sophia glanced at the stars peeking through the leafy canopy above. "That makes sense, but what about appearing out of thin air?"

"Yes, well, I can't explain everything." Celeste laughed.

***

Near the noon hour of their ninth day in the wood, they crossed onto a vast open plain. Sophia swore if the gods hid the forming fire in this land, it would be amongst that sea of golden grass. Purple clouds or hills clustered on the northern horizon.

Josiah allowed a smile, then crushed it with his warrior's

frown. "My Queen, now it becomes more dangerous. Walking will be easier, but so will observation. We'll be able to increase our pace, but Pendergast's men are likely to see our party at some point. Shall we proceed?"

Sophia looked around. Massive, old-growth oaks stood behind her. Tall dancing grass beckoned to her front. The plain was sparsely dotted with small stands of trees. The breeze fresh and clean. "I choose the route that affords the least violence and the most concealment."

Josiah's face curled into an unmerciful caricature of himself. "Placing you back on your throne will require violence on your behalf."

"If we are forced to fight, so be it. I'm not such a child as to think we can discuss the situation with Sir Mallet or his men."

Josiah bowed slightly. "Of course, my Queen. We'll be safe enough for the first day. By now Pendergast has surely purchased more hounds. The man is an ass, but he's not stupid. He must have figured out we're going to Tegine. It may end up being a footrace to our destination."

Sophia looked behind. Hounds? Were they close? Would Thomas betray them to the hounds' handlers? She raised her chin. "A wyvern does not fear hounds."

Josiah flashed a wry smile. "A wyvern can fly."

"When she chooses."

Josiah's eyes narrowed. "Tread carefully there, my Queen. You haven't demonstrated any of the wyvern's powers your lineage might suggest."

Sophia wrinkled her brow. Josiah knew of those fanciful wyvern rumors too? Foolish tales from the past. When she returned to her throne, she'd have scholars investigate and debunk those stories thoroughly. "You may lead on, Sir Josiah."

They walked on until the late afternoon. The road, no more than half a mile to the east. A scout shouted a warning and the knights and soldiers squatted out of sight. Josiah motioned for Sophia and Celeste to duck even lower. Sophia dropped to her knees, but peered to the east, her eyes level with the tall grass.

A few seconds crawled past. First a fluttering, pale-blue banner moving quickly came into view, then a moment later the crests on the riders' helmets. The horses followed. The banner streamed behind the lance it was secured to. The black stag's head stood out, even at that distance.

Josiah spit in the grass. "It would seem they ride with urgent business for Lord Pendergast. Alas, he isn't among them. If he were, we could end this here."

Sophia strained to see the men on the road. Celeste pulled on her arm. Sophia brushed her hand away.

Six of Pendergast's knights thundered down the road going toward Tegine. When the knights had ridden out of view and left dust hanging over the road, Stewart turned to Josiah.

"At that pace, they'll kill those horses long before they get to Tegine," Stewart said.

"Unless they have a relay station someplace nearby. We may have an opportunity to secure mounts for the last leg of our journey," Josiah said.

The company hunkered down in the grass and waited for Josiah's scouts to return. Celeste chewed on a long weed's stem. Sophia moved close to Stewart.

"Sir Stewart, how long can a man ride a horse at that pace without causing it harm?"

Stewart regarded her with a smile. Behind Sophia, Celeste faked a cough.

"Not more than an hour, maybe an hour and a half if the horse is well conditioned, my Queen."

Celeste whacked Sophia's wrist with the weed. "You know that perfectly well," Celeste whispered.

Sophia snarled at Celeste. "I'm just making conversation. Control yourself."

The scouts, mere boys, returned and reported their findings to Josiah. He flashed a predatory grin at Sophia. "Pendergast has a relay station with many mounts two miles from here. It's time we take some horses."

***

Observing from a copse, the relay station stood less than a quarter-mile distant. It was nothing more than a tent, a cart piled with hay, and a rope corral next to the road. A dozen horses milled about the canvas water trough in the corral. A groom worked, wiping the salty sweat lines from a horse's flanks. Sophia counted four other men working there. Surely, they were no match for her company. How would Josiah proceed? Her heartbeat quickened. Her martial training, although thorough, covered the how of fighting without dwelling on the horrible end.

Josiah assigned a boy to hold the mule, and four men to guard Sophia and Celeste, then he called for a straightforward, frontal attack on the relay station. He drew his sword, dropped to his knees and crawled, leading the rest of the company, inching toward the tent.

Sophia allowed him to get out of sight, then went to her knees and crawled after him. One of the soldiers stepped into her path.

"Get out of my way," Sophia growled.

"Your Grace, Sir Josiah said—"

"I heard what he said, but I'm the queen. Now step aside." Sophia gestured with her dagger. When the man moved away, she crawled forward. Celeste joined Sophia, staying behind her.

"What do you think you're doing?" Celeste whispered.

"What does it look like I'm doing?"

"It looks like you're making a huge mistake."

Sophia paused and looked over a shoulder at Celeste. Her

maid's eyes stood wide and imploring. "I'm not going to fight unless I have to. I want to see and be seen. Go back if you're afraid."

Celeste shook her head, then frowned. "I'm going with you. Even if you're being foolish. You know that."

Sophia's company reached the edge of the road across from the horses without raising an alarm. The animals perked their ears and looked in Sophia's direction. Her band would have to act quickly or be discovered. Josiah looked down his line in both directions. Sophia ducked avoiding his observation. She clutched her dagger and tensed her muscles.

She wanted those horses. Surprised at herself, she wanted them more than she'd wanted water a few days ago. Her breath came quick and sharp, her fingers trembled. She tightened her grip on her dagger's leather handle. The breeze carried the odor of sage while the dry earth provided a musty, but wholesome smell. Sophia's heart pounded and the crackling came to her mind's ear. She pushed the interior noise aside and looked to Josiah.

Josiah raised his sword and braced to rise on an arm. Sophia's muscles coiled, ready to leap forward. She clenched her teeth, stifling the urge to shout a battle cry.

A deep-throated hound's "barooh" cut the air behind them. Many other canine voices joined in chorus.

CHAPTER SEVEN

Josiah leapt to his feet and shouted, "Damn it all. War-dogs. Take the horses, men."

With a throaty roar the common soldiers rushed at the tent, their spears forefront. The four luckless men working there froze, a moment later they fled. The soldiers chased them down, stabbing with their spears until all movement ceased.

The groom hid among the horses' legs until he was spotted, then he fled and disappeared into the tall grass. Two of her men followed him into the weeds.

Sophia jumped forward and shouted encouragement. Richard instantly grabbed her around the waist.

"The men will take care of them, your Grace. The war-dogs are the real danger. Stay behind me, but be ready."

Sophia wrinkled her lips. Men were always taking charge of women, ordering them about under the guise of protection. By the gods, she was the queen. "I can fight."

"Now is not the time, your Grace." Richard turned away, brandishing his sword. A tattered surcoat woven in her colors covered his hauberk, testimony to their desperate situation. Her palm felt greasy on the dagger's hilt. Looking across the tall grass, a pair of black ears would pop up here, there a stubby tail, too many to count. The dogs' sounding rang loud in her ears. Men followed far behind the hounds.

Richard's shoulders stiffened. The largest dog Sophia had ever seen leapt against Richard's chest. He tried to fend it off with his sword, but the animal was on him so quickly the impact smashed him to the ground.

Sophia screamed, Richard kicked, punched, and tried to get his sword into position. Thick, padded-leather armor, painted with a yellow mountain ogre's leering face covered the dog's sides and back. A broad, spiked collar protected its neck. Foam flew from its jaws as it tried to rip Richard's throat. Its red-brown markings on jet black fur blurred together within its violent movement. The dog growled and Richard swore, though his hauberk protected him from the worst of the hound's fury.

The beast must have weighed as much as Sophia, and was armored, and outraged. She had to do something. Sophia shouted, "A wyvern fears no hounds." And leapt on the dog's back, stabbing at it with her dagger.

The hound seemed to ignore her, but still gave her a rough ride as it savaged Richard. Sophia clung to its armor with one hand and used the other for frantic stabbing. Her braid whipped back and forth as the dog snarled and shook violently. Her martial training hadn't been anything like this.

The crackling in Sophia's mind came louder than usual, more insistent. She had no time for paying it any attention.

A wounded yelp startled her. Her dagger found a gap in the dog's armor. She slammed it home. The hound leapt away, whimpered, then slunk off toward the handlers.

Sophia rose on her knees. Her chest heaving. Hot blood covered her hand and drops fell from her dagger's point. The dog collapsed a few yards away. She glanced to her left and right; twenty feet away Celeste clung to Stewart. Sophia frowned.

Richard rolled to one side then came to his feet, bloodied, but not seriously injured. He glanced after the hound, back at Sophia, then ripped off his helmet. He fell to his knees, dropped his sword on the trampled grass, and grabbed her empty hand.

"Your Grace, you've given me my life. I now re-pledge it to you. Speak your desire and I'll grant it or die in the attempt."

"Rise, Sir Richard. The enemy's minions still prowl the field. We have no time for gallant gestures. Arm yourself and heed our general's call."

A quick survey of the field showed Stewart standing with Celeste, hugging her with a powerful arm around her shoulders. Celeste twittered with laughter, but Sophia couldn't hear what they said. Stewart pointed at something across the field. He gave Celeste a quick bow, then dashed through the grass in the direction he'd pointed.

Celeste flashed a meek grin at Sophia, who turned away and helped Richard buckle his helmet.

All the war-dogs were slain, but they'd killed three of Sophia's unarmored common soldiers. The dead men's bodies were dragged to a spot near the road.

Josiah growled at some men standing nearby. "Get their names and belongings. Leave nothing to tell Pendergast who they are. We must protect their families as best we can." Josiah turned to Sophia as the men rifled through the corpse's purses and clothing. "Choose a mount, my Queen."

Sophia took a seat on a massive bay's back. Its heat penetrated her canvas trousers and soothed her tired legs. Celeste sat a roan and Josiah another bay.

Sophia looked at the men, half a score of whom had no mounts. She turned to Josiah. "We'll walk. There's no need to leave these men behind."

Josiah wheeled his mount. "Using these horses to get to Tegine as quickly as we can will serve the greater good. Most of the hounds' handlers escaped us. It won't be long before this attack is reported and reinforcements are sent."

"What of these men? What of their families?" Sophia swept her arm at the gathered soldiers, their young faces streaked with dirt, some spattered with blood.

Josiah looked down. His brows knit. "The greater good, my Queen."

She'd chosen against Josiah the last time he'd used the greater good argument. It had been a mistake. Regardless, this time he was wrong. Sophia straightened in her saddle. "We will ride at a tolerable pace. I will leave no fighting man behind. Too many were left at Persimmon. It's no wonder Sir Mallet recruited them so cheaply."

Josiah frowned. "Persimmon couldn't be helped. When your father fell—"

"I'm not casting blame, nor disparaging your honor. Merely stating a fact. We have a choice today and we'll not leave a fighting man behind."

"Pendergast will catch us."

Sophia took in the worried faces of her infantry. Mere boys really, most were younger than herself. "These men will fight at our sides and Sir Mallet will lose. Sir Josiah, I'm still learning my responsibilities, but I already know my people are the most important thing. I count for almost nothing."

Sophia frowned at Celeste's grin. Josiah looked back and forth between the women, then gestured for Sophia's attention.

"You are the queen. We've all pledged our lives to you, your reign, and your house. You can't reclaim the throne if you don't escape."

"No, Sir Josiah. I've pledged my life to the people, to these men. We must go on to Tegine, but we'll leave no soldier behind."

"You are your father's daughter. So be it." Josiah spun his mount around. "Take all the food and water. Burn the cart and the tent. Quickly men. We march to Tegine."

***

They made camp in a stand of ancient cedars clinging to the edge of a narrow creek. Nothing more than a ditch, but it offered flowing water. Josiah felt they were too close to the road to risk a fire, so they did without.

Sophia made small talk with Josiah about various fighting styles, tactics, and armor while pressing him for the political situation to get a better idea of who she could trust in her court and who she should punish. Other than Pendergast, Cavale topped the list.

Once it was fully dark, she rolled out her quilt and laid down.

Celeste came to her, her outline barely visible in the moonless night. "Will you be needing anything else tonight, my Queen?"

Sophia shook her head. After a moment Celeste pushed gently on Sophia's arm. "Are you asleep?"

"No. And I don't want anything." Sophia rolled to face the other way.

"What's wrong?"

"Nothing, I'm tired. Leave me."

"Are you sure? You've been rather quiet this evening."

"I told you to leave me. Go do whatever it is you do during the night." Sophia sniffed and wrapped the quilt tighter. A long silence passed, but Celeste didn't move away. Sophia pursed her lips and closed her eyes.

"What's that supposed to mean? I sleep at your side each night. You know it well." Celeste's voice lowered to a whisper.

Sophia lurched upright and stared at the dark outline of her maid. "I mean I saw you with Sir Stewart this afternoon. If you feel the need to entertain him, go," Sophia hissed.

"Ha!" Celeste slapped a hand over her mouth. "That's what this is about?" Celeste inched closer. "I was frightened and he made a joke. I laughed at it. There was nothing more to it."

Sophia glared even knowing her face couldn't be seen. "It looked like more than a joke."

"My Queen, I'm not just your maid, I'm your friend. I would never...Sir Stewart would never. His eyes are for you alone."

Nearby Josiah growled, "Voices carry on the night air. Sort out your romantic problems during the day. The rest of us need our sleep."

Celeste giggled, then leaned against Sophia, hugging her.

"Two hundred pardons, Sir Knight. The queen and I will keep our issues to ourselves."

Josiah's grunted reply was more a chuckle.

Sophia halfheartedly pushed Celeste away then fell back into her quilt. "Do as you please. Just leave me."

***

In the early morning Josiah led the company back to the road. They fell upon another of Pendergast's relay stations. This one was better protected. Josiah assigned four men and a knight to guard Sophia and Celeste. Sophia complained to no avail. Josiah used the argument that "losing her would be foolish," convincing her to not participate in the attack.

Despite the loss of two more men, Sophia's company prevailed and secured horses for all her remaining soldiers. Josiah suggested they split into two groups, sending one west with the plan to meet up again further north before nightfall. Sophia agreed and ordered it. Her group, with Josiah guiding, rode to the east and a smaller company, with Stewart leading, rode to the west.

Many of the common soldiers struggled to control their mounts. They had experience with draft animals, but few had ever ridden a horse. A scarcity of proper tack made the issue worse. Sophia and the knights assisted the worst afflicted. It allowed her to ignore Celeste for most of the day.

In the early afternoon, reunited with Stewart's company, they returned to the road. Cresting a low ridge, a small group of Pendergast's men surprised them. "Two hundred pardons, my Queen. I'm a fool for not sending scouts ahead," Josiah said. "It's too late to flee, the commoners would be cut down from behind."

Fifty yards away four of Pendergast's knights sat their mounts near a dilapidated wooden bridge spanning a creek. Waiting, as if they'd expected Sophia's company. Their squires were vigilant nearby.

Josiah regarded the men at their front. He turned to Sophia. "That company contains skilled men, including Cavale. What would you have us do?"

Sophia regarded the men. They remained quiet, camails hiding their faces. Their banner, pale blue with the stag's head, fluttered in the light breeze.

Sophia's seven knights against Pendergast's four, plus their squires. She set her warrior's scowl. "They are my enemies."

"It's customary to offer them the option to surrender."

"Very well, Sir Josiah, I'll leave this matter to you and the knights."

"So be it. Should we fall, don't resist. Surrender immediately. Pendergast will likely spare you as you're worth more to him as a prize than otherwise." He donned his helmet and spurred his mount without waiting for a reply. The knights went forward with him. He halted several yards from their adversaries.

"Your queen demands you pay homage and join her escort to Tegine," Josiah announced in a clear voice all could hear.

The man in the middle of their group spoke, "We don't have a queen. We have King Pendergast. Josiah, she's just a snotty bitch, will you fight for her?"

Josiah leaned back and drew down his visor. "Aye,

Dominique. As will these men. The Lady Pendergast is our queen and your life is forfeit for the insult."

"Give her to us. I'll grant you the courtesy of a two-hour start before I report you to our King. Perhaps you can return to that boy you covet before you're caught."

"That boy is a grown man, as you know well. I see you haven't brought enough men to accomplish your task, Dominique. A mistake you will not live to regret."

"I have more than enough men to scatter this rabble and slay King Pendergast's enemies."

"A fat pig's ass. Will you yield or fight?" Josiah shifted in his saddle.

Sophia's knights drew their swords, closed their visors and sat their mounts knee to knee in apparent calm. She brushed a loose strand of hair from her cheek. The horses swung their tails and stomped at flies in the heat. Sophia blew a gnat away from her lips. Her fingers twitched. Would they allow her company to pass?

Dominique looked to his left and right then drew his sword. "I've met you in the lists, Tarkenton. You've never defeated me and we are no longer playing a game."

"Truly spoken, Cavale. However, today I will kill you and tomorrow the usurper you serve."

"We shall see."

As one, Sophia's knights jammed their heels into their mounts and leapt forward. Her common soldiers fingered their weapons and licked their lips, but didn't join this battle of knight versus knight. Indeed, wearing no armor, it would be foolish of them to participate.

Sophia's knights' charge caught Pendergast's men drawing their swords. Josiah crashed into Dominique's horse and shoved his adversary from the saddle. Another knight fell among the horses' legs and was trampled in the dust.

Dominique jumped to his feet without his sword. Josiah swung his horse around, knocking Dominique down again. He scurried from under Josiah's steed's hooves. He claimed a fallen sword, then sprang to his feet. Josiah turned again and charged at Dominique. Their blades met with a clang. Dominique's weapon broke several inches above the guard. He cast it aside and grabbed his dagger. Josiah rushed forward once more and stabbed Dominique in the neck. Dominique clutched at Josiah's blade before falling. The swirling dust and stomping hooves claimed his body.

Horses screamed in pain. Many, riderless, fled the field. Of the knights, only Josiah remained in the saddle. Richard and Stewart confronted a lone knight. Josiah dashed up behind Pendergast's man and stabbed him in the back, Stewart and Richard fell upon him, finishing him with daggers and fists.

As expected, quarter was neither sought, nor granted.

Pendergast's four knights and all but one of their squires lay dead or dying. Four of Sophia's knights joined them. The lone squire was ten or twelve years old, dressed in fine mail. He dropped his spear and stared at Josiah.

Sophia examined the boy's face from the distance. He was frightened but sat his bay, straight, with bravado. Josiah reigned in next to the boy. He motioned with his sword and the boy slid from his horse, dropped to his knees, and shivered with his head down.

Josiah dismounted and stepped in front of the boy. He sheathed his sword and drew his dagger. He held the boy's shoulder and gestured at him with his weapon. The boy raised his chin exposing his neck. Josiah drew his arm back to strike.

Sophia shouted, "Wait! What are you doing?" She urged her mount forward closing the distance.

Josiah turned toward her. "He's a squire. His knight is dead. Pendergast will hold him responsible. He will be hanged. This is more merciful."

He was only a boy, for Cassandra's sake. "I am not Sir Mallet and do not subscribe to his methods. You will spare him, Sir Josiah."

Josiah paused with the point of his dagger a few inches from the boy's throat. "My Queen, he will be hanged. You know what that means. His body will jerk and spasm on the gallows for as long as a quarter-hour. Being strangled is no way for a fighting man to die. This is far more merciful and honorable."

Josiah's helmet remained closed. Sophia couldn't read his expression. She looked into the boy's cherubic face. "What is your name, young man?"

He blinked several times.

Josiah swore under his breath, dropping his dagger to his side. "Cassandra's tits. Answer her, man."

"My name is William Highsmith, but most folks call me Will. Are you really the queen?"

"I am. You must swear allegiance to me, my house, and my reign. Can you do that?" Sophia looked at the common soldiers as they fell upon the fallen knights and squires, looting their armor and weapons. They seemed to relish the task. Several weeks ago, she'd have thought them ghouls, now, it was simply the way things were.

"Yes," Will said.

Josiah scoffed as he sheathed his dagger. He cuffed the boy on the back of the head. "By the gods, man. Stand up and do it properly. Didn't Cavale train you?"

"Two hundred pardons, Sir Knight." Will hopped to his feet and approached Sophia. He placed a hand on her boot's toe and lowered his chin. "My life is yours, your Grace. Speak your desire and I'll make it so or die trying."

Sophia tousled his blond hair. "My knights have no squires, young Will. You will serve Sir Richard De Margot." She pointed at Richard. "He will see to your training and perhaps one day you will carry my scarf in the lists."

"Your Grace, he is Dominique Cavale's squire. He'll cut my throat and yours at the first opportunity," Richard said.

Sophia glanced at Will, his face chubby, dirty, but

innocent. She looked back to Richard. "Sir Richard, you fought a war dog with your bare hands. I'm certain you can manage a ten-year-old boy."

"You killed the war dog, your Grace."

"Sir Richard, I wish it so. Train him well."

Richard, his face stern, inclined his chin almost imperceptibly, then gruffly directed Will to remount and prepare to move on. The looting was complete and thorough. The naked corpses shone in the bright sun. One of the common soldiers came to Sophia with a hauberk rolled under his arm.

"Your Grace, this hauberk won't fit a grown man, but it will fit your person well." He held it out to her. Sophia accepted the armor, placing the heavy roll across her thighs.

"Thank you. What is your name?"

"I'm called John, John Astor, your Grace."

"John Astor, I'm in your debt and you are in my favor. Now, our general grows impatient, heed his orders. We must move on."

***

Choosing speed over concealment, the company trotted straight down the road. Josiah remained quiet. He responded to Sophia's questions and comments with grunts or nods.

"Sir Josiah, what's wrong? Your mind is burdened, tell me of it."

Josiah looked straight ahead. "It's nothing, my Queen. Nothing you need worry over yet."

"Is this about that boy?"

Josiah snorted.

"What purpose would killing him have served?"

Josiah remained silent as they covered several yards.

Sophia glanced at their company. "Perhaps we should speak of such things in private."

Josiah turned to Richard. "Maintain this pace, the queen and I will ride ahead."

Sophia spurred her mount to keep up with Josiah. They returned to a walk a hundred yards ahead of the company.

"What is at issue?"

Josiah glanced at her. "The boy isn't relevant except as an example."

"An example of what?"

"You are a kind person. It's in your nature. You have a good, gentle heart. A young woman's heart, much like your mother's. You—"

"You mean a girl's heart?"

Josiah glanced at her, granting a curt nod. "You must harden your heart. Grow a queen's calculating strength. Difficult decisions await you. They must be considered, weighed if you will, on their merit, without emotion. Without concern for your personal feelings."

Sophia stared at Josiah's profile. Was he speaking in general or of something specific? Josiah rarely hinted. Without emotion? Did he speak now of Stewart? Of Celeste? She turned, looking back. Celeste rode next to Richard. Stewart rode further back assisting a soldier with his horse. Seeing Sophia's gaze Celeste waved. Sophia returned it.

She returned her attention to Josiah. "My heart wishes Sir Stewart to be my consort."

Josiah grunted, looking straight ahead.

"You disapprove. Why?"

Josiah's lips tightened. "Odette is a good man. He is handsome, young, and brave. I understand your attraction to him. I sponsored his accolade, but his family brings little help to your cause."

"Politically?"

"Yes. Had your father married you to Mallet Pendergast, a horrible notion for you I realize; all of this may have been avoided." He shared a warm smile with her. "Your father knew of your desire for Odette. It weighed on his mind."

Sophia rode on in silence. Who else was there? Certainly no one among her current company. No one that stirred her insides like Stewart. Perhaps Richard, but he had a wife. That fellow John Astor was handsome enough, but he was a commoner. Was Josiah suggesting she make a bargain with Henry De Roederio? She'd never laid eyes on the man.

"What about you Sir Josiah? You have no wife. Would you be my Prince Consort?" A giggle escaped her.

Josiah scoffed. "I'm flattered at the suggestion. You are pleasant to the eye and even more so as a companion. But I'm far too old for you. And you know well, I've never favored intimacy with women. Not to mention, my name brings little benefit to your cause. There is also the scandal it would bring at court."

"Doesn't the throne decide what is or isn't a scandal at court?"

"Not in such a case. The nobles and more importantly, their wives, would whisper about undue influence. It cannot be."

"It isn't often a queen offers herself to a man. You have no idea how painful that rejection can be."

Josiah shook his stern head. "The refusal of an offer made in jest can't be taken in offense. No, I'd recommend you keep an open mind in De Roederio's court. His son is a fine man, recently widowed. His wife and child died in the birthing."

"And a betrothal to this widower would bring Tegine to my cause."

"That is how it's done. Of course, a suitable dowry will have to be promised. In this case it may be expensive."

Selling her hand and womb to a stranger to get what she wanted. It wouldn't be whoring; they were royals. It *was* how things were done. Indeed, long ago, Fraysse offered her own mother to Father to garner peace. Could she give herself to this unknown man and still have Stewart? What of her heart?

Sophia turned and looked back at her company. What if King Henry's son was ugly?

CHAPTER EIGHT

Sophia's company came in view of Tegine after dark a day later. Josiah moved them from the road to a hidden spot in the forest. The lights in the city twinkled, beckoning, while mournful music played on horns drifted across the mist-shrouded river.

Josiah advised Sophia to send Richard and two soldiers into the city to announce her and get a feel for their reception. Sophia didn't like the empty feeling in her gut, but she agreed. Guards were set and most of her company went to their blankets.

Sophia stood alone near the riverbank, gazing at the city lights. Her future lay hidden in mystery. She needed to put something in her present back to normal. Regain some control over events. To this point others had been guiding and leading her. Men, of course. Even though they were well-meaning, they still looked upon her as a woman. She wasn't some frail waif. She was the queen. A Queen of the Sword, the chosen one, she needed to show it. She picked up a stone and skipped it across the smooth water's surface.

"Five hops. Not bad," Celeste whispered as she approached.

Sophia turned to her. "I've been unkind to you the last few days. Unkind without good reason. I hope you can forgive me."

"We were friends long before you became queen. It's been a hard road so far, we're all on edge."

Sophia gestured at the river's surface. "Do you remember when we were children and we'd lay in the grass near the pond on warm summer days? Days like today was earlier. And we'd dream of handsome princes sweeping us off to the fairy lands?"

"After he'd vanquished some giant ogre or wyvern to prove his worth," Celeste said.

Sophia smiled. "Of course." She picked at a broken nail. "Wyvern-slaying princes are in short supply these days."

"Sir Stewart hasn't killed a wyvern, but he's fought many battles and been a hero in his own right. He's a fitting prince for you."

Sophia bit her lip. "I think he has eyes for you. You're beautiful and I'm plain. If you prefer, pleasant to the eye, as Sir Josiah says."

"That's not true. Either part. You're beautiful in your own way. I'd kill to have your hair, and you're the queen. I'll always be a servant in Sir Stewart's mind."

"You're wrong there. His interest is more about my station than me. Besides, other than his sword, his lineage brings nothing to my cause."

Celeste chewed her lower lip and stood silent, shifting her weight from one hip to the other. At last, she turned to Sophia. "You're not going to give up and settle for an arranged marriage, are you?"

"There was always going to be an arrangement, even if Father lived. Thinking otherwise was childish. I'm told Lord De Roederio's son is a widower and a good man. Sir Richard is opening the proposal as we speak." Sophia poked her chin at the city lights.

Celeste grunted in the darkness. "Is this prince handsome

and daring?"

"I don't know."

"What's his name?"

"It doesn't matter."

Celeste scoffed. "That's a loaded chamber pot. You should take Sir Stewart for your heart and damn tradition. Do what's right for you."

"Who then would rescue the Crows from Sir Mallet?"

"Crows? I've always hated that name. I've never heard you use it before."

"Father frowned on it, but here we are, in the wild. The rough side of life staring us in the face. I forget myself. I apologize," Sophia said.

Celeste placed a hand on Sophia's arm. "It's nothing. The common people will survive regardless. They always do. Trust me, they've survived worse than Lord Pendergast. We are like the land itself. We're always there."

"I would make their lives better."

"A noble cause, but how would you do that?"

"Father always said peace was the greatest gift the common folk could expect. I'd grant them peace and justice."

"Peace and justice? You'd have to be a noble to think of such things." Celeste bent, picked up a stone and tossed it into the river. "Common folk concern themselves with putting food in their children's bellies and providing a roof to keep them dry in winter."

Sophia glanced at the concentric rings in the water. The reflection of Celeste's beautiful face seemed undisturbed, while the ripples made her own fuzzy and distorted. Sophia snorted.

"Regardless, peace has to be bought with blood. Sir Stewart can't raise an army for me. Henry De Roederio can." Sophia frowned at the state of her nails. She sighed and looked again at the lights in Tegine. A foreign land, with alien traditions and customs. How would she cope?

"When I'm back on the throne I'll raise your station. I'll appoint you my lady-in-waiting and betroth you to Sir Stewart." She turned to Celeste and forced a pained smile. "Your children will be beautiful."

Croaking sounded at the water's edge near them. The women looked in the sound's direction.

"I'll catch him, you kiss him," Celeste said. They giggled together.

"If only it were that easy," Sophia said.

Their laughter subsided and Celeste sighed. "That's a great gift, my Queen, but I can't accept it. Regardless how many sons I give him, Sir Stewart will always love you."

Sophia glanced at Celeste's outline. Was she truly refusing? Or was she trying to appear unexcited? She must be pretending, but still... "I will think on it. We have more pressing issues right now."

Celeste stood silent for a long time. "Those musicians in Tegine could play some happier music. What's going on over there? A funeral?"

Sophia allowed a resigned chuckle. "It suits my mood." She placed a hand on Celeste's shoulder. "Come, I'd bathe and be grateful if you'd keep the guards' vigilant eyes at bay. I'm certain the sight would disappoint them in any event."

Celeste curtsied and laughed. "As you wish, but you under value yourself. I'm certain the sight would drive them all to distraction."

***

In the morning Sophia remained wrapped in her quilt.

Several common soldiers, under Celeste's direction, fashioned a screen of tree limbs and blankets to provide Sophia some privacy to dress for her meeting with Henry De Roederio. Satisfied with the construction, Celeste accompanied Sophia behind it.

Josiah sat at their small fire with Stewart and Richard, who had returned during the night. They conversed in low tones about how they'd proceed and what exactly they should offer Henry De Roederio as a dowry.

Sophia listened as she dressed. Discussing her dowry was Father's privilege. They had no right to infringe, even if Father was dead. She'd do it herself or no one would.

Celeste held up a bundle of cloth, the remnants of one of Sophia's gowns which she'd cut into strips. "Are you sure this is a good idea? It's not exactly what I'd do if I were trying to trap a husband."

"Yes." Sophia raised her arms. "I'm not looking for a husband. I'm looking for a military alliance. The husband is a by-product. Wrap it snug, but not so tight I can't breathe." Going forward she would approach all men on an equal footing. She would not allow her gender to be a distraction. She would demonstrate her status as a Queen of the Sword.

Celeste wrapped Sophia's breasts tight to her chest then helped her put on her wool jacket. Sophia wriggled into the hauberk Astor gave her. The shoulders were snug, but the length reached slightly above her knees. It would have provided outstanding protection if she'd had a gambeson. However, with her canvas trousers and shirt underneath, her protection would be adequate.

Celeste draped a quickly fashioned surcoat over the armor. During the night she'd sewn Sophia's embroidered wyvern onto the fabric. Sophia glanced at her reflection in the river. The wyvern adorned her chest and glowed in the early light. A menacing enough sight. She was the queen, chosen to fulfill prophecy. Dressed as a man, she'd take the lead like a man. She sat, allowing Celeste to comb and braid her long hair tight to the sides of her head.

A length of rope served as a belt. Sophia stuffed her dagger into it and stood. "Let's go put these men in their place."

Sophia strode to the fire. "Good morning, my loyal

gentlemen."

The knights rose and stared at her. Josiah made a long examination of her, then said, "My Queen, what are you intending?"

"Whatever do you mean, Sir Josiah?" Sophia cocked her head to one side and placed a hand on her hip.

"Something a bit more feminine would make all of this somewhat easier. De Margot reports De Roederio is in failing health and isn't keen on receiving you. Dressed as you are, he'll most certainly reject any proposal."

"I will demonstrate that I'm the Kersen Wyvern. I'll fight for my throne rather than depending on him or my future husband to do it for me. I will also deal with the negotiation of my dowry personally."

"Cassandra's teachings don't abide in Tegine. They follow Achaea. Consequently, women don't negotiate with men in Tegine. And they certainly don't wear armor. You know well it's not even common in Kersey. Your station and responsibilities allowed an exception for you."

"The men in Lord Henry's court, as well as my own, will have to learn a new skill."

"But, my Queen, we're looking for a husband, an alliance, not a day in the lists. De Roederio expects to greet a flower, not a warrior."

"I'm a Queen of the Sword, perhaps hiding a flower within my armor. Many flowers must have the petals pealed to reveal their beauty. And the most beautiful often come with thorns. Henry De Roederio and his son will recognize that or suffer the regret of a missed opportunity."

"My Queen—"

"Enough, Sir Josiah. Your objection is noted. Please lead on. I'd like to get this humiliation over with."

Josiah stared at Sophia. His eye ticked a couple times. At last, he shook his head and stomped to their meager baggage pile and rummaged in it. "If indeed this is your choice you can at least complete the ensemble," he growled over his shoulder.

He stood and held out Sophia's father's sword and baldric. "A wyvern is always well-armed."

Sophia accepted the sword. A glance verified the wyvern's head pommel and black blade, she clutched it to her breast and beamed. "Sir Josiah, I'd no idea you'd saved this. It is a treasure. Thank you."

"If my Queen insists on trying to intimidate Lord De Roederio, we may as well make it complete. It's my honor to present it to you. Your girl will need to make some adjustment to the baldric. Your father's height will make it fit you poorly."

Celeste stepped forward and made some rough measurements with her palms. "Just a few minutes and we'll have this looking proper."

Sophia turned her attention to Stewart. He avoided her eyes and made a pretense of examining the toes of his boots. Sophia stepped to his side. "What troubles you, Sir Stewart?"

He shook his head. "It's nothing, my Queen."

"My knights always seem troubled and then say it's nothing."

Stewart gazed at her with those wonderful eyes. A tremor skipped across his lower lip. "I'd thought something that cannot be. My Queen shouldn't concern herself with it."

Sophia returned her patient smile, the one she'd practiced when some servant would drop a piece of crockery. Please, Cassandra, don't let him profess his love. This was already difficult enough. What could she do, what could she say if he did? At last, she turned away. She went back to Celeste and waited there.

Celeste draped the baldric over Sophia's shoulder, then hooked the sword's scabbard to it. Sophia shrugged the baldric into a comfortable position and took a few steps. The weight and metallic clink brought a warm feeling to her chest. It was power, regal power. She could easily grow used to it.

Josiah grunted his approval. "Very well then, let's get on

with it."

The knights, the two ladies, Will, and the six best riders among the common soldiers gathered at the horses. Sophia glanced around. "We have no banners. I fear we'll appear to be a motley collection of vagabonds."

Leather creaked as Josiah swung up into the saddle. "It is what we are at the moment, my Queen. All will be set right in good time."

Sophia laughed. "Well then..." She placed a foot in the stirrup. Stewart stepped to her side and held her elbow.

"A private word, my Queen?"

Sophia looked back at him. This was it. He was going to complicate things. Make them harder than they need be. Should she ignore his request? His face implored her. She couldn't turn away. "Of course, Sir Stewart."

Josiah frowned, but held his tongue. Sophia and Stewart walked a few paces toward the river.

"I'd beg you to reconsider this decision. We can raise an army, an army from among the common folk. We don't need Lord De Roederio's help or his demands on your realm."

Sophia looked across the river. The city was bathed in bright sunlight, shining like a multi-faceted jewel set on a green background. She returned her attention to Stewart. "Sir Josiah advises me this is the best path back to the throne. I agree with him."

"Have you not felt anything for me in the time we've spent together? Have you not felt my love?"

A groan rose in Sophia's throat, she stifled it. "Until now you've said nothing to show me your heart. You've shared clever jokes and fantastic stories while I've hung on every word. Now you wish to speak of love?"

"I would if only you would hear me."

"Sir Stewart, I would hold you in my court as a trusted knight. I would have you betrothed to my maid when I've raised her station. I would have your loyalty, but I cannot have your love. Not in that way."

"That's kind of you. And cruel. Celeste is a beautiful and charming woman. But her eyes sparkle in the presence of many men. I have seen that yours have only done so in my presence. That's far more important to me."

"And I wonder, would you speak so if not for my station?"

Stewart's face grew grim. "I'm offended at such a notion. I will always speak so. Should you seek to live in a cottage in the forest and be done with all of this, so be it, as long as you choose me to accompany you."

Sophia turned her back to him and wiped at her watering eyes. Why? Why now? Why hadn't he spoken to her like this while Father was alive? What could she do now? Running away into the forest with Stewart would be so easy, but what of the people, and the prophecy?

Josiah was waiting, his face frozen in a disapproving scowl.

She was the queen, her destiny, her fate couldn't be denied. Sophia sniffed then looked over a shoulder. "Your words flatter me and they will warm my heart from this day on, but as you said yourself, it cannot be."

"I regret never speaking so before. Can you forgive me and change your mind? Is being the queen so important?"

Sophia sucked in a deep breath and held it for a moment. "A woman can forgive. A wyvern cannot. I am the queen, it's not for me to choose, the gods have spoken."

"A wyvern's breath can't match the heat rushing through my veins. I beg you to forgive me. I shouldn't have asked you to forsake your calling." Stewart lowered his chin, his broad shoulders slumped.

"You have my forgiveness, but I can't allow it to change my mind. I must go into Tegine and meet with Lord De Roederio. Know this, regaining the throne isn't for my vanity, it's for the people. Our people. I'd beg for your loyalty and understanding." Sophia turned to him. His face shone red. He looked down. His fists clenched at his sides.

"You will always have my loyalty and my heart, my Queen."

Sophia stroked his cheek. "You are my friend. I cherish that above all else." She turned away and called out, "Lead on, Sir Josiah. We have business in Tegine."

CHAPTER NINE

Sophia's small party crossed the stone bridge leading to Tegine. The clatter of their horses' hooves echoed back at them from the first buildings of the city proper.

The city, built mostly of wood, had homes and shops painted in bright colors. A contrast with Kersey. It was larger as well. Smoked meats and aromatic stewpots announced meals being prepared. Sophia's stomach growled at the smells. She dismissed the hollow feeling in her gut and smiled at those people going about their morning business, although few showed any interest in her.

A swineherd struggled to get his noisy charges out of the street while apologizing for blocking the road. Her company waited patiently. Sophia wondered at the city. How did they survive the wyverns with so many wooden structures above ground? Before an answer came to her the hogs cleared the road and her party moved on, shooing away grimy children who ran after them with outstretched hands.

They wound their way through the city streets and out the other side, where they climbed the steep road cutting through a vineyard, leading to the castle. Henry's fortress, built of black stone, shone in the sun, its glare painful to the eye. The shallow breeze fluffed its white and scarlet banners.

Sophia's company passed through the gate with no fanfare. In the bailey, grooms took charge of their animals. Josiah came to Sophia's side and pointed into the stable.

"That mount, on the end, belongs to George De August. One of Pendergast's barons. We must stay alert, my Queen," he whispered.

Sophia glanced at the big bay as her own mount was led past it. "Isn't Tegine supposed to be neutral?"

"We don't yet know if Tegine is truly neutral, my Queen."

Sophia shuddered. The game was growing more dangerous every day. She would have to search for hidden meaning in every word spoken to her.

The common soldiers were bid to enter a small door off the main building while Sophia, her knights, and maid were led into the audience hall at Castle Roederio. Many windows running down one wall lit the room well. It wore rich wood paneling accented with classic sculpture resting on small ornate tables. The air smelled of spices, leather, and men. That was it; her hall needed windows. She'd see to it as soon as she was back in power.

An ancient man sat at the far end. His throne was more elaborate than Sophia's, equipped with a padded seat and back. She strode up to him and bowed at the waist. His veiny claws gestured for her to rise. His long white hair and beard barely shivered in acknowledgment of his head movements. Perhaps he'd collect dust if his servants hadn't kept up a steady fanning of his person.

"Lord Henry De Roederio, hail and greetings," Sophia said.

"Lady Sophia Pendergast, well met." His voice soft and tremulous. "I expected more feminine attire for such an occasion."

Before answering Sophia glanced at the score or so people gathered in the hall other than her entourage. All of them men. George De August stood in the middle of the group. His bright eyes gleamed in contrast to his freshly waxed Vandyke. Four men flanked him, wearing Pendergast's heraldry. She returned her attention to Henry.

"Lord Henry, I've come dressed so to demonstrate my intent to defend my throne myself. I'll not ask you to risk your person, or that of my intended, should we come to agreement here today."

"Based on your envoy's words last night we are far from agreement." He gestured at George. "Lord Pendergast has made offers as well. His carry more substance."

"I would hope you'd hear me before agreeing to Sir Mallet's offer."

Henry appeared to glance at the ceiling. "Of course. Which of your knights will speak for you?"

"I'm the Queen; I'll speak for myself."

The old man cackled as a rustling of amusement ran through the audience. "In Tegine women do not speak for themselves, but very well. We are informal today and we are listening."

Sophia regarded the old man. His eyes didn't meet hers. His gaunt, bony fingers drummed the arm of his throne. She glanced at the dark-haired man standing next to Henry. He was about ten years her senior and clean-shaven. His eyes were red-rimmed but warm. He looked back at her with a forced half-smile. Sophia granted him a similar smile, then looked back to Henry.

"Lord De Roederio, I would offer you a full section south of the river, from your bridge extending west into the forest."

Henry exaggerated a shrug. "A thousand acres, most of which are infertile and untillable? Hardly worth the least of my servants. My son, Jean's, hand and protection are worth considerably more than that." He indicated the dark-haired man Sophia had smiled at.

Sophia bit her lip. Henry was being an ass. A section was standard and after all, she was a queen; Jean De Roederio was only a prince. What was Henry's point? What was the endgame here? Sophia looked at George. His lips curled into a smirk; a predatory gleam illuminated his face. Pendergast must be working some scheme behind the scenes.

"Very well, Lord Henry, I'll add a half section south of the first."

Henry coughed until Jean offered to pat his back. The old man waved his son away. "That land is rocky and difficult to till. Have you come to waste my time or are you going to make a serious offer?"

"I am Lady Sophia Pendergast, rightful Queen of Kersey. My offer is more than fair. I will not clear and till the land for you. If anyone is wasting time here today, it is you."

Henry sat up straight and a surprising fire flashed in his eyes. "It's been many a hard winter since anyone has dared speak to me like this, let alone a woman, much less in this hall. You are no queen. You're a homeless wanderer, a spoiled child, an outlaw. Be gone from my hall before I take further offense." Another coughing fit assaulted the king. His eyes bulged and his face turned crimson.

Sophia glared at Henry and clenched her fists, waiting for his spasm to pass. At her sides, her knights closed their hands on their sword hilts. She raised her palms to her knights.

Henry slouched in his seat; the fit subsided. A servant wiped spittle from his chin with a towel. "Be gone from my court, Queen of Crows." His breathing came labored and his voice weak.

Queen of Crows, indeed! "Lord Henry, your trust in Sir Mallet will bring you nothing but regret. When I've reclaimed my throne, and I will, I'll not forget the insults you've cast upon my person today." She turned on her heel without offering a bow, then strode from the hall. Her knights followed close behind.

Sophia's company stood in the courtyard waiting for their horses. Josiah frowned and clenched his jaw. "Well, that was certainly less cordial than planned."

"The man's a fat pig's ass. He's made some bargain with Sir Mallet and was putting on a performance for Sir George's benefit." Sophia pulled on her gloves.

"The list of suitors grows painfully short." Josiah allowed a warm grin.

Jean De Roederio strode from inside as the horses were brought into the courtyard. He approached Sophia. Stewart and Richard blocked his path. Jean displayed empty hands.

"Let the prince come," Sophia said. Her knights stood aside.

What was this? More insults? Lord Henry meant Queen of Crows as a pejorative. Sophia raised her chin. She'd make it her mantle, her calling. She would be the Queen of Crows and the champion of women in all three realms. Men might insult her, but they wouldn't defeat her. They would come to fear and respect her.

Jean inclined his head before her. "A private word, my Lady?"

Sophia glanced around, noting the stern faces in her company, then nodded. She stepped a few feet away with Jean. Her company mounted up and waited. She returned her gaze to the man. He was of average size, only a few inches taller than herself. Broad of shoulder and narrow of waist. Powerful without being huge. A handsome figure, with intelligent eyes.

"My father is ill and the past few years his social skills have left him. I must apologize for him and the crude remarks cast upon your house and person."

"Sir Jean De Roederio, you seem a decent and good man. I've been told of your recent loss. You have my sympathy."

"Thank you, that's very kind. Marta was a fine woman. I loved her and she me. You favor her to some extent. I'm disappointed we couldn't arrive at an arrangement. Perhaps, if Hecuba calls my father, an accommodation can still be made."

Sophia set her mouth, tight-lipped, "While I'm in favor of such a proposal, let us hope your father's vigor returns. However, Sir Mallet has obviously promised something of great value to block any such agreement."

"He has offered the same lands, plus another section to be drawn out later. Lord Pendergast will take my sister, Princess Phoebe, as his queen consort."

"In such a case shouldn't your father be giving a dowry?"

"One would think so. Phoebe isn't pleased. Lord Pendergast's reputation for rough treatment of women has been rumored in court for some time." Jean poked his chin at the stable. "Go carefully, Lady Sophia, his men are all about these days. Father doesn't seem to notice them. There is foul magic afoot."

Foul magic indeed. Sophia removed a glove and held out her hand. "Thank you. Until we meet again, Prince De Roederio."

***

As Sophia's company made its way back down the castle hill, armed men appeared along the way. Josiah seemed to ignore them, but Sophia couldn't. They were rabble in truth, poor men without armor, bearing farm tools as weapons. Were they hooligans or had they accepted coin from Pendergast?

At the town's edge a group of eight or ten men blocked the road. A middle-aged man wearing an eye patch and holding a wheat flail stepped forward. "There's a toll for outlaws in this city. You'll be paying the price one way or another."

Sophia looked around. Ruffians occupied the bushes on either side of the road. Pendergast must have promised a huge reward. Commoners would never stand in any knight's path otherwise. Before she could speak Stewart drew his sword, and his mount turned sideways and blew dust from its nostrils.

"You'll clear the road for our queen or you'll suffer the consequence. Show the proper respect and perhaps you'll survive your stupidity for another day, Crow," Stewart said.

"Queen? Ha. More a common whore to my eye. Indeed, she can pay the toll in yonder shack. The cinnamon-haired tart too." The man pointed to a shed a few yards away.

Sophia let her mouth open and close. No one ever dared call her a whore to her face. Father would kill that man out of hand, but....

Stewart spurred his mount and dashed at the men with sword held high. The commoners scattered and fled into the surrounding vineyard. Their spokesman failed to escape. Stewart ran him through as his horse knocked the man aside.

Sophia's horse shied. She tightened her reins.

The one-eyed man fell in the road, a startled look frozen on his face, accusing her. Sophia blinked, then dismissed the crude man's features. He'd sealed his own fate.

Stewart's horse reared and he swung his weapon overhead. Thin crimson rivulets trailed along its length. "Come and fight, you bastards. Come fight honest men in service of a real queen."

Sophia sucked in a harsh breath. The familiar warmth in her chest threatened to overwhelm her. Darling Stewart, fighting for her honor even after she'd refused his love. Her fingers trembled and mist grew in her eyes.

Josiah interrupted, "Come, we must move on, quickly. Pendergast's men are surely somewhere nearby, this rabble being only a distraction."

Sophia bumped her horse's flanks with her heels. "We will return to our camp, gather the rest of our men, and take stock."

Her small company rode quickly through the city. They jerked to a halt at the bridge. A company of infantry, numbering a score, denied them the far end. An officer led the enemy, but they were without a knight. They were, however, professional soldiers wearing thick gambesons emblazoned with Pendergast's stag's head.

Sophia reined her mount around and looked back the way they'd come. George, mounted on his large bay, was approaching at a fast trot. His four men-at-arms and a mob of field hands armed mostly with farm tools followed close behind.

"We'll press the far end of the bridge. There's no escape going back into the city," Josiah growled drawing his sword. "Odette, with me. De Margot, the queen."

Fighting with real consequences against men for the first time. Sophia drew her sword and licked her dry lips. Her horse shivered, shaking its head. Sophia blew out a long hard breath and glanced over at Celeste. Celeste's nostrils flared. Her eyes narrowed.

"Stay close, I don't know how this is going to end," Sophia said.

Celeste yanked a hunting knife from her boot. "I'm with you, my Queen."

Josiah engaged Sophia's eyes. "My Queen, dressed as you are, they won't know you. Fight your way clear and fetch the rest of our men. The knights and I will cover your escape."

"I'll fight for my realm and not ask any man to do it for me. I'm the Kersen Wyvern," Sophia growled, hoping her uncertainty didn't show on her face.

Josiah shook his head. "The men and I will clear a path for you and your girl. You have to rally the men at camp. We're outnumbered. De August is the only one who knows how you're dressed. I'll deal with him personally."

Celeste dropped her rein, reached over and grasped Sophia's elbow. "Now is not the time to be stubborn."

Sophia assessed the situation quickly. Josiah was right, she had to go to the camp and rally the rest of her men. "I understand. Lead on, Sir Josiah."

The narrow bridge allowed them to charge across two abreast. Josiah and Stewart led with Richard and Sophia close on their heels. Celeste, Will, and the half-dozen soldiers rode pell-mell, bringing up the rear. The pounding hooves, like a summer's avalanche, shook the bridge's decking.

The power of their charge raced through the rippling muscles of Sophia's horse and into her own legs. Her belly quivered as her mouth grew dry. They were committed and couldn't go back now.

Pendergast's men recoiled as Sophia's company stormed off the bridge. However, their captain rallied them, they turned and held their ground a moment later. Many of the enemy struggled to unseat the riders while others thrust their deadly spears. Sophia grunted as a spear struck her side, but failed to penetrate her mail.

She swung her sword with all her strength, first on this side, then the other. Horses were screaming, men were shouting. Her ears rang with each different sound. The crackling barged into her mind, like being close to a lightning strike. Louder than ever before. It added to the noise assaulting her senses. Each breath burned her throat with the urgency of life.

Sophia's arms and shoulders ached with the effort. Still, her heart sang and thrilled at the excitement, the immediacy, the danger. She struck with all the power she could muster, creating a clear space around her horse. A moment to breathe. A thirst, more urgent than their trek through the forest, demanded water. There was no time for it. She waded back into the enemy.

The blur of combat swirled all around as Sophia struggled to gain the edge of the fighting. A clear path for escape opened before her. She shouted a guttural noise and waved her sword above her head.

A soldier, wearing the stag's head, grabbed her rein and an ankle. He yanked with a strength Sophia hadn't thought a man could possess. She swung her sword, slashing his face as her horse screamed, threatening to roll. The man fell and her horse kept its feet. Sophia found her stirrup again, then broke free of the melee.

She spun her mount around. Enemy soldiers besieged her men. George and the rabble coming off the bridge attacked from their rear. Her men were fighting on foot among the enemy and the flailing hooves of dying horses.

Celeste, on foot, somehow stumbled out of the mob and joined Sophia on the edge of the carnage. She clutched the bloody hunting knife, her hair wild as an uncontrolled flame. Her blood-spattered breasts threatened to escape her torn shirt.

Pendergast's men surrounded Josiah, but he shouted above the din, "Flee, my Queen, these traitors are ours."

Sophia thought to charge back into the melee, but Celeste pulled on her leg. Sophia glanced at her, there was blood on Celeste's face.

"The men need help," Celeste shouted.

Celeste and Josiah were right. Sophia pulled her foot from the stirrup. Celeste claimed it and swung up behind Sophia.

"I'll be back!" Sophia gave the battle a last look, then turned her mount and galloped for their camp. She'd return with the rest of her soldiers.

CHAPTER TEN

Sophia jerked her horse to a halt a hundred yards from the campsite. The place, ransacked, their meager stores strewn about. The bodies of her men littered the ground. Some struck down from behind. Their spears and bows still neatly stacked, left unused.

Sophia's heart sank. She'd led these men to their gruesome end. She'd left more of them at the bridge. They would surely share this fate. And Stewart? Stewart was among them. Was she the cause of all this?

Large birds with obsidian wings and grotesque, featherless-red heads gathered near one of the bodies. Several more floated in lazy circles above the camp. Sophia urged her mount forward, rushing at the birds, scattering them into squawking flight.

She moved closer and counted the bodies. When she was finally at the blackened remains of their fire, she accounted for all but three of her men. She hoped those, at least, had escaped. Sophia and Celeste dismounted, the ten corpses surrounding them.

"Sir Mallet's men were here before they went to the bridge," Sophia said. "Surprised them and offered no quarter."

Celeste looked up from one of the bodies she examined. "Dead a couple hours at least. I think you're right."

"The fighting at the bridge is probably over. There's nothing we can do there now. Gather and fill any good water skins you can find, then look to the food."

Celeste picked through the flotsam, then went to the river. Sophia stared down at the mule's corpse for some time. Could Josiah and the others prevail against such horrible odds? What should she do? She and Celeste were not much of a reinforcement. The fighting, both frightful and exhilarating, had to be over. She needed to go back and see the outcome. She shuddered. She couldn't bear to stand over Stewart's lifeless body.

Celeste broke the silence, "There's a horse a short distance down the river." She tossed two plump water skins on the ground near Sophia's feet. "I'll try to catch it. Don't leave without me."

"Very well. Don't get lost or stray too far away. Stragglers from Sir Mallet's company may be skulking about."

"I'll be careful." Celeste went after the horse.

Sophia dragged most of the bodies together, lining them up as if on parade. She tried not to look at their gray, bloodless faces, but she gasped when she came across John Astor. Sophia groaned aloud and placed her hand on his forehead. Cold. She gently pushed his eyelids closed. Her heart yearned for Stewart, even knowing he was probably as dead as the corpses she'd gathered together.

Sophia stood and stretched her back with her fingers interlaced on top of her head. A powerful sob escaped her. She looked all around. Celeste was not in sight. How long had she been gone? Too long. Sophia mounted her horse, drew her sword, and rode along Celeste's path.

Sophia went less than half a mile when she came upon Celeste, sitting on a stump rubbing her ankle. No horses were in sight. "Having a rest, are we?"

"The stupid horse ran off, then I tripped and turned my ankle. Guess I'm dumber than the horse. I figured you'd get worried and come along."

"Can you get on this horse?"

Celeste pushed herself up onto one leg and hopped to Sophia's side. "We'll see."

The women rode double back to their pile of supplies. Sophia slid off the horse and motioned for Celeste to get in the saddle. Sophia fixed the supplies on the animal behind Celeste.

Celeste poked her chin at the line of corpses. "Is that all we're going to do for them?"

"Someone will find them soon enough and tend to them. We have to look to our own deportment." Sophia refused to look at them. They may be her fault, but she didn't have to stare at them. Indeed, most of their faces were etched in her memory. Ghosts to whisper to her when the nights grew cold and long.

"Ride a couple miles to the south and find a good spot. One you can watch for me from and still be hidden. I'll be along in a couple hours."

Celeste frowned. "What are you going to do? You've got that look, the one that tells me you're about to do something foolish."

Sophia patted the horse's shoulder. "I'm going to walk back toward the bridge and see what's happened. I have to see for myself. It won't take long and I'll be discreet about it."

Celeste went full nanny face. "You do realize you're the one they're after, right? From the looks of this place, they'll do pretty much anything to get you."

"All the more reason for you to move away from here. Sir Mallet's men are probably planning to come back for the weapons. Don't worry, I'll be careful." Sophia handed a spear to Celeste.

She hefted the spear. "I'll be careful? I believe they call those famous last words."

Sophia wrung her mouth into a frown. Maybe Celeste was right, but she needed to see if her knights and men had perished or somehow escaped. In spite of the danger, she had to confirm Stewart's condition. "Do as I ask. Be watching for me. I don't want us to end up separated in the wild."

"I still don't like it." Celeste turned the horse and trotted away. Sophia stood and watched until she was sure Celeste was actually doing as she'd asked. Satisfied, she grasped a spear, turned to the east, and crept along the riverbank until she could see the bridge.

An old man led two oxen dragging a dead horse across the bridge toward Tegine. Going to the butcher no doubt. Another dozen commoners gathered bodies in carts under the direction of soldiers wearing Tegine's colors. Their white surcoats with the scarlet eagle emblazoned, shone garish in the sunlight.

Many of Tegine's soldiers guarded the city end of the bridge as well. A lonely bell tolled from a sanctuary tower and black smoke smudged the sky above the sanctuary's chimney.

Sophia wrinkled her brow. She'd only been gone for an hour. What had happened? No sign of her knights or any of her soldiers. What had happened to them? What had happened to Stewart and gruff old Josiah? Were they slain and their bodies already removed? Achaea knew her reign had been a bloody disaster to this point.

She choked down bile. She'd managed to get her entire force killed. Stewart, her love, among them. How could Hecuba take so many and leave her to suffer the responsibility? The gods were unjust. Stewart, what would she do with herself? She'd spurn all others coming to court her and become a dowager queen. First, she had to regain her bloody throne or all those lost would be in vain.

She should move closer. What would Lord Henry's soldiers do if they saw her? Probably attack, as she'd been less than polite when she left his hall. It was no good; she couldn't approach any nearer without being seen.

The mystery would have to wait. It was time to go after Celeste and figure out what to do next. She gave a last, long look for Stewart. He was nowhere to be seen. She turned away from the bridge and snuck back the way she'd come.

Sophia crossed her campsite and found the horse's clear tracks left in the sod. She followed and after an hour discovered the tracks came to an abrupt halt. She leaned on her spear, looked across the grassy plain, and into the nearby forest.

Alone.

She crossed a rock-strewn hump and entered the forest's edge. Sophia looked for some sign Celeste may have left, but found nothing. Where had that foolish girl gone? Stewart was one thing, but she'd never forgive herself if Celeste had fallen into enemy hands or had some beast set upon her.

Sophia walked under the canopy, staying out of direct view from the plain. She'd gone a mile. A sharp whistle caught her attention.

Celeste waved at her from a hidden low spot in the forest floor. Sophia smiled and hurried to her, throwing her arms around the other woman, hugging her. After a moment they separated. Celeste smiled, "I knew you'd figure out I'd crossed that hard ground. You were always the smart one."

"It was a lucky guess." Sophia gestured at a water skin.

Celeste handed her one. "What happened at the bridge? I see you're still alone."

Sophia took a long drink, sat back on her haunches, then let out a powerful breath. "I don't know. There was no sign of our people or Sir Mallet's knight, just Lord Henry's soldiers and some commoners. If you thought that horn music was sad, you should've heard that bell clanking. It sounded like a real funeral dirge."

"It would seem neither of us will have Sir Stewart," Celeste said.

Sophia stifled a groan. Promising Celeste to Stewart, then

rejecting his love had made a mess of everything. He'd given his life for her reign in hopes of having her. She was a terrible queen. "Who's to say? Regardless, we have to figure out what we'll do next. How much food do we have?"

"Several days' worth, if we stay on the rations Sir Josiah set for us." Celeste rubbed her ankle.

Sophia looked away to the north. Nothing there caught her attention. "How's your ankle? Will you be able to walk?"

Celeste rolled her eyes. "I don't know. We've got a horse, why walk?"

"I think we should let the horse go in a day or two. I was able to follow it with ease and I'm neither a tracker nor a hound."

"Oh, I hadn't thought of that. I guess I can walk if I have to. I can use this spear as a cane or crutch."

"Agreed. I'll get this armor off and we'll see to arranging our load, wrap that ankle as best we can, then be on our way."

"Where are you planning to go?"

"The closest place that's at least neutral is Dearing's cottage. I think he's harmless. We can rest and recover there. After that, I'm not sure. Perhaps Oxted."

Celeste grimaced. "Do you think that carnival performer will help us?"

Sophia stood, patted the hilt of her sword and imitated Josiah's gravel voice, "Magic rarely stands up to a good blade, well employed."

The women giggled together.

Sophia led the horse while Celeste rode. They walked until dusk. They found a secluded low spot and made their camp. It grew dark soon after they'd eaten a cold meal. The impenetrable inky darkness closed around them. The horse nickered in its sleep.

Howling brought them both upright in their blankets. The northern forest was home to some of the largest, and most fierce, wolves in the three realms. Red wolves. The noise was close at hand and the horse grumbled, its eye rolling white in the darkness.

The howling ceased and after a few moments, sinister growling came from a few yards away. The horse whinnied, then bolted into the dark. Sophia grabbed her dagger. She clutched it and Celeste close as several large animals dashed through their campsite, pursuing the horse.

A few minutes later howling could be heard far away to the south. The women clung to each other in the darkness. No horse and little food left them disheartened. Knowing they were going south did nothing to relieve their gloom.

***

Over the next few days Sophia's fear of pursuit and discovery didn't materialize. Celeste struggled to walk on her swollen, bruised ankle. They sat to rest in a glen. "How much farther is it?" Celeste asked.

"Several more days, I think. I'm afraid we're making poor progress." Sophia emptied one of their water skins.

Celeste blew hair out of her eyes. "You know my mother loved you, right?"

"Of course, I loved her in return. What's that got to do with anything right now?"

Celeste shrugged. "She told me once that even though you and I were as close as sisters, one day you'd leave me behind. Not because you wanted to, but because you'd have to."

"That's an awful thing to say. I'd never leave you."

"Never is a strong word. My mother meant no insult, she was being practical. Today may be the day you need to leave me behind."

"A fat pig's ass. You're coming with me. I refuse to leave you."

"I'm not sure I can make it."

Sophia took Celeste's arm and pulled her to her feet.

"Come on. I don't like the tone of this conversation. Speak of something else."

Five days of slow, difficult, but uneventful marching brought the women to the circular clearing surrounding Dearing's cottage. The moment of truth. Would Thomas help or put a spell on them?

The late afternoon sun filtering through the trees dappled the cottage's roof. Celeste leaned on her spear and wet her lips with the tip of her tongue.

Sophia's stomach growled. They'd eaten the last of the food the day before and run out of water in the early morning. Celeste's limping had grown worse, although she didn't complain.

Sophia ignored her misgivings. She looked the place over. It appeared exactly as she'd seen it before. Once again, Dearing was not to be seen. "Thomas Dearing? Are you here? We need your help."

They went to the cottage's door. Sophia knocked lightly. "Thomas Dearing?"

A blue jay landed on the adjoining windowsill. It cocked its head back and forth several times, then hopped the length of the sill before returning and chattering at them. Its blue and white coloring reminded Sophia of her cause. Stewart had been wearing the blue surcoat with the white lion when she'd last seen him. She'd led him to his doom. The passing days had done nothing to lessen the sting. She groaned.

Celeste patted Sophia's shoulder then made to shoo the bird away, but Sophia stopped her. "Wait. Listen. Listen carefully."

"Who is calling? Thomas is engaged," the bird seemed to say.

Celeste stared wide-eyed back at Sophia. "Sorcery?"

Sophia shrugged. "Certainly magic." She looked around the clearing, then turned to the bird, "Lady Sophia Pendergast calling, and you are?"

"Ticky, Ticky. State your business," the bird squawked.

"We need Thomas's help." Sophia gestured at Celeste. "My friend is injured."

The bird cocked its head giving Celeste a thorough exam first with one of its glossy black eyes, then the other. "Wait, wait." It flew away, disappearing into the forest.

The women exchanged astounded looks. Sophia lay a hand on Celeste's arm. "That was strange."

Celeste uttered a croaking sound, something between a snicker and a groan. "The last few weeks have been strange. I say we wait inside. I need to sit down."

"We can't walk into a man's home without invitation."

"It's not like we weren't invited. Ticky said we should wait. I think he said inside." Celeste grinned as Sophia tried the door.

It swung on silent hinges. She pushed it further open and peered in. Flickering candles arranged in a circle on the floor lit the room with an orange glow. Many strange pots and vessels littered a table and sideboard. A disheveled cot stood against the far wall. Sulphur and a pungent herb wafted from the single room. Dearing knelt in the center of the circle of burning candles. A round rug with some mystic designs on it lay under his knees. His eyes were closed and his arms folded tight across his chest. A small drum lay on its side outside the circle.

Sophia took half a step in. Celeste craned her neck over Sophia's shoulder. "What in the name of all the gods is he doing."

Sophia shushed her with a finger, then took a few steps closer to Dearing. "Thomas? Are you all right?"

Dearing's eyes snapped open. He glanced around, frantic, before settling his gaze on the women. The light of recognition flashed across his features. He dropped his arms and rocked back on his behind. "What are you doing here?"

"We went to Tegine, but—"

"But you found trouble and once again, you need my help." Dearing pointed at a spot on the table, although lifting his arm seemed a struggle. A lumpy biscuit and chalice of warm wine sat there. Sophia picked up the items and stepped toward Dearing, her stomach growled again.

"Don't step beyond the candles. Hand me the bread." He accepted and bit into it, tearing off half. He chewed lazily and watched Sophia through drooping lids. He gestured for the chalice. Sophia handed it to him. Dearing gulped the wine, then belched with a grin.

"I see you've entered my protective circle again."

"What circle?"

"The circle of trees surrounding this cottage of course. Snuff the candles, Delicious, and put them on the table, then help me up." Dearing's tone sounded as if it shouldn't have needed to be said.

Sophia squinted at him. He seemed older than a few days before. She blew out the candles, then handed them one at a time to Celeste, who placed them on the table. Sophia offered a hand to Dearing. He took it with a firm grip and she pulled him to his feet. He was unsteady, as if he'd imbibed too much strong drink. Sophia helped him to the cot and assisted him to lie down.

"Eat, drink as you please. Don't touch anything. We'll talk when I wake." Dearing emitted a rumbling snore almost before he'd finished speaking.

Sophia turned to Celeste. "This quest grows stranger by the day."

Celeste's eyes grew wide. "How are we to eat and drink if we don't touch anything?"

***

Pale light crept across the floor as the crescent moon set. Sophia bolted upright at the touch on her shoulder, her dagger ready. Dearing's dark eyes glittered as he smiled. "Have a good sleep did we, Delicious? Fill your bellies, did you?"

Sophia sheathed her dagger and tossed her blanket aside. "As good as one can, sleeping on a hard floor."

Dearing chuckled as he stepped to the table. "I have a bad back. Sometimes sleeping on the floor takes the kinks out."

Sophia rose. Celeste remained asleep, wrapped in her blanket. Sophia's belongings as well as Celeste's were laid out in a neat row on the floor. How dare he rifle through her things? Sophia looked over at Dearing. He waved a hand over a candle, it erupted in sputtering red flame, before settling to a soft yellow glow.

Sophia cast a glare at the wizard. "I see your touching rules don't apply to yourself."

"Children first learn by touching, adults are no different. Many things in this room could cause you or a child harm. Merely a precaution, your Grace, as I wouldn't be available to prevent an accident."

His switching to a proper title disarmed her for a moment. "Why did you fall asleep without entertaining us?"

Dearing grinned. "Magic causes fatigue. Strong magic, strong fatigue."

Magic indeed. "What sort of magic were you working?"

Dearing waved a hand as if a gnat were pestering him. "A protection spell. My enemies will fall upon me if I don't renew the spell from time to time."

"Enemies? What sort of enemies could you possibly have?"

"Magical enemies. Enemies unlike those pursuing you."

Magical enemies? A fat pig's ass. "How do you know they're pursuing me?"

"Ticky has been keeping an eye on them. Fear not, they cannot find this place. Not yet. The usurper sent out a call for a wizard. I offered my services, but he didn't reply. Lucky for you and your house, such as it is, I'm available."

"What sort of service could you grant a sovereign?"

"Many, Delicious. Protection from magical attacks, warning of approaching dangers, such as wyverns. Advice about crops and the weather. A multitude of things."

Sophia looked into the wizard's eyes. They were unreadable, as if a veil hid them from her even though she could see them quite well. Father's wizard had done many entertaining tricks, but in the end died alongside him. Perhaps that was the most important service a wizard could provide. Comfort in the end. Could she trust Thomas? He'd tried to get patronage from Mallet. Where would his loyalty lie? Would he realize she had suspicions?

"Ticky? That little bird?" Sophia changed the subject.

"Yes. He's inquisitive, some would say nosey, but he's smart and useful. He's a cautious creature, doesn't favor people in general, but he likes you. Odd that."

The bird was a dubious ally at best. "Who has he seen?"

"Soldiers. Soldiers and knights. Knights wearing the stag's head. The new king's men. They are looking high and low for you. You're safe here, for now."

"Thank you for that." Trusting him could be foolish. What would he want as payment for his help? What did she have to pay with?

"You're welcome, Delicious. Perhaps you will learn something while you stay."

Sophia poked her chin at her effects. "Did you find what you were looking for?"

"Yes, I did. A wealth of knowledge." He stepped to her hauberk and nudged it with a toe. "A mail coat, too small for a man. Yours?"

Sophia shrugged, keeping her face a blank slate.

Dearing laughed. "Yours." He tapped her sword. "A finely crafted sword, well used. An expensive, deadly weapon. Black steel, befitting a lion and yet a wyvern's head pommel. An acknowledgment of a loved one. Your father's?"

"Mine." Sophia wrinkled her lips. Another man, thinking

he knows all.

Celeste stirred but didn't wake.

Dearing chuckled, amused at something he didn't share. "Of course, yours."

"I'd beg you, Thomas, get to the point."

"The point is knowledge. I've learned a great deal about you through careful observation. A person's things, their possessions, often speak more truth than their words. Possessions are always more honest than a person's face."

Sophia set her mouth in a stern line. Speaking in circles. Wizards always did that. Hiding their thoughts in irrelevant words and sayings. Wizard-speak, a pretense, making them feel superior to others. "And?"

Dearing grinned. "The Warrior King falls and a Queen of the Sword rises. However, she has no army. Indeed, no knights at all. A desperate situation."

He was testing her patience and it wasn't her strong suit. "There's nothing new in that. You've said it before."

Dearing chuckled again, then waddled to and pointed at Celeste as she slept. "This one cares for you. She takes great risks on your behalf. A dear friend. I wonder, would you care for her?"

Now what was he getting on about? "Celeste has my love. I always think of her and heed her counsel in any decision I make."

"She's injured. A minor affair to be true. A bit of wintergreen and a few days' rest will bring her back to vigor. I wonder, would you care for her as she heals?"

"Of course. I've been doing so since she tripped."

"Have you? Forcing her to aggravate a sore leg with further walking on it?"

"I couldn't leave her behind."

"Ah, but you wouldn't stop either."

Sophia wrinkled her brow. Getting there was her desire, did it come at Celeste's expense? Should she have waited in the forest with the wolves and other beasts, so Celeste could heal? Ridiculous, it wasn't safe out there.

"Most likely a good decision in this case, but, Delicious, you must always think a problem through."

"I don't make decisions in haste."

Thomas's eyes twinkled. "So back to the question. Will you care for your servant as she recovers?"

Sophia glanced at Celeste. She was stirring, going to wake in a moment. Sophia returned her gaze to Dearing's smug grin. "Of course, I'll care for her."

"We shall see, and perhaps knowledge will grow in us both."

CHAPTER ELEVEN

Sophia swung the heavy splitting maul for what seemed the hundredth time. The dry wood exploded into shards at the axe's impact. The tool stuck in the block with a solid thunk. She wiped her brow with a sleeve. She looked at the red blisters on her hands and swore under her breath. Her back burned with a soft fire that sleeping on the floor would surely aggravate.

Caring for Celeste was no trouble at all. Well, there was that getting wintergreen in her eye incident the first time she'd rubbed it on Celeste's ankle, but working as a servant for Thomas was growing old. With six days of weeding the garden, fetching water, feeding chickens and gathering herbs, she learned what it took to feed a family. Thomas hadn't complained about how she'd done these things. She could do anything she put her mind and back to. Sophia grimaced as she stretched her spine. At least she didn't have to cook. Her first attempt at bread, the disaster it turned into, led to Celeste banning her from the stove.

Sophia recalled overhearing one of the castle's servants saying, "Never get good at doing something you don't like." She allowed a wry grin. She certainly didn't like cooking.

Sophia gathered the wood she'd split, ignored her smarting palms and bumped the door open with her hip. She crossed the room and dropped her load into the wood box next to the stove. Dearing, his bald spot aglow, ignored them, immersed in some arcane experiment. A dank odor wafted from the bowls he fussed over.

Sophia pursed her lips and jabbed a thumb at Dearing's back. Celeste looked from the book she read and rolled her eyes. "I'm much better today. I think it's time I start earning my keep again."

Sophia smiled. "When you're ready we'll have to leave this peaceful place and get back to the work at hand."

A thump and billowing smoke drew their attention to Dearing. He coughed and waved a hand at a rotten-smelling, yellow cloud boiling from one of his bowls. "Hog's tail, what did I do wrong?" He turned to the women. "I think your presence and almost constant chattering distracts me. I'll never get anything accomplished."

"What are you doing there? Trying to burn down the cottage?" Sophia asked.

Dearing wrinkled his lips, then stroked his beard several times. "No. I'm trying to create a talisman. A protection talisman for you. You'll need it. I can't seem to get the mixture right. I thought for sure I corrected it this time, must have been too much sulfur. I'll try again tomorrow. Perhaps the two of you will take your lunch outside so I can concentrate."

"I thought wizards did their conjuring at night," Celeste said with a grin.

"That, young lady, is a fairy tale. Wizards work when duty calls."

"What's the cost of this talisman? I have nothing to pay with." The women shared a wink. Everyone knew a talisman was nothing more than superstition.

"You've already paid most of the cost. I've learned a great deal about you. Your willingness to work for your keep is a rare trait among the nobility. At least those nobles I've crossed paths with. It's been a week of learning for me and for you, I think. Knowledge, it's a treasure. Remember that."

"What else is there in this price? I've already done every household chore you could think of."

Dearing chuckled. "And done them well. I must admit, you've done them well. I'm mildly surprised."

Sophia placed her hands on her hips and stared at Dearing. One could pull a wyvern's teeth without waking it easier than get a straight answer out of him. "But there's something more isn't there?"

"When I've gotten it right, Delicious. When I've gotten it right." Dearing flashed a smile, then donned his funny hat and waltzed out the door.

Celeste burst into laughter. "He's the best huckster I've ever seen. His whole life is a show. I wonder if he can juggle too."

Dearing's large head appeared at the open window. "Wizards do not juggle, young lady."

***

Three days later Celeste packed their things into makeshift backpacks. Dearing offered them supplies, which they accepted. Sophia donned her baldric, then loosened her sword's fit in the scabbard.

Dearing, nearly weepy-eyed, watched them prepare to leave. When all was ready, he stood before Sophia and held out his closed hand. "Take these with you, Delicious. You will need them eventually."

Sophia opened her palm. Dearing dropped two small purple stones into it; they gleamed in the candlelight. "What are these? Crystals?"

Dearing shook his head. "Amethyst, much more potent. When you get to a town with a jeweler or a talented bladesmith have them mounted on your sword's blade. One on each side, near the guard will suffice. They must touch each other."

"And what do they do then?" Sophia glanced at Celeste's smirk and grinned.

Dearing cocked his head to one side. "Then? Nothing, other than looking pretty. But when you need it, place the weapon in running water for four hours. Afterward, the stones will give you the protection of a mountain ogre's strength for a matching number of hours. Choose wisely, Delicious. They will only work once."

Sophia placed a hand on her chest. A talisman, worthless in application, but comforting nonetheless. "Thank you, Thomas. I'll do as you ask. What is owed in return?"

Dearing rummaged on his tabletop and displaced many small items until he produced a tiny cloth pouch with a drawstring. He opened and sniffed it. He wrinkled his nose. "A post in your court. A monarch needs a wizard. Even if Lord Pendergast believes otherwise." He blew dust from a bowl and poured the contents of the pouch into it. An ocher-colored powder made a neat pile. He offered her the bag.

Sophia placed the stones in the pouch, drew it closed, and handed it to Celeste. "Done, Sir Thomas. I'll send word when you can report to castle Kersey and assume your duties as my royal wizard and chief enchanter."

"Very good, your Grace, but Ticky will keep me informed."

"Does he know a clear road to Oxted?"

"He does. Take a south-easterly path. You'll find a few small villages along the way. Take care crossing the main road, it's patrolled regularly. The pass at the escarpment may also be guarded. There is peril on this path, raiders, wild beasts, and even a wyvern roams the steppe, but you must take it, if indeed you want to reclaim your throne."

Raiders? A constant threat with no loyalty to anyone. Father worked ceaselessly to rid the steppe of them. Wyverns? A rare occurrence. They were usually a winter event. "To whom do these villages owe their allegiance?"

Dearing pursed his lips and pinched his eyes together. "Crows live in the villages. They have no love for Lord Pendergast, but they have no love for you either. They live as they can. If selling you to Lord Pendergast fills their pot for a day, it will be done without hesitation. Then again, if you can offer something better, well…"

Sophia carried only the promise of freedom in the future and perhaps a more just system. That was poor fare indeed when one's children were hungry. "Send Ticky to me if you have need of my assistance, Sir Thomas. Thank you for all your help and your gift."

Dearing gestured at the door. "I would go with you, but cannot yet leave the circle of trees. Soon though. Take care, Delicious, and watch the roads. Ticky tells me war is brewing in the north. Lord Pendergast may have to raise an army. If so, it may give you some room to slip past his minions. However, don't dally on the steppe, the Solstice will be upon us before you realize."

Sophia glanced at Celeste, then smiled at Dearing. The Solstice, the last festival of the year for Achaea. When vows, duties, and legitimacy are reaffirmed. Pendergast would surely take the vows in public. She would then be the usurper. They couldn't dally, indeed. They'd have to make haste.

***

The women plunged into the forest and turned southeast. Sophia set her mind to the task at hand. Get to Oxted. Once there she'd have to figure out how to gather support from the Paladin and the temple. Her claim was valid. Surely those Achaea-loving priests would support her.

On Celeste's advice, Sophia approved removing her father's heraldry from her baldric. They had a few days before they'd reach a village, they'd need to make up convincing names before then. On the one hand, it galled Sophia to take an alias, but she couldn't tell anyone who she was until she'd escaped Pendergast's reach.

Their first day in the wood passed without intrigue or event. Ticky came with them the first few miles, then disappeared among the trees. Sophia kept her eyes moving, watchful for Pendergast's soldiers, wild beasts, and that strange little bird.

The next morning came shrouded in fog. They quickly packed their damp possessions, then walked on. Sophia guessed it would take them two full days of walking to exit the forest. Their footfalls were soft and silent on the damp pine needle carpet. She feared some beast could be equally quiet and catch them unaware.

At midday the fog had gone and the mood brightened. Celeste seemed fully recovered. Her steps were light and lively. She even sang a little song they'd learned as children, for them to march to. Sophia smiled, but she found little to sing about, especially when they'd reach the end of the forest's concealment.

They arrived at the forest's edge in the early afternoon the following day. Using the sun as a guide, Sophia set a quick pace going southeast. Not knowing how far from the forest the road lay, she kept her eyes open. The horizon would grant the first sign of riders, caravans, or hamlets. Josiah's assertion that she'd failed to use the tools Father had provided came home to her now. It forced her to trek through the wilderness without knowledge of the lay of the land.

Two days march brought them in sight of the road. They stood in a copse and watched for several minutes. The road lay barren in both directions. Sophia pointed to a larger stand of trees a mile the other side of the road.

"How long do you think it'll take us to get to those trees?" Sophia said.

Celeste squinted and leaned forward. She shrugged, "Half

hour, maybe a little longer."

"That's what I was thinking too. Do you think we have half an hour of empty road?"

"I don't know. It looks like no one has come past in some time, but that's not a good judge."

"Perhaps we should wait for sunset. I'd wager we could be long out of sight before dawn."

Celeste looked both ways again. "Probably, as long as we don't lose our way in the dark."

The women settled down among the trees and waited for the night. Sophia looked over at Celeste, who dozed in the warm air. A grasshopper rubbed its legs nearby. What were they to do now? What had happened to her men at the bridge? No matter how many times she thought of them, daring, handsome Stewart, quiet Richard, or gruff Josiah, they were all still gone. Ripped away to some unknown fate. Would she lose everyone? Would she lose her closest friend as well? Would her quest to reclaim her throne cause her to lose herself?

Celeste's eyes snapped open. "I can feel you staring at me. Is there something wrong?"

Sophia shook her head. "No. I was thinking about the future."

Celeste glanced at the road, then reengaged Sophia's eyes. "Now that Jean De Roederio seems out of reach and pointless, are you going to take Sir Stewart for your own?"

Sophia sighed. "We don't know if he's alive or dead. Perhaps I'll be one of those dowager queens."

Celeste laughed. "Dowager? You? I doubt that. Men will throw themselves at your feet. For your station if nothing else."

"Yes, my station." Sophia frowned. Her station brought her much attention, but not love. And certainly not happiness.

Celeste looked away. "The smart ones will come for your beauty and wit. You may need me to sort them out for you."

Sophia allowed a chuckle. "Indeed."

Crickets replaced the grasshopper's song and the evening concealed the plain. No one had passed on the road. Judging it dark enough to conceal their crossing, the women hurried into the night. They'd gotten off the far side of the road when a full company of at least one hundred infantry came from the south. The women dropped into the tall grass and Sophia held her breath. The men trudged past, a hundred yards away. They plodded along, going north without seeming to look around, much less catch sight of the women.

Once the company stumbled out of sight, the women walked until past the midnight hour. They found a small stand of trees with reasonably soft ground and took to their blankets. Free of the large forest, they grew used to the nightly serenade of coyotes. The smaller canines rarely came close, even then they seemed only curious. Startling the women, they caused no actual harm.

Two days of uneventful, boring walking, interrupted once by the need to navigate around an immense herd of black bison, brought the women to the edge of a long untended potato field. "Why would they abandon it?" Sophia said.

Celeste whipped out her knife, then dropped to her knees and dug up a few stunted potatoes. "I don't know. No sense letting these go to waste. I'm getting tired of that hard bread and jerky." She stuffed the spoils into her pack.

Sophia leaned on her spear. "Looting is a crime."

Celeste grinned. "We're not looting. We're gleaning, there's a difference."

"That's splitting some thin hairs."

"I'm not putting them back. There's no one around to object. Indeed, your father's law said the poor can take food from a field if it's not attended. We're the definition of poor and I see no attendants."

Sophia shrugged. Not an argument worth having at the moment. Not in their present state anyway. Celeste was right.

"We can't risk a fire for cooking."

"We can eat them raw. They're still tasty and something different. Better with salt. We'd have been better served had Thomas given us salt rather than that talisman." Celeste rose and dusted off her trousers' knees.

"I can't eat raw potatoes. It's uncivilized."

"Look around. You'll find raw potatoes can be a treat after all."

Sophia turned in a circle. The sky in the west promised rain, but the warm haze of summer clung to them for the present.

Celeste shaded her eyes with a hand and pointed with her spear. "The hamlet is over there. Do you want to go meet some of the people? Perhaps we can get permission to eat the potatoes we've stolen. Or at least barter for some salt."

"I haven't stolen anything, but we haven't invented an alias yet. Do you see anyone over there?"

Celeste shook her head.

"Let's get closer, but I don't want to talk with anyone. I think we're still too close to the road to be safe from traitors. Perhaps we can use their well to refill our water skins and move on without drawing attention."

Celeste leaned her head to one side. "Among the nobility it's common to ignore those around you. Especially those of lower station. But with the commoners? They notice everyone. And even if they say nothing to us, they'll gossip among themselves. Going unnoticed isn't an option."

"Can we bypass the village? How much water do we have? I'm sure there's a creek or stream ahead." Sophia pointed at a hazy green line far away. "Those trees are probably growing along one there."

Celeste looked in the indicated direction. "It's hard to judge distance on this ground. We may run out before we get there." She dug out a rag, flipped it over her head, and tied it under her chin. "Let's call you Anna and hope the peasants keep their nosiness to themselves."

"Anna? Why Anna?"

"Because you look like an Anna. Would you prefer something different? Feel free to make up a name yourself. We've had days to do it and yet you haven't. The gods know you can be so stubborn, but now isn't a good time."

Sophia frowned. "You don't have to get nasty. Anna it is." Sophia cracked a smile. "That kerchief makes you look like a fishmonger."

Celeste shrugged. "And you look like a washerwoman with a sword, and spear, Anna. Shall we go?"

Sophia nodded. "If they must know, we're mercenaries on pilgrimage to renew our faith."

"That's fairly close to the truth."

"It's easy to remember without saying too much. Lead on."

They found a path from the field to the village and approached with care. No one appeared and as they grew closer, they saw it more clearly. Perhaps two dozen dwellings, similar to the partially underground homes of Kersey, clustered close together. More than half stood burned out. The odor of burnt wood no longer lingered. Those homes with no fire damage had partially caved in.

They came to the well in the center of the village, its cover collapsed and the windlass broken. Celeste tapped dirt from a wooden pail next to the well. Sophia looked all around. A dust devil swirled in the middle of the street. Its chalky taste clung to her tongue. Weeds and debris threatened to choke the main thoroughfare.

"This didn't just happen. Judging by the field I'd guess this happened in late winter," Sophia said as she turned a full circle. "I wonder why I didn't hear anything about this. I mean this hamlet is in my realm. Do you think Father knew of this?"

Celeste secured the pail's handle to a charred length of rope. "Hard to say. Take a look around, Anna. I'll see to the water. We can't linger, this is a bad sign."

"Do you think that influx of beggars this spring had something to do with this?"

"Maybe." Celeste gestured with the bucket. "Have a look around, but be careful."

The pail splashed behind her as Sophia approached and glanced into the first of the earthen dwellings, long ago burnt. Now dusty, rain-spoiled furniture and clothing littered the interior. She moved on, glancing back at Celeste from time to time. All the buildings shared a similar state. She came to what may have been the headman's home.

Its wooden floor had seen heavy abuse from the weather. Sophia stepped inside and found it the same as the rest. She thanked Hecuba she hadn't come across any bodies.

Over the fireplace a longbow rested on pegs. Sophia smiled and rushed over to it. She seized the weapon and rolled the string between her fingers. Still good. Should she take it? She was the queen. She could seize property if need be. It's clearly stealing not gleaning, but there was no one there. The people had left or been carried away. It didn't appear anyone would return for it. If she left it, an outlaw may come and take it. Better that she take it. So, where were the arrows?

Sophia conducted a thorough search of the house but found no arrows. She gave a shrug and returned to the well. Celeste held out a dented tin ladle filled with water. Sophia accepted and drank.

"A bow? That's expensive. Why do you think they left it?" Celeste asked, then smirked. "Have you stolen it, Anna? And where are the people anyway?"

Sophia frowned, shook her head, and returned the ladle. "I'm the queen, I didn't steal it. I borrowed it. The people? No sign of them. That's odd. Raiders always leave the dead. I didn't find any arrows."

"Raiders would've taken that bow for sure." Celeste looked around, her eyes never resting on any one object for more than a second. "This place gives me the creeps." She looked back at Sophia. "Can't you make arrows? Some fresh venison and potatoes would make for a grand meal."

Sophia shook her head. "As with sword and spear, I was taught how to use them, not how to make them. Come, let's be on our way. I agree, this place is not wholesome."

They walked away from the well going along what would have been the main street. Sophia held out a hand calling for a halt. "What is that?" She pointed at the ground.

Celeste bent and moved a blackened board. "This can't be good."

A three-foot-long track, left long ago, was partially hidden under the board. Its outside edges weathered and indistinct. Still, it showed three long, finger-like toes, ending in claws, extending from a narrow, but robust foot.

"I've never seen anything like it."

Celeste's shoulders shuddered. "I think we've been here too long."

Sophia searched the horizon and nodded. "Agreed. Let's be on our way."

Wanting to put as much distance between them and the strange village as they could before nightfall, Sophia set a fast pace. Despite a beating rain, the soft hair on her arms wouldn't lie down. Looking back failed to ease the constant wisps of faint, but unclear noise in her ears. A voice? The wind? Her imagination? Celeste denied hearing anything unusual. Sophia shuddered and walked on.

They chose a low spot far from any trees for their camp. Sophia cringed as rain continued to pelt them. She wrapped her blanket around her shoulders and frowned at the wet seeping through. Celeste lay near, often rolling over in her sleep. Sophia clutched her spear. Shadows moved in the corners of her eyes, but when she turned her head to see them, nothing.

The wind rose as the rain stopped in the midnight hour. Sophia shivered. Her drooping eyelids detected movement, and she jerked awake. Upon closer inspection, no discoveries matched those movements. Only more trepidation.

Sophia rose, casting off the heavy, waterlogged blanket. She leaned her spear against a shoulder and rubbed her upper arms vigorously. The dark night seemed to suffocate her. She felt nearly as closed in as she'd felt in the castle's storeroom. The wind carried a damp earth and grass odor. She pulled at the wet canvas clinging to her thighs.

Celeste slept but didn't appear to rest. Welcome as sleep would be, Sophia couldn't. Something was there. Something remained on the edge of sight and touch. It wasn't her imagination. How could she make it show itself? Did she want to see it, to confront it? Whatever it was.

A touch, a soft pinch on her behind. She spun and brought her spear to the ready in the same motion. Nothing. An impish giggle came to her ears. Sophia spun around again.

CHAPTER TWELVE

A shadow passed between Sophia and Celeste. Not a shadow, it was darker than a trick of the light. It had mass, but its shape was indistinct and small, no larger than a child of five or six years. Another pinch on the back of her thigh. Sophia yelped and spun around once more. A similar shadow hovered near her. Dark, featureless.

Sophia backed away from it. The shadow followed, cautiously, staying out of easy stabbing range. Sophia halted and brandished her spear as her heels bumped Celeste's blanket. "Stay back. Get away from us." Sophia struggled to keep both shadows in view.

A lilting voice came from the shadow to Sophia's front. "Too thin, too hard. Strong the fighter is. Drago it knows. The sleeper?"

"Luscious it is. Round, soft, and tasty. Much better," the other sing-songed in return.

Sophia lunged at the shadow nearest Celeste. "Leave her!" The shadow scrambled away, coming to stand next to the other. Their forms nearly mingled.

"Heavier it is. Harder to carry," one of the shadows lilted. Then they seemed to speak to each other in low tones. Sophia couldn't make out what they said. What could she do? They clearly had harmful intent. Sophia found her sword among her blankets while not taking her eyes from the shadows.

"Celeste, wake up. Wake up now." Sophia laid her spear aside, drew her sword, and threatened the shadows with it. They retreated.

"Celeste!"

"What? What is it?" Celeste rolled free of her blankets and blinked at Sophia.

"Get up and arm yourself. There's evil afoot."

Celeste looked around, then jumped to her feet. She grabbed her spear and went on guard. "What in the gods' names is that?"

"I don't know, but stay close. They keep touching us and talking like they're going to eat us."

Celeste stepped close to Sophia, bumping her arm against Sophia's side. "I'm not keen on being eaten."

"Indeed." Sophia lunged at the shadows. Her sword cut the air, humming. "Be gone foul beasts! You'll find no meals here."

The shadows separated and rushed to and fro as the women spun and stabbed at them with no apparent effect. Sophia stumbled and fell forward, her sword stuck in the soft ground. She landed on her blanket. One of the shadows leapt upon her back.

It sang a strange song with its lilting voice. It wasn't heavy, but it pinched and nipped at her behind and the backs of her legs. Sophia kicked at it, landing a solid blow with a thump. She grabbed at the shadow, getting hold of what may have been an arm.

Sophia swept her blanket over the offending creature and secured it, sack-like. The shadow struggled for several seconds, crying aloud, a mournful sound. It finally lay still. Sophia looked for Celeste. She was chasing the other shadow from their camp.

It dodged back and forth, always staying a few steps away,

but leading Celeste farther from her. Celeste stabbed at her opponent furiously, having no effect.

"Come back. Let it go, I've got one here. Help me with it," Sophia said.

Her prisoner squirmed inside the blanket. Sophia struck it with an elbow. The shadow cried aloud, "It hurts me. Save me."

Celeste rushed up and kicked the wiggling blanket. "Pinch and bite my bum, take that you disgusting beast." The shadow creature wailed. Celeste turned to Sophia, "We have it, now what do we do with it?"

Sophia leaned her weight on the shadow. "We find out what it thinks it's doing and maybe why."

"I say we kill it and be done with it."

"No!" The lilting voice sang. "I not hurt it. Let go. Treasure I have. Will trade it."

"What could you have to make a worthy ransom?" Sophia pushed against the creature again.

"Coin. Magic coin. I trade it."

Celeste grunted. "Magic coin, a fat pig's ass. It's lying, kill it."

"No. Not lie. I have. See." The bundle pushed against Sophia's stomach. A small hard object, maybe a button, pressed into her. Sophia surveyed their surroundings. The other shadow was not in sight.

Sophia glanced at Celeste. "Get my sword and stand ready. I'll let it loose for a moment. If it tries to flee…"

Celeste dropped her spear and yanked the sword free of the turf.

Sophia struggled to get hold of the shadow without releasing her grip on the blanket. Its body was solid but soft as damp clay. Sophia's fingers sunk into its flesh if she applied too much pressure. She held it as firm as she could, then removed the blanket.

The shadow's form remained indistinct, but an appendage

held a small coin. It dropped the coin in Sophia's palm. "Not lie. Trade. Now let go."

Sophia tightened her grip. She turned the coin over in her free hand. It wasn't a striking she recognized. "What sort of magic does it possess and where did you get it?"

"Drago gave it. Strong magic it has. Now you have. Let go."

Celeste threatened the shadow with the sword. "Answer the question or suffer the sharp end of this."

The creature squirmed and cringed in Sophia's grip. "I trade magic. You let go."

Sophia turned the coin again. Was this creature simple or pretending to be? They hadn't caused any real harm, beyond stealing some sleep. She looked at Celeste. "Are you injured?"

"No, just...I'm upset with all that tasting and whatnot."

Sophia turned to the shadow. "Very well, foul imp. I'll release you, but you must leave and pester us no more."

"I go."

Sophia released the creature. It faded away into the night without another word. The women stared after it for a few seconds. Celeste handed the sword to Sophia.

"Magic coin? Hog's tail. Where is it from?" Celeste asked.

"I don't know. It's different though. Warm to the touch. Here look at it." Sophia gave the coin to Celeste.

She examined it. "Never seen anything like this. What's that image? A Wyvern?"

Sophia sheathed her sword. "Perhaps. I thought it was a lizard. Regardless, it'll be clear when it gets light out." She looked around again. "I think we should move on now. I can't sleep in this place anyway."

Celeste nodded, gave the coin back to Sophia, then rolled her blanket. "We have to find someplace to hang our wet effects. There's little worse than moldy-smelling linens."

Sophia looked where she'd last seen the shadow. The grassy plain was featureless in the dark.

***

Sophia breathed deeply of the fresh, post-rain, morning air. It almost made up for the fatigue and raw spots left from marching in wet clothes. She and Celeste stopped for a rest. Sophia took in the seemingly endless grass. Had she lost her way in the dark? Was that smoke on the horizon?

Sophia pointed. "Does that look like smoke to you?"

Celeste's hair clung to her forehead. "Yes. What do you make of it?"

Sophia shrugged. "Did Sir Stewart mark the road on that map he drew?"

Celeste nodded.

"I think we've stumbled closer to the road than I'd hoped. The smoke might be a house or an inn."

Celeste rose and looked closer. "An inn? We stayed a night at an inn last year on our trip to Oxted."

Sophia grunted. "Yes, the Wheelhouse Inn. And the innkeeper was a pig. As I recall he couldn't keep his hands off you."

Celeste laughed. "I thought he had four arms. Good thing his wife caught him. I'd wager the iron pan she whacked him with raised a handsome knot on his head."

Sophia pursed her lips. "I think we should avoid it then. He may remember us. You in the least."

"We've got to get out of these wet clothes. At least long enough to let them dry."

Sophia shifted her jacket on her shoulders. "We'll make for those woods." She pointed. "We have nothing to pay an innkeeper, even if he isn't a pig."

"A night in a bed would be lovely. We have a magic coin," Celeste said.

Sophia laughed. "That coin is for the temple. With any luck at all, it actually has some value."

Celeste gazed at the smoke with a faraway look. "True. The

priests never do much of anything without payment."

They trudged on through the morning. Celeste seemed to sleep as she walked, Sophia kept a sharp eye on their surroundings. Mounted men came into view no more than a half-mile distant. They went across the women's path coming from the southeast going northwest. Sophia rushed them into a stand of scrubby poplars and watched the men pass.

A half dozen rough-looking men, wearing all manner of armor and clothing. A ragtag bunch with an assortment of un-matching arms. Raiders. Looking for easy victims. With any luck at all Pendergast's men would find them and deliver needed justice. Lawlessness ran rampant in her realm. What did Pendergast think he was doing? Father would have those men tracked down and punished for their predations. Nothing to be done about it now. Later, when she returned to the throne.

Sophia waited an hour after the men passed from view. Finally, she stood and prodded Celeste. "Come on, we have to get to Oxted before the Solstice."

Celeste groaned. "I need some sleep. In a real bed." She looked in the direction the men had gone. "I never dreamed there was so much traffic out here."

Sophia walked to the southeast. "Indeed. Come along."

The women crossed the plain and arrived at the edge of a forest in late afternoon. They hung their things, wrung out their undergarments, and tried to sleep in shifts. The view of the plain showed it empty. Hoping to dry their clothing more quickly, they lit a small fire. Then settled down for the night.

Buzzing, similar to many bees, echoed in Sophia's head. She sat bolt upright. The dawn's half-light filtered into the woods. The buzzing became the louder crackling she was accustomed to. Had a dream awakened her? No. The forest's silence, an oppressive lack of sound, roused her. She cursed herself for nodding off and closed her fist on her spear's shaft. Strong hands seized her arms as other men rushed to grab

Celeste, still wrapped in her blanket.

Sophia was yanked to her feet, her spear knocked from her hand. Two men held each of the struggling women while four others went through their belongings. The men wore dark clothing, their heads wrapped in cloth that continued around their necks, covering the lower half of their faces. They spoke to each other in a cant Sophia didn't understand.

Who were these people and what did they want? Clearly, they were from some other land. How had they found them in the dark?

The men holding Sophia had scimitars on their belts and dark eyes set below thick brows. Sophia stopped her useless struggling. "Release us. You have no right—"

One of the searchers slapped Sophia across the face. The force of the blow snapped her head to one side. A flame of pain erupted from her cheek and jaw. Her knees went weak before she could stop her descent. The men holding her arms jerked her upright.

Sophia and Celeste, in spite of their struggles, were wrestled to the ground and stripped of their undergarments. Celeste issued a torrent of curses at the men. They ignored her. Sophia shuddered. Were they about to be raped and murdered? Did these men have any idea who she was?

The men searched their torn and ripped clothing with a thief's thoroughness. Sophia groaned. Their captors' apparent leader found and pocketed the cloth pouch Thomas had given her, the stones and magic coin inside. The searchers repacked everything of any use and swung the ungainly bundles over their shoulders.

The women's wrists were bound behind their backs and ropes tied around their necks. The naked women were then half dragged, half led, on foot, out of the forest onto the plain.

CHAPTER THIRTEEN

The men and their captives marched for a mile, arriving at a camp along a sunken creek's bed. Nine faded, brownish-green tents were arranged in a line with the largest in the center. Small, smokeless fires burned in front of the tents. Many horses and donkeys occupied a rope pen that stood at the far end of the camp. A few dark-eyed children gawked at the prisoners as they passed. The buzz of conversation dwindled as the men and their prisoners reached the center of the camp. Soon silence hung heavy on the air.

Their small fire must have been seen during the night. How else would these men have found them? What would they do with them? Could Sophia talk a bargain or buy their freedom?

The group halted outside the largest tent and waited as their leader went inside. A pole stood next to the tent's entrance, topped with a fox's skull. Two bushy red tails dangled from a crosspiece. Several minutes crept by. Goosebumps crawled across Sophia's flesh as a cool breeze came up. Several children milled about. Women, dressed similarly to the men, but in lighter colors, shooed the children away. The women remained, a silent, attentive audience.

The leader came out of the tent and held the flap as an older man joined him. This man had white brows over his penetrating black eyes. He approached and lifted first Celeste's, then Sophia's chin and engaged their eyes for several moments. He directed the prisoners to turn in a full circle, first one, then the other. He grunted, stepped back, and spoke with a strong voice to the other man.

Sophia wanted to speak, to plead their case, but remembering the slap, held her tongue and looked for a way to escape. There was none.

The exchange between the old man and the other was brief, ending with the older man nodding and gesturing at the gathered women. He retreated into his tent while the five women stepped forward and took the ropes from the men and led the prisoners to a tent near the animal pen.

An oil lamp illuminated the tent's interior. A rumpled sleeping pallet sat near one wall and various utensils were stacked in neat piles on some crates. A doll made of rags lay on the pallet. The five women removed their head coverings. All but one had dark, long hair and olive skin. The last, only a couple years older than Sophia, a pale-skinned blonde.

The oldest woman jabbered at the prisoners. Sophia caught a recognizable word every so often, but not nearly enough to understand what she said. Sophia and Celeste glanced at each other, then shrugged at the speaker. The old woman gestured at the blonde, who spoke, "It's been long since I have used these words. Do you understand me?"

The prisoners nodded. Sophia smiled. "I'm—"

The blonde placed her fingers against Sophia's lips. "Do not speak, listen." The blonde nodded at the older woman, who then spoke, slow and loud, as if speaking so would grant understanding.

The blonde translated. "You are slaves. If you try to run away you will be caught, kept naked and tied until you're sold. Do as you're told and you will be released from your bonds.

Do you understand?"

Sophia and Celeste nodded in unison. Sophia looked for an escape route. Could she overpower all of these women before men could come to their aid? Probably not. Even if she could, where would she go?

The old woman brandished a riding crop with one end sporting long leather fringe, then spoke to the blonde.

"The Mother does not want to use the whip, but she will. You must do as you are told."

Once again, they nodded.

"Your fate may be sealed. Your sale at the market in Truro will help to sustain the clan for the winter season. You will bathe and clothing will be brought. Do you understand?"

"Yes, but—" Sophia said.

The old woman flicked her whip against Sophia's stomach. It stung but didn't leave a mark. Sophia looked down. The strike was a warning. How could she bargain with these people if she wasn't allowed to talk?

The other dark-haired women removed the ropes from the prisoners. A young boy brought a pail of water and a couple rags. He set them near the prisoners and flashed a grown-up leer at Celeste. A dark-haired woman instantly set upon him and chased him out of the tent.

The blonde indicated the pail. "Bathe. I will come back with clothing. If the Mother doesn't return with me, I will answer your questions."

The prisoners were left alone in the tent.

Sophia and Celeste washed. "We've got to get out of here. The Solstice won't wait for us to return to Kersey."

Celeste nodded. "I don't know where that Truro is, but it doesn't sound like a nice place."

"It's in one of the southern kingdoms," Sophia said. "We can slip out of these tents with ease. The question is, where do we go from there?"

Finished washing, Celeste tossed the rag into the pail.

"Running naked through the woods was a fun game when we were little, but now..."

Sophia nodded. "Yes, a whole different story now." Sophia dropped her rag into the pail as well. Slavers in her realm. She hadn't been told of them and had no idea. She'd have to get away from them, get back on her throne, then deal with these people in the strongest possible terms.

"Of course, we can't tell them who you are, Anna. That would open a whole new vinegar jug."

Sophia glanced at the tent's entrance flap. Would it? Maybe if she told them she was the queen they'd help them or at least let them go. "I don't know—"

"Slavers have enough problems. Taking a person of noble station? They'll kill you out of hand to be rid of any complications. Me too, so I can't tell."

Sophia would have to keep her identity a secret for the time being. A vigilant eye would show her a way to escape. She groaned. "I've never been a servant, except for those days at Thomas's cottage. What do I do? How do I act?"

Celeste groaned. "I was born a servant and now I'll be a slave's servant."

Sophia gestured at Celeste's body. "If we're sold, you'll go to some rich man to be his companion. I'll end up a washer woman or housekeeper. I may even have to cook. They may let us go if we tell them who we are."

Celeste frowned. "A fat pig's ass. Telling them will seal our death warrants. Don't be stubborn, I'm right about this."

Sophia sat back. Celeste was probably right. Still, spending the rest of her life as a servant, toiling away until she died young. "I can't be a servant. I don't know how."

"I've always been your servant. Do as I've always done. You'll be all right."

"If we get out of this in time you won't be anyone's servant. Unless you choose to serve a husband."

Celeste shook her head. "It's not that hard. Keep a blank

look on your face, do as you're told, and don't draw attention to yourself."

Sophia shifted on one of the boxes and breathed a deep sigh. "I think I've been seen naked in front of more commoners today than in the rest of my life."

Celeste laughed. "It's funny we haven't been attacked. Maybe neither of us are that interesting."

Sophia frowned. "One of us anyway. Maybe the women are protecting us. They chased that boy away."

The blonde woman returned with another young woman. They carried garments of their style. The dark woman dropped the clothing and left. The blonde lingered, holding a wool garment out to Sophia.

Sophia took it and turned it over in her hands a couple times. It seemed shapeless. "How—"

"It drapes over your head, then is wrapped once around like so." The woman indicated her own dress. "Tie it at the waist with this cord."

Sophia and Celeste dressed as shown. Sophia turned to the blonde. "What's your name and what happens to us now?"

The blonde held a hand up and cocked her head. Footfalls and giggling sounded outside the tent. After a moment she nodded. "Children playing. I am called Jenna. You will do mundane work. Mostly what others do not want to do until we arrive in Truro. There you will be sold at auction."

"My name is Anna—"

"You have no names. You are slaves. If a man chooses you, the Father will wait until the guiding star is low in the south, then he will consult the bones. They will tell him your names."

"Chooses us? What does that mean?" Sophia asked.

"Do not fret over that now. Choosing depends on the moon's phase. For now, you must do as you are told."

"When will this guiding star be in the proper place?" Sophia asked.

"Soon."

Sophia glanced at Celeste, who wrinkled her lips. "How far away is this Truro?"

"Several weeks march. We will be going there starting tomorrow."

Sophia scratched her head. "How often do you raid this realm?"

Jenna wrinkled her brow. Sophia repeated her question speaking slower. Jenna brightened. "We have not come into the northland for many years. The bones told the Father of the war further north and said slaves would be found unprotected here."

"Will you show us how to wrap the head covering?" Sophia asked.

"No. You have no man. You will not wear one."

A man's voice, sounding angry, penetrated the tent's walls. Jenna held a hand up to them. After a moment she sighed. "I must go, my man grows weary of tending the children. Take the bucket to the stream and refill it, then return here."

***

Throughout the day they gathered dry dung for fires, carried water, and fed the livestock. They were denied shoes, but otherwise had the freedom to wander about the camp as they pleased if not engaged in some task.

The children seemed enthralled with the captives and followed them about, speaking to the prisoners at every opportunity. The adults ignored them unless they had some job for the slaves to do.

Their blankets were returned and they slept in what was called the orphan's tent, sharing it with a dark-eyed five- or six-year-old girl named Darie. The girl chattered at them continuously, seeming not to notice the women didn't fully understand her.

The clan packed their camp the next day. Sophia and

Celeste received a lot of shouting and vigorous pointing during the process. Jenna did come to them and explain some of the more complicated aspects of the packing, but otherwise it was figure it out as best they could. Sophia took note of her hauberk, sword, and bow; they were kept among the clan's treasures in the Father's tent.

They moved slowly across the steppe, going generally west-southwest. Sophia cursed her luck, going in the wrong direction and wasting her precious time. She had to find a way to escape from these people.

The clan finished their preparations and moved on before midmorning, then stopped to set camp in the late afternoon. Day after day. A mundane process that blended into a blur of the same activities until it seemed one long time spent doing the repetitive. Sophia feared she'd lose track of how many days they'd been held captive.

Jenna came to the orphan's tent in the early evening. She carried a water jug and some herbs. "The moon will be at its highest point in two days."

Sophia rubbed her chin. "What does that mean?"

Jenna frowned a moment then replaced it with a smile. "The young men, those without a woman, will wash their bodies and cleanse their spirits in the moon's brightest light."

Celeste flicked a piece of dry manure from her foot's sole and rubbed at a cut she'd gotten earlier in the day. "Why is that cause for celebration?"

Jenna pinched her brows together. Then smiled again. "They will come to you after they have completed the ritual."

"Come to us?" Sophia said.

Jenna nodded vigorously. "Yes. You are the only women without a man. They will come and if they are pleased with you, they may take you as their woman."

"Pleased?"

Jenna nodded. "It will be so much better to call you sister than slave."

"I don't want to be some man's woman. In my country I can pick the man I want." Sophia ignored the half-truth of her statement.

"So, coming in the night with a clean spirit to commit rape is how courtship is done in this clan?" Celeste said.

Jenna leaned her head to one side, then crumbled the herbs into the jug before offering it to Sophia. "It is not rape. You should welcome them. They will not harm you and if one is pleased, you will be a free woman. Drink."

"Free? Like you?" Sophia sniffed the jug, it smelled like rosemary, even though the herbs had been green and leafy like basil. She took a sip, sweet. She passed it to Celeste.

"Yes. I was going to be sold. The first man to come to me was not pleased. So, I tried hard to entertain the second. It worked, he was happy, and I became his woman. He is handsome and brave and has provided a good tent for me and our children. What else can a woman ask for?"

Celeste took a sip from the jug and handed it back to Jenna. "I can ask for a lot more than that," she grunted.

Jenna took a sip, then handed the jug to Sophia. "A good man, strong children, and a stout tent. A woman can ask for nothing more. Drink."

Sophia focused on Jenna's face. It seemed to blur, then return to normal. She looked into the jug. "What is this?"

Jenna smiled. "It is the same herb the men will use in the ritual. It will allow you to please a man and he you. You must get used to it though. At first it will make you dizzy."

"It's done that sure enough," Sophia handed the jug back to Jenna. "We won't be drinking anymore of that."

"You must drink. You must please a man. If you resist, you will surely be sold. Truro is an awful place. Slaves are treated so poorly. You must drink."

"I know you believe you're doing us a kindness, but we can't allow anything to interfere with our thinking. If the men come, we'll refuse them. It must be so." Sophia needed to find a way to escape. And she needed to find it soon. Sophia glanced at Celeste, who set her lips in a grim scowl.

Jenna looked back and forth between them, then shrugged. "I will leave the elixir here. You may change your mind after thinking about it." She rose and left.

Sophia peeked out of the tent, Jenna was gone, she turned to Celeste.

"We've got to get out of here. We've got to get out of here now. I haven't seen a single handsome man anywhere in this clan," Celeste said.

"I know. I don't know how we're going to do it. Not yet anyway. Keep your eyes open tomorrow. There has to be something we're not seeing."

The following morning Sophia and Celeste were assigned tasks at opposite ends of the camp. Sophia pulled up a tent stake and let the tent she'd been sleeping in drop to the ground. After wiping her brow, she dragged the canvas to one side. A blue jay landed on the far end of a tent pole.

Sophia glanced, then looked again. "Ticky?"

The bird bobbed up and down on its legs twice, then hopped closer to Sophia. Ticky twitched his head to the west several times. "Soldiers, soldiers. Fifteen miles. West, west."

"Are you sure? Are they Sir Mallet's men? Do they wear a stag's head?" Sophia looked around, but no one from the clan paid her any attention.

Ticky seemed to nod, his obsidian eyes sparkling. "Fifteen miles. Going south."

Sophia rose and gazed to the west. Could she and Celeste get to those soldiers or at least draw their attention? She looked back to Ticky, but he was gone. She smiled to herself, then returned to her work.

The clan marched to the southwest for most of the morning, then abruptly turned due east. Sophia surveyed the countryside but saw no reason for the change in direction. She guessed they'd seen the soldiers Ticky had mentioned. The clan continued going east until they made camp for the night.

The women came together once their chores were completed. Sophia plopped down on her blanket and sighed. Celeste joined her and handed Sophia a bowl containing the awful porridge their captors fed them. Sophia thanked her.

"I've started to understand what these people are saying. Mostly from chasing the children around," Celeste said between spooning bites of her supper.

Sophia nodded. "Me too. What are you hearing?"

"Best I can figure, the Father is upset about some soldiers being on or near the road, so he's taking us to Truro the long way."

Sophia glanced out the tent's door. "Ticky was here today. He told me Sir Mallet's men are only fifteen miles west of us."

"Ticky? Are you sure?"

Sophia wrinkled her lips into a frown. "How many talking birds have you come across?"

Celeste cocked her head to one side. "Fair enough. I managed to steal a knife someone left lying about. I've got it hidden in my blankets."

"Good. We'll need a weapon when we make our escape." Sophia glanced at the tent's doorway.

Celeste followed Sophia's eyes with her own. "The moon was high last night. Promises to be higher tonight."

"I know. We're running out of time. Slavers don't rape queens in my kingdom."

Celeste grunted. "I'm not keen on being raped either."

"I know. I didn't mean anything by it." Sophia sat her empty bowl aside. "Has Jenna said anything to you about when the men will be cleansing themselves?"

Celeste shook her head as their tent mate rushed in and dropped on her pallet. The orphan smiled at the women. "Tonight the men drink," she said in Sophia's language.

Sophia smiled back at her. "You're learning how we speak, Darie. We won't be able to keep secrets from you now."

Darie nodded. "It's easy for me. I listen. The Mother asks me what you say."

A spy in their tent. "What do you tell her?"

"Nothing. I say I don't understand." Darie burst into laughter, then hugged her rag doll. "I like you sleeping here. I don't like sleeping alone. I'll sleep with Jenna's family tomorrow. The men will drink tonight, then tomorrow they'll come to this tent."

Sophia and Celeste exchanged wide eyes. Sophia turned back to Darie. "You should sleep now. We will have a long walk tomorrow."

Darie kicked off her tiny sandals before rolling into her blankets. Sophia motioned toward the door with her head. She and Celeste crept out of the tent.

CHAPTER FOURTEEN

"We've got to get away from these people and we have to do it soon. Tonight, if possible," Sophia said as they walked along the row of tents.

"I know. Getting away is easy, staying free of them is the problem."

"How much drinking do you think those men are going to do?" Sophia asked at the camp's perimeter.

A loud cheer rang from a tent at the far end of the row. Celeste looked that way. "I don't know. You'd think the Father would frown on that, what with his concern about a few soldiers."

"How did they know about the soldiers? We aren't close to the road and I haven't noticed them sending any scouts away from the camp."

Celeste shot Sophia a blank look, then rubbed a foot's sole on a stone. "I think he saw them when he used the bones. Whatever that means."

Sophia looked at the moon. It hung in the sky seeming so close one could touch it. "I'm thinking we should run for it. Tonight. We've got the moon to help guide us."

"Where? Guide us where?" Celeste huffed and paced,

waving her arms. "Everything we've done so far has turned into a disaster. Even if we get away from the camp without being noticed, where will we go?"

"To the road. Those soldiers are probably Sir Mallet's, but they don't know who we are. We can make up some story along the way. Tell them about the clan. Get them to help us. Maybe even take us all the way to the pass. We're not staying here so men can rape us, then sell us to other men."

"What about our effects? Your sword, the stones, the magic coin, and all? Don't you need those things to prove who you are?"

"It can't be helped. We'll have to leave them. Maybe one of those priests will remember us from last year. Unless you think we can sneak into the Father's tent and grab them before anyone sees us."

"I wouldn't want to depend on some priest's memory." Celeste stopped pacing and turned to Sophia. "Wait, the married men were drinking that herb water earlier. I'm pretty sure the women were too. Maybe it's part of the ritual. Maybe there's a chance we can sneak in without being noticed."

"I don't know, Jenna said people get used to that drug. Maybe it's not as intoxicating for them as it seemed to be for us."

"Don't you think we need to at least try? If we get to the temple and you can't prove who you are, where will that leave us?"

Sophia rolled it over. Celeste was right. They had to get her father's sword at the least. "Only one of us need do it. I'll go, I'm smaller. Less to hide."

"You're not going without me." Celeste stomped her foot as if it would dispel all argument.

"No, I'll go. You're clumsier than me, I can be quieter. You should gather up some food and water skins while I get our effects."

"I'm not clumsy."

"I didn't say you're clumsy. I said I was quieter."

"Now who's splitting some thin hairs?"

"Let's stand here and argue all night. Eventually the men will come and settle it for us."

Celeste didn't look convinced, but at last she nodded. "I'll try to get us something to wear on our feet too. How long until we leave?"

"Within the hour, if I don't get caught. Give me your knife, just in case."

Celeste nodded. "I'll meet you outside our tent."

Sophia passed along the row of tents without a sound. The smell of burned grass and dung hung on the quiet air. She paused, listening at the front of the Father's tent. Intimate sounds came from the tents on either side, but the Father's was silent. Sophia stepped up and peeked through the flap. The darkness inside dared her to remember where the clan's treasure pile lay.

Two young men burst from a tent at the far end of the row, laughing and shoving each other, the shorter stumbled and fell. His companion offered a hand. Sophia remained still and watched them stagger into the weeds behind their tent without any indication they'd seen her. Their voices carried across the night, laughing and swearing.

Sophia sucked in a deep breath, held it, and poked her head into the Father's tent. She paused, letting her eyes adjust. She propped the flap open, allowing a sliver of moonlight to illuminate the floor near the doorway. Another deep breath and she stepped inside.

Sophia gingerly moved out of the faint light. The Father and Mother lay together wrapped in their blankets. They both breathed slow and easy. Sophia clutched her knife. Should she kill them both now, in their sleep? It would be easy, but could she live with herself if she did? After all, killing people wasn't the plan, escape was. If she needed to kill someone to get away that was one thing. This? This would be murder.

Sophia shook her head, then located the treasure pile and inched closer, slowly, silently.

The sword was easy to find, but she had to rummage around, feeling for the small bag. She glanced over her shoulder every couple of seconds, but the tent's owners remained asleep. Sophia felt an hour had passed before her fingers closed on the pouch.

Her hand brushed across her hauberk. She wanted to take it too, but it was heavy and would certainly make some noise if she picked it up. She had to leave it.

Sophia rose and took a step. She bumped the bow she'd found and it fell, knocking a pot off a stool. The pot landed on a pile of clothing with a thump. She cursed the racket she'd made.

The Mother stirred. Sophia fought the urge to flee, remaining still and waiting, her knife at the ready. The drunken young men at the end of the aisle sang a lively song. Apparently, staying in tune wasn't the point, but they were loud and enthusiastic. The Mother groaned and rolled over, facing away from Sophia.

That was it. Last chance to get out of there without a fight. Sophia steeled herself and slipped to the tent's doorway. She paused listening to the men singing. Unsure of where they were exactly, she let her chest heave a time or two, then stepped out of the tent.

The singing stopped. Sophia didn't look for the men. She turned and strode toward her tent. One of the men called after her, his voice urgent, but his words slurred so as to be unintelligible. Stumbling footfalls behind Sophia spurred her to dash ahead. She risked a glance over her shoulder. The shorter man was coming, his arms outstretched. His face set in a slack-jawed grin.

Drunken fool. Sophia ran for her tent, the man right behind her. Sophia grasped her sword at the scabbard's center, stopped, turned, and faced the man. He tripped over

Celeste's outstretched leg and crashed onto the well-trodden grass. He slid a short distance, then rolled over laughing. A slender man, only a few years her senior. He gestured for Sophia's help to get up.

Celeste, holding a bundle against her belly, stepped forward and spoke in the man's language, "Not tonight. Tomorrow. Go back."

The man stared at her with unfocused eyes, then flashed a limp-lipped smile at them both. "Tomorrow then," he mumbled dragging himself off the ground. His companion called for him to return to their tent. The man staggered back the way he'd come. He looked over his shoulder. "I'll be back."

Sophia and Celeste waited an hour for the men's revelry to subside. The moon had begun its descent. They wrapped their feet with burlap rags and rope, then slipped away from the camp going west.

A quarter-mile from the camp, Sophia led them up a low ridge, pushing the tall grass aside as she went. At the crest a man stood a few feet from them, facing away from the camp. Sophia halted and motioned for Celeste to drop to the ground. Sophia studied the guard. Like most of the clan, a slender man, his scimitar sheathed at his belt. She risked rising enough to look around, she saw no one else. They couldn't go around him without being seen unless they took a long roundabout route. Speed was more important. Could she overpower him? Unlikely. She'd have to surprise him. Sophia placed her lips against Celeste's ear and whispered, "I'll deal with him. Stay here."

Celeste offered the knife. Sophia shook her head and silently slipped the sword from its scabbard. She turned back to the man.

He was gone.

Sophia searched the slope where she'd last seen the guard. He wasn't in sight. She crept forward slowly, making no noise. Her mouth went dry and her belly grew taught. Had he heard them? Did he move to another spot? Hecuba claim her! She shouldn't have taken her eyes off him.

Sophia inched toward the only tree nearby. He had to be hiding behind it. She begged him to show himself. At the tree she found nothing. She rose to her full height. Where did he go?

The guard rose from the grass a few feet to Sophia's left. "What are you doing, slave?"

Sophia forced a smile, then lunged at him with her sword held before her. He leapt back and whipped his scimitar from his belt, assuming a low guard.

Sophia attacked, striking at his exposed head several times. He blocked every thrust and returned strikes of his own. His eyes glittered, the scarf covered his lower face, but she knew he was smirking. Sophia set her lips in a grim frown. The man's curved weapon was new to her and his style very different from any she'd practiced against. She changed her tactics and struck at his legs, then his arms. He jumped away from her and returned strikes at her body.

The crackling invaded her mind. Her strength grew, but the fight was taking too long. Sophia feigned a strike at his head leaving herself open. He stuck, slashing her upper arm. Sophia cringed as a shocking pain rushed from shoulder to wrist, but his strike left his belly exposed. Sophia ran him through.

The man crumpled. Sophia knocked his scimitar aside and jumped on him, covering his mouth with her hand. He lay still and silent, she rose. Celeste rushed up.

"Cassandra's cradle, you're wounded. Here, sit for a minute." Celeste ripped part of the guard's robe away and wrapped it tight around Sophia's arm.

"It's not bad, just a glancing blow. We don't have time to deal with it now. We have to move on. Someone will be looking for him sooner rather than later." Sophia stood.

Celeste looked back at the camp. "That'll do for now. I'll

tend to it better when it's daylight and we stop to rest." She bent and retrieved the man's scimitar, belt and sheath.

They covered several miles before they stopped for a short rest. Celeste fussed with the makeshift bandage, then stared back the way they'd come. "I can't believe they haven't come after us already."

Sophia nodded. "I think most of them are drugged or drunk. They'll be after us at first light. You can count on that."

"I don't want to go back there." Celeste fussed with the rags she had wrapped around her feet. "How far do you think the road is from here?"

Sophia shook her head and took a sip from their water skin, before handing it to Celeste. "I don't know. I don't think it was too far away when the Father turned the clan this morning. We've got to make up that ground first, then keep going west until we get to it."

Celeste cringed. "Even so, there's no guarantee we'll find those soldiers. Who's to say that bird knows what he's talking about? When the clan comes for us, what are we going to do? Don't forget, they have horses."

Sophia stood and shrugged. What would they do? She was not a slave. She would not allow herself to be put in that position again. "Fight and kill as many as we can."

"Maybe we should've stolen a couple horses. Our escape would have a much better chance of success."

Sophia gestured for Celeste to get up. The women trudged on. "Horses are too noisy. Our departure would've aroused someone."

"My feet are going to fall off before we get to the road."

Sophia pushed on Celeste's shoulder and laughed. "You're stronger than you think. You can do this."

"Perfect." Celeste laughed too. "Throw my own words back in my face. I thought you were my friend."

Sophia set her face in a grim scowl. "I'll always be your friend. Now walk."

The sun beat down on the women for an hour before they halted for another rest. After a drink Sophia climbed a termite mound and took stock of the land. Flat to her eye, but in truth, rolling and dotted with small draws and low spots. The waist-high grass bowed in the breeze.

"Can you see them or anyone?" Celeste asked.

Sophia shook her head. She sucked in a deep breath, clean air, the smell of freedom. She wouldn't be giving it back anytime soon. "No. I don't see the road either."

Celeste rose and held a helping hand out to Sophia. "Get down from there before you fall. How far do you think we've come?"

Sophia hopped down. She sat and adjusted her rapidly deteriorating burlap footwear. "I'm not sure. Maybe five or six miles from where the clan turned yesterday. Those soldiers can't be too much farther."

"I hope they can give us a horse or a cart to ride on. All this walking is starting to wear me out." Celeste swatted at some barely visible gnat.

Sophia blew out a long breath and pulled herself to her feet. "I agree. It's been a long road, but let's not forget what lies behind us." She glanced to the east, then inclined her head to the west. "Let's go, the clan will be on us long before we want to see any of them again."

The women emptied their waterskin while the noonday sun pressed on them. The hot day attracted more insects to bedevil them and sweat caused their robes to cling to their skin. Dust and dirt streaked their faces. Still there was no sign of the road, the soldiers, or the clan.

"Are you sure we're going the right way?" Celeste complained displaying a noticeable limp before flopping on her behind in the tall grass.

"Yes. Are you alright? Do you have a better idea?"

Celeste blew at her forehead. "I'm fine. I'd hoped we would cross a stream or something. I never dreamed water would be such a rare commodity."

Sophia stood and looked around. "I know. Let's keep going. I'm glad the clan doesn't keep dogs, but we're leaving a trail that's easy to follow."

Celeste took Sophia's hand and dragged herself to her feet. "I'm beginning to think this was a bad idea."

Sophia stared at her maid. "Considering the alternative, I don't think we had much choice."

Celeste groaned. "I'm just saying, rolling around in the giggle weeds with some man wouldn't be as unpleasant as dying of thirst."

"I've no desire to roll around in any weeds and being sold into slavery isn't an option. Come, if we're going to die of thirst let's do it closer to the road."

Celeste placed her hands on her hips. "Maybe you should go on without me. If the clan finds me, they'll probably give up on you. You can get away."

Sophia grabbed Celeste's arm and squeezed. "We're going together and we're both going to escape. If not, we're going to die together. Now come on. We're getting close to the road and you're wasting time."

They plodded on for another hour. Four riders dressed in the dark robes of the clan closed in from behind. Sophia grabbed Celeste's hand and dragged her into a stumbling run. They had to find a place to make a stand, someplace where she could hold them off.

Celeste fell and Sophia lost her grip on her hand. Sophia turned and breathed deeply with her hands on her knees. "Hecuba's privy, come on. You can't give up."

Celeste shook her head. "Go on, leave me. My feet...I'll go back with them."

Sophia looked at the men, they would be on them in moments. She drew her sword. "They're not taking anyone back. I killed that guard, they're here for revenge. Get up. We'll fight it out right here."

"You have to flee. They won't follow if I give up." Celeste clambered to her feet and shoved Sophia away. "Go."

"A fat pig's ass! You're coming with me." Sophia clamped an iron grip on Celeste's forearm and dragged her. The women ran another fifty yards. A horn's tinny note ripped across the featureless sky. Their pursuers turned away, jumping to the gallop. A fully armored knight, and many mounted men-at-arms, thundered past the women and charged after the slavers.

Sophia dropped to her knees. The stag's head on the knight's surcoat had never been so welcome. Celeste plopped on the ground next to her. The women watched the soldiers chase down and attack the dark-clad men. One escaped and fled at top speed, going back the way he'd come.

A few of the soldiers pursued him, but the knight and the rest of his men returned to the women. Dust swirled around the horse's legs. It settled in a gritty layer on the women's sweat-soaked skin. The horses blew heavily from their exertion. The knight's mount shook and tossed its head several times. The knight sheathed his sword and opened his visor.

Sophia came to her feet. The man's face shone, clean-shaven, with bright dark eyes and a warm, pleasant smile. Younger than she would've guessed. Sophia bowed. "Thank you for this rescue, Sir Knight. My friend and I escaped from slavers last night. We're all but exhausted. We are in your debt."

The knight inclined his chin. "Slavers have become a plague on the southern border. My lord, King Pendergast, has charged me with ridding the land of them. I would of course prefer to be fighting the honorable knights of Tegine in the north, but one serves as one is ordered. I wouldn't have dreamed some escaped slaves would lead me to them this far north." He signaled to his men. "Give these women drink and see to their injuries." He swung down from his saddle.

Sophia accepted a skin and drank deep. The knight removed his helmet, releasing a long dark mane. Then he came and studied them. His eyes roved over their faces and dress, then lingered on Sophia's sword.

"Fighting with Tegine? Has a war started? What's its cause?" Sophia asked as she passed the skin to Celeste.

The knight raised his chin and grinned.

Sophia chastised herself. Had she shown too much interest in the affairs of state?

"Lord Henry of Tegine has died; struck down. The rumor is apoplexy after a woman challenged his authority. Prince Jean assumed the throne, then voided a contract with Lord Pendergast. War was the only option for regaining my king's honor."

Sophia looked to the north. Jean De Roederio voided the contract? How then could she get back to Tegine, should she try? She returned her attention to the knight. "To whom do I owe my gratitude, Sir Knight?" Sophia bit her tongue as the last word left her lips. She should've let Celeste do the talking. She didn't recognize this knight. What more should she say? If he knew who she was, how could she convince him to let them go?

The man inclined his head. "Gerard Kathan, recent recipient of King Pendergast's accolade. You probably don't remember me, your Grace, but I must ask, where exactly do you think you're going?"

CHAPTER FIFTEEN

"You are mistaken, Sir Knight. My name is Anna, my friend and I are on pilgrimage to the great temple. Renewing our faith. Our rescue at your hand is surely a sign from Cassandra herself."

Gerard shook his head and chuckled while removing his leather gloves. "Anna, is it? How did you wretched pilgrims come to have such a fine and recognizable sword?"

Sophia tucked the sword behind her leg and searched for an answer. Nothing came to mind.

"Those slavers had it. We stole it before we escaped," Celeste said through a wince.

One of the soldiers looked up from tending Celeste's feet. "This one shouldn't be walking for a while. She's pretty well cut up."

Gerard glanced over at Celeste and nodded. "Treat her, we'll catch the slavers' horses for them." He signaled two men to do so, then returned his attention to Sophia. "So, where did the slavers get such a fine weapon? As it isn't yours, you wouldn't mind me examining it, yes?" Gerard held out a hand.

Sophia looked at Celeste's mangled feet. She shuddered. That's what she'd meant. She'd walked holes in her burlap pads. How far had they gone with her having nothing protecting her feet?

"Anna?" Gerard smirked, his open hand still waiting.

The man's smile was disarming, but should she give her weapon to him? If she didn't, a fight would surely follow. "Oh, of course." Sophia haltingly handed the sword to him.

Gerard examined the hilt, then gave the weapon a couple of practice swings. "Well balanced, intricate tool work. Rare black steel, hard, holds a good edge, but is still resilient. And this wyvern's head pommel is quite unique. Obviously, a master craftsman created this piece. I'd guess my father made it for your fa—, er rather, the old king." He handed it back with a broad smile.

Sophia cringed as she accepted the weapon. Who was this man? He was right, she didn't recognize him. His father was a bladesmith? Father's bladesmith? She draped the baldric over her shoulder before he could change his mind about the sword.

"The slavers must have stolen it from somebody important," Celeste said.

Gerard looked at Celeste. "You think quickly, my Lady, but we know the truth here."

Celeste hung her head and said no more.

This man knew who she was. Denying it further would gain them nothing. "I am Queen Sophia. Your kindness to my lady-in-waiting has put you in my favor. What will you do with us, Sir Gerard?"

Gerard nodded. "Returning your Grace to King Pendergast will gain me his favor. I can then go to the north and fight a worthy opponent."

His soldiers gathered around the women. They murmured among themselves, but Sophia heard the word "queen" more than once. A soldier stepped up to her. He avoided making eye contact, but unwrapped Celeste's makeshift bandage and discarded it. He poked at her wound before smearing a smelly ointment on it and rewrapping it with clean material.

Sophia looked each of the men in the face. She didn't recognize any of them. Would it be so bad? Being returned to Pendergast's custody? After all, Josiah told her she was worth more alive than dead. But, what of Celeste? What was she worth to Pendergast? And it was possible her own value had changed.

"I hope you are able to rationalize your disloyalty while engaging in the combat you so earnestly seek, Sir Gerard," Sophia said.

Gerard smiled back at her. "A knight has little but his honor and loyalty. King Pendergast's accolade raised my station. I must do his bidding."

Sophia gestured for the water skin again, a soldier held it out to her, and she drank before saying, "You have a strange sense of honor, Sir Gerard. Will you fight for the usurper and deny the rightful sovereign? Escort me to Oxted and you'll be rewarded with position and favor in my court."

Gerard gestured for his men to place Celeste on one of the captured horses. He then turned to Sophia and bid her mount the other. "Discussions of politics always make my head hurt. For the moment, your Grace, you'll lead us to this slaver's camp. Once that business is concluded we'll discuss your situation more fully."

"Business? An odd choice of words, Sir Gerard."

"Slavers must be shown they have no future preying on the people of Kersey. Examples must be made. King Pendergast's orders are distasteful but clear."

Sophia glanced around. Gerard's company wasn't large enough to take the whole clan prisoner. She had no love for the clan, but there were children among them and others who probably didn't approve of the slave trade. Still, an example had to be made before the clan captured someone else.

"I will lead you to their last camp, but I won't allow you to kill them all. Innocent people are among them, women and children." Sophia hoisted her shaking, sore body into the saddle.

"Your authority here is limited at best." Gerard smiled at his men but covertly winked at her. "It's a good thing you'll be with us, your Grace. You can help sort them out."

***

The sun hung low in the west. The clan's caravan came in sight. Gerard halted on a rise. Sophia came to his side. The clan, moving slowly through a shallow draw, was strung out covering a line four hundred yards long. Children led the donkeys and mules, no fighting-age men accompanied them.

"At least a dozen men are missing and all but the Father's horse," Sophia said in a near whisper.

Gerard signaled his men to proceed. "The enemy will show themselves soon enough."

The company's whoops and cries spurred the clan to run. Starting at the rear of the line the panic spread quickly to the front. It would be to no avail. The women and children couldn't possibly outrun the mounted men. The soldiers brandished their spears and closed the distance in a blink. A pall of dust filled the draw as the pounding hooves and fleeing people trampled the dry grass.

The clan's fighting men, mounted on their fleet horses, struck from the far flank. They initially gained some ground, striking down several of Gerard's men, but Gerard quickly rallied his company and put the slavers to the sword in short order. The soldiers then turned their attention to the women and children.

Sophia and Celeste rode close to Gerard, aghast at the hazy spectacle.

The older boys brandished knives, but the well-trained soldiers butchered them without mercy.

The Father dismounted and stood with his scimitar drawn.

He gathered several children near him. The Mother hovered at his side. Some of the company's men leapt from their mounts and assaulted the screaming women. Several more confronted the Father.

The Father went on guard. The soldiers closed in. He struck one down by cleaving off an arm. A spear thrust drew blood from his thigh. The Mother screamed and tried to protect the Father with her own body. A spear to the throat was her reward, her blood, a crimson spray. She dropped to the grass. The Father fell a moment later as the soldiers speared him repeatedly until he offered no more resistance.

Sophia choked on her disgust. The breeze carried the stench of iron and copper. The soldiers gang-raped the women and murdered them. Gerard turned his back on the scene, Sophia couldn't. Murdering defenseless women and children? Is this how Pendergast rules her people? Her father would never have sanctioned such conduct. Neither would she. "Gods! What manner of example is this?"

Gerard hung his head. "King Pendergast's orders are clear. Look away, your Grace. It will be done soon enough."

"Stop this right now, Sir Gerard. I order you to stop it."

"I cannot. The king selected most of these men for their enthusiasm. This is their chosen reward. You may wish to escape now, your Grace, while they are preoccupied." Gerard bumped his horse's flanks and rode several yards away without looking back.

Escape? And leave those people to this fate? Sophia glanced at Celeste. Horror plain on her maid's face. The soldiers chased the children and butchered them. Many of the men laughed and cheered as if playing a game.

If Gerard refused to act, she would. "We'll put an end to this." Sophia drew her sword and dashed toward the nearest group of men. She rode through them striking at them with the flat of her sword. "Stop this," she shouted. "Stop this. You're Kersens, not barbarians."

The soldiers cursed and jeered. Some lashed out at her.

Sophia turned and paused. Celeste had followed but stopped near the soldier's clustered horses. The women exchanged a knowing look. Celeste was going to do something foolish. She spurred her mount into the horses, shouting, striking, and scattering them.

"Follow me," Sophia shouted over her shoulder. She rushed to the head of the clan's column. Darie stood there, weeping, holding a lead line for one of the mules. The animal's pack was full. Sophia's bow stuck out of the wrapping.

Sophia held a hand out to Darie. "Get up behind me."

The girl stood there, sobbing. Sophia cursed, then slid from her mount. She scooped the child up and deposited her on the horse. Sophia grabbed the mule's lead rope and clambered back onto her horse behind Darie.

A soldier rose from Jenna's naked, prostrate body. Sophia ignored him and made eye contact with Jenna. She wept but lay silent. The soldier adjusted his dress, then grabbed his spear from the ground. He hefted it, looming over Jenna.

Sophia dropped the lead rope, then dashed forward swinging her sword. Her aim was off, failing to adjust for the horse's movement and Darie being in her way. The man's neck erupted with a spray of scarlet. His spear clattered on the ground. He clutched his throat, then fell to his knees for a moment before dropping onto his side. His last breath a gruesome gurgle.

Darie gasped, then whispered, "You killed him. A woman killed a man."

Sophia scowled. "He sealed his own fate."

Sophia returned to the mule, leaned and got a good grip on the lead rope. With a shrill yelp, she spurred her horse to a trot. The mule balked and Sophia's arm was yanked back; she teetered in her saddle. Darie clucked her teeth and spoke to the mule. It relented and followed. Sophia sped away from the carnage. She looked back after a couple hundred yards.

Soldiers surrounded Celeste, she waved, urging Sophia to keep going. As Sophia yelled her maid's name Celeste was ripped from the saddle and disappeared among the soldiers.

Sophia shouted again. Gerard rode toward the men surrounding Celeste, he waved at Sophia to go. She shook her head. He waved more urgently. Celeste's robe fluttered to the ground outside the circle of soldiers.

An animal cry escaped Sophia's throat. Gerard rode through the circle, striking at the men with the flat of his sword, scattering them. He shouted and pointed his sword at Sophia.

He'd provided her the opportunity to escape, but she'd have to leave Celeste. Leave her closest friend to a horrible fate. What could she do? Could she prevail against twenty or more men? No, if she attacked, she'd surely fail and Celeste would still be their prisoner.

Celeste's mother had foreseen this. Sophia would have to leave Celeste. Hating herself, Sophia turned her horse and bumped it into a ground-eating lope. Celeste was tough, she'd survive. Perhaps Celeste would find it in her heart to forgive her. Sophia went southeast.

***

Sophia rode on until near the midnight hour. Sensing there was no pursuit, she stopped to rest the animals and give Darie an opportunity to walk around and wake up her numb behind. Unloading the mule's pack revealed the clan's treasure hoard including her bow and hauberk, but they had no food and only one small water skin.

Why was it so hard to keep a supply of water? When she returned to the throne, she would have engineers build wells and watering stations throughout the realm. At least they were near a stream, and the animals could drink their fill. How far from the pass were they?

"I'm hungry," Darie said after dipping her feet in the stream.

"I know. So am I, but we don't have anything to eat. Even that awful porridge would be filling right now. We'll have to drink a lot of water to make do and hope to come across something tomorrow."

"Will we be going back to the Father's protection?" The girl asked between scooping water to her mouth.

Sophia smirked at the absurdity of their conversation. Orphans lost in the wild, trying to make sense of it all. At least their meaning was clear to each other. "No, I'm sorry. The Father can't protect us anymore. We're both orphans. Orphan sisters, we'll have to depend on each other for our needs."

Darie hopped up and clung to Sophia's side, hugging her. "I'm not afraid. I'm glad you're my sister. My warrior sister. You killed a man. I've never heard of a woman killing a man."

Sophia returned her hug. "It couldn't be avoided. I'm pleased you're with me too."

Should they continue to Oxted or turn around and try to get to Tegine? What of Gerard and his company? Would they be looking for her or go back to hunting for slavers? And dear Celeste, what's become of her? The clan's treasure would give her payment for the temple, but they'd need food soon. Where could she get them something to eat?

"You should lie down and sleep for a while. We're going to get back on the move before the sun comes up."

Darie pulled away. "Where are we going?"

A good question. The temple was closer than Tegine. It had to be. Sophia chewed her lip for a moment. Tegine was tempting, Lord Jean seemed a decent, handsome man, but getting through Pendergast's army might prove impossible. The temple had to be closer. "We're going to the great temple at Oxted. We'll get help from the priests and the Paladin."

"I can't sleep without Keira."

"Keira? Who's Keira?"

"My doll. I lost her back there someplace. Can we go back and look for her?" Darie pointed the way they'd come.

Sophia shook her head. "If Celeste was here, she could sew...anyway, I lost my friend too. We'll have to get along without them." That's right, she'd have to get along without Celeste. A bitter ending to be sure. Josiah, Stewart, Richard, and now Celeste. How many more would her throne cost?

"If you'll sleep next to me, I'll be alright," Darie said.

Sophia forced a smile. "Very well then. You pick us a soft spot and I'll join you after I've hobbled the animals and had a look around."

CHAPTER SIXTEEN

Sophia flexed her stiff fingers in the predawn light. She groaned at her thighs as they tightened and stung with every movement. She'd lost count of how many bruises decorated her legs. Her arms and back were no better. Her stomach growled at her. They had to get some food before nightfall.

She trimmed down the load for the mule, leaving items she felt were of no value, but keeping the coins and artifacts. The temple would want compensation, an offering they'd call it. She found a small leather purse and placed a few coins in it before tying it around her waist.

Darie still slept, rolled in a tiny fetal ball. A troubled child's slumber. She'd witnessed her whole world murdered. Would she ever be normal after that? Sophia would be better off without the child, but she couldn't leave her there. She couldn't have left her with Gerard's men either. She'd traded Celeste for Darie, was it a good bargain? Probably not. Sophia allowed a long sigh. Sad, mournful, to her own ears.

Sophia stepped past Darie and filled the waterskin, then stood looking down at the girl. She prodded her. "Come, Sister. We have to go."

"I'm hungry," Darie said through a long yawn.

"I know you are. I'm hungry too. We'll have to tighten our belts and see what lies ahead."

Sophia set Darie on the mule, then mounted her horse. A quick glance at the rising sun and she set off going south. The road would offer the best chance to find food, but it would also provide the most danger. Gerard's men would almost certainly return to it. She'd have to stay to the wild and hope for the best.

As noon approached, Darie complained about food more loudly. The ground rose and trees grew closer together, thickening into actual forest. A purple line above and beyond the trees promised to be the escarpment.

A town came into view on the edge of the wood. A few people moved among the thirty small houses and several larger buildings. A dilapidated palisade surrounded the village, a single watch tower stood near the center. A windmill's giant panels turned slow enough the patches and tears in the blades' fabric were plain to see. Well-tended corn fields lined either side of a path leading to the village entrance, although no one was in the fields.

A body hung from a gibbet near the gate. The gallows looked new, but the man's corpse appeared long dead. The rotting body was partially clad in slavers' garb. Although grotesque, it served as a warning to any would-be slave traders.

Sophia sat her horse evaluating the lay of the land. Too early in the season to glean corn from the fields. Should she go into the town and try to buy food? Would the people want to see what she had in the mule's pack? Would they rob her, or betray her to Pendergast? If so, would Gerard allow her to escape again?

Darie came alongside. She wiped at a runny nose with the back of her hand. Sophia wrinkled her brow. "You're not getting sick, are you?"

Darie shrugged. "I'm hungry."

Sophia frowned. "You've said so every five minutes for the past hour. I swear to Cassandra, fledgling starlings show more patience." Sophia didn't have any more choices, she sighed. She and Darie were dressed in slaver fashion. She'd best go alone, leave Darie hidden in the forest.

"Come, Sister. We'll find a spot for you to rest while I go into town and get us some food."

"I want to go into town. It's been forever since I've been to a town."

"I'm sure you do, but it may be dangerous. You can see the man they hanged. I don't want anything bad to happen to you. If it's safe, I'll come back and bring you in."

Darie poked out her lower lip and frowned. They moved into a thicker stand of trees. Sophia picked a spot from which Darie could see the town, a half-mile away. "Very well then. You stay here and wait. I'll be less than an hour I expect. If two hours pass and you haven't seen me come back, get on the mule and ride to the west until you get to the road. You'll find help on the road."

"I still want to go with you. I don't like the forest."

"I know, but you'll have to pass this first test. The first test of a warrior. Being alone in the woods for a short time. Don't unpack anything. We may have to flee on short notice."

"So, this will be a warrior's test? Did you have to do this too?"

"Yes, I did. I know you'll do well." Sophia glanced at her sword. Gerard had called it recognizable. She took it off and handed it to Darie. "Use this if you have to, but don't play with it. It's not a toy."

Darie beamed. "A real sword. A real warrior's sword."

"Yes, be careful with it." Sophia rummaged in the pack and came out with a small, plain dagger. She secreted it among the folds of her robe. Her hand lingered on her little purse. She opened it. Five coins lay inside. Would that be enough? Celeste did their shopping. She never took more than five coins. It would have to do, any more and it was possible she would be waylaid. Satisfied she climbed astride her horse. "I'll be back soon. Remember, don't sleep and don't play with that sword." She tossed Dearing's pouch to Darie. "Guard this too. Don't lose it."

Darie frowned, then hefted the sword and clutched the pouch in her small hand.

Sophia turned her horse and rode to the town's gate.

The gate stood open, broken from its hinges. No barrier to anyone trying to enter. An older man armed with an ancient bronze-headed spear guarded the entrance. He thrust his spear at Sophia as if the mere threat of it would send away an intruder.

Sophia displayed empty hands. "I mean no harm, my good man. I'm hungry and seek some food. I can pay. Is there a market or public house in your town?"

"Pay? Slavers don't pay. Slavers take. And they've taken all they're going to take from Easton. Be gone before I call the militia."

"I'm no slaver. I've recently escaped from slavers, thanks to some soldiers attacking them. I'm only looking for some food and maybe some shoes."

"You look like a slaver to me."

"Is there a headman or a merchant I can talk to? I've already told you I'm not a slaver." Guards were always simple.

The old man leaned his spear against a shoulder and scratched his head. "Your story is one hard chunk to swallow. What do you have to pay with?"

Simple, but greedy. Sophia dug in her purse. She selected a small silver coin of an unknown origin. She tossed it to the old man. He caught it with a quick hand. After giving it a close look, he shoved it into a pocket and pointed at the nearest large building.

"Mercantile right there. I hope you're a good trader. Master Jacob doesn't ever lose out on a barter."

"Thank you, kind Sir." She urged her horse forward and rode to the indicated building. Wood smoke and the acrid aroma of civilization struck Sophia's nose with the shock of leaping into a freezing lake. Two women, wearing brown and gray habits, rushed a few small children from the street as Sophia approached. The women glared but said nothing. Sophia needed to get some other clothing if she could. The slaver's robe was becoming more trouble than it was worth.

She slid off her horse and dropped its rein over a post. The town was quiet, the homes squat and low. A hammer rang in a methodical beat from the blacksmith's forge across the path from the mercantile.

Down the street, a young girl threw a stick, which a wiry-haired terrier pursued, its tail a blur. Sophia smiled. She glanced at the watchtower, and a man stared at her, his scowl a badge of disgust. Sophia waved at him, then went inside the store.

Shelves lined one wall and were stacked with various bolts of bright-colored cloth and a few drab, finished garments. Candles, jars of spices, sausages, and smoked meats stood on other shelves. Their aromas mixed making her stomach growl. This place was a stark contrast to the open-air markets she was accustomed to. A counter in the center of the floor held many loaves of cornbread. Sophia's stomach gurgled again and she licked her lips.

"Hello. Master Jacob?" Sophia called.

A huge man wearing a soiled apron, came from a back room, carrying a sack of seed. He dropped it on the floor near the counter. A pleasant-looking middle-aged man with a quick smile and bright eyes. He approached and loomed over Sophia. His cheeks sported a two-day-old stubble. His smile faded.

"I don't sell to any slavers, girl. You'd best be going somewhere else."

Sophia groaned and explained her story again, being as

vague as she thought she could. The man stood with massive arms crossed on his chest. His biceps, as large as Sophia's thighs, strained his shirt's sleeves.

"Escaped, did you? And now what exactly do you want from me?"

"A few days' worth of food and perhaps some shoes. I have some coin, I can pay."

The man looked her up and down for the tenth time. "We'll see." He turned and plucked two loaves of cornbread from the pile and placed them aside on the counter. Then he sliced a few ounces of jerky from a large slab and put them with the bread. "Shoes? Hold a foot up so I can see if I've got something that'll fit."

Sophia stretched out a leg, holding her dirty foot a few inches off the floor. Jacob grunted and turned to a shelf. He returned with a pair of old sandals and held them alongside her foot, then he grunted and set them next to the food.

"Ten pieces. Real silver." He pulled off his apron and draped it on the counter.

Sophia looked at the meager pile of stores. Celeste did all the purchasing and Sophia wasn't sure if the price was correct or not. It seemed high for so little. She ventured a guess, "That's twice what things should cost."

"There's a war in the north, prices have gone up and I don't believe your story for one minute. Ten pieces, take it or leave it."

Bastard. He'd cheat someone so in need. "I have four pieces. It's all I have." Sophia emptied her purse on the counter.

The man took the coins and stuffed them in a pocket. "What have you got to trade? You still need six pieces worth."

"I don't have anything else to trade. I need my horse and tack. What will the four pieces buy?"

The man pushed the sandals to the edge of the counter. He grinned at her.

"Four pieces for a pair of used sandals. In Kersey you'd be doused in hot tar, then flogged out of the city. You've got to make a fairer bargain than this."

"We're not in Kersey, are we? Besides, the king has other problems. What I do here is of no importance to him. You want a better deal? Make a better trade or get your man to come dicker with me."

Sophia's hackles rose. Get her man indeed. She had more coins in the mule's pack. Would he let her go get them without changing the price? Would he suspect she had more and go with her? He'd find Darie then. "I have no man and nothing else to trade."

"You're a woman, aren't you?" The man moved to the door and pushed the bolt home with a click. "Young and pretty enough, but you need a bath. You're worth maybe two pieces a toss." He stood between Sophia and the door. His carnal leer undisguised.

Sophia's mind raced, the familiar crackling echoed in the back of her consciousness. Was he serious? She searched for an exit. Maybe there was one in the back room. She took a hesitant step in its direction. "I'm not that sort of...I mean, I've never..."

The man laughed. "There's a first time for everything. If you're not lying about that, I'll give you the balance for one toss. Can't be fairer than that."

Even if she agreed, this man wouldn't honor the bargain. Sophia's hand strayed to her dagger. She shook her head, taking another step backward. Jacob lunged at her, grabbing her robe above her breasts. She stumbled away from him, ripping the front of her garment. She yanked out her knife. The man slapped it from her hand and seized her wrists in the same motion.

"Damn slavers always have a knife," the man growled. "Now I'll collect payment for your last raid."

Sophia kicked at his groin, missing, as she wrenched her

arms away. The man punched her in the stomach, hard. The wind exploded from Sophia's body, she gasped, her legs wobbled and she dropped to her knees, desperate for air. Jacob pounced on her, crashing them both on the floor.

Sophia scrambled onto her belly and crawled under the counter. Jacob crushed her ankles with powerful hands. The need to escape fueled her. She had to get away, get some space to defend herself. Where was the other exit?

He dragged her from under the counter. The rough flooring snagged and pulled at her robe. She kicked and dug her nails in vain at the floorboards. He flipped her over, ripping her garment away and smashed her with his weight. His breath hot, smelling of garlic.

Splinters or nails stabbed her shoulder blades. Sophia kneed him in the crotch three times. Her position allowed no leverage, making her strikes weak and ineffective. He blocked her next attempt, swearing at her as he did. His strength and weight suffocating her, she clawed his face, drawing blood. The man cried out, a pained, angry bellow. He knocked her arms aside and struck her jaw with the heel of his hand.

Sophia's teeth slammed together with a crunching click. Copper bathed her tongue. Her eyes rolled, then refused to focus. She pushed back at the man's shoulders, he struck her again, harder. Sophia's ears rang and the fight seemed to go on in slow motion but became fuzzy and indistinct. She sucked in a breath and a horrified scream erupted from her core.

The man clamped an iron-strong hand on her throat and squeezed.

Sophia choked, gagged, and struggled for air. She tore at his wrist with both hands, her legs flailed. He laughed and squeezed harder. A collapsing tunnel of darkness closed on the man's bleeding face. Sophia squeaked a protest, then blackness threatened to take her.

Sophia blinked and coughed. She rubbed her throat and gagged. The crackling in her mind's ear roared. Jacob knelt between her bare legs. His trousers were around his knees. He grabbed her ankles, yanking her legs further apart.

"That's it, you slaver bitch, relax and enjoy. This won't take more than a few minutes. If you're good enough I'll invite my brother in for a toss. Of course, he's not as gentle as me." The man then mumbled, "Never had one fight so hard to protect something of so little value."

Sophia choked again and spit blood. Her entire body aflame with sharp, mind-numbing pain. Her dagger lay a few inches away. The crackling grew louder and insistent, even urgent. The hair on her arms stood. She looked at the man's engorged penis and swallowed hard.

The room grew dim, the background dark green, the man paler, almost yellow, standing out from the surroundings. Strength and vigor rushed through her veins like a drug. She brought her knees to her chest and kicked his shoulders with both feet, then grabbed the knife.

"I'm the Kersen Wyvern, not an object to use and cast aside," she croaked, then emitted a sound she'd never heard come from any man or beast. She flung herself onto his back and stabbed at his neck and belly while biting anything she could sink her teeth into. She wrapped her legs around his waist and hammered his crotch with her heels. Her dagger found the mark twice, digging deep into his flesh.

The man carried her with him as he staggered to his feet, roaring. He blocked her knife arm with his hand. His grip a steel vise, he flung her aside. Sophia slammed into one of the shelves. A cascade of earthenware jars crashed to the floor, some breaking, spilling their aromatic contents. Spices filled her nose, an odd companion to the work at hand. The crackling continued its roar in her mind. Something jabbed her in the back near a shoulder blade. But she ignored the pain.

Jacob took a hobbled step toward her, and blood spurted from his neck, staining the floorboards six feet from him. He clamped a hand on his throat and lunged for his butcher's knife. His heartbeat on display, once, twice; blood squirted from between his fingers.

Sophia growled deep in her core. He wasn't going to get that knife. She leapt on him again, delivering another mortal stab, this one to the liver. The man shoved her away again and issued an angry groan. Sophia sprawled on the floor. She steeled her legs for another pounce.

Jacob turned slowly away from her before collapsing, his pants still around his knees. Sophia jumped to her feet, wary. The man mumbled something she didn't understand, then he sighed, a rattle deep in his throat. His fingers twitched, then became still. A dark puddle spread from beneath his head.

The strange power abandoned Sophia as suddenly as it had come. The room's colors returned to normal. Her chest heaved. She dropped the dagger. Her entire body quivered from her injuries and exertion. She staggered to the counter on wobbly knees.

She was naked, bruised, and bloodied. People were sure to come investigate the noise. Being a stranger, they would most likely not care that he'd attacked her. They'd want revenge for one of their own. She would surely join the wretch hanging outside the gate. What if they found Darie? She had to flee while she had the chance.

Sophia picked up the tattered remains of her robe as well as Jacob's apron. She gathered the stores he had placed on the counter, then wrapped them in the garments. She took a quick look around, then grabbed two more loaves and the slab of jerky, adding them to her bundle.

She cradled the package and looked at the door. No one here knew she was the queen. She'd just be a naked woman running away from their town. Two deep breaths, then she left the mercantile's door open, stumbling to her horse. A few men approaching from the blacksmith's forge paused in the street and looked at her with curious stares. Sophia ignored them, crawled onto the horse's back, and turned it toward the gate.

Sophia bumped the horse's flanks and charged from the town. As she thundered past, the old man standing guard shouted something about putting on clothes.

CHAPTER SEVENTEEN

Sophia leaned on her horse's neck, savoring the heat rolling from it. She'd come to a halt in the glen where she'd left Darie.

The girl rushed to her side, stared wide-eyed, then gasped, "You're naked. What happened?"

Sophia dropped her bundle, then slid off the horse. "I'll explain later. Pack these things, quickly. We have to get away from here. Was anyone following me?"

The girl shook her head. Sophia dumped the items on the ground. She picked up her robe, torn and spattered with rusty brown spots. Still, it was all she had to wear. She dragged it over her head and pulled on the sandals. They had thick wood soles with rope straps. Only slightly too large, better than nothing.

Darie picked up a loaf, took a bite from the middle, then pointed. "Your neck is purple and there's blood on your leg," she said through her chewing.

Sophia glanced at her thighs, decorated with smears of drying blood. Her tongue was swollen and the copper heat of her injuries filled her mouth. "It's alright, I'll be fine. Come, Sister, we must flee this place and find a spot where I can catch my breath and bathe."

A rush of nausea swept through her guts. Sophia gagged, then dropped to her knees and vomited. Nothing came out but a little stringy yellow liquid. The thought of what had nearly transpired in the mercantile caused her to shake uncontrolled. She retched, then spit the bitter taste from her mouth. Her lungs screamed for air. She couldn't draw in enough. Her belly convulsed, she vomited again. More stringy liquid.

Darie came to her and rubbed her back. "Are you going to die, Sister?"

Sophia wiped her mouth with the back of her hand, then patted the girl's arm. Her throat and lungs burned. The quaking in her core receded. "No, of course not. I'll be alright in a bit."

"Everyone I've ever seen do that dies." Darie's voice trembled.

"I'm not going to die. Not today."

Sophia staggered to her feet, used her sword to cut a piece of rope and secured the cord around her waist. Then she pushed Darie onto the mule's back and led her deeper into the forest.

Perhaps eight hours of daylight remained. Sophia moved as fast as she thought safe. Many times, whiplike tree limbs whacked her in the face. She pushed on, going east. The ground rose and the trees thinned. Rocks and boulders grew more common. Before night cast deep shadows along the escarpment, Sophia spotted a cave entrance large enough to allow the animals to pass through.

Sophia slid off her mount and looked into the darkness. Men called back and forth, far away, following Sophia and Darie's path. This would have to do. She'd sell their lives dearly in this narrow opening. She turned to Darie.

"We're in danger. I killed a man in that town and took some of his things, although I'd paid for them. I'm sure the men following us are seeking revenge. We'll hide from them here. If they find us, we can defend this cave for a long time."

Darie hopped down from the mule. "I'm scared. Are they the same men that came after the clan?"

"No, they're different men, but their intent is the same." Sophia gestured for Darie to lead the mule into the cave. The animal resisted. Sophia gave it a swat on the rump to get it moving, then she led her horse into the dark.

They found a dogleg turn, but the cave wasn't near as deep or narrow as Sophia had hoped. They huddled together on the rock-strewn floor, their animals behind them. Sophia kept an eye on the opening, a paler dark than their surroundings. An hour crept by. Sophia's injuries stiffened and ached. She flexed her fingers on the hilt of the sword. Did she have the strength for one more fight? She had to find it somehow. She had to keep Darie safe from them.

Torchlight danced to and fro among the trees. Men called to other men. The townsfolk gathered close to the cave's entrance but remained out of sight. The light from their torches cast long shadows on the cave's walls.

Darie breathed slow and soft. Sophia begged Cassandra and Hecuba to keep the men from finding them. A man's baritone rose above the other voices.

"There can only be a few caves she can hide in. Split up and check them all. Sing out if you find her."

Muttering followed, but the shadows revealed people moving around, getting closer to her hiding spot. Two men paused at the entrance. Each held a torch. They didn't appear to be armed. One man moved a couple steps into the cave, then turned to his companion.

"A fat pig's ass if I'll be singing out. I hope she's gotten clean away. Jacob had worse than that coming. The bastard."

"Maybe," the other said looking over his shoulder. "Jeremy is sure being a ram's pizzle about this. I guess if it were my brother, I'd feel the same."

The torch held aloft between them. Sophia couldn't make

out the man's features. She guessed he couldn't see her either, but a couple more steps and he'd be in easy sword range. The torch's burning pitch sputtered and filled the small space with a greasy odor. Its smoke coated the back of her tongue with an oily film. She sucked in a breath, held it, and flexed her grip on the sword's hilt.

"How'd you feel if it was your wife or sister? You know he forced himself on her. You saw her outside the mercantile. Looked like she had the tar beat out of her," the nearest man said.

"Yeah, but she was a slaver. Don't know they're decent folk to begin with."

"Old Willard said she claimed to have escaped from slavers. Besides, doesn't matter who she is, don't make it right. What was she, the third one in two years? Jacob got what he deserved. I hope Hecuba has him shoveling wyvern shit for eternity."

"I know, but—"

Sophia's horse grumbled deep in its chest and stomped a hoof.

The men's casual deportment leapt to stiff and alert. They peered into the cave. "What was that?"

The closest man lowered his torch and made eye contact with Sophia. She adjusted her grip on the sword and tensed her legs. A cold, distant calm settled on her as the crackling returned to her mind. She would kill them both. Then take the fight to the rest of them. They wouldn't harm Darie.

The man held up a hand, shaking his head. "I don't know, Mort. Maybe a...bear. Yep. Won't be no woman hiding in a bear's den and I'm not trying to fight one off with a torch and a knife." The man backed away, raising his torch again. Sophia let her breath leak from her lungs.

"Are you sure? It sounded like a horse to me."

The closest man continued to retreat, ushering his friend ahead of him. "You're wrong, Mort. Bear for sure. Let's get out of here while the getting is good."

Sophia relaxed her sore muscles and let the searchers retreat. Maybe there were some good and decent men in her realm. Of course, they could change their minds if offered some treasure or prize. How far away did they go? She needed to wait until they'd gone, then she'd have to move on. Find someplace to rest and figure out how far from the pass they were.

A few minutes later a muted meeting took place out of sight and barely in earshot. The commanding voice sounded angry, "She's got to be here somewhere. The weather's going to get nasty. Looks like a thunderstorm coming. We'll hole up in that big cave over there."

"You can if you want to, Jeremy, but there's a bear in that one," a familiar voice called out. "That'll make for an entertaining evening."

"A bear? Well, sure as Hecuba's privy we don't want to tangle with a bear in the dark. We'll pull back into the woods for shelter and look for her in the morning," said the commanding voice again.

There was no guarantee they wouldn't check the caves again with the daylight. Sophia would have to risk moving at night in a storm.

At the midnight hour Sophia woke Darie and led her and their animals out of the cave. Thunder boomed, a physical force, bouncing from the granite cliff face. Windswept rain lashed at them, pelting their skin like tiny darts. Trees swayed, groaning in resistance, while roaring torrents of water gushed from cracks in the escarpment.

The animals shied with each flash of lightning. Sophia made Darie walk, fearing the mule might bolt away at any moment. Her only consolation: the town's men would be hunkered down, trying to stay warm and dry.

Sophia's leaden limbs balked at every step. In minutes she was muddy to the knees and cold to the bone. Only her will to escape drove her forward. Pain wracked her back and her mind. Although the storm abated with the dawn, the morning sun did nothing to alleviate her suffering. The cooing of mourning doves mocked her, cheerful against her depressed mood.

They came to a ravine that blocked their path. How far west would she have to go to get around it? Could she navigate straight through it? The sides were steep, rain-slick, and treacherous. She'd have to go around.

Darie complained of being cold and hungry. Sophia took the time to stop and eat a meal. The food welcome in her gut, her jittery belly soothed. She couldn't recall her last meal. Even so, the breakfast did little to rejuvenate her energy. Long before she was rested, they plodded on.

The ravine's steep sides flattened out. Sophia turned into the ravine at that point. Reaching its floor, they found a stream running high with the rain, its water the color of milk mixed with cocoa. The animals drank, then Sophia moved on following the stream, looking for a crossing point. At midday they came to a small cottage tucked away in the trees and scrub that clung to the stream's far bank.

Sophia drew her sword as a tall gray-haired woman peered at them from the cottage door. Sophia's sword weighed a hundred pounds; she couldn't lift it again. The weapon slipped from her weary fingers and clattered on the stream's stone bank. She surrendered, her eyes closed, and exhaustion took her.

***

Sophia woke with a start. The woman she'd seen stood a few feet away, tending a pot heating over a small flame in the fireplace. Her silver hair, wild, looked windblown. Sophia was in a bed, naked, covered with a heavy down quilt. She rose on an elbow.

A single window lit the dim room. Piles of bird feathers and various vegetables covered most of the counter and tabletops. A few well-worn books were mixed in. Many empty vessels, some glass, some earthenware, and others metal, occupied the shelves across from the rope bed she lay on. Her mule's pack and belongings sat on the floor near the door.

"Back among the waking, I see. Back from the safety of the dreamland," the woman said in a smooth, soothing voice. She used a ladle to fill a stone mug from the pot she tended. She cracked a smile, missing a tooth. She came to Sophia's side. "The place of dreams doesn't allow a man to harm you, does it?"

"What? Where's Darie?" Sophia engaged the woman's startling blue eyes. Clear as a summer sky in Kersey.

"The child? She's gathering some herbs from the garden. She'll be back in a few minutes. Here, drink this." The woman pushed the mug at Sophia.

Sophia sniffed, pungent, awful. "Garlic? I'll never eat garlic again. What is this and who are you?"

"I'm called Meredith. Drink it all. Garlic or not, you need it. It's medicine, of a sort."

Sophia sipped the caustic brew and cringed. "It's awful."

"Drink it all down. It won't work in the cup, only in your belly."

Sophia choked it down. She wiped the inside of her mouth with her tongue and handed the cup back to Meredith. She coughed a time or two, her throat scratchy. "I'm in your debt, but I must get up and move on. Men are after us. They'll surely find this place and you'll be punished for helping me."

Meredith laughed, a warm, but haunting sound that lingered in the rafters. "The forest close to the escarpment is a strange place, young lady. Men and wyverns often lose their way here. We have nothing to fear from either of them."

"Men." Sophia lay back, staring at the thatched roof. Every nerve in her body throbbed, providing a dull, nagging reminder of her trials. "I have no use for men."

Meredith patted Sophia's shoulder and cocked her head to one side. "No use at all?"

"None. Men have failed or betrayed me my whole life. They have only one use."

Meredith laughed again. "Lovers or killers?"

Sophia glanced at the woman. Her blue eyes gleamed in the low light. "Soldiers, and even then, they aren't to be trusted. I must get up and be on my way. I have to get to Oxted. I need the Paladin's help."

"All in good time. I've examined you thoroughly. Your body's wounds are minor and will heal in a few days. The cut on your arm is several days old, but I cleaned and dressed it properly. You should rest. Oxted and the Paladin will still be there when you arrive."

"If my injuries are minor, what was that awful drink you forced on me? It tasted like lamp oil." Sophia winced, a cramp, not unlike her moon phase, tightened her abdomen.

"That will cleanse your womb. You don't want to be burdened with a child after such an unwanted encounter. Do you?" Meredith stood and pulled a small table to the bedside. A chalky powder filled the bottom of a glass. An earthen pitcher stood next to it. "I have to go find that child. If you should start to bleed, fill this glass and drink it down. It'll save your life."

Meredith turned and left without waiting for more questions.

Sophia stared at the closed door. Pregnancy was out of the question. She'd stopped him before...she hadn't thought about how close it'd been. In truth she hadn't thought about much of anything, except escape and keeping Darie safe. How long had it been since the attack? A day, two? She wasn't sure. Tears welled and her guts churned, accompanying her thoughts.

Sophia rolled on her side facing the wall. She drew her

knees to her chest and gripped the blanket until her knuckles blanched. The image of her assailant's face burned in her mind. The bastard. Sophia allowed her sobs to grow. Nearly everything bad that could happen, short of dying, had come to pass. She was the chosen one. Was her throne worth all this? Maybe she should have taken Stewart's suggestion and slunk off into the forest with him to never be seen again. And poor Celeste, she'd dragged her dearest friend to a miserable end. Darie? Had her actions only postponed the inevitable for the little girl?

She cursed Achaea and Cassandra. Why would they demand she face these trials and suffer so for them? Only Hecuba seemed to pity her and yet, even she hadn't called her to the tower.

Sophia's mind begged for sleep. For time to adjust. She allowed it to come.

***

Meredith wiped Sophia's face with a warm, damp cloth. Darie, gleeful, flung a rag doll about the room, her giggling incessant.

Meredith smiled her fleshy grin. "There's a sound you can't help but love. A child at play."

Sophia rubbed a hand across her forehead and regretted it. Lumps and heat met her palm.

"Tell me about your encounter with this man," Meredith said.

"Why? Will speaking of it make it go away?"

"No, of course not. That which is done cannot be changed. Although in some cases, it can be put right. No, maybe it'll help you understand what happened and how to avoid such a thing in the future."

Sophia scrunched her eyes closed. She recounted the assault as best she could, including the strange green lighting and surge of strength.

Meredith nodded, attentive to each word. Sophia finished speaking. Meredith leaned back and smiled. "You've had your first good cry. That's progress of a sort. The first step, some say." The old woman tossed the cloth into a basin. She nudged Sophia's hip and sat on the edge of the bed.

"How long was I asleep?" Sophia asked.

"A few hours. I see you've had no bleeding. That's also a good thing. You're a lucky girl. Most women fail to fight off such an attack. Cassandra has smiled on you."

Sophia wanted to scream, but relented and eyed her host. Something about her promoted confidence and trust. The eyes? The calm voice? Who could say? Sophia rolled her head back and forth on the pillow. "Lucky? My throne taken. My friends and family enslaved and murdered. I've been beaten, made a slave, and pursued through the wild. All at the hands of men. At their behest. It seems Cassandra is fickle at best."

Meredith raised an eyebrow. "So, you're the one. The child queen. It all makes sense now." She brushed her calloused fingertips along Sophia's jawline. "I believe there's a bit of the wyvern in you, your mother's side no doubt. It's where your strength comes from. You must embrace that wyvern if you're to succeed, but don't hold it so close you lose yourself."

"Wizard-speak. I hate that." Sophia turned her face to the wall.

Meredith laughed. "Wizard-speak? Hardly child. But hate is a strong word. The wyvern uses that word."

"The wyvern?"

"You know of it. You know the truth which lies within. You may not want to admit it, but tell me this, how could you have come this far without it?"

"My goal is the throne. And the peace promised by prophecy. This place isn't remotely close to my receiving hall in Castle Kersey." Sophia sniffed. Had it been the wyvern that gave her strength in the mercantile? Did Mother know of it, even guard against it? Ridiculous, a tale to entertain and frighten children.

Meredith patted Sophia's thigh. "Perhaps your journey isn't over."

Darie came to the foot of the bed and squeezed Sophia's toes through the blanket. Her dark eyes were wide and bright. "My sister is a wanderer, a warrior, and a queen. How exciting."

Meredith smiled at Darie, "All true. Go play outside, child. Your sister needs to rest. Do not cross the stream. Men from Easton are over there."

Darie sped from the room, leaving the door ajar. Meredith watched her go, then turned back to Sophia. She squeezed Sophia's shoulder a time or two.

"If there is some wyvern in me, why didn't it prevent the attack?" Sophia said.

Meredith shrugged. "Magical creatures often work in strange ways. Maybe you had to be attacked to bring it out. Maybe you had to be a certain age. Who's to say?"

"You can sense this wyvern?"

Meredith nodded.

"Can others?"

Meredith wrinkled her brows into a single gray line above her eyes. "Galen Goshawk will recognize the wyvern. His eyes are both open and seeing, but he won't help you unless you can control it. Call it forth and use it. Release, but control your inner self. Even then he may not help."

Sophia pursed her lips and glanced at the stew pot. A vegetable soup simmered, releasing an herbal tang into the air. A piece of glowing wood popped. Sparks bounced on the hearth. "Who's Galen Goshawk?"

Meredith laughed until tears came to her eyes. "You don't know who Galen Goshawk is, even as you seek his help? That's rich, that's rich indeed."

Sophia shrugged. Meredith's chuckling subsided.

"Galen Goshawk is the great Paladin at Oxted. The protector of the faith, the faithful, and the helpless." Meredith finished her announcement with a flourishing hand gesture. "Which will you be?"

Sophia flashed a meek smile, more an embarrassed cringe. Which would she be indeed? A good question. One for which she had no answer. "Funny. I never realized he'd have a name. Everyone in Kersey calls him the Paladin."

"No one, not even the mighty Galen Goshawk, springs from the earth or the wind. We all come from a line of some sort. We all have a history. Are you hungry yet?"

Sophia sat up and placed her feet on the floor as her head spun. She drew the blanket around her shoulders. The aroma of carrots, onions, and potatoes wafted from the pot hung in the fireplace. Wood smoke blended with the damp earth. Sophia rubbed her arms, safe and warm. She forced a swollen smile. "I'm famished."

Meredith patted Sophia's knee, rose, and went to the steaming pot. "Good. Another good sign. You have many good signs."

"How do you know so much about the Paladin?" Sophia asked. She cradled the bowl of hot soup. Her mouth watered and stomach growled.

Meredith chuckled and sat close with her own bowl. "I wasn't always the old hag you see before you. No. At one time I was like you, young and beautiful." She dropped a hunk of cornbread in Sophia's bowl. "Galen Goshawk is just a man after all. A man who tickled my fancy for a moment in time."

Sophia paused with her spoon halfway to her mouth. "You took the Paladin as a lover? I don't believe it. Isn't that sacrilege?"

Meredith shrugged. "Believe what you will. He was a gallant and handsome wyvern hunter before he took up the mantle. Besides, one man's sin is another's joy."

Wyvern hunters were the stuff of legend. She'd never

thought them real. "Who are you?"

Meredith chuckled. "Some call me a hermit. Some call me a crazy old woman. Others call me a witch. And again, believe what you choose. I've told you, I'm Meredith." She blew on her spoon.

Darie rushed in, breathless. The doll carelessly dangled by an arm, "Men are on the other side of the river. They looked right at me, but they didn't see me. Is that soup? I'm hungry too."

Meredith nodded. "Sit, I'll get you a bowl. Don't worry about those men. They're lost and although their eyes are open, they cannot see. They'll find their way back to their homes soon enough."

"How do you know such things?" Sophia asked.

Another nod. Meredith placed a bowl in front of Darie. "This child has a man-sized appetite." She turned to Sophia and winked. "I'm a witch. These are my woods. If one isn't welcome, one doesn't see." She wagged a finger at Darie. "Off your knees, sit like a young lady."

"I thought witches were ugly and mean," Darie said, stirring the soup as she moved to sit properly. "You aren't either of those."

Sophia rubbed her chin; it hurt. "I thought all the witches were banished from Kersey's lands."

"It's possible neither of you are as well informed as you think. It's not surprising. People fear what they don't understand. They create a view of their world that suits them. That's why they can't see. Eat."

"Have you put a spell on us?"

"No, of course not. That would be unethical."

"But the men cannot see."

"The enchantment, spell if you will, hasn't been put on them either. Eat now, then rest."

CHAPTER EIGHTEEN

Sophia slid her sword from its scabbard and sneaked across the stream. The forest lay quiet. An occasional bird chirped itself awake. The stream gurgled its soft song and the air smelled damp. A warm breeze blew toward the far side of the creek. She stood breathing deep. No men were in sight.

Sophia cursed the coarse wool habit Meredith gave her. It added to her itching as her wounds healed. Sophia put discomfort aside and looked for any sign of the men from Easton. She placed her feet with care, as silently as possible. After an hour she returned to the cabin without having seen another person. Meredith sat on the log bench near the garden.

"Good morning, your Grace. Did you find what you were looking for?"

Sophia tried to rub a sore spot on her back as she shook her head. She pointed with her sword. "The men are all gone."

Meredith set her lips in a tight grim line. "A good thing, I think. You can't hope to kill them all, you know? Some are innocent."

"A fat pig's ass. There are no innocent men. Only those who haven't been caught."

"What about your father? Was he guilty too?"

Sophia paced on the path before the bench. "Father wasn't as bad as most, but after Mother died, he carried on with young women. Leading them on with his station and charm."

"You believe that?"

"So I was told."

"By a jealous woman I'd guess. Well, I don't believe it. Your father was a good man and a good king. It's a shame you can't see that any longer."

Sophia dropped her sword on the ground, then shook her fist at Meredith. "What do you know about it? You never met him and you weren't attacked in Easton. I was. I'll set things right."

Meredith shared a knowing smirk which infuriated Sophia further. "How exactly do you plan to set things right?"

Sophia's chest heaved and her heart raced. She sputtered. Frustration brought tears. "I don't know."

Meredith rose and hugged Sophia. "Come inside. Let's have some tea."

"Tea won't make it any better."

"It won't make it any worse either."

Sophia and Darie stayed five days with Meredith. Sophia healed and spent time exercising, going through the sword manipulation drills she'd learned early in her childhood. She interspersed those training exercises with hours spent chopping and splitting wood for Meredith's fireplace. Bouts of uncontrolled sobbing accompanied her quiet moments. Darie always seemed to know about those times and would seek Sophia out to console her.

Sophia's strength returned. She gained the upper hand on her crying with a renewed focus on her objective: getting to Oxted and enlisting the Paladin's aid. Prophecy would be brought to fruition.

On the eve of Sophia and Darie's planned departure, they sat at the table eating supper. Sophia fussed with her ill-fitting, scratchy garment.

"I've come to realize you won't answer any questions about yourself or how you live here in the wild, but will you at least tell us how far away the pass is?" Sophia asked at their meal's conclusion.

Meredith sipped her tea. "Certainly. The pass is three days cautious riding from here. Follow the edge of the forest, keep the escarpment in view on your left, and you'll come to it. Can't be missed."

"Good. Then Oxted is only a few days' ride beyond that."

Meredith's brow knit together. "Take care there though. The wind tells me Kersey guards the pass. Lord Pendergast has brought the Paladin's attention to Kersey. The wind says Lord Pendergast seeks a certain person."

"Father never guarded that pass. Indeed, it was never mentioned in any meetings I had with my advisers either."

"Perhaps you and your father didn't go out of your way to offend and oppress the commoners."

"I didn't sit the throne long enough to offend anyone other than Sir Mallet. What has he done?"

"That's not for me to say. But you must know, it's you he seeks." Meredith turned to Darie. "Clear the table, child. I'll tend the mess later. You can spend a last evening playing in the garden. Your sister and I must speak of grown-up things without interruption."

Darie opened her lips as if to object but apparently thought better of it. She placed the dishes in Meredith's washing tub before dashing out of the house.

Sophia watched her go then turned to Meredith. "I'd hoped to leave her here with you. She likes you and you've been kind to her. I don't know what the path ahead holds. She'd be safer here."

Meredith's knowing grin shone in the fireplace's glow. "That's an appealing thought. Nothing keeps a heart young like the company of a child. However, she won't grow to her full potential here. There's much ahead for that child, out there." She waved a hand at the door.

"Out there? Pain, death, men, and the deceit they bring. She doesn't need any more of that."

Meredith paused with her lips parted. "That's all part of life. So is the warmth of a man's arms and the love of children born and raised in partnership with a man's love. You'd rob her of that?"

"I've felt no warmth in a man's embrace. Only pain."

"Never?"

"Never. I'd protect Darie from that."

"Your offender has paid in full, but you can't forsake them all. Have you not had a desire for a man? A longing so strong it makes your belly tremble and knees weak?"

Sophia shrugged. "Once, when I was a child. I thought I wanted Sir Stewart Odette more than anything. Now he's dead. And in spite of his lies to the contrary, his only interest in me was my station. He didn't truly love me in return."

Meredith patted Sophia's hand. "Then you must find another. One with a true heart. You must know a man's love. You can't reach your potential without having that feeling at least once."

"Spoken by a hermit living in the wild." Sophia cursed the bitterness in her voice.

"Of course, your Grace is free to reject any advice given. Who sits the throne doesn't affect me or my life." Meredith rose, went to the fireplace and removed the pail of water. She poured it into the tub. Steam swirled about her head.

Sophia watched the woman's back for a few moments before joining her at the dish washing. "I didn't intend to offend. I'm sorry. I'm having trouble, in my mind. Things have happened to me, my friends, and I don't know what to feel about them. I'm not certain I'm following the right path. Am I?"

"I can't answer that."

Sophia scowled. Of course not. She placed the dried dishes back in the cabinet. "Are you sure you won't let Darie stay?"

"That's not up to me. It's up to her destiny. I don't see her achieving it here."

Sophia went to the window and looked out. Darie sat in the garden, talking to and feeding one of the small deer which frequented the clearing. "Those deer walk right up to her. Me, they don't flee, but they don't approach."

"She has the gift of trust and understanding. All animals, even the little ones sense it in her. In you they feel the wyvern. Muted, but there regardless."

Sophia nodded. She might need to embrace the wyvern to recover her throne and protect herself and Darie from men. "I see. What does she call that doll you made?"

"Keira, I believe. Why?"

Sophia shook her head. "No reason. When I was her age Father placed a wooden sword in my hand. Before the tenth celebration of my birth, I was proficient in its use. Some of my teachers called me 'gifted' with it and tactical concerns. I don't recall playing with dolls."

"That's a shame. A child should be able to play and laugh. Did your father let you laugh? Did he hug you and tell you he loved you?"

Sophia frowned without removing her eyes from Darie. "Yes, of course he did. He wasn't a monster, but he knew I'd sit the throne one day. I'd have to be strong and able to fight for myself."

"Everyone needs help from time to time. You are no different."

Sophia turned to face Meredith. The old woman hung her apron and finger-combed her hair.

"Will you come to Oxted with us?"

"No. I can't. I have to tend to things here, my garden, the birds, and those tiny deer."

Sophia stared at the floor. "Tell me what I should do."

Meredith groaned, a mournful sound. "I can't. You have to listen to your heart. The heart you had before. The one you're listening to now has been poisoned, wounded. It's unsure. The wyvern is working to escape even as one of full blood seeks its legacy." Meredith bit her lip before she continued. "You must never forget what happened, but you must move on. I can't help you with that."

Sophia toyed with her sleeve. A full-blood? A wyvern? What legacy? Ridiculous. Wizard-speak, even if Meredith would deny it. She couldn't let herself be distracted. Not now. "What should I say to Galen Goshawk? What can I say to bring him to my cause?"

"Galen?" Meredith smiled. "Be direct. Say what you want and why. Why may be the most difficult thing to say, but it may be the most important. He's a man of few words. Don't assault him with oratory."

Sophia looked up at the rafters and shrugged. "I don't know why I'm doing any of this." She exhaled forcefully, then engaged Meredith's gaze. "Thank you for your advice and kindness. I'll grant you any item from our baggage, except my father's sword, as payment."

"I need no payment. I only wish Cassandra treats you well."

"Sleep on the idea. Even a witch has need of material things."

Meredith laughed. "I will. Now, call in the child. It'll be dark soon."

***

Sophia, dressed in her armor, nodded her satisfaction with the load's security on their mule's back. She turned to Darie, "Come, Sister, we have to be going."

"Do we have to? Meredith makes good food and tells wonderful stories."

Sophia smiled. "Yes, she does, but we have our business to tend and Meredith has hers."

Darie ran to Meredith and hugged the old woman. "Can I keep the doll you made?"

Meredith beamed. "Of course, you can. I made her just for you."

Sophia came and joined the hug. "Have you changed your mind about a payment?"

Meredith nodded. "I have. I'll accept a lock of your hair as payment."

Sophia leaned back. "My hair?"

"Yes. One never knows when one may need a bit of wyvern's hair to put the right polish on a potion. Especially if the lock is given freely."

"Very well then." Sophia allowed a nervous giggle. Magic was so strange and dangerous. What sort of potion would Meredith make? She turned her back to the older woman. "Choose what you will."

Meredith produced a scissor from her apron pocket and snipped an inch of hair from near the nape of Sophia's neck. She placed it in her pocket with the tool. "The bird that's been keeping an eye on you was here this morning."

Sophia turned to Meredith. "Ticky?"

Meredith nodded.

Sophia bit her lip. "Why didn't he help me in Easton? Or at least warn me?"

"I don't know. Perhaps he'd gone back to his master. Those sorts of incantations need to be renewed from time to time. I frown on them. The forest's creatures should be allowed to choose their allegiance."

Sophia wrinkled her brow, then glanced at Darie. The girl yawned. Sophia returned her attention to Meredith. "What did Ticky have to say?"

"He said the town's men have returned to their homes. You should be safe for the first hour of your journey. After that you'll be outside my protection, and beyond the distance that bird can travel. Stay to the trees and be wary of anyone you cross paths with. I sense dark souls afoot. Some will seem fair."

"We will. Thank you again." Sophia boosted Darie onto her seat atop the baggage. The girl clung to her doll and waved at Meredith. The old woman waved in return.

"You will also cross paths with those in need. Don't forget, kindness will always be repaid. If you have the opportunity, be kind," Meredith said.

"I will." Sophia swung into her saddle and after another farewell to their benefactor, turned her horse to the south.

Sophia kept her horse on a tight rein. Its nervous energy radiated through her legs. Fully rested, the animal was ready to run. They made their way through the trees. On the one hand, Sophia wanted to get to Oxted as soon as possible; on the other, the forest was calming. A light breeze moved the damp boughs, creating a soothing music all its own. A gentle backdrop to her troubled mind.

The day wore on and the never-changing landscape, tall trees, and leaf-litter-covered forest floor became monotonous. The warm humid air worked as a sedative. Darie drowsed in her seat and the animals plodded along, droopy, and seemingly uninterested in their surroundings. Sophia kept a watchful eye for them all.

Had Celeste suffered a worse violation at the hands of Pendergast's men? Worse than she had in Easton? Did she survive? If she did, would being abandoned cause Celeste to hate her? Would she ever be able to wash the blood from her hands? Killing her attacker—justified. But what of Josiah, Stewart, and Richard? Not to mention the rest of them and that poor boy, Will. Another child rescued from a storm only to be swept away later. If she could return to Tegine would Jean De Roederio accept her after being nearly violated? Should she tell him of it?

Sophia blinked back tears. She chose anger. Meredith was wrong. She didn't need a man in her life. No woman did.

Her world was all about men. Their greed and lust for power. The male need to dominate those around them. Things they could seize like so many chickens in a coop. Men, and their lack of compassion or empathy, caused all the strife in the world. Even Josiah, who didn't fancy women, had been ambitious and ruthless. Women should rule in the three enlightened realms, in all the world's kingdoms. Enlightenment, peace, and safety would be much more common if it were so.

Galen Goshawk was a man. She'd need to sway him to her cause, but he must be made to understand that she'd not be a prize or dalliance for any man. Nor would her realm.

Sophia sniffed and shook her head. A low buzzing, more a pitiful groan, seemed to fill the air, coming from all directions. The sound similar to that which had come to her in Easton, but not quite the same. Quieter, more mournful than angry. The sound resonated deep in her core, waking compassion. Compelling, yet more familiar than foreign. Sophia jerked her horse to a halt. The mule bumped into the rear of her mount. Darie snapped awake complaining at the mule.

"Quiet Darie, listen. Have you heard such a sound before?"

Darie cocked her head to one side, a serious look of concentration crossed her face. She shook her head. "What do you think it is? A monster?"

Sophia stood in her stirrups and looked all around. "I don't know. Doesn't sound particularly threatening, but I've no idea what it is."

"Maybe we should go back." Darie licked her lips, her eyes wide.

Sophia resumed her seat, smiled, then shook her head. "We can't go back. We must be brave and continue our quest."

After a moment's listening, Sophia couldn't shake the similarity of this sound and the crackling she'd had in her head for most of her life. Was the inner wyvern encouraging her to investigate? She urged her mount in what she'd determined to be the sound's direction. She rode slow and cautious. Meredith's words of warning about foul souls came to mind.

They went a short distance. Sophia halted again. A steel cage, not large enough for a horse, but certainly big enough to contain a sizable animal or several people, stood tucked in among some brush and scrub. A large creature occupied the cage.

Darie leaned around Sophia and gasped. "A bear trap. But that's not a bear."

"No, it's not. I've never seen a bear trap before, but that one looks well-made and expensive. There must be men somewhere nearby. We should move on." Sophia glanced all around but saw no other people.

"What have they caught?"

Sophia bumped her horse's flanks and moved a few steps closer. The moaning stopped as the creature in the cage turned and glared at her with large, goat-like yellow eyes. It snorted a puff of gray smoke from its nostrils. She'd never dreamed of seeing one so close, but there it was. "That, my little sister, is a wyvern."

CHAPTER NINETEEN

"A wyvern! I want to see it." Darie urged the mule forward, but it balked and brayed, a fearful sound.

Sophia blocked Darie's path. "Wait, it's not safe. Wyverns are dangerous." So she'd heard in every story told during her childhood. Still, it was trapped and seemed harmless at the moment. And quite beautiful, with emerald-green scales edged in gold twinkling in the light penetrating the camouflage piled on the trap.

Not as tall as her horse, the creature was longer, bent back on itself. The leathery wings flexed, striking the roof and sides of the cage to no avail. How could something so small be so frightening to so many? It was almost dog-like in a way, batting its eyes and rubbing its snout on the bars.

"I want to see it." Darie slid from her mount and rushed toward the cage.

Sophia jumped down, grasping her reins and catching Darie's arm. "Wait. It may set you on fire. The grass is wilted and some of the bushes are burnt. It's dangerous. You can see it from here."

Darie laughed and pointed. "The men wanted to catch a bear and they caught a wyvern. They'll be surprised."

"Indeed."

The wyvern clawed at the door and snorted again.

"We should let it go. The men will find their cage empty and their bait gone. It'll be a funny joke." Darie's dark eyes sparkled, her hands in constant motion.

Sophia shook her head. "No. We'd have to get too close to release it. And if we did, it might attack us. We should move on. Come, get back on the mule. We'll go."

Darie stomped her feet and pulled from Sophia's grasp. "No. We should let it go. It hasn't hurt anyone."

"You don't know that. It's a wyvern. Hurting people is what it does. Haven't you heard any stories about them?"

Darie stared at the creature. "It's a baby. It's sad and frightened. If we let it go, it'll go to its mother. It'll fly away. We'll get to see it fly."

"If it doesn't set us both on fire and eat our mounts. Come, get back on the mule."

"Look, it's crying. You have to let it go. You're a warrior. You've killed men. Men kill wyverns. It won't hurt us."

Sophia turned to the wyvern. An orange tear rolled down its face like a bit of molten iron. It spattered on contact with the ground. She shook her head. For the love of the gods, now what should she do? Josiah would tell her to harden her heart and leave, but it looked helpless. Her belly quaked. She'd been trapped in the mercantile.

"Anna, let it go." Darie wrung her hands and stared at the wyvern. "The men will kill it when they find it."

Sophia bit her lip. True enough, the men would most likely kill it. She couldn't change what had happened to her, but she could change this creature's fate. In the short term, at least. She and Darie probably wouldn't live long enough to regret it. "I haven't been completely truthful with you. My real name is Sophia Pendergast. I want you to know, in case I get killed. Hold the horses. Hold them tight. When the wyvern gets loose, they'll try to run away."

Darie jumped up and down. "It's going to fly."

Sophia took Darie under the arms and placed her on the mule. "Hold my horse's rein. If the animals spook, at least you'll be on one of them." She turned to face the cage. She loosened her sword in its scabbard, then approached the wyvern with hesitant steps. She located the pins and springs holding the door closed. She'd have to get right next to the creature to open the door. She looked over her shoulder. Darie beamed and nodded.

"This is a mistake," Sophia muttered, then reached for the first latch. She pulled it open and hooked it on the cage's frame. The wyvern pressed against the bars. Sophia inhaled a strong ozone odor as she moved to the other side of the door. With one hand on her sword, she pulled open the other latch.

The wyvern erupted from the cage, banging the door on its hinges. Sophia staggered back, tripped, and fell. The wyvern curled back toward the trap, serpent-like, and leapt on her, pressing a foot to her chest, pinning her sword arm and nearly crushing the breath from her. Sophia pushed against its hot body, but it was hopeless. Its weight was too great.

Sophia clenched her eyes closed and turned her face from the wyvern. She struggled to force the image of the would-be rapist from her mind. The wyvern sniffed a deep, grass-wilting breath, fluffing her hair in an artificial, ozone-laden wind. Its heat brought Sophia back to the present reality.

Darie laughed. "It likes you, Sister, it's wagging its tail."

Nothing more happened. The wyvern breathed several times. Sophia dared a peek out the corner of her eye. The wyvern stared but didn't strike. A lilting musical voice came into her mind, more a feeling than words. "Thank you, Cousin."

The wyvern curled on itself again, moving away, regarding the sky. Sophia sat up. Without warning the wyvern's long, bronze-colored wings flapped once and it sprang into the air. It flew right over Darie and the horses. Sophia's mount bolted away and dashed into the forest.

Darie clapped and laughed while her mule shied and ran several yards off the trail before stopping to look back. Sophia clambered to her feet. The wyvern made a circle high above them, its scales flashing in the fading light. It disappeared going northeast.

Sophia dusted herself off. Darie continued clapping and cheering, staring at the empty, darkening sky. "Did you see it? It flew away, right over my head. Whoosh."

"I saw it. Did you see where my horse went? The one you were supposed to be holding."

Darie made a vague hand gesture. "I think it went that way. Did you see the wyvern fly? I've never seen a wyvern before. It was so wonderful. I'll remember it my whole life."

Sophia's horse wasn't in sight. Hog's tail. She knew letting that thing loose was a mistake. Kindness repaid? Now she'd be stuck walking to Oxted. And what was that "cousin" thing about? She'd have to think about it later. Right now, they had to get away from the trap before men came to check it.

"Come, Sister. We have to move on."

Darie continued to bubble about their encounter as Sophia led the mule back to the path they'd been following. She plodded on for an hour after it grew full dark. Not knowing where the trappers were, she elected to keep a dark camp. Their campsite stood at the crest of a low ridge.

Two miles distant, someone else's campfire burned bright. Probably the trappers. Regardless, she couldn't trust them, whoever they were. She checked the mule's hobble twice. Couldn't afford to lose the animal and its cargo. She fed Darie before sending her to her blankets.

Sophia set her mind to sleeping in short naps. All the while keeping a wary eye on the distant campfire. She snapped awake in the wee hour before dawn. The air was chill and clear. She draped her blanket across her shoulders and eyed the unknown people's campfire. It was a barely discernible glow. The hair on her arms stood and the crackling in her mind bid her stand and look around.

She checked the mule's hobble again. Faint shouting in the distance caught her attention, as the crackling came upon her in a loud rush. She stood with a hand on the mule's shoulder. A dreadful trembling assaulted her knees.

Something flew across the sky between her and the distant fire. It moved faster than any bird or bat. So large it blocked the waning moon from view for a moment. A narrow stream of blue flame belched from the black sky. Sophia jumped with a start. The shouting became screams of fear and pain, far enough distant to be muted while still being recognizable. The blue flame disappeared as suddenly as it had come. The screams died away.

Downslope a large swath of the forest and scrub glowed with embers; the starry sky pulled down to earth. Here and there a licking flame struggled to grow. Smoke, darker than the night, crawled like a lazy serpent toward the stars.

Sophia shivered. The dark mass of an enormous animal rushed overhead for an instant, then it was gone. She turned to follow its flight path. Her knees shook and stomach rolled over. The mule cow-hopped several yards away from her. The flying creature returned, landing on the path not fifty feet from her. It brushed mature trees aside as chaff. This wyvern, much larger than the one she'd released from the trap, stared with its amber eyes. Sophia closed her hand on her sword's hilt, then released it. The weapon would be less than useless.

The mule brayed and jumped around. It would break the hobble or worse, a leg, if she couldn't calm it. Frozen to the spot, she stared back at the wyvern. It scratched a leathery wing with one of its bronze-colored horns. "Tend your animal," came into her head. Sophia grabbed at the mule's halter and hung on, speaking in low, reassuring tones. It took a few moments and a carrot bribe, but the animal returned to its normal, calm self.

The wyvern rose on its hind legs, its green scales iridescent in the pale, growing light. Heat radiated from its massive body, wilting the nearest leaves. The creature glowed as if it stoked an inner flame. Its tail flicked, breaking a limb from a tree. "Those few who can claim to have met me call me Serek-jen, Scourge of the East. You are?"

She should be afraid, but calm seeped into her mind. The wyvern was a beacon, a lantern shining from a dark place. It offered safety while grave danger lurked within its being. She felt compelled to answer, as a child might a parent. "Lady Sophia Pendergast, rightful Queen of Kersey."

"Why are you in my lands, Queen of Kersey?" Serek-jen leaned onto all fours and swung her massive head close to Sophia. The mule shied but didn't flee.

What should she answer? The truth? A lie? A wyvern shouldn't be trifled with. "I'm going to Oxted to ask for help reclaiming my throne. Is there a tariff for crossing your lands?"

Serek-jen chuckled, a deep rumble in her long throat. Her eyes came to rest on Darie where she slept. The wyvern exaggerated a sniff in Darie's direction. "What do you have there?"

"A child, rescued from the usurper's men. She's not part of this bargain if we are to arrive at terms." Sophia's knees shook violently as they always had when Father caught her in a lie. She changed her stance to steady herself.

"The child is a translator, a communicator, a valuable commodity," Serek-jen said. "She could serve me or any sovereign well."

"She's not for sale." Sophia tightened her grip on her sword.

Serek-jen's gaze returned to Sophia. "Even queens do not tell me what terms I'll demand."

Sophia needed to play her hand without overstepping it. What had the small wyvern said? Cousin? Not really knowing what it meant, she might be able to use it now. "I'm asking for a fair bargain, Cousin. I don't intend to cheat you."

Serek-jen breathed deep, then what passed for a smile came to her lips. Ivory teeth, as long as Sophia's hand, glistened in the dawn. "The tiny bit of blood we share matters not. Your rescue of my legacy is all that keeps you alive."

Was the story about her ancestor true then? She needed to pay attention to the here and now. She could search her genealogy later. "I'd trade that favor for passage then."

"You've stolen a piece from my collection. I want it returned." Smoke boiled from Serek-jen's nostrils.

"I've stolen nothing from you." Sophia's knees shivered and a shudder dashed across her shoulders. What could she have stolen? She'd never laid eyes on this or any wyvern before.

"I can smell it on you. If not stolen, how did you come to have it?"

Sophia looked around in the dawn's half-light. She shoved a hand in her pocket and fingered Dearing's tiny pouch. The coin she'd gotten from the imp was inside. That must be what Serek-jen was talking about. "I took an odd piece from an imp in exchange for releasing it."

"A likely story. An imp? Why didn't you say a faun? Thieves conjure any lie they can to hide their wicked deeds."

Sophia squared her shoulders and stiffened her spine. "I know nothing of fauns. I'm the Queen of Kersey. I don't steal and I don't lie."

A deep rumble echoed from inside Serek-jen's throat. A physical force that shivered the ground where Sophia stood.

The wyvern's hot breath warmed Sophia's cheeks. "Royals lie as often as they stuff their faces."

"Men perhaps, but I do not. I'll trade you the piece for passage. Your issue is with the imp, not with me."

The dinner-plate-sized eyes were unreadable as the wyvern stared for a long minute. At last, what passed for a chuckle came from Serek-jen. "I sense a real queen in you. Therefore, you shall pay a single piece. You know of what I speak."

Sophia pulled Dearing's pouch from her pocket. She'd hoped to use the imp's coin to pay the priests at the temple. But if Serek-jen killed her here, it wouldn't matter. She held out the strange coin. "This is the fare I offer. Do we have terms?"

"We have terms." Serek-jen rolled her head from side to side. The coin vanished from Sophia's palm. "You may proceed, Cousin. Tread carefully, the pass is guarded. Perhaps when I find the time, I will do something about that."

Sophia blinked at her empty hand. Magic was so strange. She returned her attention to the green and gold creature before her. "Thank you, Cousin. I will heed your advice."

"See that you do." Serek-jen leapt into the air and flew away without another word. Sophia staggered from the wind the wyvern's wings generated. She caught her balance next to the mule. She patted its shoulder and gazed at the sky where she'd last seen the giant creature, her knees still shook.

Now that, little sister, was a *wyvern*.

CHAPTER TWENTY

Sophia said nothing to Darie about meeting Serek-jen or the destruction she'd wrought. They loaded their stores on the mule and walked to the southwest, following the edge of the forest. After midday Sophia led them out of a draw and onto a sharp ridge. They reached the crest. A man sat on a log drinking from a canteen. He smiled and shared a greeting. Sophia stopped in her tracks. The man rose, not fifty feet away.

"Nice day for a walk in the forest. Never dreamed I'd meet two lovely ladies out here," the man said, brandishing an ear-to-ear grin.

Sophia looked around. The man was alone. Could she pass him without getting too near? No, the game trail would carry them right past his log. Why didn't she see him before they got that close? "Yes, a nice day indeed," she said.

"I was about to have my luncheon. I'd be honored if you'd share it with me. Eating alone is boring and for some reason, not as filling. It's as if conversation is food in itself."

"That's kind of you, sir, but we've had our meal and our business is pressing. We'll move on. Good day." Sophia steered Darie to the far side of the trail as she stepped forward and tugged the mule's lead line.

"We haven't eaten yet," Darie said as they neared the man.

His grin never faded. "Ah. From the mouths of children. Now I must insist you dine with me. In Tar Flats it's customary to accept an invitation to share bread."

Sophia looked the man over. Maybe thirty, well-groomed and wearing expensive knee-high boots. "We're not in Tar Flats, sir. I intend no insult, but our business is urgent."

"Too late, I'm offended. The only remedy is for you both to dine with me." His eyes sparkled almost playful. "Just because one is in the forest, doesn't mean the manners of civilization need be cast aside."

"We don't know you, sir, and we must be on our way." Sophia moved her hand to her sword. Who did this man think he was? He had no right to order her or anyone else around. Not out in the wild.

He rose and bowed at the waist. "Mica, at your service, and you are?"

Darie let go of Sophia's hand and stepped toward the man. "I'm Darie and my sister's name is Sophia. She's a queen."

Mica smiled. "A queen? Well, that makes you a princess, doesn't it? Pleased to meet you, your Grace." He held a hand out toward the little girl. Darie drew close to him.

Sophia pushed between them. "Don't touch her." She whipped her sword from its scabbard.

Mica withdrew his hand. "I mean no harm. I'm just trying to be friendly." His eyes strayed to his quarterstaff, leaning against the log a couple of steps away.

"Don't," Sophia snarled. "Darie, take the mule and go on ahead. I'll be along in a few minutes."

"But we haven't eaten yet, Sister."

"Don't argue. We'll eat later. Take the mule. I'll catch up to you." Sophia didn't remove her eyes from Mica. He stood stock-still with eyes mere slits. Darie grumbled her discontent, but yanked on the mule's lead and wandered down the path.

Sophia set her most poisonous scowl. "We've had more than enough friendly men in our lives. Following us will cost more than you're willing to pay."

Mica held his hands in front of his chest, palms toward her. "I'm trying to get along with people and find the witch some say lives in this forest. I'm not going to follow you."

Sophia wanted to believe him, but she couldn't trust him. Not if she wanted to keep Darie safe. "They say if you're welcome at a witch's cottage, you'll find it."

Mica's smile was no longer friendly. "You know where she is, don't you?"

Sophia shook her head and took a step away from the man. "Our business doesn't involve witches."

"Witches are my business. If you show me where she is, I'll forget your name as well as ever seeing you."

A witch hunter. A scoundrel. Probably in Pendergast's employ. They came and went in the night, with their wooden weapons, seeking bounties. Father always let them eat, then sent them away. This one would never find Meredith without her help. "Tell your master what you wish, but I can't help you." Sophia retreated another step.

Mica glanced at his staff again. "I don't care about you. I want the witch. What's she to you?"

She'd give him nothing. She owed Meredith that in the least. "Not knowing anything about a witch leaves me caring not, one way or the other."

"In my business one gains a feel for liars. I knew you were a liar the moment you opened your mouth. That child merely confirmed it. Show me and I'll leave you in peace, but I don't have all day. The offer will fade away quickly." Mica took a step toward his staff.

"Touch that weapon and you'll die, sir. Go back to your hunting and I'll go back to my business."

"But your help would make my job so much easier—" Mica's hand jerked. A crack and bright flash garnered billowing smoke, which hid him from view. Sophia leapt back, raising her sword in a two-handed high guard.

Mica lunged out of the smoke, thrusting his staff, spear-like, at her belly.

Sophia deftly blocked his clumsy attack and struck at his left shoulder in the same motion. Mica dodged, deflecting the blow with the other end of his staff. He smiled at her.

"Trained, I see. So be it. The first to draw blood gets their way." Mica assumed a more professional grip on the staff and turned his body, one foot in front of the other, then bounced on the balls of his feet.

"Parlor tricks won't save you." Sophia lunged at him, striking at his knees and upper arms in quick succession. Mica blocked and retreated, all the while keeping one end of the staff between them.

She couldn't get frustrated. Frustration led to mistakes. Mistakes led to bad ends. Sophia circled the man keeping her sword high and eyes on his belly. The quiet crackling distracted her; she almost went for his head fake but caught herself. His miss left him off balance and an arm exposed. She slashed it. His staff rattled on the hard ground. Mica clamped a hand on the bloody wound.

"Gods. A woman bested me. Hecuba's privy, a girl."

Sophia didn't lower her guard. She stepped toward Mica. The crackling rose in volume, becoming a torrent of sound. The hair on her arms rose and heat scorched the base of her skull. Mica's features appeared pale green. "Your witch-hunting days are finished."

Mica glanced at his fallen staff. "We had an agreement, your Grace."

Sophia steeled her lips in a tight frown. "Agreements among men mean nothing. Men have no honor and don't deserve honorable treatment. Besides, I didn't agree in the first place."

Mica lunged for his weapon. Sophia stabbed him in the

throat. His eyes went wide and he grabbed her blade. She snatched it away, severing two of his fingers. Mica gasped and tried to speak before falling backwards, his knees bent at an unnatural angle.

Sophia's chest heaved. The hairs on her arms relaxed and the crackling subsided. She licked her lips. The copper taste of blood mixed with fear's bile drenched her tongue for a moment, then faded.

Sophia stared at Mica's corpse for a minute. He looked small and much less than he'd been in life. Had she murdered the man? Was the wyvern taking control of her? She sheathed her sword and grunted as she dragged his body off the path. He would've killed Meredith. He got what he deserved. She cursed his feet being too large. She left his boots. After rummaging through his pack and taking what food he had, she threw the pack into the underbrush, then ran after Darie.

Sophia trotted along the path. She timed her breathing with her footfalls. Josiah would surely have killed him. Stewart would've also. It couldn't be taken back now. She had to concentrate on getting to Oxted's temple. On getting the Paladin to help her.

Meredith warned her many times about the wyvern residing within, but she'd decided Mica's fate. The wyvern had nothing to do with it. Injustice, that's what it was about. That's what it was all about. As the queen, setting justice right and heeding prophecy would be her calling. Stern, but just.

Darie skipped along the path tugging on the mule's lead line to keep it moving. Sophia stopped next to her. "There you are. I was worrying you'd left me far behind."

"You said I should go on. When will we eat? That nice man was going to have lunch. Can we have lunch?"

"He wasn't a nice man."

"He called me a princess, that's nice."

"Sometimes bad men say pleasant things to make you think they're nice. He was a bad man, a witch hunter. He wanted to hurt Meredith. Now he won't"

"Why would he want to hurt Meredith? She's nice."

Sophia knelt and grasped Darie's shoulders. "Sister, men can't be trusted. You must always think they're going to do bad things until they prove otherwise. Do you understand?"

Darie nodded, but her eyes spoke a different answer.

"Look, women, like you and me, we're better people than men. Men are glory seekers. They fight and carouse. They make noise and drink strong liquors. They take things, things they shouldn't take without asking. You have to be careful around men. Never trust a man until he proves his worth."

Darie looked all around, her eyes wide. "All right, I'll try to be careful."

Sophia squeezed the girl's shoulders. "That's all I'm asking. Come, we need to put a few miles behind us before we can eat."

Darie pulled the mule's lead and stepped forward. "Are all witch hunters bad?"

"Yes. They're evil men who think they do good. Let's talk of other things now."

***

The late afternoon of their third day out from Meredith's cottage brought Sophia and Darie to the last ridge before the pass cutting through the escarpment. The stone-paved road snaked through a narrow gash in the cliff. It appeared to end sixty feet above the plain, but she knew it continued on to Oxted.

Two hastily constructed log guard towers flanked the road near the pass. Several tents with a rope corral appeared to provide shelter for a small garrison. No knight's banner flew among those tents.

Sophia frowned. She could go around, but that would take her weeks out of her way and the Solstice would be long past before she got to the temple. No, she'd have to get past these men and take the road to have any hope of returning to Kersey in time.

She'd wait for nightfall. The moon was still in its waning phase. Maybe it would rain. High thin clouds drifted slowly across an otherwise featureless sky. Now, when she needed some rain to help conceal her, there would be none. Should she wait a day or two for the weather to change? She shook her head. Running out of time. They'd have to go that night; win or lose, they'd have to risk it.

Sophia knelt and squeezed Darie's hand. "The men in that camp and those towers are the same that attacked the clan. We have to get past them. I can't fight them all and win. We'll have to try to slip past them without their notice. You'll need to be quiet when we go. If they stop us and ask what we're doing we'll tell them we're pilgrims going to the temple to confirm our faith."

"But that's not true. You said we have to be honest with each other. Like when you told me your real name." Darie cocked her head to one side.

"These men are going to try to stop us. We have to fool them or we won't get to the temple. This time it's alright to tell a lie. Besides, if they don't see us, we won't have to tell them anything."

"You're the queen. You can tell them to let us go."

Sophia shook her head. "They don't believe I'm the queen. And you shouldn't tell people about that. It's a secret until we get back to Kersey."

"I can keep a secret. Secrets aren't lies."

"Most of the time. So tonight, we'll keep secrets."

An hour after sunset Sophia took Darie's hand and the lead rope. They went as close to the escarpment as they could before turning toward the pass. The ground was rough and strewn with boulders and scrub. Sophia cursed herself for the noise they made. The guards would certainly hear them long before they saw them.

Sophia set a path to pass between the escarpment and the east-most guard tower. If they could make it to the road without being seen, they could run for it. Most likely the soldiers wouldn't pursue her into Oxted's territory. They picked their way among the boulders until they were adjacent to the tower.

"Hold there," a man shouted from the tower. "What's your business out here in the night?"

Sophia looked for him, but couldn't see him in the tower's dark house. Footfalls on the road and the clinking of arms announced the approach of more troops.

"We're pilgrims going to Oxted. Is there something wrong?" Sophia called into the darkness. The road lay fifty yards away.

"Most pilgrims use the road. They don't skulk about in the night. Stay right there. I've got a cocked crossbow, don't move."

He'd have to be a good shot to hit them from that distance in the dark, but the mule was a big target. Sophia cursed her luck. Six spearmen crossed in front of the tower and approached her and Darie, their spears lowered and ready. Sophia gripped her sword and looked for an escape route. A few more men blocked the road. Her only path to safety led back the way she'd come. She couldn't go that way. Once the soldiers were close to her the threat of the crossbow would be removed. She didn't like the way this was going, but she had no choice. She'd have to fight it out. Her belly tightened as she waited.

The spearmen halted three yards from her. Their leader took a couple more steps. Sophia had difficulty seeing his face, but his brass badge of rank twinkled in the night. A lower-ranking officer. He gestured at her with his spear. "You don't look like any pilgrim I've ever seen."

Sophia sized him up. Taking him down would be crucial.

If he fell his men might rout. "Believers come in all forms, good Sir. I'd ask to be allowed to continue on my way."

"The king demands a tariff for all pilgrims coming and going on this road."

"What is the fare?"

"Five pieces for each animal or cart. Three for a person and one for a child. Can you pay?"

"Yes." Sophia had enough in her purse to cover it. If she paid, would they really allow her to pass?

"Show me your coin." He turned to one of his men, "Bring up a torch. Let's have a better look at these pilgrims."

Sophia fished the coins from her purse and offered them on her palm. The torch showed the man to be middle-aged with dark eyes. He glanced at her, then looked again.

"You look familiar. Where have I seen you before?" Recognition flickered in his eyes.

Sophia's mind was assaulted with the same crackling she'd had before Serek-jen's appearance. The hair on her arms rose and her ears burned. She fought off her inner wyvern's approach. If she could talk her way out of this, she would.

From the far end of the camp, a frantic alarm ripped across the night.

CHAPTER TWENTY-ONE

Sophia and the soldiers looked toward the shouting. A sudden rush of wind pelted them with sand and twigs as a massive creature flew overhead at high speed. Serek-jen belched her blue flame, igniting the tents in an instant. A moment later she turned, disappearing above the escarpment. Men, their clothing aflame, stumbled from the incinerated tents, screaming before falling and going silent. Darie tightened her grip on Sophia's hand.

The soldiers stood with mouths agape. Serek-jen returned, setting the closest tower on fire before darting out of sight to the west. The crossbowman leapt to his death, a screaming falling star.

Sophia shook herself from awe-struck inaction, swept Darie up, and deposited her on the mule's back. She pulled on the lead rope and stepped toward the road. The officer took note and blocked her passing with his spear.

"I know who you are," he said.

Sophia pushed the spear aside and moved on. "I think you have more important issues to deal with."

The man shouldered his spear before looking at the sky. "Go, your Grace. Go now while there's still time."

Serek-jen flew past, immolating the last tower, then vanished over the escarpment again. Sophia wasted no time. She trotted to the road. The towers, now giant torches, lit her path. The road climbed after only a few yards. In a few minutes she'd gone beyond sight of the camp. The burning towers cast bright pillars into the night sky.

Sophia paused at the top of the pass and looked back at her realm. The towers still gave off a glow; nothing more could be seen. Had Serek-jen helped her or had the monster started a reign of terror? Would her reign be sullied by the wyvern? There was no way to know. The breeze brushed her face with the comfortable odor of wood smoke and the disturbing stench of burnt meat. Sophia frowned, then turned toward Oxted. The first order of business was convincing the Paladin to help her.

Sophia and Darie traveled less than a mile. Serek-jen flew over, coming to rest on the ground a dozen yards away. The mule brayed and stomped. Darie hopped down, speaking to the mule in low tones until it settled. The gift, Meredith called it.

Serek-jen appeared to yawn. "Those animals are such a bother. I'd offer to eat it for you, but alas, I've already dined on those at the bottom of the pass."

The mule calmed sufficiently to allow Darie to hold it. Sophia walked toward the wyvern, stopping halfway. Serek-jen's green scales glowed as if backlit. Ozone lingered on the night air. "Why did you attack those soldiers?"

The wyvern blinked before answering. "Because I felt like it. Because I could. Because I had a taste for horse. Because it amused me. Does it matter?"

The wyvern version of wizard-speak. "I see. Do you intend to become a scourge on Kersey?"

"Men bring the scourge of wyverns upon themselves. Each of them thinks he is Achaea, or a hunter, and can thus slay a wyvern. I and my sisters teach them differently. Regardless, my plans are my own. You should thank me. I've allowed you to escape your former minions."

"Those men were never my minions, but you have my thanks. I expect to arrive in Oxted without further issue."

"If they aren't your men, you should arm yourself. They are coming."

Sophia looked the way she'd come. Shadowy figures were approaching. She groaned before setting her lips in a thin scowl. She drew her sword and asked over her shoulder, "Will you help me with these men?"

Serek-jen took to the sky in a single bound. "No. You claim to be the queen, prove it is your destiny. Provide for your house and in so doing ensure the future of your people. Prophecy is in the balance. My sisters and I will be watching." She disappeared going to the northeast.

Provide for her house? What in Cassandra's name could that mean? Her house was in shambles. Was her house to be the future of her people? The men approaching were of more immediate concern.

Darie craned her neck watching Serek-jen fly away. "Did you see that wyvern, Sister? It was so big. It was the little one's mother. I think she likes you."

Sophia motioned for Darie to go down the road with the mule. "Stay on the road. I'll see what these men want. I'll catch up to you again."

"You said that about the witch hunter too. I want to stay and help. It's dark down the road."

"Alright then. Get off the road in those trees and hide until I call for you." Sophia pointed.

Darie grumbled under her breath and led the mule into the trees. Sophia turned back as the first of the men halted ten yards from her. She raised her sword, assuming the high guard. "If you've come to do Sir Mallet's bidding, you'll find I'm not easy to subdue."

Six men gathered behind the first. All stood silent looking

at Sophia, their spears and shields held loose but ready. The first man took another step forward. "Queen Sophia?"

Sophia wrinkled her brow but remained on guard. "We are no longer in Kersey's territory. What do you want?"

He took another step closer, then dropped to a knee, laying his spear on the ground. He bowed his head, then lifted it again. Sophia blinked. He was the officer who had stopped her at the bottom of the pass. "I served your father as his shield-bearer. I was with him at Persimmon. I would serve you now."

Sophia lowered her sword. "What is your name?"

"I'm called Orin Feathers, your Grace."

She gestured with her sword. "And the men with you?"

"Loyal to your house."

"And yet you all wear the stag's head."

The other six men all dropped to their knees as well.

"A man can kneel before the headsman or swear to serve. We chose to live. Had all who supported you refused to live, who now would take up arms for you, your Grace?" Orin said.

Sophia shook her head. Shifting loyalties at best. She couldn't trust them. Not yet. She sheathed her sword and stepped back. "Darie, come back now," Sophia called. She returned to Orin. "I can't trust you fully, but I can't keep you from going to Oxted if that's your desire. For now, I'm willing to share the road."

***

Sophia woke with a start. One of the soldiers stood silhouetted against the rising sun. His spear resting butt-end on the ground. She looked around. Darie slept, curled up against Sophia's side. The other soldiers slept a few yards away. She groaned and approached him. The soldier snapped to rigid attention.

"All is well, your Grace. Nothing to report," he said.

Sophia nodded. "No wyverns attacking, I see."

The boy shook his head. "Gods, no. What happened at the pass was horrible."

"It was indeed." Sophia stretched her arms above her head, fingers interlaced. She took a couple steps away.

"We saw you, your Grace. We saw you talking to the wyvern. It was a sign from the gods. If I may be so bold to say, you're destined for greatness. No one can talk to a wyvern and live. I think Achaea chose us to survive so that we might serve you."

Sophia shrugged. "It was more a case of the wyvern talking to me. I said little."

"Even so, it was a thing I hope to tell my future children."

"Being in my service has ended badly for many men and women. You may want to rethink that." Sophia allowed a smile. "Let us hope you live long enough to have those children."

Orin approached. "Your Grace, we have a good archer in our company. If he could use your bow, he can take down some coneys or other game for our larder."

Sophia gazed at the man. He'd served Father. She couldn't place his face. Had she been guilty of Celeste's claim and gone about her life without even looking at those of a lower station? Another thing she needed to get better at. Should she trust him? The inner wyvern lay silent, but he was a man. Meredith had warned about those who felt fair. "I have no arrows to go with the bow."

"Cassandra provides. Our bowman saved a few shafts, but not his bow."

Perhaps Meredith was wrong, or maybe he was what he claimed to be. She couldn't do everything on her own. She'd have to relent and trust someone at some point. As Darie said, 'They can't all be bad.' Sophia stared into Orin's eyes for a minute. She found no lies there, then sighed. "Very well. I'll get it for you."

They went to the mule's pack where Sophia yanked the

bow from the pile. She turned to Orin. Should she help arm these men? They were already too close to her and Darie. If they had bad intentions they'd have to act soon. Oxted was only a few days' march away. Still, they would need food. Her supplies wouldn't sustain them all for more than a day. "Let's hope his aim is true."

Orin accepted the bow. "I'll be sure he uses this wisely, your Grace."

Sophia and Darie ate a sparse breakfast, then loaded the mule and moved on. Her little company of men followed fifty yards behind. At midday they stopped near a small shrine decorated with the tri-corner representation of the three gods. A few coins lay near Hecuba's form, offerings for loved ones no doubt. A spring trickled cool clear water in the midst of the decor. The men took turns bowing at the shrine and filling their water skins. The archer returned with several coneys, which were hung from the mule's pack before they moved on.

In the late afternoon Sophia's company stood aside to allow a long merchant's caravan, going opposite their march, to pass. Oxen pulled six heavy wagons. Fifteen armed guards accompanied the merchants. The merchant leader reported the road was clear to Oxted and the temple was preparing for the festivities surrounding the Solstice. She purchased two bottles of wine, giving one to Orin for the men, keeping the other for Darie and herself.

They camped for the night. The men started a large fire. Sophia and Darie sat several yards away. Orin came and built a small fire for the ladies.

"I want to sit with the men," Darie complained. "They have meat. I want to eat some meat."

"We have our own food. Besides we can't trust those men yet," Sophia answered.

"They've been nice and I'm tired of eating carrots."

"Carrots are good for you. Just because they've been nice so far doesn't mean we can trust them."

Orin came to them carrying two bits of meat stuck on a thin stick. He offered the stick to Sophia. "A bit of the spoils, your Grace."

Sophia shook her head. "The men need the meat. Let them eat it."

"It tastes good, no salt, but still not bad."

Sophia smiled. "I'm sure it's quite good, but the men gathered it. They should have it."

"They insist, your Grace. Consider it a trade for the wine." Orin smiled.

Sophia allowed her face to soften. He was a handsome, dirty-faced rogue, and yet rather gallant. And he'd done nothing to arouse her inner companion. She reached for the offered stick. "Very well. In exchange for the wine." She offered a piece to Darie as Orin bowed and went back to the men. "There, now you have some meat."

Darie plucked the morsel from the stick. She tossed it back and forth between her hands before popping it into her mouth. She spoke around it. "Can we sit with the men? I'll bet they're telling tales. I haven't heard a story since we left Meredith."

Sophia shook her head and looked over at the men. She popped the hot, succulent morsel into her mouth. "No. We have to get some rest. There's a long way to walk tomorrow. We can hear their stories when we get to Oxted."

They went to their blankets. Sophia kept a nodding eye on the men. She snapped awake with the primal crackling ringing loud in her mind. A figure loomed over her in the dark.

CHAPTER TWENTY-TWO

The figure raised an arm. A dagger's blade gleamed in his hand. Sophia rolled to one side and blocked the poorly aimed attack. She kicked the side of his knee. Pain seared her arm from elbow to wrist. The man raised the weapon again. Sophia scrambled to her knees. She had to get hold of his arm and get the dagger from him. On the edge of her consciousness, Darie screamed.

Sophia and the assassin engaged in a grunting wrestling match, each trying to get control of the dagger. He wrenched his arm away, then drew it back to strike again.

The man's eyes went wide as a spear point protruded from his chest. He slumped with a groan, falling on Sophia. His weight carried her to the ground. She shoved at his shoulders. Panic gripped her mind. The man struggled to breathe, his gasps becoming a gurgle. She had to get out from under him. She screamed at him and kicked with all her might.

Orin grabbed the assassin's arm and dragged him aside. "It's over, your Grace. It's over. Are you injured?" He cast his bloodied spear aside.

Sophia kicked at the man's body and pushed with her heels until she came to Darie's side. She clung to the girl and stared at Orin. His face twisted in confusion.

"There's blood." Darie's voice wavered.

All the men gathered round. Orin stepped toward Sophia. "Let me see the wound, your Grace. Someone fetch a torch."

Sophia recoiled from Orin. His face morphed into that of her would-be rapist's. She glared at the dead man. He too wore Jacob's visage. Sophia drew her dagger and menaced Orin as Darie clung to her arm.

"It's her arm. My sister is bleeding, help her."

A torch was brought, casting its red light all around. Sophia stared at the assassin's dead body. She half expected him to rise up and attack again. Orin waved a hand before her eyes, catching her attention.

"Your Grace, it's a serious wound. You must let us tend to it."

Sophia pried her eyes from the corpse. Orin's face returned to normal and pleaded, but he kept his distance. The light flickered. She'd let the men get too close. Another mistake. What should she do now? Wounded, she had to do the right thing. The right thing for Darie and for herself. She dropped her weapon. It took her two tries, but she held out her injured arm.

He ripped her sleeve, exposing a long cut on the fleshy part of her forearm. He pinched it and looked under her arm as well. Sophia flinched and tried to jerk her arm away, but he held it firm. Orin gestured at Darie. "Fetch that wine bottle, girl."

Darie hopped up and quickly returned with the bottle. Orin smiled at her and accepted the offered vessel. He pulled the cork with his teeth and dumped a generous splash of it on the wound. Sophia groaned through clenched teeth. Orin ignored her and turned to one of his men, speaking around the cork. "Wound salve and some bandage material. Be quick about it."

A man rushed back to their fire.

"Take the cork and the bottle, girl. Set them aside for now," Orin said to Darie. She complied, giggling as he winked when she plucked the cork from between his lips. He touched Darie's nose with a finger. "I have one much like you at home."

Sophia breathed deep. Her arm throbbed and her stomach roiled. Was she going to faint? She couldn't swoon. Not with the men so close. She had to keep her wits about her. "How bad?"

Orin shook his head. "It should be stitched, but we don't have a priest. I'll wrap it tight. The priests at Oxted will tend it properly."

Orin dabbed an oily-smelling ointment on her arm then wrapped it with linen strips. Sophia let her head loll to one side. "Stupid of me, falling asleep with you and your men so close."

"It's my failing, your Grace." Orin poked his chin at the corpse. "That one always seemed too fond of the king. I should've kept a closer eye on him. Your instincts and skills held him off long enough for me to come to your aid. Our orders were to capture you, but now it seems King Pendergast has changed his mind."

Sophia sat up and stared into Orin's eyes. Try as she might, she found no deception. She moved her arm back to her side and winced. Orin smiled and gestured at Darie for the bottle. He pulled the cork again, then offered the bottle to Sophia.

"A couple swallows to take the edge off, but no more."

Sophia took two healthy swigs, then handed the bottle back to Orin.

One of the men tore his surcoat into a large triangle and held it out toward Sophia. "By your leave, your Grace?" He asked.

Sophia nodded. The man stepped behind her and tied the sling so her arm rested comfortably on her belly. She leaned back against his legs. Darie took her good hand and squeezed it.

"You were with my father at Persimmon. What happened there?"

Orin nodded but looked down. "It was a mess. Traitors ruined your father's plan. If I could have taken his place I would've done so without regret. Perhaps Hecuba spared me so I might serve you now."

"So many of my loyal men and friends have perished. I don't have words to express my gratitude. Had Sir Josiah lived, he would say it better than I."

"Sir Josiah Tarkenton?"

Sophia nodded.

"He's alive. He fights for Tegine."

"Sir Josiah lives? Truly? You do not jest?" Sophia sat straight. "Are there others?"

Orin nodded. "I speak the truth, your Grace. Sir Josiah lives and fights for Tegine. I've heard he's a constant thorn in the king's side. They say there is another, but I don't know the truth of it." He took a sip of the wine, corked the bottle and handed it to Darie.

"Who is the other?" Sophia couldn't stop her heart from skipping. Cassandra let it be Stewart. Her fingers trembled even as her arm throbbed anew. Was it her injury, the wine, or something else?

Orin shook his head. "I haven't heard a name put to him. Sometimes he's with Sir Josiah and other times he leads raids in other areas."

"Are you sure? There's been no mention of Sir Stewart or Sir Richard?"

Orin engaged Sophia's eyes. His face grim. "None. This knight may not be one of your loyal men. He may be a knight from Tegine's house. You shouldn't worry over that now. Rest, you haven't slept in two days. I'll personally stand guard over you for the night. You have my word, I'll not let anything happen to you or your ward."

"How does the war go? Are the people suffering?"

Orin's face grew even more stern. "Kersey is losing. It's rumored Fraysse will send help, but of course there will be demands on the realm as payment. I'm not privy to such details. The Crows suffer, as they always do in times like these."

"They're not Crows, they're the people." Sophia's nostrils flared with her deep inhalation.

Orin inclined his head and stared at the ground. "Of course, your Grace. Two hundred pardons."

Sophia regarded him through narrow eyes as she lay back. "Very well. I place myself and the fate of my reign in your hands, Orin Feathers."

Orin rose. "Your confidence is appreciated. I'll do all I can to ensure it's not ill-placed." He gave orders for two men to drag the assassin's corpse into the woods, then he stood nearby with his spear and shield at the ready. Sophia gave in to the demands of her heavy eyelids and fell asleep.

The next day Sophia's company got an early start and at midmorning saw the towers and yellow banners affixed to the temple's corners. A few minutes later the tops of Oxted's white walls came into view as well. Sophia halted her company and ordered them to throw away their surcoats bearing Pendergast's livery.

The paved road led directly to the main gate. Although guards were present, the company passed through without issue. The odor of civilization assaulted their noses. Open toilets, livestock, cooking, and humanity blended into an odious stew. Weeks spent in the fresh air of the wild intensified the stench. Sophia made directly for the inner wall surrounding the temple itself.

Sophia laughed at Darie. "You can blink, Sister. It's a city, much like a village only larger."

Darie shook her head. "I've never seen such things. Did you see all that food in the square?"

"I did. We'll buy some after our business with the Paladin

is concluded."

Guards at the temple gate signaled for them to stop. "The high priest has declared the temple grounds full for today. You'll have to return tomorrow," the guard said.

Sophia looked past the man. The garden inside the walls stood empty. "But we've come from far away and we must be allowed to confirm our faith."

"Be gone. You're not the only pilgrims coming from afar. You can enter in the morning. The gods won't mind another day's delay in your worship."

Best she not push the issue, not there anyway. They still had time to gather support and march on Kersey before the Solstice. "Where do the pilgrims stay when they can't gain entry?"

The guard pointed. "If you have coin, inns will take you. If you can't pay there's an open space near the outer wall. You can camp there. Use the fountain and bathe. You all reek." The other guard chuckled as he looked away.

Sophia pursed her lips. Her arm throbbed and her patience reached its end. She was the queen, but not there; the high priest ruled there. "Very well. My company and I will accept your gracious invitation."

They found the camping area and picked a spot among the other pilgrims. Sophia frowned at some people gathered nearby. Ruffians and thieves from the look of them. Her company would be lucky to survive the night without being robbed or murdered in their sleep.

Orin grunted. "I'll have the men remain on guard all night. Two on a shift. That should keep the riffraff at bay. Unless you'd prefer we go kill a few of them. Just to show them we're not to be trifled with."

Sophia growled. "We'll defend ourselves, but there'll be no killing unless it's necessary."

"Of course, your Grace."

"Have the men wash up as well. No need to give the guards

more excuses to deny us entry to the temple."

"As you wish. I'll see to it."

CHAPTER TWENTY-THREE

Sophia and her company survived the night without incident. She'd gotten Darie to help her wriggle out of her hauberk. It pained her, but she didn't want to meet with the priests appearing to be a threat. She washed her and Darie's face and hands as well.

Sophia draped her worn baldric over her shoulder and fussed getting her sword to hang properly in spite of her arm's sling. Her sword; Father's sword, Gerard had called it recognizable. Now it, and her hope at least one of the priests would remember her, were all she had to identify herself. To prove her claim.

The company finished the last of their food, then marched through the busy streets to the temple gate. They passed through crowded alleyways where destitute people held out hands. Stray dogs and cats competed for the scraps that equally stray humans discarded. Rotting garbage and offal penetrated her sinuses, leaving an unsavory taste on the back of her tongue.

Sophia thought of the mud homes many of her subjects lived in and the stark contrast of those with the small wooden homes people in Tegine built. She'd have to make sure appalling conditions like these wouldn't occur in Kersey.

The company passed through the temple gate without comment from the guards. Sophia found a spot in the crowded courtyard and unloaded the mule. She organized about half the stolen trinkets and treasures into a pile, then wrapped them in her blanket. She swung the ungainly package over her shoulder and turned to Orin.

"Remain here with the men. Guard the rest of these valuables and the mule. We'll need it to trade for equipment and lodging. Darie and I'll go in and meet with the Paladin."

"Consider it done. Do you think the Paladin will help? Will he bring the monks to our cause?"

Sophia hiked the bundle higher on her shoulder. The same worry she'd had since leaving Thomas's cottage. Would the Paladin help her? "That's why we're here." She turned and called Darie to accompany her. They went directly to the temple's entrance.

Sophia chafed. The year before she'd been led into a side, private entrance. Today she stood waiting in line behind other pilgrims at the main door. The giant wooden door had relief carvings of Achaea, Cassandra, and Hecuba looking over the land, the forming fire behind them. Cassandra's swollen belly shone, worn smooth and glossy by thousands of women's fingers as they prayed for healthy children.

Sophia assuaged her feelings. When they found out who she was, the priests would be embarrassed. Finally, she was allowed into the holiest of places and stood before an ancient priest, who was seated behind a low rostrum. Sophia recognized him from her last visit, but couldn't remember his name. The name thing again. She had to get better at that.

The old man examined Sophia and Darie's dress with his dark eyes and a wrinkled brow. His hair matched his white vestments. He clutched a new quill in a gnarled hand and dipped it in an ornate well. At last, he returned his judgmental visage to Sophia, his hand poised over a parchment. "Your names and place you've come from."

"Lady Sophia Pendergast, Queen of Kersey. We met last year. My ward and six loyal men-at-arms are in my company. I have an offering and seek an audience with the Paladin." Sophia dropped her bundle on the marble floor. The contents rattled inside the soft wrapping. She sucked in a deep breath of the incense-laden air.

The priest's eyebrows merged with his hairline. "Queen of Kersey indeed. I don't recall ever meeting you." He glanced at Darie. "Your ward is dressed as a slaver. Your offering notwithstanding, your claim is absurd."

Sophia pursed her lips. "If you do not recall our meeting, perhaps you remember my father's sword." Sophia turned so the priest could easily see the weapon's hilt. "I'm the anointed sovereign of Kersey. A usurper has ousted me and I've suffered many dangers, hardships, and insults to my person to be here. Summon a younger priest, one without a faulty memory."

The priest's eyes narrowed. He gestured for two guards to join him. "Spoken with authority. Authority you do not have in this place. However, I'll humor your request. Name this younger priest and I'll send for him."

Sophia clamped her lips together and cursed herself. A name, what for all the gods' sake was that priest's name? "I'm not in the habit of keeping the names of men I meet. He was tall with straw-colored hair and blue eyes. Perhaps ten years my senior. He guided me through the pillars and accepted my prayers. I'm certain you know of whom I speak."

The old priest emitted an annoyed chuckle. "It seems I'm not the only one with a faulty memory."

Sophia groaned. Would she need to beg? "If you can't call for this other priest, then summon the Paladin. I'll prove my claim to him."

The priest turned and gestured to a servant. "Take this woman's offering, then ask Brother Jonas to join us." The servant gathered up the blanket, then left through a side door.

The priest looked back at Sophia. "Where did you come upon such a waif to be your ward?"

Darie stabbed her hands onto her hips. "I'm not a waif and my sister is a queen. A warrior queen. We're not to be trifled with."

Sophia patted Darie's shoulder. The priest allowed a cautious grin.

"She has been rescued from Sir Mallet's men. She's an orphan from a slaver clan. Now she is my ward and I call her sister."

"Sister, indeed," the old priest said.

Sophia glanced at the gold-encrusted altar standing at the far end of the room. Larger-than-life renderings of Achaea, Cassandra, and Hecuba along with the forming fire flanked the altar. The figures were plated in silver. Achaea's muscled chest, Cassandra's ridiculously large breasts, and Hecuba's grim frown all shone in the light of oil lamps. Servants tended to cleaning soot from the various artifacts as pilgrims bowed and prayed.

A blond priest came into the hall and walked directly up to Sophia. He patted the older man's shoulder, crossed his arms on his chest and looked Sophia up and down.

A smile crept across Jonas's face. "Lady Sophia, so good to see you again. Have you come to walk the pillars once more? It would certainly help you regain your throne. Particularly paying attention to Achaea's stations." He turned to the old man. "I'll tend to this, Brother Tobias, you may return to recording the faithful."

"Thank you, Brother Jonas. While I'd forgotten your name, I hadn't forgotten your face. You have my sincere apology. I'll certainly tend to the requirements of my faith, but I'm in need of a meeting with the Paladin." Sophia held out her hand. Jonas took it and gently squeezed her fingers.

"All in good time, your Grace. You've been injured. You can introduce me to your companion while I escort you to the infirmary. We need to tend to your wound before all else."

Sophia and Darie followed Jonas as Tobias scowled, but he waved his guards away. Jonas led them through an ornate door and down an artifact-lined hallway. An herbal odor wafted from Jonas's vestments while an unseen flutist played a lighthearted tune. After making several turns, they arrived in a wide room filled with bright sunlight.

Camphor lingered in the air. The room had many cabinets along one wall and windows at the far end. Three neatly made beds rested beneath the windows. A sun-bathed counter on the other wall held planting pots, herbs of various types and use growing in them. Four small tables with chairs sat in the middle of the floor.

Sophia's party entered. A priest and two acolytes looked up from crushing herbs in mortars. After a brief exchange with Jonas, the priest motioned for Sophia to sit at one of the tables. Jonas left them, promising to return shortly.

The priest fussed with removing her sling and gently peeled the field dressing from her arm. Darie wandered about peeking in the cabinets. One of the acolytes pursued her, shooing her away from them. The other acolyte hovered near the priest, assisting as he could.

"Wicked business that, but not serious, I think. It should have been stitched, but it's healing now, your Grace." The priest squeezed and poked at the wound. Sophia flinched, then concentrated on holding still. "Whoever put on that dressing did a good job. We'll clean it, then put a new bandage on it. Should be right as Achaea in a few days."

Jonas returned as the priest finished his work. A proper sling was affixed and Sophia was returned to Jonas's care. The trio stepped into the hall and Jonas led them on a winding path through the bowels of the temple.

"I've come from speaking to his Lordship. He has agreed to speak to you. In fact, he said he knew you were coming. Odd that, I haven't known him to possess any skills in divination.

Regardless, I'm taking you there now."

"Thank you, Brother Jonas. I'm in your debt. I'd ask you to see to my company being fed and provided a place to rest. We've been on short rations for several days. They wait in the courtyard."

Jonas indicated a closed door. "We've arrived. I'll see to your men. And I'll expect to see you at dawn in the hall of pillars."

Sophia thanked him again. Jonas left them in the hall outside the door. She watched him go. How had the Paladin known she was coming? It was difficult to say. The gods often seemed more mysterious than magic. Sophia sucked in a deep breath and knocked.

A moment later the door opened. A smiling, young priest in drab, everyday vestments greeted them. He gestured for them to enter. They stood in an unadorned vestibule. The priest led them into the next room. It was decorated with the various trappings of war and soldiering. A hauberk gleamed on a stand, crossed swords hung over the fireplace, and maps were on the other walls. The furnishings were large and sturdy. A table, several chairs, and a divan filled the floor space.

"My Lord, Lady Sophia and her ward, Darie," the young priest announced.

Galen Goshawk rose at the far end of the table. He placed a wooden, cube-shaped puzzle on the table and bowed slightly at the waist. Handsome, probably in his late fifties. His bald head shone, reflecting the lamp light. His deep voice rumbled in the confined space, "Welcome, your Grace. Please come in, sit." He indicated a chair near his. "I've been expecting you."

A more massive man than she'd anticipated. Indeed, she'd always imagined him being much like Josiah. She couldn't have been more wrong, not only larger but younger as well. Sophia stepped forward and looked up at the man. She held out a hand. His smothered hers as he bent to place a quick, dry kiss on her wrist.

"I'm pleased to finally meet your renowned self, my Lord." Sophia took the indicated seat.

Galen sat, his hand covering the puzzle like a tent. "Political niceties complete. Although I was told of your coming, I wasn't told of your intent. What do you want?" He raised a hand and stroked his close-cut white chin whiskers, a stark contrast to his olive skin.

Galen's eyes, the color of hardened steel, bored into Sophia's. She swallowed in spite of her dry tongue and pulled at her habit's neck. A glance at the fireplace showed no flames there. She stared back at him. "I've come to ask for your support and assistance regaining my throne."

Darie rushed forward and stood next to Galen. She patted his arm. "My sister says you're the greatest warrior in all the world. Is that true? And knights everywhere are afraid of you. You don't look scary to me."

Galen turned his gaze to the child. "I can hold my own, young lady." He looked to the priest. "Brother Charles, take this young lady and see that she's bathed and dressed appropriate to her station as the queen's ward. Find her a sweet treat as well."

Brother Charles herded a complaining Darie from the room. Galen turned his visage on Sophia once again. "Normally I don't concern myself with the petty arguments of the various thrones."

"And yet you agreed to see me."

Galen's face betrayed nothing. "I have it on impeccable authority that you harbor the wyvern. I wish to see for myself."

"Authority? Who would that be, Meredith?" Couldn't be. How would the old woman have spoken to him? Still, she was a witch.

Galen's eyes softened for a moment. "No, but you must've met her. How does she fare?"

"She seems well. Vigorous and busy with her vegetables and animals. Will you help me defeat the usurper?"

"What will my help gain?" Galen tapped a finger on the table next to the puzzle. He had only three fingers on that hand, the smallest being missing. Charles returned and stood nearby.

Sophia swallowed again. "The usurper taxes the faithful on route to this temple. I'll abolish that. He has closed the grievance courts, taking the common folk's voice from them. I'd reinstate them. He has ordered the murder of women and children in their beds. He has—"

Galen held a hand up to her. "Tell me what you gain from this and why I should participate."

"I regain my throne, my family's honor, and avenge my father's death." Sophia glanced at her dirty feet clad in the ill-fitting sandals. What did she gain from all this?

"You mean you regain power. What does the temple gain? How is Achaea served?" Galen gestured at the priest. The Paladin's bell sleeves rippled with his arm movement. "Brother Charles, if you'd be so kind, bring us tea."

"As you wish, my Lord." The priest slipped away again.

Sophia watched Charles leave, then looked back at Galen. "Of course, power is returned to me. The power to do good things for the people of Kersey. It is the first step in prophecy. I would think that would please the gods. And by extension, the temple."

His face betrayed nothing. "What are the three principles of combat?"

Sophia glanced around the room. "What?"

"I spoke clearly. The three principles?"

Sophia blinked as she searched for her tutors' words. She knew this. Even Mallet had all but clubbed her over the head with it. Part of her tactical training. She raised a finger for each point as she recited, "Use the minimum force necessary. Stay in contact with the enemy until the issue is decided. Seek the ideal range for your weapons while denying it to the enemy."

Galen sat, tapping the tabletop, his gaze stabbing Sophia's soul. At last Charles returned with a tray and served them. Sophia sipped the tea, savoring its heat and strong flavor. What should she say next? Had she answered incorrectly?

"I will test you." Galen stared over the rim of his cup.

"My Lord, Lady Sophia is wounded, she can't possibly pass the test," Charles said in a hushed voice, stepping toward the table.

Galen didn't look at him but held an open palm toward the boy.

Charles bowed and retreated. "Two hundred pardons, my Lord."

"You may decline the test. There's no dishonor in that. However, there is no help from me either."

Sophia set her cup aside. What sort of test? Could she pass a physical contest? Her reign and the future of her people depended on it. "I accept your challenge, my Lord. Let us get on with it."

Galen raised one side of his lips for an instant. "Very well, follow me." He rose and strode toward a plain wooden door.

CHAPTER TWENTY-FOUR

Sophia followed Galen into the next room. It was a large rectangle with many windows along one of the long walls. Four oil lamps, secured in plain iron sconces along the opposite wall, provided good lighting. The floor, made of unfinished wood, lay mostly empty. Thousands of unknown bare feet over the centuries had polished it to a glossy hue. A cool breeze carrying the scent of the garden wafted in through the glassless windows.

Several monks, wearing yellow and white kilts, fought mock battles with wooden weapons in the center of the floor. Galen waved an arm at them. "Clear the floor."

The monks stopped fighting and retreated to the walls, many of them sitting on the windowsills.

A rack of wooden weapons stood against the wall beneath the sconces. Galen stopped in front of the rack. He casually undressed, hanging his garments on a hook. Sophia looked away, then back again. The backs of his legs, buttocks, and shoulders bulged with powerful muscle as he moved. Indeed, he was chiseled in granite from bare feet to burnished bald head. But he was a man. An old man at that. Why did she find that so...interesting? Heat scorched the outer rims of her ears.

He lifted a yellow and white kilt from the rack and wrapped it around his waist, fixing it with a leather belt before he turned to face her. Three parallel white scars ran two inches apart, from his left hip to his right armpit. Galen gestured at another kilt, hanging next to the weapons. "Disrobe and put on appropriate attire for this contest."

Galen took an old wooden sword from the rack and stepped into the middle of the room. Sophia walked to the kilt, her hard-soled sandals clacking on the floor. She fingered the kilt's material. Soft wool, probably warm. Decorated with alternating yellow and white diamond shapes. Why would he have her wear this? She could fight in her own clothes. "I've never worn such a skirt."

"It's tradition. It proves neither of us has concealed an advantage. Prepare or decline the test."

Sophia looked over her shoulder. The monks showed no intention of averting their gaze. Nudity wasn't uncommon in the temple. Indeed, one would walk the pillars while nude. Being so brought one closer to the gods. But her belly trembled anyway.

Galen stood, legs apart, arms at his sides. The wooden sword he held in a loose grip, its point resting on the floor. His eyes were closed, his chest expanding and contracting in a slow rhythm.

She turned to the wall, sucked in a deep breath, and removed her sling, baldric, and frayed habit, keeping her back to the silent audience. She stepped out of her sandals. The kilt fit her and the belt was also the correct length. He'd said he knew she was coming. How could he have known? Had someone been following her? A mystery for another time. She turned and faced Galen. Goosebumps marched across her bare breasts.

"Choose a weapon, then come stand opposite me," Galen said without opening his eyes.

Sophia examined the available weapons. Several staffs and

clubs of various sizes filled the slots. There were only two swords. Prove worthy of his help he'd said. Face the Paladin in mock combat. Would it be mock? Would a quarterstaff or spear grant her an advantage?

She glanced at her sword's hilt where it hung against the wall, the amber stones in the steel wyvern's head stared through her. No, a sword. The Paladin chose a sword. Win or lose, so would she. Sophia's hand lingered near the newer looking of the two. She glanced at Galen, he hadn't moved or opened his eyes. She took the older, more well-used weapon and hefted it. Heavy, but well balanced. She went to stand in front of the Paladin. The smooth floor was cool on the soles of her feet. She blocked the monks from her mind, concentrating on Galen.

"Control your breathing. Focus. Concentrate on the fight. Avoid distraction. If you cannot do this, there is no point in proceeding," Galen said.

"What are the rules?" Sophia said.

Galen's eyes snapped open. "This is combat. This is killing. Rules do not apply. Consider only the three principles."

Sophia stared at his unsmiling, inscrutable face for a moment. She held her breath, then let it leak out slowly. She raised her sword in a two-hand grip. She assumed the high guard position, shifting her feet, left foot forward, right behind. An electric twinge rippled through her injured arm. Galen didn't move. He only closed his eyes.

Two minutes crawled past. Galen rolled his head from side to side, then opened his eyes. "Attack."

Sophia lunged at him, striking first at his right shoulder, then his left. Galen blocked both thrusts and side-stepped from her attack. Sophia rained blows and stabs as quickly as she could, continuing to advance on him. She alternated her blows from his legs to his arms to his head. Galen parried and side-stepped deftly.

Sophia paused, catching her breath.

"You've spent too much energy. Defend." He struck at her head.

Sophia blocked and parried furiously as she retreated from his rapid, powerful attacks. She bumped into the wall, ducked, and slipped past him, striking at his rear as she passed. He blocked the blow, but a smile came to his lips. He resumed the attack. Sophia retreated across the room once more. His attacks grew in strength, and her arms ached.

Galen stopped in the middle of the floor. "Show me the wyvern. Attack."

Sophia wiped sweat from her forehead. She was losing. She needed to win, but she had to keep her patience and remember her lessons. She couldn't overcome his strength, so she had to rely on speed and technique.

She sprang forward. The crackling she'd heard in the mercantile came to her mind in a flood. Her vision narrowed. Galen appeared as a pale tint of green on a darker background. She pressed him. Vigor rushed through her body. Her sword became weightless and her blade crashed against his. Splinters flew. Galen retreated, blocking as he went. Sophia executed her best head fake. Galen went with it. She struck his right arm with a strong stab. She went for the kill.

Galen recovered and blocked her strike, knocking the sword from her hands. It skittered across the floor. Sophia leapt back, her fingers numb. Galen returned to his normal color and her arms felt heavy as she dodged his first return strike, a classic riposte. The crackling faded. Galen lunged again and slapped his blade across her belly below the ribs. Sophia wobbled, then lost her feet. She fell to her knees gasping. Her knuckles bled, her head and arm throbbed. A groan escaped her.

Galen towered over her. He touched her throat with the point of his sword. "You're dead. Pick up your weapon and defend."

Sophia staggered to her feet. Was that uncomfortable

throne worth this? She stumbled to her sword, still gasping. She turned and faced the Paladin. She couldn't call the strange force that had fueled her last attack to return. Her breaths came labored while her arms and thighs trembled. A sob escaped her as she resumed the high guard. "Attack," she whispered.

Galen approached. "Your tears mean nothing to me."

"They mean nothing to me either. Attack."

Galen did. He pounded Sophia from every angle. She sidestepped and retreated, but he disarmed her again.

Sophia clenched her fists before her and growled, "You'll not take me for your pleasure."

Galen paused, allowing his sword point to touch the floor, then he grunted. "You flatter yourself. I don't want you." His eyes flashed bright, then he slammed the flat of his sword against Sophia's cheek. Stars erupted in her vision. They were replaced with a sense of falling and black nothingness.

***

People muttered on the edge of Sophia's consciousness. Pain scalded her cheek and something tugged at the skin on her face while strong fingers held her head motionless. She pried her eyes open as a moan escaped her dry lips. Brother Charles stood smiling at her. He wore his formal vestments and yet looked even younger than he had earlier. An older priest was stitching the wound on her cheek.

"Awake now, are you?" Charles asked.

Sophia jerked her head away and tried to rise. "Get away from me. No man will touch me."

"Be still, your Grace. I'd hoped to finish this before you started moving around. I need to put in one more stitch," the older man said through tight lips.

An older female servant patted Sophia's shoulder. "You're safe, your Grace. Let the priest finish his work."

Sophia lay on a divan in a small but well-appointed apartment. The kilt gone. A yellow robe made of a soft fabric replaced it. A glance showed her feet encased in silk slippers. She smelled of floral soap. She'd been bathed. Had the woman tended to that? "What happened?" She croaked, her throat tight and dry. She lay back against the pillow.

Charles beamed and looked over a shoulder before leaning close to answer. "You hit him. No one has ever hit him. Well, not in the practice hall anyway."

The older man grunted. "Made him angry is what you did. He's never drawn blood from anyone in there before either."

Sophia flinched as the needle penetrated her flesh again. Made him angry? Gods. Now he'd never support her cause. Another disaster. "Where is Darie?"

Charles jerked his head toward a window. "Your ward? She's playing in the garden's fountain. One of the servants fashioned a boat from some twigs and tree bark. She's been playing there for quite some time."

The older priest secured a knot and leaned back. He tossed the spool of gut, and the curved needle onto a side table, then opened a tin of red ointment, which smelled of fish oil and hazel. "There, your Grace, it's done. If you were a prince, I'd have used four stitches. Princes like a neat scar they can brag about, but I put in seven. Perhaps the scar will be less noticeable." He dabbed a bit of the ointment and smeared it along the wound with his thumb. "In five or six days you'll be good as the day you were born."

"Hardly, but you have my thanks." Sophia rose to a sitting position. Vertigo assailed her and she reached out, taking hold of the older priest's arm.

He patted her hand. "Rest. You'll feel better after a good rest."

"I must speak with Galen Goshawk." Sophia lay back and groaned.

"All in good time. He's expecting you to dine with him this

evening. Rest now." He offered her a goblet containing water.

Sophia drank, then settled on the divan and watched the priests gather their healing supplies and leave. The woman went with them.

Sophia gazed out the window. The tops of faraway trees swayed in the wind. Rain was coming. Rain. It seemed it was always raining on her. Raining on her life, her plans, her future. What could she say to the Paladin? Did she need his help? Did she need to get back on Kersey's throne? It was comfortable here. Could she accept being a ward of the temple? A servant to Cassandra?

Whatever numbing agent the priest had used wore off. Her cheek ached, tight and tender to the touch. Sophia rose and took a few unsteady steps to a wall mirror. She gasped. The left side of her face shone a regal shade of purple with the gooey red ointment smeared in the middle. Her eye a mere slit in the bruise's puffy expanse. The cut ran an inch from the corner of her eye onto her normally prominent cheekbone. She opened the robe. A hot red welt decorated her belly. The wounds from the assassin and the slavers' guard hadn't fully healed yet either.

Sophia groaned. She felt like one of those straw men looked; those the soldiers beat on to practice their skills.

She went to the window. Lightning flashed. Many seconds passed before the low rumble of the accompanying thunder reached her. What should she do? What would her friends advise her to do? Josiah would certainly tell her to fight on, as he was doing. And Stewart? What would he say? Run away and live a fairytale life in the forest. Celeste? That cinnamon-haired woman would never give up. What would Serek-jen advise? Sophia shrugged. Who knew how a wyvern thought in the first place? Regardless, none of them stood there to help. She had to find her own way.

Sophia gently touched her face, then spared a glance at her sword in its scabbard. The cold steel wyvern's head seemed to snarl at her. It was an answer in itself. She'd fight on. If she didn't, then her friends' sacrifices would've been for nothing. Father's hopes for her would never be realized. She and her people would never truly be free. If Galen Goshawk refused her, then she would have to find another way. She could raise an army from among the common folk. An army of Crows and she was their queen. The Queen of Crows.

Sophia stood staring at the approaching storm until the day faded to gray. She turned at soft knocking on the door.

CHAPTER TWENTY-FIVE

Sophia waited as the door swung open. An acolyte, framed in the doorway, bowed. "My Lady, his Lordship requests you join him for dinner. I'm to show you the way."

"I haven't seen or spoken to my ward in some time. Do you know where she is?"

The boy nodded. "She has been sent for and will join you at table."

Sophia tried a smile. Half her face responded, while the other tightened and stabbed at her. Could she even eat a meal with that injury? A glance at a well-stocked vanity showed many different powders and other cosmetics. Should she try to hide the bruise? Hide it from whom? No, she'd let those in attendance see the Paladin's work. She opened the wardrobe; a yellow gown hung there. She took it and stepped behind a standing screen. "I'll be a moment."

"Of course, my Lady." The acolyte returned to the hall and closed the door.

Behind the screen Sophia found several undergarments. She picked one that felt soft on her fingers and smiled. She hadn't felt anything so soothing on her skin in weeks. Her apartment in Castle Kersey came to mind. Were her clothes and other things still there? Her head reeled; dizzy, she placed a hand on the wall for a moment. When the spasm passed, she dressed and checked herself in the mirror. She tied her hair back with a ribbon. As good as it was going to get. She stepped into the hall and addressed the acolyte. "What is your name?"

The boy responded. Sophia nodded. "Very well, Walter, you may lead on."

Sophia followed the acolyte to a receiving room decorated with many gilded artifacts representing the gods and their blessings. The room was warm and busy with several bishops, their wives, and some other high-ranking priests. All seeming to speak, within their various cliques, at the same time. Galen Goshawk made eye contact from across the room, then approached her. He presented a goblet of white wine. Sophia accepted it.

"Two hundred pardons, your Grace. It wasn't my intention to injure you. Needless to say, viewing the wyvern brought out my aggression."

His face betrayed genuine concern. Sophia nodded but sipped the wine before answering. Its tart warmth landed hard in her empty belly. She'd need to go easy on that. "It seems we both have a bit of the wyvern to deal with. However, all is well, my Lord. A lesson given that I shall not soon forget."

Galen smiled. "That's kind, but I wasn't trying to give a lesson either. Come, have you been introduced to his Holiness?" He stepped aside and led the way for her with an outstretched arm.

Galen introduced her. The high priest granted a smarmy smile. His hand was sweaty and slick as he squeezed her offered fingers. Sophia's skin crawled and she fought off the urge to recoil. In spite of his appearance, his voice rumbled with a warm resonance. "Your Grace, welcome to the people's temple. I must say it's been long since one so renowned has granted us their company." His black, rodent-like eyes roved over her from head to foot and back.

Sophia curtsied as best she could with her arm in a sling and her head slowly spinning from the bit of wine. "I am in awe of this meeting, your Holiness."

Darie rushed in, dressed in a gown similar to Sophia's, and her face scrubbed to a shine. She threw her arms around Sophia's waist and clung to her. Sophia winced and groaned.

"Sister, there you are. I was alone all day. What happened to your face?"

"It's all right. I've had an accident. I'll be fine."

Darie stepped back and pointed at Galen. "He didn't hurt you like the man at the village, did he?"

Sophia shook her head and forced half a smile. "No. Of course not. It was an accident. Have you met his Holiness?"

Darie gave a clumsy curtsy as Sophia introduced her to the high priest. Darie placed her hands on her hips and said, "What do you do here?"

The high priest pulled his hand back and smiled with a blank look in his eyes. "I guide the faithful, of course. And speak for Achaea." He turned to Sophia. "I'd no idea your ward was so young a child."

Sophia placed a hand on Darie's shoulder. "She's recently rescued from slavers. She's seen much a child shouldn't see. We're still working on her manners, your Holiness."

"I saw a wyvern a few days ago. It burned the men at the pass," Darie said, her eyes alight with excitement.

The high priest clenched and released a fist. "I see. Excuse me." He moved away.

Galen squatted next to Darie. He plucked a strawberry from a servant's tray and offered it. Darie accepted. "Young lady, in temple, we don't speak of the wyvern over dinner. It's considered rude, but tomorrow come to my study and tell me all about this encounter."

Darie bit the treat in half.

Galen glanced at Sophia. "I've found a child will always speak of events without an adult's confusion."

"Why is it rude? It was exciting and scary," Darie said.

Galen returned his attention to the girl. "Because the priests don't believe the gods made the wyverns. They've never had a good answer for their existence."

Darie grinned. "Well, I think they're strange and beautiful. Maybe that's all they're for."

Galen smiled. "Perhaps you're right, but we'll speak of them tomorrow."

"I'll come to your room right after breakfast." Darie looked to Sophia.

"That will be fine," Sophia said.

"It's settled then." Galen rose.

Sophia scrunched her eyebrows in spite of the swelling. Wyverns and great deeds were common dinner conversation in her home. The purpose of their being was never considered. Wyverns were just wyverns. Or were they?

A servant announced they could move into the dining room. Galen caught her eye.

"You and your ward will sit with me. His Holiness will address your request after we've dined."

Sophia glanced into the dining room. The tables were set with finery and heaps of food of all kinds. She turned to Galen, "My Lord, I can't possibly enjoy such a repast not knowing if my men are cared for."

"They are in barracks with my own monks. Their bellies are full and their kit and persons cleaned. Come. Let us eat."

Sophia took Darie's hand and preceded Galen into the dining room. He showed them to their seats, several chairs from the high priest, who sat at the table's head. Little was said as they were served courses of roasted game birds, fishes, and pastries. Sophia concentrated on wrangling Darie's cutlery and showing her the proper manners for eating at a state dinner. Servants cleared away the dishes from dessert, then poured after-dinner wine.

The high priest looked over at Sophia but spoke to the

room at large. "Lady Sophia, what exactly is it you want from the temple?"

Sophia wiped custard from Darie's lips and placed the napkin on the table. "Your Holiness, I've asked for the Paladin and a battalion of his monks to assist me in removing Sir Mallet Pendergast from my throne. I've given a generous offering to the temple and will consider any and all requests regarding future offerings."

"I've been told of your offering, generous indeed. Beside this offering, what does the temple gain for this political stance?"

Sophia glanced at the diners. Most stared back at her with hard eyes. She found Tobias among them and smirked when he looked away. Galen allowed a half-smile but said nothing. She looked at the high priest. He yawned. The crackling tried to encroach on her mind, and she shoved it aside. He was a pig's ass, but she needed to court that ass for the moment. "There has never been a question of my or my father's faith. I'd renew that faith here and allow pilgrims to travel the roads in Kersey without penalty of a tariff."

"A grand gesture indeed. However, King Pendergast has already agreed to do away with such taxes."

"He hasn't told his road agents of that decision. They attempted to extort coin for my passage a few days ago." It would be best she not mention Serek-jen. "An unexpected intervention prevented it and allowed me to arrive here safely."

"I'm sure the king will see to his minions following his instructions."

Sophia frowned. "You refer to him as king. He is a usurper and has no legitimate claim to Kersey's throne while I live."

The high priest shrugged. "Merely a title of convenience, your Grace."

"A title he has no rightful claim to." Sophia spoke louder than she'd intended. She gripped the linen napkin, squeezing it in her good hand.

The high priest smiled a greasy grin. "Even so, the Solstice approaches. Achaea has decreed that he who stands before the people then is the legitimate ruler. I don't know that you or Galen Goshawk can depose Lord Pendergast before that happens."

"The gods will recognize a usurper simply because of where he stands on a given day?"

"In so much as they recognize the accident of any legacy's birth." The high priest smiled.

"Accident?"

The high priest nodded. "But for providence, who's to say the child next to you may have been born in your station and you in hers?"

Wizard-speak, of course. Priests, witches, and wizards, different limbs of the same tree. Sophia looked at Galen. He shared a conspiratorial wink, but otherwise his visage may as well have been cast in iron.

Had Pendergast sent a more generous gift to the temple, making amends? Doubtful, he'd been worried about the temple. Could she frighten the high priest into helping her? He was a toad-faced man. A man toying with her because she was a woman. Doing so because she allowed him to.

She shoved her chair away with the backs of her legs as she rose. The chair fell over. A servant gasped, then stood the chair back up. Sophia held her good hand out toward the high priest. "I'm the Kersen wyvern. You have little idea the patience I've exhausted tonight. If you will not assist me, say so. I have no time for your word games."

The bishops and their wives recoiled as if she'd slapped them all across their faces. The high priest's dark eyes narrowed. Galen smirked.

"Speaking of the wyvern is forbidden, it's sacrilege. You must walk the pillars four times to cleanse your spirit," the high priest said.

"My spirit is clean. I've come to you in good faith, but I see faith has little to do with the reality of this temple. Good evening. I and my company will bother you no longer. We will depart the grounds in the morning." Sophia grabbed Darie's hand and half dragged her from her seat.

"I haven't granted you permission to leave my table."

Sophia glared at him. The room grew green. She fought that off, but still raised her wrist to her chin and wiggled her fingers at the floor. The high priest jerked back in his seat, his frown so deep it may have touched his belt. Sophia made to spit on the floor but stopped herself. A bridge had been burned, no need to make it final. Bridges could be rebuilt. She turned on her heel and pushed Darie ahead of her into the hall.

Sophia led Darie through the maze of hallways until they'd gotten to the apartment she'd been in earlier. They entered and Sophia bolted the door. She turned to Darie, "We'll be leaving soon. Tomorrow we'll trade for supplies and proper traveling clothes."

Darie stared wide-eyed. "You hung the beard. That's very bad."

"I know. I'm sorry you saw that. We will have to get our things and gather our men."

A knock at the door interrupted them. Sophia demanded to know who was there.

"I'd be in your debt if you'd speak with me."

Galen. Had the high priest sent him to punish her for her disrespect? Sophia's eyes lingered on the wardrobe. Her sword was inside. She quietly slipped it from its scabbard then opened the door. "Have you come to kill me? Spare my sister if that's your intent."

Galen chuckled. His massive hand pushed the door fully open. "Kill you? Hardly." He tossed a strawberry to Darie; the girl caught it and beamed. He pointed at her sword. "You won't be needing that tonight, but if I'm going to help you, I need to know some details before you leave the temple tomorrow."

"But I hung the beard. You'd still help me?"

Galen burst into laughter. "Until today, only Meredith had the nerve to do that to him."

"But the high priest denied me any help."

"I'm the Paladin. I decide where and when the temple's monks fight. Granted, I can't give you a battalion, but I can bring a potent force."

"You'd defy his Holiness? Why?"

"Because Mallet Pendergast is a pig's ass and you are the Kersen wyvern. I'd have been entertained had you turned it loose in there. Remind those pompous asses of what real people have to deal with day to day. Regardless, sometimes prophecy needs a push for it to come to pass. And Pendergast? If he should win his war with Tegine, he'll turn his eyes to Fraysse. If successful there, he'll look to the temple. Pendergast's charming words seem to have enthralled the high priest. I am not so easily impressed."

Sophia placed her sword on the divan. She needed assistance. "My Lord, I'll accept any help I can get and yours above all else."

Galen smiled, broad and warm. "So, tell me, how did you find Meredith?"

CHAPTER TWENTY-SIX

The following morning Sophia stopped briefly in the monks' barracks and spoke with Orin, informing him of their situation.

"You are your father's daughter, your Grace."

Sophia smiled, then shrugged. Father had a well-known stubborn streak. "Well, there is that."

Sophia followed Galen's directions to a bladesmith and made arrangement to have her sword modified as Dearing had directed. She spent most of the morning making sure her men would be properly equipped for the campaign to come, as well as buying proper traveling clothes for herself and Darie. With little treasure left she returned to the Paladin's quarters.

When she arrived, Galen bid Sophia to sit. Dealing with logistics had never been her favorite endeavor. Josiah always dealt with supplying the army and Celeste made sure her apartment was properly stocked. Sophia complained to Galen about prices and the time the bladesmith required.

"If you want the end result to be proper, you have to allow a craftsman to do his work," Galen said.

Sophia nodded, rose, and stepped to the window. Servants tended a flower garden crammed with late summer blooms.

Darie dashed across her view before disappearing into some bushes. Sophia grinned. The girl's energy seemed boundless. "Did Darie give you a good account of our meeting Serek-jen?"

"She did. She also told me of the small wyvern. Most would've left it to die. You have a kind heart."

"I've been told it's a girl's heart. Like my mother's."

"Kindness is as important as wisdom and strength. Kindness leads to justice and mercy. It's not an accident the gods have those traits spread among them. A person must emulate them all to be fully whole."

Sophia turned and flopped in one of the large chairs. She drummed her fingers on the tabletop. "Do you think I should try to make amends with the high priest? Get those gods back on my side? Especially Achaea."

Galen chuckled. "Win the coming fight and his holiness will get over it without any effort on your part."

"But what of the gods?"

Galen poured tea from a ceramic pot and handed her a cup. "In my experience, the outcome of battle depends more on leadership, training, and healthy men than it does on the gods. You should look to those things first. The gods will care for themselves."

Sophia squelched a groan. The protector of the faith didn't think the gods influenced battles? "My Lord, I don't see any route to victory which doesn't have Achaea's assistance in the least. Indeed, my company consists of one sword, five spears and a single archer. Add a little girl and one mule, all of which will be adequately equipped at best."

Galen wrinkled his lips into that inscrutable grin. "That's better than nothing." He rose and unrolled a map on the table near Sophia, holding its corners flat with the puzzle and his teacup. She leaned forward as he tapped on the marking for Kersey.

"Pendergast has suffered a major defeat against Tegine's army here. Apparently, the previous war with Fraysse sapped much of the strength and will from Kersey's men." He moved his finger to a spot north of Kersey.

Sophia pointed at the marking for Fraysse. "I've been told Bruce De Leon will assist his lackey with an army and supplies."

"Perhaps, but De Leon has problems of his own further west. Tegine marches on Kersey and Pendergast falls back toward the city." Galen tapped on Kersey again.

Sophia looked at him. "Then I should march on Kersey as well, join Jean De Roederio in the siege."

Galen nodded. "Indeed. You will need to recruit men along the way. Peasants and common folk. I hope to arrive at Kersey with a force of at least a hundred men from the surrounding villages and farms. The fields are nearly ripe, so provisions shouldn't be a major issue."

"Water can be a problem. I'll remedy that once I regain the throne."

"One step at a time, your Grace. First you must finish your preparations here and move out of the temple. My monks will be provisioned so you need only concern yourself with your company. Be wary, Pendergast's agents lurk in the city. Perhaps assassins as well. Take care in your deportment, draw little attention to yourself, and you should be safe enough for a few days. When you are ready, I'll join you."

Sophia rose. "May I keep this map, my Lord? I feel the need to study it in more detail." Galen nodded, rolled, and handed it to her. "Thank you."

"Don't fret over your injuries. I'll have a healer with me, an unfortunate necessity."

***

Sophia and her company spent three days camping in the pilgrims' plaza waiting for her sword to be finished. They spent most of their time protecting their stores from would-be thieves and entertaining Darie. Sophia took note of a few men who lingered, watching. Thinking they were Pendergast's agents she pointed them out to Orin. He didn't say anything, but the next morning those men were gone.

Finally, word came from the bladesmith. Her sword was ready.

Sophia and Orin approached the bladesmith's shop. It stood in a noisy alley. The building front was adorned with a faded anvil carved from wood, and the single window blackened with soot from untold years of forging. A few men loitered several doors down, in front of a pub. She touched Orin's arm and poked her chin at them. His eyes narrowed and he set a grim frown on his face.

Sophia went in as Orin stood guard outside. The proprietor's smoke-darkened face erupted in a smile at her approach.

"Ah, my Lady, your sword is done. And may I say it was a pleasure to work on such a fine piece. The quality struck me. I suspect Darnell Kathan made this sword. Is that so?"

Sophia accepted the weapon from the smith. "His surname is Kathan, but I don't recall his given name. He made the sword for my father. It's now an heirloom and my protector." Sophia turned the blade in her hand, checking that both purple stones were visible on each side near the hilt.

"A tricky bit of work that was. I trust those stones carry some great magic."

Sophia draped the baldric over her shoulder and sheathed the sword. "They are a talisman, installed as an accommodation for a friend. If I recall correctly, the agreed-upon price was six pieces, yes?"

The smith shook his head. "That was the agreement, my Lady, but the work was more difficult and involved than I'd first thought. The black steel is hard to drill. I'll be needing eight pieces."

Sophia frowned. Galen said the man was skilled but

somewhat slippery. Now the cheating begins. "Are you amending the agreement?"

"If my Lady has no argument. I believe eight is a fair price for the work done."

Orin joined them. He shifted his hand down on his spear's shaft. Sophia held a hand up to him and draped her other on the sword's pommel. "I do object, sir. You said six, I've waited three days. Days I couldn't afford to spend. And now you say eight."

The smith wrung his hands on a filthy rag before casting it aside. "My Lady, you'd rob me in the shadow of the temple?"

Sophia dug out six coins and balanced them on the anvil's toe. "You'd try to rob me in the shadow of the temple?"

The smith's eyes shifted from the coins to Sophia. Orin tapped the stump below the anvil with the butt of his spear. "Coin in the hand, man. And it's the agreed-on price," Orin said.

The smith swallowed hard. "I guess there's no reason to call for the magistrate. It was the agreed-on price." He swept the coins from the anvil into his pocket.

Sophia turned to leave, then paused. She fished another coin from her purse and placed it on the anvil. "One more to cover your costs when the money changer cheats you." She spun on her heel and strode from the forge.

On the street Sophia turned to Orin, "I'll not have a man do my negotiating for me. I can and will do it myself."

Orin looked at the ground. "Two hundred pardons, your Grace. I was only trying to help, reminding him he was a thief. I was your father's shield-bearer, now I'm yours. It's proper that I help in any way I can."

"I have no shield, but now you are my right hand. I only demand that you allow me to deal with circumstances in my own way. If I need assistance, I'll request it."

"As you wish, your Grace. And thank you for your confidence."

Sophia regarded him for a moment. "Come, I have another bit of supply to claim from a tailor. We shouldn't have need of threats there."

They retrieved two bundles wrapped in rough cloth from the tailor without incident, then returned to their camp in the plaza. Galen, fifteen monks, and Brother Charles waited there.

Sophia looked Galen's force over and shook her head. "I know you couldn't bring a battalion, my Lord, but you haven't even brought a company."

Galen's smirk seemed more annoyed than amused. "I must still answer to the high priest to some extent. He has allowed you the use of my initiates only. They will prove their value to the temple or perish. That's the way of it."

Sophia glanced at the midmorning sun. Initiates. Trained, but untested. Her own experience exceeded theirs. She returned her gaze to Galen. "Your help is all that matters, my Lord."

Galen nodded. "We shall see, your Grace."

Sophia removed a brilliant white surcoat with a blue wyvern on the chest from one of the tailor's bundles. She draped it over her shoulders before she summoned her men to her. She directed them to stand in a line shoulder to shoulder. She inspected their faces. All but Orin were young, probably no more experienced than the initiates. They were the men she had. They'd have to do.

"My loyal men, I have little to offer you at this time. What I do have to grant is title and expectation. Loyal service will be rewarded with lands and respect. This accolade won't be as ornate as it should, but it is still binding." She opened the other bundle and took a blue surcoat from it. She unrolled it as she stepped to Orin. He bent so she could place the surcoat over his head. A white wyvern on the blue background glared from his breast. He dropped to a knee.

"I declare you Sir Orin Feathers. A knight of my house." Sophia slapped him across the face. "Rise, Sir Orin, and let no man or woman strike you freely ever again."

Orin rose and stood with head bowed. "Thank you, your Grace."

Sophia repeated the ritual with each of her men. At last, she turned to Galen. "Father said knights always fight better. We shall see how these six serve me."

Galen grinned. "He was right. Now, before we march, we must drink from Achaea's barrel. It's one tradition I'm rather fond of." He waved a hand at his initiates and they brought forth a small hogshead. With a spray of foam, it was tapped and beer was handed out among the men. Galen presented Sophia and Darie both with a cup. He raised his. "May the wyvern fly at the Queen of Crows' side."

Sophia sniffed the rare treat. Its foam tickled her nose. Hoppy, but smooth, well crafted. She smiled and drank it down. She handed the cup back to Galen, then winked at Darie.

Darie sniffed as well. "Beer is for special occasions. Is it somebody's birthday?"

Galen laughed. "In a manner of speaking, it is." He turned to his men. "Give what's left to those pilgrims." He pointed, then turned to Sophia. "I've taken the liberty of sending riders into your realm. They are to spread the news that the Kersen Wyvern is marching to her castle. Loyal men will come to her, spies will report her progress to the usurper."

Sophia shook her head but grinned. "With any luck we'll gather a strong force before Sir Mallet can organize resistance."

"Time is short. The festivities for the Solstice will be upon us in twenty days. We must be on our way, your Grace."

CHAPTER TWENTY-SEVEN

They carried no ensigns or banners. Sophia led her company and the Paladin as they strode from Oxted's white gate. They went straight down the road toward the pass, their spirits high. Darie insisted on walking between Galen and Sophia. The six Kersen knights followed close at hand, while Galen's initiates kept a tight rein on their four heavily laden mules. Brother Charles led the initiates.

The recent rains cleansed the air allowing the surrounding fields of heather to impose their sweet aroma on her breathing. Darie skipped and laughed, gleeful in the bright sun. Galen seemed taken with her antics.

Sophia slowed and let them proceed. She renewed her pace alongside Brother Charles. "How is it the high priest has allowed you to accompany my expedition?"

Brother Charles's boyish, chubby face grew grim. "His Lordship overheard my bragging of your success against him in the practice hall. He decreed I would benefit from seeing you in action."

Sophia laughed. "So, it's punishment that brings you along and not a higher calling?"

Charles smiled and shook his head. "Your Grace, I prefer

to call it a new experience."

"Very well then." She placed a hand on his arm. "My face and arm still ache. Do you have something in your kit to alleviate that without robbing me of my senses?"

Charles brightened as he drew his bag up and dug in it. He produced a piece of black root and a small knife. He cut a pea-sized piece of the root, letting it drop into Sophia's palm. "This is Gobi root. It has a strong spicy flavor. Crush it with your teeth and let it rest against your cheek. When the taste fades, spit it out. Don't swallow it."

"A proper lady does not spit."

Charles grinned. "A proper lady doesn't hang the beard at the high priest either. However, do what you must, but don't swallow it. The Gobi root is a strange bit of medicine. Its juice is safe and pain-numbing, but the pulp if ingested is poisonous."

Sophia eyed the tiny bit of root in her palm as she strode along. She barely knew the boy. Should she trust him? The Paladin wouldn't expose her to an assassin, but Charles hadn't chosen to join them.

Charles seemed to sense her thoughts. His face dropped. "I'm with you, your Grace. I'm on your side in this endeavor. I'll not bring any harm to you."

Sophia glanced askance at him. She'd grudgingly come to trust Orin, the others and Galen. A leader, any leader, had to trust at least most of those close to them. She took a deep breath and popped the tiny bit of root into her mouth. A strong, hot-sweet taste flooded her tongue. After sucking in a tight breath, she crammed the morsel against her cheek.

"This tastes horrible."

Charles nodded. "I don't care for it either, but the strength of the taste will fade."

Sophia wiped at a sudden runny nose. "And this?"

Charles grinned. "A side effect. It will pass soon enough."

Sophia thanked him, then trotted ahead to rejoin Darie

and Galen.

Galen glanced at Sophia. "I see you found a bit of trust for Brother Charles."

Sophia didn't answer but gazed down the road. Going forward trust would always be a commodity in short supply. Her attacker's garlic breath and flared nostrils invaded her mind. Would Jacob, the bastard, always be there, lurking in the dark recesses? The rapist bastard, tolerated in his community. Because of his station, perhaps even encouraged? That would change once she was back in power. Bastards like him would be brought to justice, even if she had to tend to it personally. She shuddered and looked back at Galen. "He seems to have a true enough heart."

A concerned light glowed in Galen's eyes for a moment. Did he suspect what had happened to her or did he worry about the wyvern?

"Brother Charles is a true believer. Young and inexperienced outside the temple, but he'll be a steady supporter. He's a skilled healer. You have nothing to fear from him."

Midmorning the third day out from Oxted saw Sophia's company pause for a rest at the top of the pass. Sophia stood alone staring at the golden plain spreading away from the escarpment. The blackness of thick forest bordered it on the west. The road to Kersey, a great serpent, separated the different terrain. She stood on the edge of her realm. A few more yards and she would be on Kersen soil again. She breathed deep and allowed a sigh. Butterflies worried her stomach. Soon she'd be back at Kersey and her forces would have to defeat Pendergast's army. It was absurd, she'd have to lead her men to kill their fellow Kersens. And there would be so much to do after...

"By your leave, your Grace." Charles approached from behind. "I'd like to remove the stitches Brother Aaron used to close your wound. Your face is much closer to its normal color and the swelling is all but gone."

Sophia turned to face him. "Very well. You may proceed."

Charles bid Sophia take a seat on a boulder before he produced tweezers and a knife. It took a couple minutes. He leaned back. "There. Good as new. The scar is small. Brother Aaron is quite good at his craft."

Sophia thanked him and asked for a looking glass. Charles held up a rectangle of thin polished steel. Sophia regarded her reflection in its surface. The thin pink scar looked dainty and almost dignified, considering the thick ugly rope adorning Josiah's face. She returned the mirror.

"How has the arm been? I noticed you've discarded the sling."

Sophia rubbed the injury and looked past Charles. "It's much better. Somewhat stiff, but the strength has returned."

Galen approached. Darie rode on his back. "Your Grace, may we have permission to enter your realm?"

Sophia laughed but told Darie to get down. The little girl obeyed, then ran back toward the knights. Sophia returned her attention to Galen.

"Of course, my Lord."

Galen turned his head and gazed at the plain, his brows nearly touching. "May I suggest we don our armor and proceed armed?"

Sophia looked over the plain. Nothing caught her attention. "What do you see?"

Galen frowned. "Nothing. I feel..." He allowed a meek grin as he looked at her. "I feel danger. Has the wyvern spoken to you?"

She hadn't thought of the wyvern in days. "Serek-jen? No. I haven't seen or heard anything from her since before I arrived at temple."

Galen frowned. "She hasn't spoken to me either."

Sophia's eyes went wide. Serek-jen speaks to the Paladin? Is that how he knew she was coming? "Do you share blood with the wyvern?"

Galen touched the scars on his abdomen. "In a manner of speaking. Regardless, we should be safe for the first few miles. Pendergast's attention is most surely focused on Tegine."

Darie rushed up and stood between them. "Are we going to eat while we're here? I'm hungry."

Sophia patted Darie's shoulder. "No, we'll eat our next meal in Kersen territory." Then she turned to Orin and ordered her men to dress for battle. They complied without comment.

With everything ready, the company proceeded down the road through the pass. The remains of the towers lay in a jumbled heap of blackened logs on either side of the road. The fire's odor still lingered. Here and there lay a charred bit of bone or equipment. Sophia shuddered and increased her pace, putting the scene behind her in short order.

They went no more than two miles. Whoops and war cries reverberated from the surrounding forest.

A score of horsemen rushed at the company from the cover of the trees, several of them archers. Arrows buzzed through the air. One lodged in an initiate's throat. The man fell without a sound. A belated alarm went up. Sophia whipped her sword from its scabbard and pressed Darie close behind her.

Galen bellowed a throaty cry urging his men to stand their ground. Sophia repeated it for her knights. The horsemen swept through Sophia's ragged line, losing only one member of their company. Sophia turned and ushered Darie around behind her again as the enemy flashed by.

Raiders. Of all the times to have them fall upon her. They'd need to dispose of them quickly. "Gather round, semi-circle!" Sophia shouted at her knights. They quickly formed close to her, creating a bristling wall of spear points.

The raiders wheeled their mounts and charged again. Their guttural screams echoed across the road like the wails of demons being driven before their devil masters. Most headed straight for Sophia's small contingent.

"Steady!" Sophia shouted, her mouth dry and her palms sweaty.

"Now!" Galen shouted. The initiates loosed two quick volleys of arrows at the oncoming raiders. A third of their number fell from the saddle or were carried to the ground on stumbling horses. The rest pressed their attack on Sophia's group.

Sophia wished Darie had been near Galen when the attack started. Now she had to keep herself between the raiders and the little girl.

Orin raised his spear above his head. "Defend the queen, advance!"

Her knights moved forward in unison, their shields presenting a barrier, their spear points gleaming their promise of blood.

The horsemen collided with the spearmen. Shouts and threats rang out as the raiders forced their way through the spearmen's defenses. Horses screamed and men cursed. Spears shattered and shields flew into the air. Men were torn from the saddle and horses leapt over the fallen before dashing away from the chaos. A raider landed face down in front of Sophia. There was no time for mercy. She stabbed, pinning him to the ground.

The raider's leader, a large man wearing a spectacle helmet with a horsehair crest, shouted for his men to retreat. The remaining dozen fled going north on the road. A volley of arrows pursued them, felling another raider. The knights and initiates went among the fallen. The moans of several wounded men played on Sophia's ears as she breathed heavily. Her men granted no quarter, quickly dispatching those raiders that hadn't been killed outright.

Galen strode past Sophia with a longbow taller than her. He paused in the middle of the road and drew the bow to full bend with ease. A moment later he loosed a shaft. Sophia watched it streak across the distance. The man with the horse-hair crest fell from his mount and rolled several times in a cloud of dust. His men didn't stop or look back.

Galen walked back past Sophia. He pointed at four horses milling nearby. "Catch those horses." Four initiates moved to obey.

Sophia checked with Darie. The child was unharmed. Then she surveyed the field. Five initiates lay dead. Charles tended to another of Galen's men. Two of her knights, Ruben and Anton, also lay dead.

Galen came to her side. "Odd. It seems they were waiting for us."

Sophia wrinkled her most confounded frown. "So it would seem. Sir Mallet's spies must abound."

Orin stood with one of the initiates. "Your Grace, come look at this."

Sophia and Galen approached. Orin pointed at a marking on a captured horse's shoulder. Sophia sucked in a sudden breath. "That's a horse out of the royal stable at Kersey."

"It is," Orin said.

Galen grunted. "It seems Pendergast has purchased some assistance."

"We've lost nearly a third of our strength. What should we do now?" Sophia looked all around again.

Charles came to them. He groaned and wiped his lips with the back of a bloodied hand. "That man can't walk. Hecuba knows he'll probably die in a week."

They looked back at the wounded man. Galen spoke. "Should we end it then?"

"Gods, no. But he can't walk. We need to make some sort of transport for him."

Galen turned to Sophia. "Do you trust my judgment, your Grace?"

Sophia glanced at her knights. Most were armed with

weapons taken from the raiders, their surcoats stained with freckles of blood. She returned her eyes to the Paladin. "I do."

Galen smiled a genuine smile. "We are sorely short of fighting men." He turned to his men, pointing at two. "Take supplies. Use a horse each. One of you scout to the east, the other west. Rally men to the queen's cause. Offer standard payment. Embellish the temple's commitment to her Grace if payment doesn't move them. Meet us in front of Kersey in ten days."

The two men bowed and went to the mules. They gathered their supplies and departed, leaving trails of dust clinging in the air.

Sophia looked at Orin. "Fashion a sling or litter of some sort for the wounded man. We must move on. Lay our dead in a line off the road. We'll return and tend to them properly later."

"Whoever holds the ground after battle is responsible for tending to the fallen. It's only civilized. Leaving them lowers us to the enemy's level," Galen said.

Sophia faced the Paladin. "We have no time for that now. The Solstice won't wait for my arrival at Kersey. I've said we'll return for them."

Galen crossed his arms on his chest. "Even the wyverns tend to those whose magic has failed."

"What would you have us do? We have no digging tools."

Galen gestured at the nearby trees. "A pyre will suffice. Brother Charles can tend to the spiritual needs."

Sophia glanced at the sky. Would they ever get to Kersey? "Very well, my Lord. We'll tend to them."

Sophia stood silent, pouting at the delay. She held Darie's hand as the men gathered wood for covering the bodies. Two of her knights, Ruben and Anton, were added to the growing list of those fallen for her cause. She didn't know the initiates at all. She had to stop making personal connections with so many. When she was back on the throne, ghosts would certainly walk the halls of Castle Kersey. She'd never want for company.

The fire was lit and Charles intoned prayers and a repetitive chant as he paced around the fire three times. "Hecuba judge our brothers well, Hecuba judge our enemies fairly, Hecuba accept this offering." Charles tossed a coin into the fire at the end of each recitation. Finally, he announced he'd done all he could.

Sophia turned her back on the fire, then stepped to the horse and ran her fingers over the brand on its shoulder. The animal stomped and grumbled at her. She didn't know this horse, but its marking showed beyond doubt that it belonged to her. She patted its neck. A blue jay landed on its rump and squawked at her.

"Ticky?"

The horse swatted at the bird with its tail. The bird hopped onto the cantle, then bobbed up and down.

Sophia stepped closer. "Do you have news?"

"Thomas waits. Thomas waits."

"Where? Where is Thomas?"

"Wheelhouse, Wheelhouse." Ticky launched himself into the air and flew away, going straight down the road. Sophia called after him, but he didn't return.

Sophia turned at Galen's voice.

"A friend, I take it."

Sophia looked past the Paladin. The men were preparing to leave. Charles supervised the loading of the wounded man onto a frame attached to the remaining horse's saddle. She returned her attention to Galen. "He tells me my wizard is waiting at the inn."

"A wizard? If he has the power he may be of help."

"He has the power, but it works in strange ways. When it works." Sophia turned to Orin as he approached.

"All is ready, your Grace. We can proceed at your leisure," Orin said.

Sophia called Darie to her, then placed the child on the horse. "You may lead on, Sir Orin. We make for the Wheelhouse Inn."

CHAPTER TWENTY-EIGHT

At the intersection of the main road and the fork leading to Truro, Sophia's company approached the Wheelhouse Inn. The inn's whitewashed walls and thick thatched roof offered a welcoming air, although an oppressive silence clung to the place. No people milled about and the front door stood closed. One could see the undulating terrain of the great steppe to the east on the far side of a thin belt of trees. To the west the forest grew thick and dark. Wood smoke hung on the still air.

There had been no more visits from Ticky, nor any word from Galen's scouts. Sophia approached the inn's main entrance. She looked for any sign of Thomas or the bird.

There were none.

Doubt crept in. Was it safe? She breathed in deep and glanced at Galen. The Paladin's face was an inscrutable blank. Sophia tried the door handle. It was locked. She yanked once on the bellpull hanging near the door. A faint clank sounded in the recesses of the building.

A full minute crawled past. The door opened a crack, then was flung wide. A rotund woman dressed in blue wool cracked a wide smile before frowning. "So, it's true. The queen is returning."

"Indeed," Sophia said trying to see past the woman.

"You place me in a predicament, your Grace. If you return to power, I'm a loyal subject. If you're defeated, I'm a traitor to the king. If I turn you away now, and you win, I'm a traitor to you. You see my dilemma."

Sophia nodded. "I don't intend to cause you troubles. If you'd announce to Sir Thomas Dearing that we're here, we'll be on our way."

The woman's eyes strayed around the yard as her fingers worried some object in her pocket. "King Pendergast's men were here yesterday. They took the wizard to Kersey."

Sophia glanced at Galen, but he said nothing.

"Was he their prisoner or a willing guest?" Sophia asked.

The woman's eyes went wide. "They beat him, then dragged him behind their horses. It was an awful thing for my small children to see."

Taken? How would Pendergast know he was allied with her and how did they find him? Sophia looked at the woman's hand still worrying some object. "What do you have in your pocket?"

The woman produced a coin and showed it to Sophia. "Payment. I'm to release their pigeon when you arrive. What should I do, your Grace?"

Sophia glanced around the inn's grounds. She pointed to the well inside the low fence. "You will craft a note for Sir Mallet. You will say we forced you to give us water and other comforts. You'll ask for protection in exchange for your loyal service. Attach the note to the pigeon and release it. We will use your well and trouble you no more."

"Thank you, your Grace. There is fodder in the barn and vegetables in the garden. Take what you need. I'll pray for your victory."

"That's kind of you. Where is your man?"

The woman watched as the monks and knights went to the well and watered the animals. She returned her attention to

Sophia. "My husband and oldest son have been pressed into King Pendergast's army. I feared for our safety. Raiders were lurking about. But a knight, Sir Gerard, and some soldiers came and sent most of the raiders packing. Achaea surely sent him."

"Sir Gerard?" Sophia placed her fingers on the back of the woman's hand. "Did he have any prisoners with him? A red-headed woman perhaps?"

The innkeeper shook her head. "No."

Sophia's heart fell. She looked at the ground and sighed. Celeste must have been killed or at best sent to Kersey in chains. "I suppose it was Sir Gerard's men that took Sir Thomas."

The innkeeper shook her head. "No. It was another bunch. Looked more like raiders to my eye, but they claimed to be from the king's court. Lowlife mercenaries if you ask me."

Gods. Raiders working as mercenaries? Thomas would be lucky to survive the trip to Kersey if indeed they were taking him there. Sophia thanked the woman again then joined her men at the well. "I'd hoped to find Sir Thomas here."

The Paladin grinned. "Perhaps a wizard incapable of preventing his capture by some ruffians isn't necessarily a potent ally."

Charles stepped up. "Two hundred pardons, my Lord, our wounded comrade is starting to show some improvement. I'd like to ask the innkeeper to take charge of him. He'll be better off not being dragged along behind us and we'll be able to increase our pace."

Galen nodded. "See to it. Give the innkeeper his horse as payment."

Charles bowed, then went inside the inn.

Sophia glanced at Darie. The girl crawled about on hands and knees, playing a marble game with the innkeeper's two other children. Sophia turned to Galen. "Perhaps you're right. Dear Celeste always said Sir Thomas was nothing more than a carnival performer, but his presence brought me comfort."

Galen accepted a tin ladle of water from one of his monks, then drank. "Comfort does have some value. Do you know this knight, Gerard?"

Sophia took a drink, then nodded. "A new knight in Sir Mallet's court. He allowed me to escape even though he knew who I was. I'd hoped he had Celeste with him, but..."

Galen looked down the road toward Kersey. "If he allowed you to escape, perhaps he will be an ally we can bring to your cause."

"We certainly need the help." Sophia called for Darie to finish her turn, then join them as they resumed the march.

***

Sophia's company marched straight down the tree-lined road. She'd sent Orin ahead on their only remaining horse to scout the path. As she strode along doubts crept into her mind. Should she turn from her goal and seek to rescue Thomas or press on and leave him to his fate? Knowing Josiah and Galen's thoughts, she should press on. Regain the throne, then do what she could for those supporters who'd survived. That thought granted little comfort as she rummaged through the memory of those who'd already fallen. Would those ghosts linger in the halls at Castle Kersey, haunting her forever?

Orin returned at a run. Sophia escaped her thoughts. He reined in beside her and leapt down before bowing slightly. "Your Grace, there is a small camp about five miles ahead. They are Pendergast's men, perhaps a dozen, no more. They didn't see me. A knight's banner flies near one of the tents."

Sophia gazed down the road. "Did you recognize the knight's heraldry?"

Orin shook his head, then took a drink from his canteen.

Galen poked his chin at the path ahead of them. "Gerard?"

Sophia stepped forward, hands on hips. "Perhaps. We'll

cover the five miles in about two hours." She turned to Orin. "I know the danger you'll be in, but I wish you to ride ahead and make contact with these men. Find out who they are and whose side they're on. Return with an answer. If you don't return...that will be answer enough."

Orin bowed. "Of course, your Grace. If need be, I'll stay alive long enough for you to rescue me." He sprang back into the saddle and galloped back the way he'd come.

Sophia signaled for her company to move on. She glanced at Galen. "I hate sending good men to their doom."

Galen set his lips tight. "A sad necessity. Sometimes the greater good is so served."

Sophia looked askance at him. "One of my knights is fond of the 'greater good' argument."

Galen laughed. "I'd wager that's Tarkenton."

Sophia allowed a broad smile as she nodded. "Do you know him?"

Galen shrugged. "By reputation. I understand he's a good man."

"He is, although I sometimes fear he'd sacrifice every fighting man in the realm to keep me on the throne. Thus, leaving me no realm to lead."

Galen glanced at her as he kicked a stone from the path. "Prophecy states that real power and prosperity lie in the hands of women. That's why the wyverns and their activities are linked to women. Men are expendable."

"I don't think that's a prophecy taught in the temple."

Galen smiled. "Of course not. The temple exists to glorify the deeds of the gods, Achaea in particular, but a man or woman should educate themselves beyond the teachings of the temple or the realm."

Sophia regarded Galen through narrow eyes. "Are you not the protector of the faith?"

"I am. That responsibility doesn't preclude my being educated. Indeed, it requires a more rounded knowledge of things and events beyond the temple walls. The same as your Grace requires knowledge outside her realm's borders. Remember, most of the commoners believe wholeheartedly. The nobility rarely believes, unless they need to gain some political advantage over a rival. Then of course, the gods are on their side."

Sophia looked down the road. It was true enough. She'd rarely gone to the sanctuary unless Father commanded it. Did she know enough about events and other things to rule effectively? Josiah as well as Thomas had tried to show her the way. She would have to heed their advice more closely in the future. "So, tell me, my Lord, how did you know of my coming to ask for your help? You mentioned a reliable source, which would that be?"

"Does it matter?" Galen turned without breaking stride. He signaled to an initiate to dash ahead and relieve the man scouting before them.

"A curiosity. Humor me."

Galen glanced at her, then chuckled deep in his chest. "Serek-jen occasionally visits me."

Sophia released Darie's hand and stopped in the middle of the road facing Galen. "Serek-jen? Truly?"

Darie hopped up and down. "You've talked to the big wyvern?"

Galen waved a hand in the direction they'd been traveling, urging them to continue. "Yes. You don't think you're the only one with a relationship with the wyvern, do you?"

Galen speaks with the wyvern? Wyvern blood must be more common than she thought. Perhaps that's why he agreed to help her. Another cousin, so to speak? "Yes, actually. I did think that was the case. What sort of relationship do you have with Serek-jen?"

Galen rubbed his chest absently and his eyes faded into a memory. He shook his head. "It's one of mutual respect."

They marched on in silence for a hundred yards halting

when three riders approached. Sophia eyed them. Orin and Gerard, but the third wore a closed helm and sported heraldry she didn't recognize. The riders reined in. Orin and Gerard dismounted and approached. The last remained seated watching from behind his helmet's camail.

Gerard dropped to a knee and lowered his eyes. "Your Grace, I've prayed against all hope you would find your way to safety and return to us unharmed. Let me now pledge my and my men's loyalty to you."

Sophia looked to the other rider. He hadn't moved. She returned her gaze to Gerard. "When last we spoke you said Sir Mallet was your sovereign. Now you would support me?"

Gerard looked up. Muted anger flashed in his eyes. "The so-called king has abandoned all decency. He's hired raiders as mercenaries. Hecuba's privy, criminals. He has imprisoned the family members of my men to ensure our loyalty. He has executed my father as an example. Half my men wanted to return to Kersey to display their loyalty to the king. Seeking his favor, they tried to take us as a prize. Those loyal to you and decency won that fight. Now we will fight for you, if your Grace will have us."

Sophia glanced at Galen. Although his eyes gleamed, he only nodded. She looked back at Gerard. "Rise, Sir Gerard, know I take you and your men into my house."

Gerard stood and thanked her. He gestured at the last rider. "Do you have a question for her Grace?"

The rider removed the helmet. The breeze tousled a wildfire of red hair that escaped. Celeste flashed a deep frown. "My Queen, who in Cassandra's name has been caring for your hair?"

CHAPTER TWENTY-NINE

Sophia stared at Celeste with her jaw slack. Foolish grins occupied the faces of her men. Sophia shook her surprise aside and rushed to Celeste's side as Celeste stepped down from her horse. "By the gods, I'd thought you'd been murdered or worse."

Celeste laughed as Sophia embraced her. "I'm not so easy to kill."

"By all the gods I'd thought you gone forever. I couldn't find a way to forgive myself for leaving you. You can't imagine how happy I am, finding you alive and well. It's akin to being brought back from Hecuba's tower. Can you forgive me?" Sophia buried her face in the redhead's hair.

"My mother said you'd have to leave me at some point, remember?"

Sophia clung to Celeste tighter, nodding.

"I've worried about you too. I know well the trouble you can get into without me to watch over you," Celeste whispered.

"I've been through a lot. Not all of it good."

Celeste leaned back. "Well, you're here with me again safe and sound. It's worked out for the best, I think."

"We'll see. How did you escape the slavers' fate?"

"Sir Gerard protected me. He's rather a handsome man, don't you think?"

Sophia hugged Celeste again, then turned to Gerard. "Thank you for sparing my friend a horrible fate, Sir Knight."

Gerard's face reddened. "You're welcome, your Grace. But I must admit to having selfish reasons for doing so." He looked at Celeste. She and Gerard stared at each other, seeming not to notice the others gathered around them.

Sophia looked back and forth between Celeste and Gerard, then shook her head before grabbing and hugging Celeste again. "I see we have to talk, but not now."

Galen stepped close. "Well spoken, your Grace. We should move on. I suggest we spend the night at Sir Gerard's camp, then continue the march to Kersey in the morning."

As evening fell the company arrived at Gerard's camp. Sophia called her first war council around the fire. Celeste withdrew with Darie leaving Sophia with Galen, Gerard, Charles, and her knights.

Sophia looked around the group pausing to examine each face. They were unwashed and grim. "Where do we stand?"

Galen pulled at his mustache. "I have seven monks here with two more away gathering commoners. Brother Charles?"

The priest shrugged. "The gods are quiet. I believe Achaea waits for a sign of devotion before committing to either side."

Sophia gestured at Gerard, who cleared his throat and pushed a stick into the fire with his boot's toe. "I have fourteen men-at-arms. I can vouch for most of them. Each man has a horse, but we have no remounts. We are well-supplied at present. I also have a few camp followers, perhaps ten women and children."

"I have Sir Orin and three others." Sophia gestured at them standing on the firelight's edge. "Do we know how large Tegine's force is?"

Gerard shook his head. "Rumors only. Pendergast has

withdrawn to a point near the city. We believe he is fortifying a position on Fish Hook Ridge. He has pressed men from the commoners living near the city. His raiders have abducted a few men from the countryside. It seems he will try to force an action east of the city proper."

Orin squared his shoulders. "With a few more men we could get between Pendergast and the city. We'd be the anvil for Tegine's hammer."

Galen nodded. "It could be a good plan. Assuming we can get on good ground in time."

Sophia rose. She paced near the edge of the light. The men watched her with grim expressions. "Uncertainties in this plan abound. As much as we know of the enemy's maneuvers, it's prudent to expect him to know of us and that we threaten his rear. He will leave a force to block our approach. He'd have to. As a friend once told me, Sir Mallet is an ass, but not a stupid ass. What of Fraysse? Have they come to Sir Mallet's aid?"

Gerard glanced around the circle. "Nothing is known yet. It's not the proper season, but a rumor says a wyvern has set upon Fraysse in the far west. Pendergast is hard-pressed without Fraysse's help."

Sophia faced her men. If Josiah were there, she'd have a better feeling of what to do. "What can we do if we assume our current force is all we'll have when we get to Kersey? How can we best harm the enemy?"

"We can prey upon his supply lines and attack isolated outposts. Distract his attention and perhaps pull men from his main force," Galen said. The other men grunted their agreement.

Sophia bit her lower lip. Not an ideal plan. If carried out, it would leave Tegine and Jean De Roederio to put her back on the throne, if indeed that were his plan. Still, it would be something and her small force was certainly limited in the scope of its actions. "It's decided then. Let's get some sleep and move toward Kersey tomorrow. If we gather more men, we can modify our course as necessary."

The meeting broke up with the men going to their blankets. Sophia paused at the entrance to the small tent Celeste told her would be her sleeping place. Galen stood nearby. His smile barely discernible in the dark. "You've made a good decision, your Grace."

"The near future will judge, my Lord. If I could replace Sir Mallet without a single drop of blood spent, I'd do so in an instant."

Galen nodded. "I understand. It's good you understand that it's not possible in any other way."

Meredith told her all things were possible. Perhaps Sophia could depose the usurper without bloodshed. She'd have to consider how exactly it could be done. For now, she had only the sword. She allowed a grim smile. "Goodnight, my Lord." She ducked and entered the dimly lit tent.

Darie and Celeste looked up from their dinner. Celeste held out a tin plate containing a hunk of aromatic cheese and several slices of a hard sausage. "Eat this, my Queen. You look like you've lost too much weight in my absence."

Sophia accepted the plate and thanked Celeste as she sat next to Darie. The girl grinned and spoke around some morsel she was chewing. "I love cheese."

Sophia squeezed Darie's lips with two fingers. "A proper lady doesn't speak with food in her mouth."

Celeste burst into laughter and pointed at Darie. "I told you so."

Darie shrugged and swallowed. "I still love cheese. Do we have more?"

Celeste shook her head as Sophia broke hers in half and placed a piece on Darie's plate. The girl took a big bite of it.

"That's all I could steal from the supply master. Funny how he always watches me but never sees what I'm doing," Celeste said as she poured wine from a clay amphora into earthenware cups.

Sophia laughed. "He sees, but he doesn't say anything. Trying to curry your favor."

Celeste giggled as she handed the cups to the others. "I know, but my story is better than what's actually going on."

Sophia sipped her wine. Not from Burkett, but still good. "What is going on here? I mean between you and Sir Gerard?"

Celeste blushed in the sputtering candlelight. She fussed with the wick, avoiding Sophia's inspection. "He is a good man. He rescued Jenna as well. She's with the camp followers working as a cook."

"That was gallant of him. I must see her tomorrow and ask how she is."

Celeste avoided looking directly at Sophia. "I pray Sir Gerard will not be harmed helping you."

Sophia gestured with her cup as Celeste sat back. "Please, do go on."

Celeste looked askance at Darie, then back at Sophia. "I've lain with him. His child may be with me."

"Carrying his child? How could that happen?" Sophia wrinkled her brow.

Celeste set her lips in a thin line and cocked her head to one side. "You're asking that?"

Sophia glanced at Darie. The girl rolled her eyes. "Men and women sleep in the same blankets, then Cassandra gives them babies. Everyone knows that."

Sophia turned back to Celeste. "Are you sure?"

Celeste beamed. "It's early, but my moon phase has passed with no cramps or bleeding. So..."

Sophia studied her friend's face. Would her court be plagued with scandal from the start? Herself nearly raped; the perpetrator a commoner. Her lady-in-waiting pregnant while unwed. She shook her head. No. Things would change. Society would change once she returned to the throne. Galen said women were the future. So they'd be in her realm. She embraced Celeste. "You must love this man. It sounds as if you gave yourself willingly. Does he return your affection?"

"I do and he is a wonderful partner. I've been happy the past few weeks. The only thing that would've made me happier would've been knowing you were safe."

"And what of Sir Stewart? It's possible he lives. Sir Josiah does."

"We don't know what has become of Sir Stewart. Besides, he was always in love with you. Sir Gerard is the man I want."

Sophia smiled at Celeste. "Your face tells the tale." She turned to Darie. "Sister, run out and fetch Sir Gerard to us."

The girl tossed the last of the cheese into her mouth, then rushed from the tent. Sophia watched her go and then turned to Celeste, but lowered her eyes, staring at the trampled earth near the blanket she sat on. Celeste had found love while she'd found pain and injustice. Did the gods require such irony? Should she interfere in her friend's happiness just to cause her pain? No. The gods had cast Celeste's lot. It wasn't her place to cause harm. She was the queen. She was supposed to make people's lives better. Sophia sighed and glanced at the tent's doorway.

"A commoner attempted to rape me the day after I left you. I think it was Cassandra's punishment for my cowardice." She looked at Celeste. "She has rewarded your courage with a loving man and a child. I think that is as it should be."

Celeste stared. Her lips parted. Her pink tongue flicked across her lips, then she jumped forward and embraced Sophia. "By the gods, raped? Are you all right?"

Sophia returned the hug. "Yes, I'm fine. He didn't complete the task. I killed him in the act. I've had good luck since. Finding you well has surpassed all of that."

"Tell me all of it."

Sophia recalled all that had passed since leaving Celeste. When the tale was finished, Celeste sat back, her chest heaving. She traced her fingers along the scar on Sophia's face. "What a pig's ass I've been. Falling in love and enjoying myself while you've struggled so."

"Other than doubting I'll ever fully trust a man again, I've made it through no worse for the experience. Besides, you can't imagine the majesty and wonder of speaking to a wyvern. It was so surprising and amazing. Akin to discovering a stranger has left you a most desired gift. Of course, it was more than a little frightening as well."

"By the gods, my Queen, you know the prophecy. Is it about to come true?"

"I don't know. If a wyvern truly worries Fraysse, then perhaps."

Gerard and Darie came into the tent. Gerard wore an undershirt and was barefoot, but held his sword. "What do you need, your Grace?" he asked, yawning.

Darie hopped on her knees across her pallet and kicked her sandals into the air. Sophia batted a sandal aside and glared at Darie. "Sir Gerard." She gestured at Celeste. "This woman is my lady-in-waiting. If you have objection to taking her as your wife, I'd hear it now."

Gerard cleared his throat, then again. He glanced at Celeste who looked away. "Your Grace, I have no objection. Indeed, I've prayed to Cassandra asking for guidance about the proper time to approach you with such a request. We're at war. I'd thought to wait for a resolution before asking you."

"If one waits for the end of war, one will wait until the wyverns are tamed. We must do what we must while the opportunity is present."

Gerard smiled at Celeste, she looked away again, blushing. "So be it, your Grace. I'd ask now, then."

Sophia laughed. "Poorly spoken Sir Gerard, but I'll let that pass. It's done. You are betrothed to Celeste Tucker, my lady-in-waiting."

Gerard bowed, then smiled. "Is there anything else, your Grace?"

Sophia shook her head. "No. You may return to your rest."

Gerard withdrew. Darie hopped about, then stopped in front of Sophia. "Will there be a wedding? I love weddings."

***

The following morning camp was struck and the march resumed. Gerard insisted Sophia ride his horse. After some fuss, she acquiesced and mounted the massive charger. Darie rode behind her. They held an easy pace, allowing the infantry to keep up.

They paused at midday. One of Galen's scouts returned, bringing about forty commoners into the fold. Farmers, woodsmen, and miners. Mostly boys from the look of them, few if any older than herself. Already dirty and dust-covered from their trek to join her and armed with an array of old bronze-headed spears and farm implements, their faces were eager for adventure. Here and there an old mail coat draped over a threadbare gambeson or a rusty steel helmet, worn with pride.

Sophia welcomed them and bid them fall in line, adding to her company. She faced the front and led toward Kersey. How many would perish in the next few days? Did any of them realize what lay ahead? Boys, excited, dreaming of great deeds. Hoping their deeds would be worthy of songs. Forgetting that most of the rhymes spoke of dead heroes, swept away in torrents of violence.

They marched on for two days. Galen's other scout rejoined them, bringing a similar collection of men to her cause. Sophia's army camped for the night knowing Kersey lay only a few miles ahead. Scouts were sent out to look for Pendergast's defenses and agents. An eerie quiet settled over the camp. Sophia sat with Celeste and Darie at a small fire.

Ticky joined them, landing first on Darie's head, then hopping to her arm. The girl twittered with joy at the meeting. The bird's feathers were ruffled and its top knot shorter than

Sophia remembered. "Do you have news, Sir Ticky?"

The bird hopped about fluttering its wings before settling on Darie's shoulder. Ticky bobbed a few times. "Soldiers, soldiers."

"Soldiers? Where? Are they Sir Mallet's men?"

"Soldiers, soldiers. Five miles. On the hill. Waiting, waiting."

Sophia turned to Celeste. "Go fetch his Lordship and the knights. They must hear about this."

Celeste rose and sped into the darkness. Sophia turned back to Ticky. "What of Thomas? Where is Sir Thomas?"

Ticky fluffed his neck and combed a wing with his beak. His obsidian eye blinked once. "Dungeon, dungeon."

Darie beamed. "A magical bird. I've never seen such a thing." She rubbed Ticky's chest with a finger. He allowed it. He even closed his eyes as if savoring the experience.

Sophia looked up at the stars. Thomas in the dungeon. What an awful place it was. Even when Father was alive it smelled of putrid clothing, rotten food, and offal. She shuddered. What could she do to get him out of there? Her knights and the Paladin would say, "win the coming battle." Perhaps they were right.

The approach of her men brought Sophia back to the present. She briefed them on what Ticky had reported.

"Did the bird say how many men and where exactly they are?" Galen asked.

Sophia shook her head. "He is a bird. He gives a good accounting of distance, but otherwise..." She looked over at Orin. "What hill lies five miles from us now? Do you know it?"

Orin nodded. "Pelican Hill. Steep on this side, gentle on the other. A good place to block the road to Kersey. Good, but not impregnable."

"It seems the field is set and battle is at hand," Galen said. "With luck our scouts will return with more detailed information."

Orin picked up a stick and drew on the ground as two men lifted brands to light his drawing. "This is what the lay of the land at Pelican Hill is like."

CHAPTER THIRTY

The following morning Darie and Celeste assisted Sophia as she dressed for battle. When ready, they went to meet the knights and Galen. After a quick briefing on what the scouts had reported, she used Orin's drawing from the previous night to explain her plan.

"Pelican Hill sits east of the road with the steep slope facing west. We'll attack in the late afternoon so the sun will be at our backs." Sophia tapped on the hill's marking with a thin stick. "Sir Orin, we have what, around eighty armed commoners?"

Orin nodded. "That's correct."

"They are inexperienced and may not understand the plan. When battle is joined, they may find they don't have the stomach for it. Pick two who are swift of foot to serve me as messengers, then split the others into four equal groups. One of our knights will lead each group."

"It's necessary a guard for your person be formed, your Grace. I'd volunteer my men for that honor," Gerard said.

Sophia shook her head, her lips tight. "Thank you, Sir Gerard, but no. You and your men will ride, unseen, around behind the hill. There the slope is gentle enough for horses to climb. We will fix the enemy with our frontal attack. At the sound of battle, you will strike from their rear. It will be over before they know what is happening."

Gerard smiled. "Very good, your Grace, but what about your guard?"

"This is but a skirmish. I'll not need a guard. The two messengers will suffice. I'll be at the middle of our line. The men will be able to see me. Hopefully they'll be inspired."

"And what will you have me do for you, your Grace?" Galen asked.

Sophia looked at the Paladin. "My Lord, you may position yourself and your men where you think they will do the most good. It's no secret, this is my first battle plan. I'll trust you to fill the gaps in it."

"Our scouts have reported the enemy is nearly equal in strength. Even so, it's a good plan. I'll take position on the far left of your line and assault the steepest portion of the hill."

Sophia raised a hand to Charles. "Brother Charles, have the gods spoken to you?"

Charles wrung his hands, he glanced at Galen, then back to Sophia. "Achaea and Hecuba watch. Cassandra weeps. They know the outcome, but have not shared it."

Priests and their version of wizard-speak. Whatever the battle's outcome, he'd claim having foreseen it. At least Charles was a good healer, making himself of some use. "So be it."

Sophia nodded. Achaea and Hecuba, the warrior and the reaper. Cassandra, the mother. Had she thought this through? A million things could go wrong. The enemy could move away or be greater in number than expected. It was too late now, she was committed. She raised a finger. "One more thing, gentlemen, Kersens wishing to surrender will be granted quarter. There will be no slaughter of the innocent or unarmed. Raiders, on the other hand.... If possible, I want Sir Mallet's knights taken alive. Questions?"

Darie patted Sophia's arm. "What do you want me to do, Sister?"

Sophia looked at the girl, her pleading eyes so big, dark, and intelligent. A precious child who, if allowed, would grow to be a beautiful woman. "You and Ticky will stay in the camp with Jenna. You will help her and Brother Charles with preparing bandages and caring for those who are hurt. It's an important task."

"But I want to be a warrior. When you left me alone in the forest, you said I took the warrior test."

Sophia knelt and hugged the girl. Darie resisted, but couldn't pull away from Sophia's tight grip. "A warrior has to pass many tests. Sometimes restraint is more crucial than action. This is one of those times."

"But everyone else is going to be in the battle."

Sophia glanced around. The men all stood with faces of stone. Celeste bit her lip. Ticky flapped his wings as he perched, riding up and down on a flimsy branch nearby. "You must stay with Jenna and Ticky. Remember, Ticky has lost his friend Sir Thomas but has found a new one in you. He couldn't bear it if something happened to you and neither could I."

Sophia leaned back but maintained a loose grip on Darie's shoulders. Ticky landed on the girl's head and chattered excitedly before hopping to her outstretched arm. "Stay, Stay."

Sophia flashed a broad smile. "You see? Ticky needs you to be safe."

Darie looked back and forth between Sophia and the bird. "I guess I can stay. I think if Ticky and Jenna need me I can miss the battle."

Sophia rose and rubbed the girl's head. "Unfortunately, there will be other battles, Sister."

***

The sun rode low in the west. Sophia's army closed on Pelican Hill. The enemy stood silent in close ordered ranks near the hill's crest. Apparently, they'd been warned of Sophia's approach. She raised her arms and the men spread out to either side. The enemy offered no sign that they would come down from the hill. Sophia's men would have to go up and meet them.

What could she do to stop this? Sophia looked down the lines of her men. Many mumbled prayers or stared at the ground, no doubt hoping the enemy would be gone when they looked up. Sophia stared at the ground for a few seconds as well. She raised her eyes. The enemy was still there. She was committed to the fight. Gerard would be in position waiting for the sound of battle. There was nothing left to be done.

Celeste, clad in armor, with her helmet and spear, approached.

"What do you think you're doing?" Sophia asked.

"I'm your personal guard."

"No, you're my lady-in-waiting. Does Sir Gerard know you're here?"

Celeste shook her head. "He has allowed me to fight at his side. He'll be pleased I'm fighting at your side today."

"Have you told him you're carrying his child?"

Celeste shook her head. "I'm waiting for the right time to tell him."

"I can't let you take this risk. Return to the rear and assist Brother Charles."

Celeste wrinkled her lips. Sophia cut off her coming argument. "I'll not discuss this now. I'm certain if your betrothed knew of the child, he'd object in the strongest terms. Go now. You know you have my love, but I have enough to worry me today. I don't need you adding to it."

Celeste lowered her chin. After a moment she looked Sophia in the eye. Her lips parted for a second, but she clamped them closed and turned away. Sophia watched her go for a minute, then turned to the enemy's line. Several banners fluttered in the breeze. They showed her more than one knight opposed her. She sighed and motioned to her messengers. "Do you believe Hecuba will reward you in the afterlife?"

Both men nodded.

Sophia closed her eyes and propped her chin on her chest. Of course, the gods remain silent. They're always silent. Thank you, Hecuba, for not making this an easy choice. She opened her eyes. She may be sending one of these men to his death. She had no choice, she had to trust the gods and the men. She gestured at the man on her right. "What is your name?"

The man answered. Sophia regarded his smooth face, his beard merely blond fuzz. "Very well, Donald, I wish you to go to the enemy's line and deliver this message: Any knight who chooses to stand with me will be granted clemency along with his men-at-arms. There is no other option."

Donald bowed, then ran ahead. Pausing near the enemy's position. His voice could be heard, although Sophia couldn't make out his exact words. A knight she didn't know strode from the enemy's line and stabbed Donald in the throat, Sophia shuddered. The messenger fell aside and the knight held his bloodied sword up in defiance, then hung the beard at her army.

Sophia gritted her teeth. So that's how it was going to go. She drew her sword and waved it above her head. "Advance!"

Sophia's men lurched into motion. She strode forward, her white surcoat emblazoned with the blue wyvern, stark against the golden, late-summer grass. Sophia's men closed with the enemy. Both armies paused and shouted taunts and jeers. They were afraid, bolstering their nerve with bravado. Sophia's mouth grew dry and her belly tightened, but she had to press on. Her throne and the end of this brutality lay beyond the hill's crest. The enemy hurled a blinding fusillade of stones. Her line faltered. A stone struck Sophia on the shoulder, painful, but harmless.

Sophia shouted encouragement and advanced with her sword held high. Her line went with her. The armies met with the roar of two hundred voices. The knights assaulted their counterparts while the commoners attacked the commoners in the enemy's ranks. The two forces soon intermingled, making identifying friend from foe difficult.

Sophia lunged at the nearest enemy knight, the one who had killed Donald. The knight's face was hidden behind steel, but he wore Pendergast's light blue surcoat with the stag's head. He met her attack assuming a high guard. He blocked her first thrusts, then repelled her with brute strength. All around the clamor of fighting drowned out all but the closest voices. The knight facing her abandoned his men, pressing Sophia back down the slope. She gave ground avoiding his blows. She had to stop his advance before her men noticed her retreating. It might lead to a rout. Josiah had told her most of the killing took place during the rout. She ducked under a swift swing, then commanded the wyvern to come to her.

The crackling in her mind rose to a deafening crescendo in an instant. The background of her field of vision changed to the green she'd become accustomed to, her opponent a lighter shade. Sophia blocked a thrust, issued a strong riposte, and advanced, forcing her opponent back up the hill. The knight gave ground, blocking her strikes frantically. The battle grew silent. The thumping of her adversary's heart rang loud in her head, her chest, even her limbs vibrated with his life's urgency. The acrid bile of his sudden fear flooded her tongue. Sophia savored its taste and pressed in on him. He backed away, then tripped on a body. Sophia slammed the sword from his hand, then ran him through. His pain flashed through her, then disappeared. Her heart grew light, her throat drank his life's essence as it melted away. She ripped her sword from his body and thirsted for another victim.

A group of commoners threw away their weapons and turned, fleeing from her. Sophia waded among them, cutting down any in reach. She feasted on their fear and pain. The taste of it drove her forward, seeking more to slay. She cursed their cowardice, daring them to return. A strong hand landed on her shoulder spinning her around.

Sophia drew her sword back to strike. Galen stood before her. His armor and surcoat speckled with blood. "Control, your Grace. You must regain control of yourself."

Sophia struck at him. Galen blocked her blow and instantly flicked his weapon against hers, sending hers flying away. Sophia lunged at him with her fists clenched. He held her at bay with an outstretched arm. She clawed at his mail-covered bicep.

"Control, your Grace. Order the wyvern to stand down."

Recognition clicked in her mind. Sophia clung to Galen's arm and commanded the wyvern to recede. The anger, power, and violent lust drained from her. Fatigue crushed her shoulders even as nausea welled in her core. The wyvern lingered on the edge of her mind, seething. It breathed fire against her will. Galen reached to hold her up, but Sophia dropped to a knee.

She clenched her eyes shut, driving the wyvern away. Commanding it back into the dark recesses of her mind. It resisted, insisting she release it. Sophia vomited, then again commanded it to recede. It obeyed at last.

What had she done? What had she become? She'd attacked an ally. Could she control the wyvern? Her breaths came in loud rasping pants. A man approached, his boots crunching the dry grass.

"The field is ours, your Grace. You've won a great victory. What should we do with the prisoners?" Orin asked, nearly breathless.

Sophia opened her eyes. The toes of Galen's boots were their normal color. She breathed deep and raised her head. The groans of the wounded came from all around as she grasped Galen's forearm and pulled herself up. She expanded her chest as far as possible, then turned a full circle and wiped her mouth, the taste of fear now bitter and disgusting. The dirty faces of her troops beamed with the courage and confidence victory granted. A cheer went up. Sophia raised her hands, calling for their attention.

"Bring up our baggage train and the healer. Tend to the wounded, my brave, loyal men. Honor the fallen as we should." Sophia shouted. The wyvern prodded her, clawing at her willpower, burning the base of her skull. She had to ignore it. She spit in the grass. The affairs of state required her attention. She turned to Orin. "How many have been taken alive?"

"Half of them, your Grace. About forty commoners and three knights, including their captain. A few were allowed to escape to carry the news of the defeat to Pendergast." Orin smirked, then grew serious. "Will you make an example of the enemy's knights?"

Galen removed his helmet. Sophia avoided his eyes.

"I trust I did not harm you, my Lord. You have my apology. It will not happen again."

"You must tread a fine line. It's all about the will and the need." He returned her sword. Sophia took it and wiped the blade on the bottom of her surcoat before returning it to its scabbard. She glanced at the blood-speckled mail covering her arms and shoulders. She failed to suppress a shudder.

She turned to Orin again. "Take me to them."

Orin led while Sophia followed on unsteady knees. She clamped her hands together, stopping the trembling assaulting her fingers. Why did she feel so drained and weak?

Near the hill's crest Gerard met them. He inclined his head. "Your Grace, congratulations on a decisive victory. I've taken the liberty of sending a scout to meet with Tegine's army and share the news as well as gain insight for what they are planning."

"Very good, Sir Gerard." She motioned for Orin to

continue.

Pendergast's three knights ringed a small fire. Sophia strode past them. They rose and bowed their heads. She granted them a nod, then stood before the commoners. The commoners sat on the ground together in three roughly straight lines. Many wore the red wool trousers the lumbermen of Kersey prided themselves in. Several were wounded, the rest dirty and panting, with dull, blank eyes. Sophia made eye contact with many of them, then took a deep breath.

"I am Lady Sophia Pendergast, the Kersen Wyvern. I am the rightful ruler of Kersey. Some call me the Queen of Crows. You have taken up arms against me. Perhaps some by choice, perhaps others not. Regardless, you will be fed and your wounds tended. If you choose to join me your weapons will be returned and nothing more will be said of this day. If you cannot join me, you may go to your homes on the condition you never take up arms against me again. I grant you ten minutes to decide." Sophia turned away from the commoners and addressed Orin, "We've captured their baggage train and supplies?"

Orin nodded.

"See they are fed, have water, and Brother Charles tends to those in need."

"As you wish, your Grace." Orin stepped away.

Sophia went to the knights. Galen joined her but said nothing. The setting sun cast long shadows on the ground and the failing light brought an eerie hush to the battlefield. The muted groans of the seriously wounded seemed far away, not actually on the same field. Perhaps they were the moans of those already ghosts, choosing to remain in this haunt.

She looked the knights over, recognizing the heraldry of two, if not their faces. Minor nobles, rarely at the castle except for formal affairs. "You have chosen poorly, gentlemen."

They lowered their heads but didn't speak. Sophia crossed

her arms on her chest. "My father's punishment for such an offense would be to strip you of land and title. To exile you and your families to one of those barbaric southern kingdoms. Kingdoms where men without title are bought and sold as slaves. Kingdoms that worship false gods and carry out horrific sacrifices. If a knight were to beg for mercy, he would be granted a swift and honorable execution."

The enemy's captain raised his head. His face was set in resigned sorrow. "Does your Grace desire such begging?"

Sophia glanced at Galen, again he offered nothing beyond a stern, tight-lipped glare. Orin and her knights gathered nearby. She turned back to Pendergast's knights. "I am not my father. I will allow you to retain half your lands if you swear allegiance to my house and join me in the coming fight."

"Your Grace, you cannot trust these men. They have no honor. Leave them to me and the knights. They will trouble you no more," Orin said from behind her.

Sophia held up a hand. "This is one of those times I do not require assistance, Sir Orin."

"Two hundred pardons, your Grace."

The captain glanced at his men, then back to Sophia. "And the option if we choose otherwise?"

"In all the enlightened realms treason is punished severely. It can be no other way. Should you remain traitors to me, you will be executed and all of your lands seized for my loyal knights. Your families will be spared but exiled to Tegine or Fraysse, whichever will have them. You have the same ten minutes I granted the Crows." Sophia turned and strode down the hill.

CHAPTER THIRTY-ONE

Sophia's army, including all three of Pendergast's knights and most of his commoners, camped in sight of Kersey. Pendergast's remaining troops occupied the fish hook-shaped ridge between Sophia's army and the city. Tegine's army stood camped on Sophia's right, aligned against the shank of the hook.

Sophia paced outside her flimsy tent. A delegation from Tegine was expected. Would Josiah be with them and what would she tell him? Should she reopen the negotiation about a possible marriage to cement the alliance? What would Jean demand in compensation for his assistance?

Sophia's single trumpeter had claimed a dented horn from the battlefield. He now played a poor fanfare with it. Several riders approached. Galen, Charles, and Orin joined her. Celeste and Darie arrived a moment later.

The riders, all clad in armor with white surcoats displaying Tegine's scarlet eagle, dismounted. Three strode toward Sophia. She swallowed hard, clamping her trembling fingers into fists. Flanking Josiah were Stewart and the young squire. Will shared a broad smile. Josiah stopped at three paces and dropped to a knee. The others trailed behind.

"My Queen, I am pleased to find you well and in command of such a fine force. The presence of his Lordship, the Paladin, indicates Achaea has surely smiled upon you. Victory is at hand," Josiah said.

Sophia gazed at Stewart's handsome face. He had more lines than she remembered. Certainly, war and the troubles she'd survived had changed her in his eyes too, although his still sparkled with the same light she'd been so fond of. She returned her attention to Josiah and bid him rise before gesturing at a few hastily arranged camp chairs and logs placed around a fire. They all took seats.

Sophia smiled at Stewart while she commanded the butterflies in her stomach to cease their flight. They ignored her. Stewart returned her smile and engaged her eyes. Josiah cleared his throat. Sophia turned to him. "So, tell me, Sir Josiah, what is our situation?"

"Didn't Dearing deliver our message? Where is he anyway?" Josiah stretched his neck, looking around. "I led a raid to his cottage, assuming you'd be there. When we found you weren't there, he was compelled to join us."

"His familiar is here." Sophia indicated Ticky, perched on Darie's shoulder. "Sir Mallet's men captured Sir Thomas and took him to Kersey. I fear for his condition."

Josiah growled. "Taken? Dearing has knowledge of our plans and deportment. That's a wicked blow indeed. It's my fault, I should've sent men-at-arms with him."

"Nothing can be done about it now. With luck we'll rescue him before it's too late."

Josiah leaned forward. His eyes narrow. "So be it. Well, my Queen, providence has worked in its way. Jean De Roederio fell in battle two days past. His sister, Phoebe, in spite of some court in-fighting, has assumed the throne. Prophecy is at hand. We will defeat Pendergast quickly. With the Paladin's assistance we cannot lose."

Jean De Roederio dead? His sister on the throne. The tide

was turning, but Pendergast still had allies. "What of Fraysse?"

Josiah grinned an evil smirk. "It's prophecy at work, two battalions set upon at the river. Burned to cinders. It's rumored Bruce De Leon is among the slain. The wyverns have risen. It would seem they have chosen sides. The side of prophecy and your reign. This rumor has quelled dissent in Queen Phoebe's camp. Even the most ardent supporters of Achaea realize prophecy is coming to pass."

Sophia smiled, a closed-lip affair. "If we defeat the army poised against us, then Sir Mallet will have no choice but to surrender. Most of those on the ridge opposing us are commoners from Kersey, yes?"

"So it would seem."

"I would address them under rules of parlay."

The scar on Josiah's face seemed to glow, framing his grim expression. "That is highly dangerous. You would be exposed to enemy archers. And those archers aren't rabble, they're soldiers. Soldiers we must assume are loyal to Pendergast. What do you hope to accomplish taking such a risk?"

"I want to end this affair with no more Kersen blood being shed. Indeed, far too much has been spent already."

"I must oppose this course." Josiah gestured for support from Galen. "My Lord, you know well, Pendergast won't honor any parlay. He'll use our exposure to attack and try to end this through treachery."

Galen nodded. "It may be an unnecessary risk, your Grace."

"The risk isn't any greater than I'm asking the men to take if we should join in battle." Sophia rose and crossed her arms as she spoke.

"Granted, but if you are lost so is the throne and the prophecy. You have no heir." Josiah punctuated his words with a clenched fist.

Sophia placed her hands on her hips, then looked each of

her advisers in the eye. Meredith said Darie had a destiny, would it be this? She sucked in a deep breath. "Prophecy will take care of itself. My heir sits at my side. I believe her to be prophecy's chosen child." Sophia gestured at Darie.

The men voiced their alarm all at once, angry grumbling circled the fire. Celeste stared wide-eyed but said nothing. Josiah called for quiet. The arguing stumbled to an expectant silence.

"My Queen, this child is too young to sit the throne. Not to mention she is a commoner and we know nothing of her nature. It's customary to choose a blood relative or some noble close to the throne. A trusted person," Josiah said.

"If Bruce De Leon is indeed dead, I have no blood relation other than Sir Mallet. Darie and I are orphans, one doesn't get any closer than that. Her nature is as noble as any other. She has a talent for language, communication, and divination. Valuable skills in a ruler. I've been told providence placed me on the throne and it could as easily have placed Darie there. Regardless, if I fall, she will have all of you to guide her into adulthood. Her council of regents will be you, Sir Josiah, as well as Sir Orin, Lady Celeste, and if he still lives, Sir Thomas. I can think of nothing more promising for the future of our people."

"Naming an heir is your right. Achaea knows it's your responsibility. But because you've named an heir doesn't mean you're free to risk your life on a fool's errand," Josiah said.

"I don't perceive trying to save lives among my subjects to be foolish."

Josiah clamped his lips in a vice-like frown. The fire's flickering flames reflected in his eyes. Galen leaned back, a bemused smirk on his face. Josiah sputtered for a moment then asked, "What will you say to them?"

"I will say the same to them as I said at Pelican Hill. Fully a third of this army opposed me there. Perhaps they will join us or at least lay down their arms."

"Can I not sway you from this course, my Queen?"

"You cannot."

Josiah gave a curt nod, his frown carved in stone. "You are your father's daughter. Tomorrow at dawn?"

Sophia smiled, then patted Josiah's shoulder. "Midmorning. Arrange the army for battle so all may see our resolve. Then I will address them. Return to Queen Phoebe and carry my condolences for the loss of Lord Jean. Tell the queen I will grant her the same lands I offered when proposing to her brother. I will also entertain any other demands she may have once this business is concluded."

"So be it." Josiah rose.

The men, some grumbling to each other, wandered away into the evening. Galen lingered near the three women. "Your Grace, a bit of advice for tomorrow?"

Sophia nodded. "Of course, my Lord."

"Close your mail tight at the throat." Galen grinned. "And carry a shield." He turned and walked into the darkness.

***

Stewart's voice sounded outside Sophia's tent. She looked up from washing her legs. Celeste hopped to the tent's opening and stuck her head through the flap. "Her Grace is indisposed, Sir Knight. She can't accept visitors."

"I won't take much of her time, but I must speak to her," Stewart said.

"The queen is bathing. Come back in the morning," Celeste whispered.

"Lady Celeste, please—"

"It's all right, Celeste. Give me a moment, then let him come." Sophia glanced around the candlelit tent, then kicked her undergarment out of sight, beneath her cot. She stood and wrapped herself in a blanket. "I'm ready."

Celeste stepped aside. Stewart ducked through the doorway turning his broad shoulders sideways. Sophia clutched her blanket tight. His smile warmed her insides, and she fought off a barrage of trembling. Her chest tightened, her breathing rapid and shallow. His approach heightened her tremors, which snaked along a knife's edge between giddy joy and paralyzing fear.

Stewart dropped to a knee before her, his eyes engaging hers. "My Queen, I didn't get a chance to tell you personally how grateful I am to Cassandra that you've come back to us safely. All these weeks I've been fighting, fueled by the hope I'd serve you again."

"My heart is filled with joy at seeing you well and saddened to hear of Sir Richard falling at the bridge."

Stewart rose and hung his head for a moment. "He was a gallant supporter of your house. And he has been sorely missed."

Sophia studied his square chin, thin mustache and dangling black ringlets. He was more handsome now than she remembered. With Jean De Roederio among the fallen, she was free to choose another for her consort. Did she need a consort? Meredith said she needed a man or she would fail in her destiny. She needed a loving man. Was Stewart that man?

"I've revoked your betrothal to Lady Celeste and promised her to Sir Gerard." Sophia covered her lips with her fingers. Why had she blurted that? He might think she was throwing herself at him. Was she throwing herself at him? Cassandra knew that wasn't the case. Didn't she?

"Indeed? Shall I seek out Kathan and demand satisfaction?" A playful smile brightened his face.

Sophia looked past Stewart's shoulder. Celeste stood near the entrance with a hand over her mouth, but her eyes were laughing. "Please leave us. I'd like a few minutes privacy."

Celeste winked. "I'll find Darie and we'll spend the night in Sir Gerard's tent."

"That's not necessary—"

Celeste slipped away.

"Nothing has changed since we spoke on the banks of the Rolling River, my Queen."

Sophia returned her eyes to his. "That's not true, Sir Knight. Many things have changed. I have changed."

"Have you lost your love for me?"

Sophia tore her eyes away and stared at the ground. Heat grew in her belly and spread to her limbs. "I...I don't know. Things have happened. I want to love you, dear Stewart, but I'm not sure. I'm not sure I can love any man. Not in a way he would want." She risked a peek at him from beneath her brow.

Stewart took a step closer. The warmth of his smile radiated into the air itself. "I don't understand."

Sophia's knees trembled again. She turned her back to him. Could she make him understand? She couldn't lie to him, but would the truth change his feelings? An hour ago she'd had purpose, focus, her throne in sight. Now...could her responsibility to the people be tempered with a bit of happiness? Meredith, Josiah, even Serek-jen spoke of love, her house, and legacy. Stewart claimed to still love her, the truth would be a powerful test. She lowered her head, took an unsteady breath and whispered, "I carry a wyvern inside. It sometimes controls my emotions."

His silence crushed upon her. People spoke outside near the fires, but their words were indistinct murmurs. The candle sputtered. Now what should she say? A full minute crept by. He hadn't moved or spoken.

"Has this wyvern chosen another?" He whispered.

Sophia shook her head. "Of course not. But it saved me from being raped by a commoner. I now have difficulty trusting men."

"Two hundred pardons, my Queen. I spoke poorly. I'm truly humbled that you'd share something so...intimate." He took a shuffling step forward. So close his chest's heat penetrated his hauberk and her blanket. "I would never harm you. What must I do to prove my love and gain your trust?"

The smoldering embers of her attraction hadn't faded. Sophia sniffed. She refused to cry, not here, not now. Could she lay with a man after all that had happened? If only Cassandra would give her a sign.

That awful knife's edge shone bright in her mind. Could she embrace Stewart and know joy and love or would the rapist bastard rise within her mind to paralyze her with fear and doubt? Would his memory destroy her chance at this little bit of happiness? Would the wyvern rise and cause her to harm Stewart?

Tears came despite her command that they not. Healing her wounds, inside and out, was her task, but Meredith said she could seek help from a trusted man. Trust, she had to trust someone. She had to trust Stewart. She had to trust the wyvern to subdue the bastard. She would put her fate in love's hands.

Sophia faced Stewart. The tips of her ears burned. She savored his scent: fresh sweat, oiled mail, and aged leather. She bathed in the comfort of his accepting gaze. What would Cassandra have her do? Stewart was a fierce warrior, but he'd always been gentle, kind, and even playful when alone with her. Sophia accepted the wyvern's direct approach and rolled her shoulders, letting the blanket fall away.

Stewart's gaze roved over her, returning to her face. He allowed a meek smile, then wiped a tear from her cheek with his thumb, letting his thumb linger on the delicate scar near her eye. "You aren't worried about scandal?"

"Are you worried I may set you afire?"

Stewart shook his head.

Sophia wrapped her arms around his neck. "Then you are my Prince Consort. The people would expect nothing less."

Stewart covered her hands with his, granting a gentle squeeze. He pressed his soft lips to hers.

Sophia lost herself in the sweet taste of his mouth and the feel of his broad chest against her. The wyvern stirred and her belly quaked. She leaned away. "I'm frightened."

Stewart smiled and embraced her, pulling her close. "As am I. Perhaps we should proceed together."

CHAPTER THIRTY-TWO

Sophia was dressing. Celeste came into the tent sporting a conspiratorial grin. "I just passed a certain knight displaying a lively spring in his step. I doubt his breakfast provided that."

Sophia paused with her arm half in a sleeve. "You are so crude."

They giggled together. "You must tell me all about it. Was it wonderful?"

Sophia rolled her eyes. "How was your evening? And where is Darie?" She finished buttoning her shirt.

"She's coming. The Paladin was showing her how to solve that dumb puzzle thing he's been fooling with." Celeste placed a hand on Sophia's arm. "Now tell me, are you well?"

Sophia shrugged. "The rapist will always be with me, but I feel...safer, stronger, in control now."

Celeste hugged her. "I'm so happy for you. After all that's happened, you deserve a bit of joy. And Sir Stewart is quite the catch. Your children are going to be beautiful."

"Well, there's still a civil war to be won."

"Will we have a double wedding?"

"Lady Celeste, the war."

Darie rushed in. "Sister, Sister, look what his Lordship

showed me." She held two intricately intertwined pieces of stiff wire that seemed to form an inseparable chain. Her tiny tongue covered her upper lip as she twisted the wires on themselves. A few moments later she beamed, holding a single piece in each hand. "It's a trick, you see. Once you know the secret it's easy."

"That's clever of you. Come we need to dress for the battle. Now that you're my heir you must be properly attired and stay in a safe place," Sophia said.

"You're going to make me miss the battle again aren't you?" Darie poked her lips out and stared into Sophia's eyes. Sophia knelt and flashed a smile.

"Yes. We can't have both of us taking risks. What would happen to the people if we both fell? There would be no one to lead them."

"Why can't the people lead themselves?"

Sophia glanced at Celeste who cocked her head to one side. Sophia returned her gaze to Darie. "Perhaps one day they will. Maybe it's your destiny to teach them, but for now they need their queen to protect them from the wyverns. You and Celeste will stay with Jenna and the rest. Men will be charged with protecting you and the others."

"I'll never get to be in a battle."

"I hope that's true. If we have some luck, today there won't be a battle. But I doubt it will come to pass. There will always be men who think they should lead. That they know better. That Achaea knows better than Cassandra. Men who seek adventure and glory. Now, help me with my armor, then we'll see to some breakfast."

***

With breakfast and Darie's complaining finished, Sophia stood among her gathered knights. Josiah and Stewart wore their tattered old blue surcoats bearing the white lion.

"My Queen, Queen Phoebe has released us from her service so we return to yours. Our heraldry will be updated when time permits," Josiah said.

Sophia let her eyes linger on the boy, Will. She glanced at Stewart. "Young William is now your squire?"

"Yes, my Queen," Stewart said.

"Has he tasted battle and is he competent with blade and spear?"

"He is."

Will pumped out his chest and smiled.

Sophia scanned the skies. Thin clouds strolled high above them like gigantic dandelion seeds, the pale blue belying the heat to come once the day wore on. The future of her kingdom lay with those children, those the war had blown about like so many seeds on the wind. She returned her attention to Stewart. "Young William will join those guarding my heir. The Princess Darie's safety is his personal responsibility."

"As you wish, my Queen," Stewart said.

Will's eyes scanned the gathered hard faces, then landed on Sophia's. He bowed his head. "It's an honor to serve, your Grace."

"Very well, off with you then."

Will bowed and left them.

Josiah watched him go before turning to Sophia. "Well played, my Queen. I've grown rather fond of that boy."

Sophia smiled. "Probably unnecessary, if the parlay goes as I hope."

Josiah frowned. "Pendergast has refused the parlay. His response was...somewhat vulgar."

Sophia looked to the enemy's line. They stood in neat, well-ordered ranks, waiting. Their light blue banners hung limp on the still air. "I'll go forward to speak with them anyway."

The gathered knights all grumbled their dissent as one. Josiah called for silence. "My Queen, we can't allow you to do that. Pendergast will not honor any such parlay. He will certainly attack you."

"Is this the point where you bring up the 'greater good' argument, Sir Josiah?"

Josiah nodded. "Word is already spreading through the army and the realm that you've chosen an heir as well as your prince consort. The people are expecting your victory. Hope is rekindled. If you proceed with your plan, we'll be holding a state funeral before that pig faces the gallows."

"If there's a chance to spare Kersen lives and indeed those from Tegine, then I must at least try."

Galen cleared his throat, all eyes turned to him. "If your Grace is intent on this course, I'll accompany you. Any attack on us will be seen as an attack on the temple. The risk of a blasphemy charge can be a powerful motivator. Especially among the commoners."

"Thank you, my Lord, but I believe the temple would frown on you taking such a risk."

"You've fought, suffered, and struggled to ask for my help. This is the point where my assistance will weigh the most. If you choose to continue, I must go with you," Galen said.

Sophia took in their faces again. Grim, hard eyes, and tight lips all. She lingered on Stewart's face. Worry clouded his brow. A vision of his touch, his weight, and the tangled linens they'd shared overnight flashed in her mind's eye. "Very well, my Lord. Sir Josiah, a small honor guard that doesn't include Sir Stewart."

Stewart stepped toward her, opening his mouth, but Sophia stopped him with a hand. He clamped his lips shut. Sophia softened her war face. "No, my love. There will be other times for you to accompany me. In our absence you will command the army. If we are attacked, I expect you to come to our rescue. Regardless of what happens during the parlay, when the sun goes down, we will own that ridge."

Stewart clenched his jaw tight and stepped back.

Josiah thrust a spectacle helmet with camail at her. "At least agree to protect yourself."

Sophia smiled. "I doubt that will fit."

He grinned at her. "It's not your father's coronet. The armorer has adjusted the band and suspension. It should fit you well."

Sophia accepted the helmet and tucked it under her arm. "I will carry it, but the men must see that it's indeed me. They must know the words come from my own mouth. Let us proceed before the day wanes and we lose the chance to avoid a battle."

Sophia rode toward the ridge. Her toes gripped the soles of her boots tighter the closer they got. Galen rode on her left and Josiah on his. Gerard and Orin followed close behind with half a dozen men-at-arms. Shouts went up along the enemy line. Sophia and her riders stopped outside easy bow range. Sophia raised her empty hand and shouted, "Parlay with Sir Mallet Pendergast."

"Come closer, we'll grant you parlay." The voice was not Pendergast's.

Galen rose in his stirrups, his yellow surcoat garish among the blue of Sophia's men. "I am Galen Goshawk, Paladin and Protector of the faith, out of the temple at Oxted, and friend of Queen Sophia of Kersey. Achaea smiles on me. You will parlay in good faith or suffer the consequence."

The voice shouted again, "What consequence would that be?"

"Hecuba waits with open arms. She's marked those she has condemned. I'm her instrument," Galen shouted in return.

A long minute crawled past. Horns sounded in the enemy's line. Pendergast's voice cut across the still air, "I'll parlay with the Paladin, but not with that woman. She has no standing here."

Galen dropped into his saddle. He leaned toward Sophia. "He may think he'll talk to me, but I have nothing to say to that pig's pizzle. You'll have to carry the conversation, your Grace."

Sophia smirked. "Very well, my Lord. Thank you."

Another minute and riders came from the enemy's line. A force of equal size to Sophia's. The last rider dragged a burden, perhaps a man, behind his mount. They halted thirty yards away. The bundle being towed was indeed a man, wrapped in a battered cow hide. His bare feet protruded from the wrapping.

Pendergast, his face hidden beneath the camail, reined his mount hard to one side. He pointed at Sophia, "That woman has no place here. Send her away and we'll talk."

Josiah grunted, "You have no place in any of the enlightened realms yet here you are."

Sophia held a hand up to Josiah. "Sir Josiah, I'll speak to the usurper." She turned her eyes to Pendergast.

Pendergast erupted in a rich laugh. "Yes Tarkenton, take your orders from a woman. Tell me, does she share her bed in exchange for your obedience? I forget myself. You don't fancy women. Has she given you a new boy? Cavale's squire, perhaps?"

Josiah growled deep in his throat as he gripped the hilt of his sword. Sophia motioned for him to stand down, then she bumped her horse's flanks and advanced several yards. "Sir Mallet, in spite of your coarse insults I'll grant you this offer. If you surrender now, sparing the men of Kersey the price of battle, I'll allow you to escape in exile to one of the southern kingdoms. If you refuse you will suffer a traitor's fate."

Pendergast sat silent, toying with his horse's rein. Sophia rose in her stirrups, then shouted. "Clemency will be granted to all commoners that quit the field now." A buzz of voices rushed through Pendergast's line.

Pendergast's eyes couldn't be seen, but they burned Sophia's cheeks. "Achaea has said women do not make demands of kings in the enlightened realms, nor offer terms to his army. I'll humor your offer with this counteroffer." He raised an arm. Two men dismounted and wrestled the prisoner out of the cow hide, then dragged him to Pendergast's side. They yanked him to his feet and held him up. The naked man bled from many minor wounds and abrasions. He was Thomas Dearing.

"Your army will quit this field and you will surrender to me," Pendergast said. "Or I will execute your so-called wizard where he stands. Then I will crush this army of yours. You have one minute to decide."

Sophia glanced at Galen and Josiah. Their faces were set in grim frowns. She looked at Dearing. He forced a weak smile but breathed heavily.

"You bathe your reign in honor, Cousin. You've murdered many a good man and yet you cannot bring Achaea to share your cause. Why haven't you called for mountain ogres to be your allies? Surely they carry more honor than this rabble you've assembled."

Pendergast gestured at his men. They pushed Dearing to his knees. One of the guards drew his dagger and looked to his lord. Pendergast held up a hand. "You have thirty seconds."

Sophia raised her eyes to the sky. A passing raven's obsidian wing glinted in the sun. A raven, a noble crow, here to escort the lost to Hecuba's tower. She returned her eyes to Pendergast. Would Cassandra grant her mercy when Hecuba finally called for her? "Sir Thomas's blood will serve the greater good. Your army watches and their nerve wavers. They know this is extortion, not parlay."

Pendergast dropped his hand. The guard drew his arm back to strike. A mass of black wings following a streak of blue flashed past Sophia, surrounding the would-be executioner in a cacophony of screams and squawking. He struck wildly at the birds as they dove and darted among the men. Horses reared and bellowed. Ticky landed on Sophia's rein.

"Thomas, Thomas, save him," the bird squawked.

Pendergast yanked out his sword and shouted, "Treachery and sorcery! Kill them all!" He turned his horse and fled toward his line. Most of his men followed.

Galen's horse leapt forward. The Paladin cut down the executioner as he tried to remount. His blood splattered across his saddle before he fell away. His horse reared, then bolted. The birds scattered, calling back and forth. The rising shouts of men ahead and behind muted the bird's shrill voices.

Josiah pursued Pendergast, his sword held high. Arrows rained around Sophia's party. The horses screamed and men shouted. Gerard dashed toward Sophia, extending his shield. The enemy's shafts slammed into the ground looking like new crops springing from the earth.

Among the falling arrows, Josiah gave up his chase and returned. A demonic roar rolled up the ridge. Sophia looked back at her army. Stewart and her infantry charged forward. A glance to the left revealed Tegine's white- and scarlet-clad soldiers charging as well.

Sophia drew her sword and waved it above her head. The battle was joined. Her hopes for saving lives dashed. She had tried Cassandra's way, now it would be Achaea's. She set her face in a grim frown. There was terrible work to be done.

Dearing fell face-first onto the ground. An arrow protruded from his rump. Sophia pushed forward, placing her horse between the archers and Dearing. Orin came with her. Sophia sheathed her sword, then donned her helmet behind the protection of Galen and Orin's shields. She buckled the chin strap and shifted the camail onto her shoulders. "See that this man is carried to Brother Charles as soon as possible."

Another barrage of arrows greeted her infantry as they swarmed around her. Many fell, screaming, grasping at the long shafts. Of those hit, most writhed on the ground, but others lay completely still. Sophia waved her sword and spurred her horse toward the enemy. The sooner they closed the distance the sooner the archers' effectiveness would be reduced. "Follow me to the top!" she shouted.

The helmet interfered with Sophia's vision. She had to turn her head to see anything to either side. Looking to the right, Tegine's troops unleashed a fusillade of archery before contacting the enemy line. She searched in vain for Pendergast's banner as her own troops crashed into the enemy.

Orin protected her left side. The wyvern rushed to the forefront of her mind. She wouldn't grant it control again. She couldn't, not this time. If she expected to lead her people, she had to remain in command of herself. The crackling deafened her, drowning out the battle sounds. Sophia pushed back at it, refusing to allow it free. The wyvern seethed, insisting, breathing fire on her willpower. She commanded it back into the recesses. It lingered, burning her skull near the base, but at last it obeyed.

Sophia panted in the wake of her inner victory. She sucked in a deep breath and shouted encouragement to her men. She struck at a man near her then paused and surveyed the field. Tegine had overwhelmed the line in front of them. Her own troops pushed the enemy back. Beyond the confused lines, she caught a glimpse of Pendergast and many of his knights fleeing the field, going straight toward Castle Kersey.

"Sir Mallet is fleeing, Pendergast has fled," Sophia shouted. The cry spread along the line. The commoners arrayed against her broke and ran from their attackers. The rout had begun. Sophia shouted for her men to grant quarter and take prisoners. The gleeful cheers of victory drowned her out.

Arrows and stones buzzed in all directions. The men closest to her grappled with each other. Sophia looked beyond the carnage surrounding her. The last of Pendergast's entourage thundered across the ancient planks into the castle. The drawbridge slowly retracted until fully seated against the outer wall.

Something heavy slammed into her helmet. Sophia shook her head. Dazed, her sword slipped from her fingers and she swooned. Her horse reared, uncontrolled. She fell from the saddle.

CHAPTER THIRTY-THREE

Sophia was dragged to her feet. She held Orin's arm and shook her head. Her helmet had turned and she couldn't see out of one of the eye slits. Josiah and Stewart voiced concerns, but their questions held no meaning. Her shoulder ached and the cobwebs in her mind refused to recede. She shook her head again. Someone crammed her sword back into its scabbard.

"Take the queen to the healer. We'll see to finishing this business," Josiah shouted, sounding far away.

Many hands took hold of Sophia's arms and she was whisked away from the noise of battle and led, stumbling, down the ridge. She resisted, coming to a stop. She unbuckled the helmet and removed it. Other than Orin, Sophia didn't know the men surrounding her. Young faces, all showing concern.

"Wait, I must return to the fight." Sophia stood among a cluster of wounded. She dropped her helmet. It rolled up against one of the dead. The casualties were the enemy's as well as her own. There was no difference in their groans, both being pitiful and urgent.

"Your Grace, we've been tasked with taking you back. You

must let the healer tend to you," one of the men said.

"It's a minor wound. I'm all right."

Orin shook his head and indicated a stump close at hand. "Sit, your Grace. We'll bring the healer to you. If not for your helmet you'd be dead. Come, sit down. The knights are winning the fight for you."

Sophia glanced at the helmet. It sported a fist-sized dent. She touched her forehead. Her fingers dampened with blood. Orin stood next to her and gestured at the stump again. She nodded. "Very well, but I'll not be removed from this field until the battle is decided and these men have been tended."

Her men guided her to the stump and assisted her in sitting on it. The thunder of battle carried beyond the ridge. Black smoke rose in several places on the far side. Black smoke was always bad.

"Of course, your Grace. The healer is coming." An unfamiliar voice.

Sophia studied the man as he looked downslope. A commoner, solidly built. Good-looking, but plain. A man, like so many others. Still, he looked familiar. A rope surrounding his waist held up his red wool trousers. A woodsman's hatchet was tucked into the rope.

"You stood against me at Pelican Hill a few days ago." Sophia grasped her sword's hilt.

The man lowered his eyes. "I did, your Grace. The king threatened many of our families. Choices aren't always as tasteful as one would like."

Sophia released her grip on the sword. More of Pendergast's threats and objectionable conduct. Perhaps, as Meredith suggested, the commoners got on with their lives and didn't care much about who sat the throne. "I'm grateful you're with me now. What is your name?"

The man answered, then stood aside. Charles, Celeste, Darie, and their guards rushed up. Charles dropped to a knee and examined Sophia's scalp. Darie clung to Sophia's arm while Celeste stood with hands on her hips. Charles grunted, then stared into each of Sophia's eyes one at a time, pulling down on her lower lid with a thumb.

"My head has cleared, Brother Charles. I think it's a minor thing."

Charles grunted again, then rummaged in his bag. He blotted at her hairline with a clean bit of cloth. "I agree, your Grace, it looks much worse than it is. Thank Achaea you were wearing a helmet."

"Another scar. I'll be known as the Queen of Scars." Sophia grimaced. A subdued chuckle raced among the gathered common soldiers.

"Princes love scars," Celeste said, grinning.

"I now have those aplenty."

"Are you injured anywhere else?" Charles asked.

Sophia shook her head and immediately regretted it. Her head seemed to continue moving even after she'd stopped it. She groaned as she lifted a hand toward her helmet, and asked for its return. She accepted the helmet from a soldier, then turned to Charles.

He pointed at her shoulder. "Did you land on that arm?"

"I'm not sure what happened."

Charles examined her shoulder and arm as best he could through her hauberk and the thick padding under it. Sophia grunted. Shocks zinged from her fingers to her neck. At last Charles sat back on his heels.

"Nothing broken, and the shoulder isn't dislocated. Most likely bruised. If you give it a few days rest it'll be fine."

Resting wasn't an option. She needed to change the subject before another argument about her safety came up. "How fares Sir Thomas?"

"He is alive, your Grace. He's a tougher old bird than he appears. Regardless, the king's hospitality was hard on him."

Sophia nodded. "And the arrow?"

"A needle-bodkin. The wound is minor, all things

considered. However, your Grace, you must rest. We can take you to him. He has inquired about you. Strange though, he keeps calling you 'Delicious.'"

Sophia smiled, then used Charles's shoulder as a crutch and propelled herself to her feet. She gripped his shoulder tight until a mild dizziness passed. "We don't have time for rest right now. We have a battle to win." She gingerly put on the helmet. Her shoulder objected but she worked through it. "All able-bodied men come with me. We must add our weight to the fight."

"You're in no condition to fight," Celeste said. "I'd object to your attending a formal ball in this shape, much less a battle. Let the men finish it for you."

Sophia glanced around her attending soldiers and friends. "I'll not allow any man or woman to risk their person while I keep mine safe. It's my throne, I'll fight for it."

Celeste crossed her arms on her chest. "The battle is all but won anyway. You must protect yourself."

"Enough. You and Lady Darie return to your duties caring for the injured. Thanks to Sir Mallet, far too many are in need. The rest of you, follow me."

Sophia led her small band up the ridge. Her army's fighting had carried over the crest and into the dirt streets of the city itself. Looking across the mound homes through the growing smoke, she noted Tegine's forces closing in on the castle. They quickly blocked the roads leading to the north and west. Pendergast's banners and flags still rode above the castle walls.

Sophia turned to Orin. "Go find Sir Josiah and the Paladin. Tell them to press on to the castle as quickly as possible. I want them to block the roads leading south and east out of the fortress. And if they can spare some men, start fighting those fires before the whole city burns down."

He bowed and ran ahead, down the slope. Sophia urged her band on, going south and west, skirting around the city.

She rubbed her shoulder as she walked. Perhaps she should have asked Brother Charles for some of that Gobi root. Too late now.

Sophia came upon a force of twenty enemy soldiers cowering behind a goat pen's mud and stick wall. The enemy company was twice the size of her own. She stepped forward and called to them. "Kersens, look to the castle. The usurper has abandoned you. You have only one chance to save your lives and return to your homes. Join me now. Help me lay siege and restore the rightful heir to the throne."

Their leader slowly stood, then looked around. His eyes lingered on the castle's gray walls. "It seems you speak the truth, your Grace. Will we receive a fair treatment?"

"I've already said you will. My word is binding."

He signaled his men to rise. "Then we'll join you. If you seek to close on the castle's wall, I can show you a path that's unguarded."

Sophia looked askance at her man with the red trousers. "Michael, do you know this man?" She pointed at the other group's leader. "Can he be trusted?"

Michael shook his head. "I don't know him. I'd proceed with caution, your Grace."

Sophia looked over the city again. Women and children would be cowering in their homes, praying for Cassandra to save them. Hoping Hecuba hadn't yet laid her eyes upon them. Certainly, fearing the fires if nothing else. This madness had to be stopped. Stopped as soon as possible. She looked back at the enemy's leader. "Very well, you may lead on."

The new group filed out of the goat pen. Commoners, mostly tradesmen or laborers. Men, but like her own little band, not real soldiers. They followed their leader going mostly southwest. Sophia held her men back, ensuring they didn't intermingle with the newcomers. "Keep a sharp eye out. We may find others who are not so willing to join us."

Sophia and her band arrived at the permanent stone

bridge connecting the city with the small island before Castle Kersey. Josiah, Galen, and her knights had already established a ramshackle palisade on the island beyond the bridge. Sophia dropped onto a camp chair, removed her helmet, and sighed.

Galen handed her a wineskin. She thanked him and took a sip. Its tart flavor burned going down, and she winced. She hadn't realized how thirsty she was. Josiah sat across from her.

"My Queen, we've been worried about you. Scouts have been sent to find you. That priest you brought along said you were badly injured. We couldn't help thinking the worst," Josiah said.

Sophia rubbed her shoulder. "I'm fine. I was led on a roundabout route to get here, but I'm here now. What's our situation?"

"Pendergast's men have secured the castle against our entry, but Tegine and we have sealed it from their escape. Rumor has it Pendergast ordered stockpiles of food and other supplies brought into the castle a week or more ago. This could be a long siege."

"I don't want a long engagement. Indeed, we're not equipped for a long siege. The townsfolk and the men have to get back to their fields before harvest time. We certainly don't want a famine the first winter of my reign." Sophia examined their makeshift base. "Where is Sir Stewart?"

"I've sent him and a few men to scout the secret tunnel. If Pendergast hasn't found it we may be able to use it to gain access to the inner courtyard. That would put a real twist in his codpiece."

Sophia smiled. "Understood. What can we do to shorten the time we spend here?"

Josiah shrugged, offering nothing.

Galen gestured at the castle. "Get Pendergast to come out or find a way to get a large body of men inside."

"How can we do that?"

"The tunnel Tarkenton spoke of sounds promising."

"My Queen, there you are." Stewart and Orin approached, their faces streaked with sweat and soot, their surcoats blood-spattered. "We've been worried about you." Stewart dropped to a knee and grasped her hand. He kissed it while eyeing her through his damp ringlets.

"I'm well, thank you. What did you find at the tunnel?" Sophia traced a finger along his firm jaw.

He grinned back at her and winked before looking around the council. "It seems Pendergast hasn't found it. I went all the way to the outer wall. The door is still intact. It may be a way in. Not wanting to show our intention I didn't open it."

Sophia bit her lower lip. "It may be a trap. Sir Mallet is no fool. He has to know we didn't fly over the wall when we made our escape. He's had weeks to find it."

"True enough. I've stationed men at the door. They have instructions to remain quiet and listen for any sounds coming from within." Stewart smiled at Sophia again, then blushed and looked away. "They will also raise the alarm if Pendergast attempts to sally from the tunnel."

Sophia gazed up at her castle's battlements. Pendergast may know of the tunnel, but he probably wouldn't come out. He was a badger caught in his den. He'd lash out if approached, but not try to escape until his larder was empty. She could try to goad him into coming out, but her knights would never allow it. It was risky, but she'd have to try. She needed to distract her men for a minute. She flashed a broad smile all around, then strode toward the palisade.

The men sat frozen for a moment, then rushed to Sophia's side.

"What are you doing, my Queen?" Josiah demanded.

"Ending this."

Josiah stepped into her path. Sophia paused behind the palisade.

"Get out of my way, Sir Josiah."

"I will not. Beyond this wall you'll be in easy bow range." Josiah's eyes pleaded.

"Am I your queen? Do you believe the prophecy's time has come?"

Josiah nodded. His lips tight.

"Then obey and step aside."

Josiah stared her in the face. Defiance loomed there for an instant, then it was gone. He stepped aside. "Shields, men, quickly!"

Sophia strode to within fifty feet of the castle's bridge landing. The men scrambled, throwing up shields before and around her. She surveyed the gatehouse above the bridge. Pendergast appeared there, twenty feet above her, only his helmetless head exposed.

Sophia pushed a shield out of her way, cupped her hands around her mouth and shouted, "Cousin, you see how this will end. The siege engines are being built, it's only a matter of time before we breach the walls and slay every knight and man-at-arms inside. If you want mercy, end this. Surrender now."

"Women don't issue orders to men. Come in and get me if you think you can," Pendergast shouted back.

"Fraysse will not help you. A wyvern has destroyed their army. You know what that means."

A long minute passed. Pendergast's head ducked behind the wall.

Sophia sniffed the light wind for a minute. It carried a worrisome smoke. "Sir Mallet, we can settle this in the old way. Come out and face me in single combat."

Stewart hissed in her ear, "You can't be serious, my love. Pendergast is a skilled knight and you're wounded."

"Enough, Sir Stewart. The challenge has already been made. If he has any honor at all he must come out."

"Here is my reply," Pendergast shouted.

Arrows flashed from the wall. They fell among and around

Sophia's guards. They impacted the shields like heavy rain on a tin roof. Several men fell, crying out. A brilliant pain scorched her thigh. A shaft lodged there. Sophia cried out and fell, grasping the arrow. Her men re-covered her with their shields while others jerked her arms and dragged her back toward their palisade.

The shadow of a massive flying creature darkened the gatehouse. Serek-jen loomed above the walls.

CHAPTER THIRTY-FOUR

Sophia was borne on a litter to a secluded spot in an empty animal pen with low mud walls surrounding it. The ground reeked of manure and urine-soaked straw. She clutched the arrow's shaft and groaned aloud. Her knights fretted, patted her shoulders and talked all at once, reassuring she'd be fine. Sophia brushed their hands away between groans. She glanced at the wyvern's massive frame as it loitered above, turning wide slow circles against the smoke-darkened sky. Had she failed Serek-jen's expectations? An arrow struck and bounced harmlessly off the wyvern's tough scales.

Sophia rose on an elbow while still clinging to the shaft. Serek-jen altered her flight path, rolling to one side, her gold-edged scales glittering. She belched blue fire at the gatehouse. The screams of men carried over the distance. Licking flames clung to much of the woodwork along the edge of the battlement. Serek-jen swooped and landed near Sophia's company. They were pelted with canes of straw and bits of gravel. A puff of ozone-flavored smoke rolled from her nostrils.

"Only fools launch arrows at me. Perhaps they have learned a lesson," Serek-jen spoke into Sophia's mind.

Sophia's men drew weapons and placed themselves between her and Serek-jen. They glanced at Sophia, their eyes narrow and sweat on their brows.

Hecuba no, Serek-jen would kill them all. "It's all right. Serek-jen is a friend. Leave her in peace." Sophia said. Her men slowly returned their weapons to their scabbards and stood aside. The muted hum of wonder and fear surrounded her.

"The test is before you, Queen of Kersey. If prophecy is to be fulfilled, you must make it so." Serek-jen whispered in her mind.

Sophia grimaced, her thigh sending an occasional flash of sharp pain out of the throbbing numbness. "I don't know that I can do it," Sophia answered aloud.

"If you cannot, no one can. Hecuba's patience is at an end. At the sun's zenith tomorrow, my sisters will join me. If there has been no resolution, Kersey will be no more." Serek-jen scratched a leathery wing with one of her horns.

"You can't do that. The people are innocent."

"We will have prophecy or we will have chaos. Our master, Hecuba, has decreed it. Men must submit or be punished. We do not care either way."

Sophia's head throbbed. Serek-jen's words and her own inner wyvern assaulted her willpower, both urging her to act even as her fatigue and confidence encouraged her to relent, to sleep. She had to rest. They had to grant her some peace. "Enough. I understand."

"See that you do."

The gathered men and Sophia watched in awe as Serek-jen took to the sky. She flew a lazy circle around the castle, then sped away to the east, and passed from sight.

Sophia looked to her knights. "I must get up and meet Sir Mallet. I must meet him before the noon sun tomorrow."

Josiah knelt at her side, gripping her forearm with a firm squeeze. "My Queen, you are wounded twice, you can't possibly expect to meet Pendergast on a level field. It's two days to the Solstice. Let us gut that pig for you."

"No. I must do it." Sophia's wounds jabbed at her, and she fought off tears.

Stewart held her hand as she lay back. His eyes wide, begging for her attention. "My Queen, let me force an entrance through the tunnel. We can push him out into the open. Then if need be, you can meet him with our help."

Sophia touched her palm to his cheek. "Dear Stewart, I can't allow it. The tunnel has to be a trap. There is no other explanation for its being apparently unguarded. You and any I'd send with you would surely perish in that dark place. No, I must meet him, alone. The wyverns and Hecuba will have it no other way." A new, sharper pain wracked her thigh, and she cringed. "Where is Brother Charles?"

"He is coming, your Grace. Rest now." Galen offered her a skin. Sophia drank and returned it, then let her head drop onto the litter.

Minutes dragged away until Charles, Celeste, and Darie rushed into the pen. Charles instantly shooed the knights aside before dropping to his knees and gently removing Sophia's hand from the arrow shaft. Using his small knife, he cut her trousers' leg open beneath her mail, enough to examine the wound.

Celeste stood aside with tight lips. She seemed to purposely look away from what Charles was doing. Darie grabbed Sophia's hand and squeezed as tears stained her plump cheeks. Will, soldiers, and camp followers gathered around the outside of the pen.

Charles looked up. "Your Grace, it's serious, but not mortal. Looks to be a needle-bodkin. Your hauberk slowed it enough it hasn't lodged in the bone. However, it will have to come out. We'll have to pull it back along the path it's made."

"Of course it must be removed. Get on with it." Sophia groaned and waved for Galen's wineskin. He pulled the cork and held the skin to her lips.

"Not too much of that," Charles said. He gestured at the knights. "Pick her up, let's get the queen into a house, out of view. We're going to need some privacy."

Stewart, Orin, and two others lifted the litter, while Charles kept a firm grip on the arrow's shaft. Josiah led them into the street and to the front door of a small stone-walled home. He pounded on the door. There was no answer, so he pushed the door open. The knights struggled to get the litter through the narrow doorway without spilling Sophia onto the floor.

A woman with two small children stared wide-eyed as her house filled with armed men and women. Josiah turned to her. "Two hundred pardons, we need to use your table. The queen will see you compensated for the trouble."

The woman nodded, her mouth hanging open. She fiddled with the neck of her plain wool shift, clutching her children to her side. At last, she blinked and pointed at Sophia, "Is she the queen? The one who would save us from the wyverns?"

The knights placed the litter on the table, removing the chairs to the walls. Their footfalls were loud on the old planks of the floor. Josiah grinned at the woman, "She is. If you would, please put a kettle on to boil. I'm sure the healer is going to need it. If nothing else we can all use some tea."

Charles chimed in, "Yes indeed, lots of water please." He then turned to Celeste and asked her to hold the skirt of Sophia's hauberk, which the arrow had penetrated, off of her leg. Celeste complied but looked away.

"Lady Celeste, it can't be that bad. Surely, you've seen worse," Sophia said.

Celeste looked at Sophia. "I have, but not as concerns someone I love. You've got to stop taking these risks."

Darie patted Sophia's shoulder. "Are you going to die, Sister?"

Sophia shook her head. "No, of course not. Brother Charles

will patch me up good as I ever was." The crowded room hummed with noise. Men whispering, feet shuffling on the plank floor. The house matron's children scurried up the ladder into the loft. They watched from above, wide-eyed, curious, but like forest nymphs, removed from it all.

At Charles's direction, a lamp was lit and placed on the table near Sophia's hip. He dug in his satchel, then laid out some bandage material and a few bits of herb, as well as a mortar and pestle. He asked the woman of the house for some flour or corn meal. While she got the requested item from a cupboard, he crushed the herb in the mortar. He mixed the herb with the flour and some water then applied the paste to the bandage. He looked at Sophia. "A poultice to draw out any poison."

Sophia, exhausted, let her head thump on the table. Her eyes burned, demanding sleep. She closed them. Her inner wyvern remained strangely silent. Was it a petty creature, pouting? She rolled her head back and forth.

"We're ready to proceed," Charles said. "A man on each shoulder and knee if you please. Another on this hip." He waited. More furniture was scraped across the floor as men moved about. Stewart took her hand and smiled as he pressed down on a shoulder. Josiah took the other. Men gripped her legs as well. A finger lightly touched her forehead. Sophia looked. Galen held a leather belt.

"Bite down on this, your Grace." He placed the sweat-smelling piece of leather between her teeth. It tasted of oil and dirt. She groaned, then nodded at Charles.

Using a firm steady pull Charles removed the arrow from Sophia's leg in a single motion. Sophia grunted, leaving teeth marks in the belt. The flame of pain scorching her thigh intensified, and she struggled against the men restraining her. Charles slapped the poultice on the wound, pressing with one hand.

"Good news, your Grace, it came out in one piece. No need

to dig around looking for the head." Charles held the blood-stained shaft for her to see. The iron point glistened. He set the shaft aside then tightened the bandage around Sofia's leg. She cringed but pushed the belt from her mouth.

"Do you have something for the pain?" Sophia asked.

Charles dug in his bag. "I do, Anthall leaf, it's powerful and usually induces sleep. I'd recommend we use it. You need the rest." He washed his mortar then dried it on a clean cloth.

Sophia raised her head. Stewart gripped her hand tight and kissed her forehead. He propped her head up with a hand behind her neck. Josiah demanded the room be cleared out. The men jostled each other as they jockeyed for the door.

Sophia's thigh and shoulder throbbed. Her head spun and ached. Still the wyvern remained silent. A small blessing in the least, she couldn't bear subduing it while dealing with her injuries. Celeste and Darie helped the house woman prepare tea for the remaining knights.

"I can't sleep. Not yet. Do you have more of that Gobi root?"

Charles shook his head. "There have been many injured in the last few days. I've used up my supply."

Celeste held a steaming cup to Sophia's lips. "You should rest. Take the drug. Let the men dig that beast out of the castle for you."

Sophia shook her head. "No, I must do it. The wyverns are coming. I must do it for the people." She looked at Charles. "A lesser dose, enough to allow me to stand on the leg. I can't fall asleep."

Charles looked to the Paladin. Sophia followed Charles's eyes. Galen's face reflected a hard edge. "The queen must finish this. That said, there will be no more fighting today. It will be dark soon. Give her a lesser amount. Enough to allow her to sleep comfortably, but rise in the morning with a clear head. No more than that." He turned to Sophia. "You must rest, your Grace. You cannot expect to accomplish your task in this condition."

Sophia glanced around the room, Galen, Josiah, Stewart, Orin, and Gerard all nodded at her. Stewart squeezed her hand tighter. "I will stay at your side through the night, my Queen. No harm will come to you. I swear it. Tomorrow I will accompany you onto the field to ensure a fair contest."

"We all will, my Queen," Josiah said. "If you do not kill that jackass, we will."

Sophia blinked several times. A tear ran down her cheek. She licked it away. "Has Sir Mallett agreed to come out?"

Josiah shook his head. "He remains in hiding. We will try to pry him out with taunts and insults to his person. Perhaps his pride will overrule his wisdom. It's possible his knights will cast him out, wishing to save their own skins."

Sophia groaned. "That's a terrible plan. He'll never agree to it." She looked to Galen. "My Lord, can you ask Serek-jen to return in the early morning, before her sisters join her?"

Galen inclined his chin once. "I can try, but she doesn't always heed my requests."

Sophia cringed again then held her breath for a moment. She drew strength from Stewart's grip. "I'd have you try in the least." She turned to Charles. "A reduced dose if you will. The pain is becoming annoying."

Charles tore the leaves in half and placed them in the mortar. After crushing them he scraped the green flakes into the cup Celeste held. "This should be adequate, your Grace."

Celeste placed the cup to Sophia's lips. She gulped the concoction down in a single swallow. In a few minutes the room faded away.

CHAPTER THIRTY-FIVE

The dawn broke promising a glorious day. The sun was a brilliant orange disk marching into a deep blue sky, casting its light through the window and across Sophia's torso. Stewart slept in a chair next to the litter, his hand holding hers and head resting on the table. Sophia smiled at him, then cringed at the electric stabbing, tingling through her entire leg. She waited for the pain to fade. She traced her finger across his parted lips, then nudged him awake. He yawned as he sprang to his feet.

"Two hundred pardons, I didn't intend to fall asleep."

Sophia smiled again. "It's quite all right, my love. You were as exhausted as I was. I'm refreshed now, but I need to tend to nature's call. Will you wake Celeste so she can assist me in getting to the privy?" Sophia pointed to where Celeste and Darie lay on the floor, curled together in a blanket.

Celeste rose, recovered Darie, then came to the table. With Stewart's help they got Sophia upright on the floor.

Sophia tested the leg with her weight. Celeste hooked her arm and supported Sophia as she took a few furtive steps. She found walking difficult, but possible. Pain lanced her from a myriad of wounds, some only now recognized. The thigh was the worst of them.

"I must look a wreck," she said.

Celeste clicked her tongue before answering. "Don't worry. You're a beautiful warrior."

When she and Celeste returned to the home, Thomas greeted them. He wore a plain shirt and a pair of woodsman's red trousers. He smiled in spite of a cracked lip, which must have been painful. Even though he was covered in dabs of red wound salve, giving him the look of having the plague, and smelled of fish oil and hazel, Sophia embraced the old wizard.

"Ah, there you are, Delicious. I've been worried about you."

"And I you. Join me for breakfast. You can tell us how you've come to be here as well as what is to come."

The rest of her knights straggled into the house in ones and twos. The room sweltered as the group grew to ten or eleven unwashed bodies. The lady of the house set a table with cornbread and butter. A steaming pot of tea rounded out the meal. Sophia thanked her several times for her hospitality.

Sophia's knights bandied varying ideas of how to get Pendergast to come out of the castle. All incorporated some form of attack against the walls and insults to Pendergast's honor. None of which offered any real hope of ending Pendergast's reign before the sun reached its highest point.

Sophia called for silence, then looked at Galen. "My Lord, will Serek-jen come this morning?"

Galen shook his head as he spoke. "I've burned the requisite herbs and the smoke has taken flight. If she comes, then she is wont to. If not..."

Sophia frowned and looked from face to face around the room. "Serek-jen told me her sisters will join her today. If Sir Mallet isn't defeated before the noon hour, they will raze all of Kersey, consuming all who dare remain here."

A murmur of concern swept around the room. Sophia held up her hands silencing them. "I intend to ask Serek-jen, assuming she comes to his Lordship's call, to convince the men in the castle to expel Sir Mallet so I may meet and slay him in single combat. Her presence will have more impact than any army's."

The men seemed to weigh her words, waiting for her to go on. Josiah rose and clenched a fist before his chest. "My Queen, you cannot face Pendergast alone. You've been seriously wounded. He is a potent knight. Your life would be forfeit and we'd still be left facing this wyvern storm."

"I must face him, Sir Josiah. Hecuba demands it, the wyverns will enforce it. Even so, I want our men to spread this decree. The people are to leave the city and take refuge in the forest. See they are told within the hour. Once the issue is decided they can return." Sophia glanced all around again. "The real danger comes if Sir Mallet refuses to come out. Then our fight will be to save the people from Hecuba's rage. We'll have to defeat the wyverns." A powerful twinge of pain raced from ankle to hip as she shifted her weight on the chair.

Thomas raised a finger. "Your Grace, assuming Pendergast comes out, have you prepared the talisman I gave you?"

Sophia looked at the old man and shook her head. She fingered her sword's hilt. "The stones are in place, but I'd quite forgotten about them."

"We have barely enough time to put them to use." Thomas's eyes gleamed with the mischievous fire Sophia had seen at his cottage. He gestured for the weapon. Sophia gave it to him. He examined it. "Yes, well done. They will work perfectly. They'll grant some relief of your pain and give you strength."

Sophia instructed Will to take her sword to the river and place it in the water and guard it, then return it to her in four hours. He stated his understanding, repeated the instructions, then left with the sword. She returned her attention to her council. "Still, Sir Thomas, there is no guarantee Sir Mallet will come out."

"My recent visit to the castle revealed Pendergast's tenuous hold on power. His men are not confident. Indeed, the only reason I'm still in one piece is because his torturer wasn't zealous in following his instructions. Not to mention, during interrogation, I may have embellished your connection to the wyverns. His men are fearful of that in itself."

"Do you think they'll rebel and cast him out if Serek-jen threatens them?"

Thomas nodded. "I do, Delicious. And with the talisman, even injured, you will defeat him."

"Even if Pendergast comes out, you will be at a disadvantage, my Queen, A talisman is hardly the stuff a queen can hang her reign upon," Stewart said. "In the least, let us fire some arrows at him. If one hits him, then the field will level."

Sophia shook her head. "No, my loyal men, we will not sink to his level. Deceit and treachery are the tools of the usurper. I will face him and I will prevail. If not, then I charge you all with placing Darie on the throne and doing what you can to spare the people from Hecuba's wrath."

Josiah frowned, but turned to men standing outside the window and issued orders to evacuate the women and children. The war council returned to angry argument over how best to get Pendergast to come out of the castle.

Sophia closed her eyes, shutting out the angry voices. She grasped Stewart's hand and allowed his fantasy of a cottage in the forest to whisk her away from all the noise and strife. She smiled at the image.

Alarmed shouting outside caught their attention. Sophia struggled to her feet. Josiah leapt to the window. A moment later he turned to the room. "It seems Serek-jen has arrived, my Queen."

Sophia limped to the riverbank. Her war council accompanied her. Serek-jen stood, baring her teeth and snorting smoke. She seemed to enjoy frightening the few people brave enough to satisfy their curiosity and gather nearby. Her green scales were aglow with the morning sun, while her ozone odor clashed with the musk of water meeting earth.

Darie clamped her fingers around Sophia's hand. The amber eyes came to rest on Sophia. A puff of smoke from Serek-jen's nostrils framed her long face. She shifted her gaze to Galen. "What does Achaea's Paladin want from me?" Serek-jen asked aloud, her voice a harp's chord.

"I've asked you here on behalf of Kersey's queen, Great One." Galen gestured toward Sophia.

The penetrating stare returned to Sophia. The wyvern spoke in her mind. "What do you want?"

"I'm asking you to compel the usurper to come out of the fortress and face me."

"I cannot. I am forbidden from taking sides until prophecy comes to pass."

"You've already chosen sides. You helped me at the pass and stopped Fraysse's army from reinforcing Sir Mallet."

"I had nothing to do with Fraysse. Argent-wan will be chastised for her interference."

"Well, what of the pass then?"

"A lark, which I will not repeat. I cannot help you."

"It seems a simple choice. What is stopping you?"

"Hecuba, the mother, stops me."

"I thought Cassandra was the mother."

"She is your mother, not mine."

Sophia wrinkled her brow and shifted her weight. What did Serek-jen mean? A question for Brother Charles, she had other things to ponder at the moment. "If you don't help how will prophecy come to pass?"

"It is not for me to say. You claim to be the queen, the burden to prove it belongs to you." Serek-jen hissed. Smoke rolled from her nostrils, then she rose on her hind legs staring into the sky.

Sophia shielded her eyes with a hand. The crackling of her inner wyvern rose to a drowning barrage of noise in her head. She rubbed her throbbing temples.

Another wyvern streaked toward them. This one the same size, but nearly the opposite color of Serek-jen. Yellow scales outlined in green. The sun glared from her sides, the bright flashes adding to Sophia's headache.

The new wyvern swooped low over them, then back into the sky. Serek-jen growled deep in her long throat, then leapt after the other. Sophia staggered back from the concussion Serek-jen's launch left behind.

The newcomer rolled, and twisted, climbed, and dived. An incredible display of nimble acrobatics for so ponderous a creature. Serek-jen mimicked those maneuvers, getting ever closer to the other. They met high above the city, grasping and clawing at each other as they plummeted toward the ground. Leathery wings beating frantically. They released their grapple and swooped back into the sky with only a hundred feet to spare.

Galen and Stewart came to Sophia's side, each supporting one of her arms. The wyverns came together again and repeated the falling wrestling match before streaking back into the sky. "What in Hecuba's name is going on?" Sophia asked, watching the spectacle.

Thomas grinned and limped to her side. He leaned on a makeshift cane, then used the cane to point into the sky. "The rogue, Argent-wan. It seems she and Serek-jen have a difference of opinion."

Sophia glanced at Thomas. He grinned. "I'm a wizard. Wyvern lore is a required study."

Sophia returned her gaze to the wyverns. They fell once more, a thin trail of smoke scarring the sky. Serek-jen continued to fall even as Argent-wan pulled up. Serek-jen crashed into the poorer side of the city. A plume of dust and smoke billowed into the sky. A thunderous thump echoed across the dwellings' domes. Sophia prayed the people had left their homes in time. Several seconds passed. Argent-wan circled above, then Serek-jen flashed into the sky, fleeing to the east. Argent-wan pursued.

Sophia and her council stood in silence for several minutes. Then a cacophony of fear and wonder at what they'd seen erupted. A chair was brought and Sophia sat, resting her injuries. Charles changed the bandage on her thigh.

"I don't know what we've witnessed means," Sophia said, the throbbing moved from her temples to a spot above one eye. Her men and women gathered around her.

Another wyvern chased Serek-jen away. Had she been about to help Sophia? The prophecy was Hecuba's. If she wanted it to come to pass, why would she interfere? The inner wyvern scalded her skull, demanding, but unclear as to what it wanted. Sophia shoved it back into the recesses. "Without Serek-jen's help, I don't see how we can compel Sir Mallet to come out of the fortress. I fear for the future of our people. I'm open to suggestions."

All those gathered nearby spoke at once. Some shouting to be heard. Sophia called for calm. She glanced at the sun. It was only three hours until it would be at its zenith. She looked to her advisers. "We are running out of time. Soon the wyverns will come. If Sir Mallet hasn't been removed, they will become a scourge upon Kersey. A bane on all the three kingdoms."

Josiah set a grim frown, then strode toward the castle walls. Sophia watched him for a moment, then waved for Orin and Stewart to follow him. They jumped to obey. Sophia turned in her seat. Josiah and the others halted outside of bow range. Josiah cupped his hands around his mouth, then shouted, "Cast the usurper out to us. The queen has granted clemency to all who lay down their arms. You have one hour to comply."

"Go back to your whore and tell her to surrender,"

Pendergast shouted. "You'll get no quarter here."

Josiah stood with hands on hips for a long minute, then turned on his heel and strode back to Sophia. "I suggest we try the tunnel, my Queen. That pig's ass won't come out. We'll have to go in and get him."

A collective gasp ripped through the gathered soldiers and knights. Argent-wan flashed low overhead. Sticks and sand pelted all those near the river. She flew over the castle then returned and landed near Sophia's company. Sophia struggled to her feet, placing a hand on Darie's shoulder. The wyvern surveyed the company, then glared at Sophia.

"Fruit of my house, Queen of Kersey, will you see prophecy come to pass?"

Fruit of my house? An archaic term, not used in generations. Still, wyverns live for centuries. Sophia held her chin aloft. "I would if Mallet Pendergast can be brought to battle."

Argent-wan swung her head toward the knights. "Achaea's Paladin is here with many brave knights of Kersey." She returned her gaze to Sophia. "I can only defy the mother so much, therefore I cannot kill him for you. What is your plan?"

"I will face Sir Mallet in single combat. We are stymied at getting him to come out."

Argent-wan turned her gaze on Castle Kersey. "Let us see if we can do something about that." She leapt into the air. Men staggered away from the thrust her wings generated. Sophia shaded her eyes with a hand and watched. Argent-wan swooped low over the castle. Arrows pelted her harmlessly before she breathed blue fire into the courtyard. She turned and flew high into the air. The stench of charred flesh accompanied the aroma of burnt wood drifting from the castle.

Argent-wan swept back across the walls, igniting any wooden structures the masonry protected. She paused above one of the towers, her wings fanning the growing flames. Her voice, carried on the breeze, accompanying the electric odor of her flame. "Expel Mallet Pendergast from these walls so that he may meet his destiny. Do so now, or face my wrath for I will raze this castle to the ground. All inside will face Hecuba's judgment."

Sophia watched, holding her breath. Even if Pendergast was cast out, would she be able to defeat him? Argent-wan returned to the riverside, landing near Sophia's party. Sophia turned to her.

"Now we will see if those men love their lives more than they love Mallet Pendergast," Argent-wan said in Sophia's mind.

Sophia thanked her, then returned her gaze to the castle walls. She'd sleep tonight in her own bed or in her grave.

CHAPTER THIRTY-SIX

Long minutes crept past. No evidence of Pendergast coming out manifested. Sophia checked the sky again, only two hours left. She turned to Argent-wan, but before she could speak, Will rushed up to her. He knelt and raised her sword before her, laying it flat across his palms. Sophia reached, but Thomas hobbled forward and took the sword from Will.

Thomas hefted the sword, then swung it twice in the air. He bobbed his head with his lips set in a smug grin. "Well done, young man. Very well indeed. The talisman is working as designed. A fine piece of craft, if I must say so myself." He handed the weapon to Sophia.

Sophia held the sword, it felt as it always did. She glanced at Celeste. Her lady-in-waiting rolled her eyes and shrugged. Sophia smiled, then sheathed the sword. "All we need now is Sir Mallet."

Stewart frowned. "Even if he comes out, you can't face him alone. Let me stand for you, my Queen."

Sophia glanced at Argent-wan, the wyvern blinked several times but said nothing. Sophia returned her eyes to Stewart. "I must face him, my love. Prophecy can't be fulfilled unless I do it."

Stewart's face grew grim. Josiah patted him on the shoulder.

"Listen to reason, my Queen," Josiah said. "You stand little chance in your weakened state. You must choose a champion to represent you."

Sophia took in the dark faces of her advisers and friends. Even Darie's lips were set in a scowl. Only Thomas seemed confident. "My friends, my loyal friends. You have my love, but things greater than all of us are at work here today. Tomorrow is the Solstice, and rather than preparing for the celebration we are caught up in this civil war. It can only be resolved if I end it. None of you can stand for me. Hecuba will not allow it."

Galen made to speak, but turned his eyes, along with everyone else, to the groaning of the drawbridge hawsers. Their creaking signaled the extending of the ancient planks. Argent-wan rose on her hind legs, smoke swirled from her nostrils.

Sophia shuddered. What or who would come out of the castle? Was it a full-scale attack or would Pendergast come out alone? She tested her leg. Pain flashed from the wound. She sucked in a sharp breath, trying to dispel it. It didn't work. She took a few furtive steps while the bridge seemed to take hours to reach its moorings. Josiah blocked her path.

"Wait. It may be a trick. Knowing Pendergast it probably is."

Sophia limped around him. Her eyes fixed on the bridge. She paused at the stone bridge separating her party from the castle's island foreyard. Knights dressed in Pendergast's livery came from the castle and fanned out along the water's edge. They stood silent, their spears at their sides and shields resting on the ground before them. Sophia poked her chin at the flat ground which lay beyond the palisade.

The Paladin and her knights as well as Celeste and Darie accompanied her. Sophia stood as straight as she could, limping to a spot she liked. She halted and waited.

The slow creep of time made the nearby sparrows' chirping seem far away. Sophia licked at the sweat forming on her upper lip. She shifted her weight to her good leg and closed her eyes, trusting her men to sound the alarm should anyone sally from the castle. She groped for and found Celeste and Darie's hands. She squeezed their fingers. Let the power of women united come to her and see her through this contest.

"This is not going to end well," Celeste whispered.

Sophia peeked at her companion. The redhead chewed her lip, staring at the drawbridge. "Regardless, we are committed."

"At last, the pig's ass comes," Josiah's voice was flat.

Sophia opened her eyes. Pendergast strode across the drawbridge. Several knights followed him, stopping on the road as soon as they'd gotten off the planks. Kersey's Lord Bishop and his acolyte, their vestments tattered and soiled, stood on the drawbridge. Pendergast came on a few more yards. Sophia's knights spread out on either side of her.

"If killing that snotty bitch brings this affair to an end, then so be it. Send her forth," Pendergast called.

Sophia glanced at the rolling black smoke still billowing above her castle's bailey. Common soldiers worked behind Pendergast's knights, forming a bucket line from the moat into the castle. She looked across the thirty yards separating her company from Pendergast's. "When I have killed Sir Mallet, clemency will be granted to all who lay down their arms. Justice will be quickly dispensed to those who do not."

Pendergast laughed. "There will be no mercy for the dogs that've supported you. Lead on to the lists. My luncheon awaits me."

Sophia glanced over her shoulder. Argent-wan snorted smoke but held her place on the far side of the river. Sophia returned her gaze to Pendergast. He'd been her tutor and trainer. None knew her fighting style as well as he. Could the student defeat the master? "There is no need to use the lists. I will slay you here so that no one need bear your vile head farther than yonder post." Sophia pointed at the stake which weeks before had held her father's head.

"Your confidence is misplaced. So be it." Pendergast closed his visor and drew his sword.

Sophia released her grip on the other women's hands and took a step forward. This time Stewart stepped into her path. "I cannot allow you to do this, my love. I again beg you to let me stand for you."

Sophia placed her palm on his cheek. "Dear Stewart, you can't do this for me. You must step aside."

"I will not. Be reasonable, you may be with child." Stewart crossed his arms on his chest and jutted his jaw.

Sophia rose on her toes and kissed him. Then she looked to Orin and Gerard, gesturing at Stewart with her chin. "Hold him if you please."

Orin and Gerard each grasped one of Stewart's arms. Sophia stepped around him.

Josiah held a hand up to her. "A moment, my Queen." He shoved a dagger into her belt and patted it a couple times. "A gift to me from your father. It has served me well. See that it finds a fitting home."

"I will."

Galen held out her helmet, then offered a shield as Sophia donned it. "Pendergast has no respect for your skills. He'll be aggressive and try to end this quickly. He'll use his size and weight to force you into a disadvantageous position. Stay to his left, force him to strike across his body. Make him tire himself. Your fighting style is vulnerable to being disarmed with a riposte. Be aware when he tries."

Sophia took the shield and drew her sword. "Thank you, my Lord." She sucked in a deep breath and limped toward Pendergast. Stewart bellowed and struggled against the men holding him.

Sophia paused then turned back to her company. "Know this, you all have my love. If I fall, serve the people." She turned on a heel and advanced.

Sophia's every step toward Pendergast came easier than the one before. Was the talisman working? An arrow to the thigh would be a minor wound to an ogre. She hefted her sword as she moved discreetly to his left. Strength and vitality grew with each step. Thomas's talisman *was* working. She inquired of her inner wyvern, but it remained silent, perhaps pouting. The ogre's protection it would be. She paused a few feet from Pendergast. She wished to make one last plea for him to surrender but was forced to defend as he lunged forward striking at her head.

Sophia blocked his strike with her shield and side-stepped to Pendergast's left. He struck again, advancing, using his strength to push her back. She tried to move to his left. He seemed to realize her intent and blocked her movement in that direction.

Other than Pendergast's and her own grunts and labored breathing, the field lay eerily silent. Neither her men nor her adversary's cheered. All stood with grim faces. Sophia could give them only a glance before Pendergast renewed his assault.

Sophia slipped to Pendergast's left, avoiding a powerful thrust at her gut. He hunkered down behind his shield, breathing hard. "If you'd go away, I could strike a bargain with these wyverns. Save the Crows, that's what you want isn't it?" Pendergast asked between breaths.

Sophia licked her lips. "You can't bargain with Hecuba." She struck at his exposed thigh, scoring a superficial wound. Pendergast grunted and tried to snatch her sword away with his riposte. Sophia jumped back, keeping her weapon and shield before her.

Pendergast roared, "Just die!" He rushed at her, hammering blows from every direction in quick succession.

Sophia retreated, splinters flying from her shield and her sword's steel ringing with each parry. Pendergast paused to breathe. Sophia unleashed the power of Thomas's talisman. It felt different from the wyvern, more subtle, less controlling. She advanced while raining blows on Pendergast's shield and thrusting at any exposed portion of his body. He defended flawlessly as he gave ground.

Pendergast cast his mangled shield aside. He called for a new shield, but his men stood still and silent as stones. The breeze ruffling their surcoats as it might topiaries in a garden. He muttered a curse and taking his sword in both hands he assumed the high guard. "Is that the best you can muster, woman?"

Sophia said nothing. She struck at his legs, drawing his guard down. A slash, which he partially blocked, opened a rent in his camail. A frantic parry on his part prevented her from piercing his throat. Pendergast backed away, cautiously circling to her right, keeping her from gaining his left side.

Sophia stalked him, testing his guard. Pendergast would have none of it. He blocked every probe. She searched her mind for the words or emotion to summon the wyvern, but couldn't find them. It refused her. She would have to find another way. She studied Pendergast, his shoulders slumped and his steps were flat-footed. His breathing was loud and ragged, matching her own. Even so, he kept the high guard in place, checking her moves.

She lunged at him, striking at his belly. He blocked the move and flicked his sword against hers. A classic riposte. As Galen had warned, her grip loosened and the sword flew from her hand. She jumped away from him. Weariness and pain crashed upon her senses. Her thigh throbbed and shoulders ached. She had no time for it. Pendergast pressed his attack. Sophia backed away, trying to get the dagger from her belt while keeping her shield between herself and Pendergast's blade.

Sophia tripped and fell backwards. She kept her shield in front of her as Pendergast leapt forward and thrust at her belly. The strike glanced off her shield and penetrated her armor above her right hip. A searing flame roared through her core. She failed to stop the gasp which escaped her lips. Pendergast yanked his sword back, changed his grip, and stabbed at her from above his head with both hands.

"Now die!" He shouted. His blade gleamed as it descended. Sophia shifted her shield to deflect the blow. The sword slid off the shield's edge and stuck in the ground next to her. Sophia kicked Pendergast's groin and rolled onto his blade, breaking it.

Pendergast stumbled back, swearing. Sophia yanked the dagger from her belt and sat up. A sharp, crippling pain ripped through her gut. She gasped again but kept a clear eye on Pendergast. He bellowed a vile curse and leapt upon her, striking with the broken shard his sword had become.

Sophia fell back under his weight. His cursing was an incoherent string of unconnected obscenities. In her mind's eye the gleaming face of his helmet morphed into that of her would-be rapist, the bastard. She felt his rough unshaven face and the heat of his garlic breath. Pendergast's weight smothered her. Ignoring her pain, she screamed a guttural panicked oath at him and struck frantically with her dagger. It glanced off his helmet several times before finding the eye slit. She shoved it home.

Pendergast grunted and went limp against her shield. Blood gushed from his helmet's eye opening, splashing her face. She spit the hot liquid from her mouth.

Sophia shoved his gurgling corpse aside. She groaned as she came to her feet. A cheer went up from her men. She turned, picked up Pendergast's broken sword, and cleaved his right hand. She grasped the dismembered hand and snatched the signet ring from a finger, then dropped the horrid appendage. She raised the ring for all to see, then collapsed.

***

Sophia blinked as the noon sun shone down on her. The helmet gone, her head rested on a soft pad of cloth. Her men were gathered round her. Celeste and Darie, tears staining their faces, clung to her hands.

Charles looked up from her wounded side and frowned.

"So many long faces. Have we won the day?" Sophia croaked through dry lips.

Josiah nodded. "You have won the day, my Queen. Pendergast's knights have surrendered. All of them."

Sophia rolled her head back and forth on the makeshift pillow. "Then the bloodshed is over. Thanks be to Hecuba."

Argent-wan loomed over the heads of those gathered round. "Prophecy is now fulfilled, Queen of Kersey. The sisters are gathering to celebrate."

Sophia forced a smile. "Brother Charles, what have you found with your fussing down there?"

Charles looked up and frowned more deeply. "I fear it's mortal, your Grace. Even as he paid the price, Pendergast has killed you."

Sophia nodded. "Darie must be taken to the Lord Bishop. She must accept the throne so the prophecy may live on. It must be so, for the good of the people." She coughed. A taste of hot copper assailed her tongue.

Celeste sniffed and turned to Thomas. "Is there not some magic you can do to save her?"

Thomas shook his head. "That power is beyond me. Only the gods can intervene."

Darie sobbed. "You can't die, Sister. You told me you weren't going to die."

"It's not up to me, dear Sister."

"But I'll be alone."

"No, you won't. You'll have all of these new friends at your side. They'll be your family, they'll help you."

"But—"

Celeste scooped Darie up and crushed her in her arms. The girl hid her face in Celeste's hair.

Sophia looked at Stewart. He stood silent, tears welled, clouding his blue eyes. "Do not mourn, my dear Stewart. Our time was brief, but it was ours. Live your life in happiness. Promise me you'll do that."

Stewart nodded but didn't speak.

Argent-wan opened her maw, emitting a cloud of smoke. "This is not your end, fruit of my house. The mother provides another way."

Everyone looked to the wyvern. Argent-wan closed her eyes and waggled her head back and forth.

Sophia felt a warm spot in her palm. A coin appeared there. A coin like the one she'd returned to Serek-jen. She raised her gaze to Argent-wan.

"Grip the coin tight and call that which lives inside you, my dear grandchild. Join me in Hecuba's service."

Sophia looked at the coin again and accepted the truth of it. She slipped the signet ring from her thumb and placed it in Darie's hand. "Serve the people well, Sister. This is not the end."

Josiah set his lips tight. He closed his strong hand on Darie's and nodded. "It will be done, my Queen."

Heat grew in Sophia's palm. She gripped the coin tight and called for the wyvern. It rushed into her mind sweeping her away as if flying over the land. She saw the three realms from far above, tinted with a pale green filter, then shared a last smile with her friends.

Her people stood back as Sophia's body grew pale, then translucent. Her clothing collapsed into a flat pile as a swirl of Kersen-blue mist formed where she had lain. The mist merged into the outline of a small beautiful-blue wyvern for a moment, then disappeared on the breeze.

Argent-wan took to the air and circled low over Darie's party. "Fear not, Queen of Kersey. She who calls you sister will return when your need is dire."

GLOSSARY

Accolade: The ceremony bestowing knighthood on a squire or man at arms.

Achaea: The primary god of men/warriors. Respects pragmatism, glory, and strength.

Anthall leaf: A fictional medicinal plant.

Bailey: The open space inside a castle between the battlement and the keep. A courtyard.

Baldric: A belt of leather or fabric worn over one shoulder and across the breast to support a sword, bugle, or other heavy equipment.

Battlement: The outer fortified wall of a castle.

Camail: A mail skirt attached to a helmet, protecting the neck and shoulders.

Cassandra: God of home and hearth. Achaea's mate and mother to all women.

Coronet: A crown.

Crier: A common man with some form of disability who is charged with walking the bailey and main city street announcing the time of day.

Gambeson: A coat of thick cloth or leather, padded, and quilted. Often worn under a hauberk.

Gatehouse: A fortified opening in the battlement, often containing a portcullis.

Gobi root: A fictional medicinal plant.

Hauberk: A coat of mail having long sleeves, but no hood. Typically extends to mid-thigh.

Hawser: A heavy rope of large diameter.

Hecuba: God of the dead. Mother of wyverns.

Keep: The fortress inside the battlement.

Lists: A field used for jousting and hand-to-hand combat tournaments.

Loiter-sack: A lazy person, a slacker.

Mail: Circular links of steel laced and riveted together in a pattern to provide flexible armor.

Needle-bodkin: A barbless arrowhead, designed to penetrate mail.

Parry: To block a thrust or slash from a sword or other hand weapon.

Pizzle: An animal's penis.

Portcullis: A grate of strong wood or iron bars that can be let down suddenly to block a portal.

Riposte: A quick return thrust with a sword, following a parry.

Sanctuary: A chapel inside the battlement.

Scimitar: In this story, a heavy, curved blade, single-edged sword, used primarily for cutting/slashing.

Spectacle helmet: A dome-shaped helmet protecting the top of the head, with a plate covering the eyes and nose, but still allowing vision.

Surcoat: A loose cloak-like garment worn over armor. Typically in the colors and adorned with the heraldry of the wearer's house/faction.

Sword: In this story, a long narrow bladed weapon. Double-edged, used primarily for stabbing, but can also slash/cut.

Talisman: A magical item of limited power or one-time use.

Witch: A female magic user, often drawing her power from weather, nature, and herbs, etc.

Wizard: A male magic user, skilled in spells, lore, and alchemy.

Wyvern: A typical European-style dragon, having its wings' leading edge attached to its forelegs.

ACKNOWLEDGEMENTS

Too many people to mention assisted and supported me in bringing this book's long journey to fruition. I'd like to thank them all and these folks in particular: Karen Wilton, Angela Rydell, Robin Gardner, Julie Wilton Zack, Jennifer Rupp, Dennis (Moe) Moore, Megan A. Hurley, Chelsi Hicks, MaryKate DeJardin, Wendy Wimmer Schuchart, Suzanne Schairer Olajos, Phillip N. Martin, S.J. Rozan, Dave Rank, Tim Mackesey, and of course, Mom.

ABOUT ATMOSPHERE PRESS

Atmosphere Press is an independent, full-service publisher for excellent books in all genres and for all audiences. Learn more about what we do at atmospherepress.com.

We encourage you to check out some of Atmosphere's latest releases, which are available at Amazon.com and via order from your local bookstore:

Saints and Martyrs: A Novel, by Aaron Roe

When I Am Ashes, a novel by Amber Rose

Melancholy Vision: A Revolution Series Novel, by L.C. Hamilton

The Recoleta Stories, by Bryon Esmond Butler

Voodoo Hideaway, a novel by Vance Cariaga

Hart Street and Main, a novel by Tabitha Sprunger

The Weed Lady, a novel by Shea R. Embry

A Book of Life, a novel by David Ellis

It Was Called a Home, a novel by Brian Nisun

Grace, a novel by Nancy Allen

Shifted, a novel by KristaLyn A. Vetovich

Because the Sky is a Thousand Soft Hurts, stories by Elizabeth Kirschner

ABOUT THE AUTHOR

S. L. Wilton is a retired, former non-commissioned officer in the United States Army. He is a current member of both the Chicago Writers Association and the Wisconsin Writers Association. He lives in rural, central Wisconsin with his wife, Karen, and their Chihuahua, Willie.

CPSIA information can be obtained
at www.ICGtesting.com
Printed in the USA
FSHW010956310821
84427FS